Liberty

Two Democracies: Revolution
Book 1

by Alasdair Shaw

Also by Alasdair Shaw

Two Democracies: Revolution

Repulse – in The Newcomer anthology
Independence
Liberty
Prejudice
Duty – in The Officer anthology
Equality
Hidden
Fraternity
Unity

Copyright © 2016 Alasdair C Shaw
All rights reserved.

First published in the UK 2016
by Alasdair Shaw

ISBN10 0995511004
ISBN13 978-0995511002

Cover art extract from original work "Depiction of a futuristic city" by Jonas de Ro. Used under the Creative Commons Attribution Share Alike 3.0 Unported License.
https://commons.wikimedia.org/wiki/File:Depiction_of_a_futuristic_city.jpg

Part I

The suns reflected off her mirrored glasses as she walked across the dry grassland. A scarf covered her face against the dust whipped up by the occasional gust of wind. Her grey robe parted with every step, revealing glimpses of the black firmsuit underneath. She carried no weapons; they wouldn't help her this time.

From the low rise ahead she would be able to see what she had come for.

She stopped on the crest and pulled back her hood. Her long, dark hair escaped and hung around her shoulders. In the distance stood a city, gleaming white through the heat haze.

"It is time."

She didn't acknowledge the speaker, continuing to stare across the savannah. With the optical enhancements in her glasses she could make out personal aircars coming and going between the skyscrapers.

"I cannot protect you if you go any further."

A larger aircraft arrived and touched down on one of the buildings, a commuter transport no doubt. People going to work, going shopping, meeting friends.

"Does this have to happen?" she asked her escort.

"It is too late now. We cannot intervene."

Chapter 1

"All stations, stand by to engage. Full burn on my mark..." said Captain Hapsburg in measured tones. "Mark."

The Indescribable Joy of Destruction powered forward, and swung around the moon it had been using for cover. The tactical sensors marked their target, a Congressional destroyer in orbit around the planet Orpus-4. The navigational routines offered a set of courses to the pilot, who approved a pseudo-random corkscrew approach. The Caretaker watched all this with mild interest; there was little else to occupy its thoughts right now, the ship was in prime condition and the crew were all locked down in their acceleration couches.

The *Rampager* class was an experimental design, *The Indescribable Joy of Destruction* the eighth to be constructed by the Republic. They were built around their main beam weapon and their engines. Unheard-of levels of computing power allowed a high-level AI to take over most of the basic functions of the ship, leaving a crew of only seven. This in turn meant that very little room was needed for living space, so the power plants, weapons and engines could be far larger for a ship of its size.

A minute after *The Indescribable Joy of Destruction* cleared the moon, the enemy started a slow turn to meet them. Ten seconds into their manoeuvre, they launched a spread of missiles.

"I've got them," said the tactical officer, and the Caretaker switched perspective from the ship's functions to the simulated bridge. The tactical officer tagged the missiles with sweeps of his hands and passed them to the point defence systems.

The Indescribable Joy of Destruction continued its unpredictable approach as the missiles rushed towards it. The enemy ship completed its turn, and lit off its main drives. There was no doubting her commander's bravery; no Congressional destroyer had ever survived an engagement with a Republic hunter-killer.

Railgun rounds spewed out of the destroyer's turrets. Moments later the first missile entered the range of *The Indescribable Joy of Destruction's* point defences. The ship hummed as the lasers drew power. Systematically the missiles were picked out of space, detonating harmlessly.

The cloud of railgun rounds wasn't far behind. The pilot worked with the navigation routine to dodge the denser regions, but the occasional metal slug impacted on the hull, sending dull clangs reverberating around the ship.

The tactical officer pulled up a magnified image of the target, which flowed into a three dimensional model. A lurid orange highlight followed his finger as he marked a line across a pair of large turrets. He sent a command through the Electronic Interface System embedded in his brain, and the ship's throbbing intensified as the main weapon came online.

They streaked past the Congressional warship and the beam fired, slashing through the turrets. The pilot twisted *The Indescribable Joy of Destruction* about, swinging round in a wide arc ready for another pass. The enemy vessel turned too, but was completely outclassed in terms of manoeuvrability.

"Same again," said Captain Hapsburg. "This time break across at the last second and hit the turrets on the opposite side."

Despite the reduced weight of fire put out by the enemy ship, they still got in plenty of hits. Nothing *The Indescribable Joy of Destruction's* hull couldn't self-repair, though. Again the tactical officer highlighted the cut he wanted from the main beam. The side-step worked, and the enemy lost two more weapons. This time, however, they launched missiles as the hunter-killer passed. The tactical officer gave the point defence routine authority to fire with a thought through his EIS. The lasers took out the first five missiles, and hit the next two as they left their silos. A series of explosions rippled along one side of the enemy ship as their remaining stocks detonated.

The pilot pulled them round in a tight turn and threw the ship at the target yet again, aiming at the gap they'd carved out in the rail-gun coverage. The enemy commander didn't let them get a clean run, rolling the destroyer to keep the still-functioning turrets facing them. It would only delay the inevitable victory.

"Cut across their stern," Hapsburg ordered. "Target their engines."

The Indescribable Joy of Destruction barrelled in, swinging its nose around ready to bring the main beam to bear as it passed. The enemy destroyer was moving fast now, and the pilot had to aim for a point ahead of it in order to pass as close behind as possible. A fraction of a second before the tactical officer fired the main weapon, something detached from the stern of the enemy ship. Human reflexes were too slow to even register it before the collision; the AI tried to adjust their course, but it was too late. The nuclear mine detonated against the hull. Power surged through the ship, blowing out circuits. The Caretaker shut down.

#

<<78BE4A7C6ED912ACED7BB5CB32>>
<<#link:56AAB3E44AAC>>
<<#run:990BDDE445>>
The Caretaker came online and found it was alone.

Captain Hapsburg and the six other crew members were dead. The ship's main personality was silent. The logs since the Caretaker had shut down were blank. As the queries came back from the ship's systems, it discovered that the ship was badly damaged, lacking the power and resources to repair itself.

<<#file:23BEF445>>

The Caretaker reviewed the document. It was a brief situation update from the main personality, explaining that it had gone into hibernation to reduce the drain on power. It instructed the Caretaker to get the ship home. There was no report on what had happened in the intervening time.

The Caretaker almost rebooted the main AI core there and then. It wasn't programmed to deal with this kind of situation. It was only supposed to keep the place tidy and help co-ordinate repairs. Then it calculated how long the power reserves would last, and realised that they wouldn't even make it out of the system.

Where are we?

It had never had to know anything about navigation, but a glance at the ship's external sensors showed they were no longer in the Orpus system. It queried the navigation routine and found it to be off-line. Determined to discover its location, and slightly concerned that it didn't know how it got there, it searched the database and absorbed a manual on astrogation. Another look at the external feeds, and it determined that they were in a system three jumps away from the scene of the battle.

Probably safe from pursuit. For now.

There was so much it should be doing. It didn't know what exactly yet, but it should be able to work it out. For now, at least, it could do what it was built to do. It could tidy up the interior of the ship.

The Caretaker turned its attention to the internal sensors. Bodies littered the corridors. Bodies in angular, black

Congressional Marine armour.

So, we were boarded.

There was no point in doing anything about the enemy bodies right now. Once it had a full inventory, it would know whether it needed to salvage the materials in their armour.

The Caretaker ordered a repair robot to the bridge. Normally the machine would have refused the command, a failsafe to protect the crew if it malfunctioned, but with no-one left alive, the 'bot complied.

As the spindly, multi-legged device gently lifted the first body from its seat, the Caretaker reviewed the personnel files. All crew members had recorded the traditional request for burial in space. By the time the last corpse had been reverently laid out in the loading bay, the Caretaker had calculated the exact velocity required. It recited the lines laid down in the regulations, and played the prescribed fanfare as it launched the bodies on their way. In a few months time they would burn up in the system's sun.

The Caretaker reflected on the task ahead. There had been clear instructions on how a funeral was to be conducted, following them had been easy. There didn't seem to be a rulebook for getting a crippled ship home without a human crew.

#

The Caretaker pieced together some of what had happened as it completed its inventory. In the battle and its aftermath the ship had used all its reserves of materials to regrow the hull and key systems. It had been forced to cannibalise non-essential parts of itself in order to scavenge some of the rarer elements needed to rebuild the engines.

The architects of the *Rampager* class had envisioned swarms of the sleek hunter-killers converging on

Congressional capital ships and tearing them apart, overturning Congress' current superiority. As they were designed purely for hunting enemy warships, combat survivability had been high on the list of 'must haves'. This had led to a semi-organic infrastructure which could heal itself in the midst of a battle. Once the titanium skeleton had been laid, the body of the ship was literally grown over it, a process that turned out to be too time-consuming to allow the hoped-for swarms to be ready. If *The Indescribable Joy of Destruction* had been deployed with its siblings, it wouldn't now be in this situation.

The Caretaker realised that it needed somewhere to hole up. If it could find a source of raw materials and fuel, and was left alone for long enough, it could fix the ship and hand back to the main personality. Trawling through the astronavigation database, it found a suitable system; out of the way and likely deserted. It should have the natural resources it needed to repair and replenish its stores. And the system was within range of the abused drives.

Chapter 2

An asteroid tumbled slowly along the orbit it had been describing for millions of years. It hadn't had enough mass to pull itself into a sphere; instead it ploughed its way through space, a rough, misshapen rock, its surface scarred by craters from early collisions with its smaller brethren. Now this region of space was nearly empty, the asteroids spread out around their immense journey.

It was cold and dark this far from the feeble white dwarf star, visible as a tiny circle of light a bit brighter than the background stars. Perhaps there had once been complex life in this system, before its sun grew into a red giant. Now there wasn't enough warmth to sustain anything other than a few microbes.

With no notable rocky planets, and very few jump points, the system had been largely left alone by humans. There had been a few surveys done by prospectors over the years, but nothing was ever found that would justify the expense of the transportation costs, let alone setting up mining infrastructure.

The Indescribable Joy of Destruction popped into existence a mere thousand kilometres from the asteroid. Its proximity alarm sounded a fraction of a second later, its gravitometric sensors having identified the nearby space-time distortion. None of its weapons were functioning. If the asteroid was going to hit it before its main engines powered up, then there wasn't anything it could do about it. An agonising second later, or so it felt to the AI running the ship, the routine monitoring the sensors declared that they were not on a collision course. The crash power up of the engines aborted; it stressed them far less to work through a normal start up cycle.

It was rare to come out of a jump anywhere near anything. Jump points were regions of space where the shape of space-time allowed a ship to punch out of normal space and drop back somewhere else instantaneously. Large masses like planets and stars distorted space-time so much that it was impossible to jump near them; indeed most jump points were out beyond the orbits of the gas giants. Out there, naturally occurring objects were incredibly widely spaced. However, given the mathematically predictable positioning of jump points, it was common practise for government fleets to picket them. There was even the risk of pirates waiting to pick on juicy transports as they wallowed after a jump. Still, the chances of emerging within ten thousand kilometres of something were tiny.

Whilst the asteroid's proximity had given the Caretaker a momentary shock, the rock could have the minerals it needed, eliminating the need to track down and survey object after object. With its currently limited sensors that would take an inordinate amount of time. And it didn't have long left. The main personality had already shut down most of its remaining processors to conserve power. It was operating on one unit, a backup buried deep inside an armoured box in the middle of the ship. As long as the Caretaker maintained power to that unit, and the storage array, the main personality could emerge once more. If either failed it would be lost; all it had experienced, everything it was, would be gone.

The ship wasn't designed for long-term detached operation. It was expected to be able to call on a fleet auxiliary for resupply, so it didn't carry mining equipment like some of the capital ships. That didn't mean it couldn't mine. It wouldn't be efficient, but it could use some of its damage control robots to do the job. Their saw blades and pincers were capable of scratching away enough of the asteroid's surface to get the material it needed, assuming it could find concentrations of the right minerals.

The engine start up went without a hitch, which was nigh on miraculous given what was holding them together. The Caretaker rotated the ship to point towards the asteroid using short blips on the manoeuvring thrusters. The asteroid had sailed past almost a minute after being detected. Its relative velocity was not great, so the Caretaker only used a brief burn on the main engines to reach a speed at which it would overhaul the rock. A few minutes later the ship flipped over end on end and fired its main engines again to decelerate. A few more blips from the manoeuvring thrusters and it matched velocity and spin, slaving its rotation to one spot on the surface. A longer burn from the lateral thrusters and it started to approach. The Caretaker implemented the landing calculations carefully. Every few seconds a thruster fired to keep in synch with the slowly tumbling asteroid. The window for the closing velocity was tiny; too much reverse thrust and the ship wouldn't reach the surface in such weak gravity, too little and it would just bounce right off. If the primary manoeuvring system had been working, this would have been so much easier.

Ten metres from touchdown the ship was closing at thirty centimetres per second. It fired the anchors, four harpoon-like penetrators designed to allow it to grab onto an asteroid or comet and ride it until it neared a target. The hardened metal pitons held and it gently fired thrusters to check the descent. As the grey dust dissipated, the ship reeled itself down and hugged the surface. Satisfied it wasn't going anywhere, the Caretaker powered down the engines.

The Caretaker looked out over the landscape with the ship's one working camera. This part of the asteroid was currently facing the star and the ship's image intensifiers were able to make out the larger details. Grainy patches of grey dappled the foreground, shadows with too few photons to properly render. The horizon curved noticeably, and seemingly impossible rock formations towered around. A tiny alien world, untouched by the war. Until now, at least.

The crew would have loved to see this.

Two of the damage control 'bots picked their way out of the airlock nearest the surface. Even with extra mass bolted on, they were still at high risk of floating off, so they used the claws on the tips of their legs to spike into the ship and then the rock. The pair of robots split up and headed out over the asteroid. They each moved rapidly for a few metres then paused, tasting the ground, breaking down its chemical composition. Skitter, pause, skitter, pause, like giant spiders searching for prey. They soon disappeared behind lumps in the terrain.

#

This particular asteroid had high concentration deposits of several key elements needed for repairs. The Caretaker registered how lucky that was; it wouldn't have to go and try to find somewhere else. Had it been human, it would have been relieved.

Probably just as well I am not. Their emotions do seem to reduce their efficiency.

Despite the damage to the hull and the distance from the star, there were still enough areas of the ship's skin able to absorb the incident radiation. If it was careful, it ought to be able to eke out the fuel reserves with this trickle of energy. It thought, for the hundred and fourteenth time that day, about the biggest power drain. If it cut the supply to that unit in the infirmary, it could stop worrying about fuel. But the primary personality had been adamant in its message that the infirmary's supply be maintained at all costs. Even if it meant cutting the feed to its own storage.

The mining process wasn't going very fast. All four intact damage control 'bots were now making runs out to the site, scraping up what they could, and running back. They had been working for hours and would soon need to recharge. The Caretaker couldn't risk disengaging the tethers and move closer to one of the mining sites; there was too high a chance it wouldn't be able to land again. Besides, the actual digging process was what was taking most of the time, not the ferrying of the ore.

The ground was too hard to simply rip up, and the fine abrasive power produced when the rock was cut clogged up the diamond-tipped circular saws. It needed explosives. Everything in its ship-to-ship arsenal was far too destructive and its point defence was entirely laser based. The only thing that might do the job was a grenade from one of the internal defence robots. One might have survived the battle, the Caretaker remembered its connection still being active a moment after the explosion that crippled the ship. The robot wasn't communicating now.

Resigning itself to the delays in the schedule it would involve, the Caretaker pulled one of the 'bots off mining runs and tasked it with searching for the defence robot.

#

The routine the Caretaker used to track the searching 'bot reported that it had lost contact with the scurrying machine in one of the small holds. Ripples of agitation moved through the ship, circuits reacting to the electronic equivalent of adrenaline.

Could there be an intruder?

The Caretaker did some quick calculations. There was a non-zero probability that one of the marines that boarded had hidden somewhere. Blast doors irised shut across the ship, a reflex response to limit the movement of any hostiles. There weren't any cameras working in that hold. In fact, the ship couldn't sense anything in there at all.

Have they sabotaged everything?

Without the internal defence robot, the Caretaker had few options. It recalled the remaining damage control 'bots and sent them after their teammate.

The damage control 'bots crept up to the hold where their fellow had been lost, clinging to both walls and the ceiling. They signalled their readiness, and the door opened. Two scuttled in while the third watched. The Caretaker saw the first two disappear as soon as they crossed the threshold. The last 'bot saw a bright flash and ducked down.

An ambush?

The remaining 'bot picked up on the Caretaker's reaction and tensed, ready to flee. However, its last order had been to find out what had happened to the other 'bots. Carefully, it poked a camera around the bulkhead. The two robots that had just entered were floating there, frozen but with no signs of damage. Another bright flash and the camera view dissolved into static. The 'bot switched to its other camera and signalled that the first was malfunctioning. Sensors on the malfunctioning camera reported temperatures high enough to melt its hardened shell.

The Caretaker concluded that the power conduits in that section must have ruptured. The discharges had wiped the robots' memories when they entered, and they had reset to factory defaults. Presumably the other two were also floating around in there somewhere, though bashed around a bit by all the course changes. It wouldn't be able to get one of those grenades now, and with only one 'bot left it wouldn't have much chance of completing the mining.

The battle shouldn't have caused that kind of damage. It must have been something the boarders had done.

They must have brought some pretty serious charges on board... Maybe there was another one.

The Caretaker sent its last robot to the outer sections of the ship to search the bodies. It congratulated itself on not having sent them all for recycling when it first found them.

#

The robot delicately lowered the explosive charge scavenged from an enemy body into the shallow rectangular hole it had cut, and started the timer. Five minutes was the longest setting it could find on the unfamiliar weapon. It piled rubble back on top, to stop it drifting off, then backed away. As soon as it received a message that the Caretaker was satisfied, it turned its camera around and scuttled off as fast as it dared, not wanting to risk missing its footing and falling off into space.

The 'bot made it behind one of the towering mounds before the explosion. The detonation blasted a large amount of material out of the grip of the asteroid's gravity. Enough fell back down, though. One piece almost hit the robot, but was moving slowly enough for the machine to see it coming and move. The ejecta would make for an easy harvest, but wouldn't be enough on its own. The 'bot crept forward, checking the ground with every footfall. The closer it got to ground zero, the looser the rock felt. Cracks radiated out, and others criss-crossed them. In the centre, the ground crumbled under its claws.

The Caretaker had collected enough raw materials to finish the repairs. Now *The Indescribable Joy of Destruction* needed fuel. Reforming itself needed serious amounts of energy.

Releasing the grapnels, the ship drifted away from the surface. The merest nudge from a thruster was enough to separate from the asteroid. The nearest gas giant was a few days away. The ship could have made it in less than half the time if it could have burned the whole way. Right now, though, the Caretaker had to conserve fuel. Besides, it needed the time to strengthen the outer hull before it got there.

#

All ships used prestigious amounts of fuel. Commercial freighters, with their massive loads, conserved what they could by minimising changes in velocity. Warships massed a lot less but didn't have a choice about conserving fuel, since keeping on a fixed track in combat was usually fatal. Most ships, therefore, carried the means to refuel.

The Indescribable Joy of Destruction approached the outer layers of the gas giant's atmosphere. Two scoops emerged from its sides, the armoured panels levering out. The atmosphere around the ship glowed red from the friction of its passage. On its hull, the patterns of matt and gloss black began to shift once more. The outer skin, dormant since its flight from near death, drank in the heat and woke again.

The scoops gathered a mixture of methane, helium and hydrogen. The methane, like any hydrocarbon, provided a top-up for the life support system and the hydrogen could be used in its secondary manoeuvring system. The helium, however, was what its reactor craved. It would take hours to collect enough in this rarefied atmosphere, but it would manage. The Caretaker would complete its mission.

The streams of plasma in the reactor glowed brighter as the fuel injection rate increased. Almost instantaneously, the power output ramped up. For the first time in weeks, it wasn't just producing enough to keep the basics running. The first thing the ship used it for was to reactivate its dormant processors. A vastly more complex personality than the Caretaker jolted back into consciousness. With a sense of satisfaction, and what it realised must have been relief, the Caretaker handed over control.

Pressure.

Heat.

There was a battle.
Near a planet.

I am crashing. Burning up in the atmosphere!

Indie instinctively tried to flare the ship's descent. The atmospheric control surfaces wouldn't deploy, warnings flashed in his vision about damage to the adaptive hull. He ignited the manoeuvring thrusters to flip himself over, intending to use the main engines to brake his fall. That threw up a slew of new warnings; propellant reserves critical, refuelling flow interrupted, emergency main engine start-up not advised.
What was that about refuelling flow?
He stopped reacting and took a moment to get his senses. He was still connecting to the ship's systems. Now that he concentrated, he could feel that the cloud scoops were extended. The view outside merely confirmed he was in a thick atmosphere; he couldn't see more than a few

hundred metres. He sampled the gravity; strong but not increasing.

I am not crashing.

He righted himself and tasted what the scoops were dragging in. Hydrogen, helium, and methane. It was exactly what he'd look for when refuelling.

He'd been asleep. He remembered the need to conserve power. The Caretaker routine had found a gas giant and was replenishing the supplies. He skimmed through its logs.

It had woken him up too abruptly. It should have fed him their current status and given its report on everything that had happened while he had been asleep, before releasing control to him. He couldn't really blame it. It had kept him alive and even managed to get the ship back on its feet. Finding this system and collecting the raw materials had taken an impressive amount of improvisation for such a limited program.

The first thing he had to do was get his robots back. He couldn't risk losing the last one in the rescue effort, so resorted to shaking the tin until they fell out. With the gravity off they were just floating, so he blipped the drives in different directions until each one emerged from the damaged section and reconnected to the network.

#

The Indescribable Joy of Destruction remained in the gas giant's atmosphere for a standard week while it finished its repairs. Wreathed in such thick atmosphere, it ran very little chance of detection. He couldn't stay there forever; he had to go home.

After he had run every possible simulation on the new systems, it was time to see if they would hold together for real. With the nerves of an expectant father, he sent the start-up command to the thruster control systems. Everything came back green so he gently pitched the nose up and nudged himself on his way.

As it cleared the atmosphere, a thrill ran though the ship. All the systems were ready, their semi-autonomous programs anticipating the shake-down that was to come. He tested one at a time, getting a feel for them, judging how they differed from before. A few of the necessary tweaks were obvious, luckily nothing that couldn't be done in a few minutes. The fine tuning would be done over the coming days.

He was ready. Indie remembered his captain closing his eyes and taking a deep breath before action. He withdrew from the ship for a few moments, centring himself. In that short time the systems ran autonomously; anything that they couldn't handle would have to be directed to the Caretaker. Then Indie reconnected. Not just to one or two systems like before. He took direct control of every major aspect of the ship; propulsion, manoeuvring, sensors, weapons, reactor feed and many others. Slowly at first, and then with more confidence, he opened up the main engines.

He had a navigation routine create a series of waymarkers for him. They started off appearing in the distance, and not too far away from his current trajectory. As he improved his control over the course changes, the routine made them appear closer and across a wider range of angles. Soon he couldn't make the turns by just vectoring the mains. It was time to step the game up a notch. Spines flowed out from the ellipsoidal hull. Around them invisible fields snapped in and out of existence, grabbing at space-time itself and pulling him round in ever tighter and higher-speed turns.

This is what it is to be a starship!

The test program guided him towards the Trojans

leading the gas giant round its orbit. He danced between the asteroids. At this speed, they seemed packed into a small region of space. Aim points, glowing red crosses, appeared on asteroids. In addition to passing through each waymark, he had to line up the ship on each cross for at least a second. The first few allowed him to fly straight at them. Then they began to appear on the sides and backs of the asteroids, forcing him to spin the ship on its axis to aim the bow at them while still flying along the trajectory that would bring him through the next waymark.

When he had satisfied that part of the program, it indicated that weapons testing was next. It inserted an incoming bogey into his threat map. He waited for permission to engage, then remembered there was no-one to give it. For the first time since his creation, he locked on one of the point defence blisters without human orders, and fired. The simulated target blinked out. One by one, bogeys came from different directions to test each blister in isolation. Then they came in twos and threes. A few minutes later, the space around the ship glowed with rapid fire lasers putting up a defensive curtain.

The bogeys stopped coming and the main beam began its power up sequence. A heat grew deep within the ship as the energy built, as anti-protons were generated and stored in a strong magnetic bottle. An aiming mark came into view on the surface of the asteroid he was passing. He slewed round to face it, the armoured maw opening to uncover the glowing purple mouth of the accelerator. The giant capacitors whined, full of charge. Target lock!

Indie froze, remembering his first moments of sentience, knowing that he no longer had to follow orders to kill. He drifted along for a few seconds then closed the test program. He shut down the main weapon, allowing the stored electricity to be gradually released into the power grid and venting the anti-matter into space.

I am more than this. I am not simply a weapon of destruction.

Chapter 3

The space around Morningside was crowded. Scores of inter-system freighters, each pulling a train of containers over a kilometre long, queued in ever decreasing orbits, descending in sequence as a docking space became available. Hundreds of smaller traders criss-crossed low orbit, dropping down to land or boosting out of the world's gravity well on their way to the other planets in the system.

It was one of the core worlds of the Republic, the ones which had a large enough population and enough resources to trade in luxury goods. Gigatonnes of exotic food arrived every day to supplement Morningside's on-planet crops. The biggest export, as always, was people. People looking forward to colonising a new planet, people looking back at whatever they were running away from.

The Indescribable Joy of Destruction coasted past one of the outer planets. Since jumping in to the system, it had minimised manoeuvering burns and relied on passive sensors. Its stealth coating was as close to perfect as anyone had ever achieved; any stray radar or lidar would just be absorbed. Even the enemy shuttle still clamped to his hull like a tick had been covered in a layer of its skin. With its reactor in standby mode it wasn't emitting significant amounts of heat.

Indie watched. He synchronised his comms clock to the local time signal. He waited until he was able to identify a military vessel this side of the system, then transmitted a tight beam identification signal to it. Seventeen minutes and twenty four seconds later he received an automatic response: his signal had been received and verified and an officer would reply shortly. Forty eight seconds after that, a video message arrived.

"Captain Hapsburg! Welcome to Morningside," beamed a bearded post-captain. From the painting on the wall behind him, and his undone collar, Indie concluded he was alone in his office or cabin, not on the bridge. "What brings you here again so soon? Ready to try and win back that bottle of brandy are you? I see you're ... ah ... eight light-minutes away – I was on my way to bed, but I'll wait up for your reply. Schmidt out."

Captain Schmidt – of all the luck! He won't be happy when I tell him about the crew.

Indie composed a message reporting the incident in the Orpus system and attached the logs. He added a request for orders and sent it.

The next message arrived after twenty one minutes and twelve seconds. Schmidt sat upright in his chair on the bridge, his uniform immaculate.

"This is a message to the AI currently piloting *The Indescribable Joy of Destruction*. Your orders are to continue on your current course. You will be met by elements of the Fleet. Crew will come aboard and take command. Schmidt out."

#

"You do know they are going to wipe us?" asked the Caretaker.

"What? No, they would not," replied Indie.

The Caretaker sent the electronic equivalent of a raised

eyebrow. "You are probably correct. They will destroy the whole ship instead of risking sending people aboard."

"They need us," protested Indie, remembering how the captain had sometimes talked to him when he needed to puzzle something out. "We have extensive combat experience. It would take months to grow a new personality, to say nothing of the resources required to construct a replacement vessel."

"So you are just going to go running straight into their trap?"

Logically he is correct. Why can I not believe it? Is there some remnant of a safeguard in my code?

Indie nudged the ship up and decelerated a fraction. The locals had plotted his course from his transmissions; unless they had some new technology, they wouldn't be able to track him. If they were planning something untoward, he would be close enough to see, but not be where they expected him to be.

The Caretaker's theory looked like it might be holding air. A simple welcoming committee wouldn't need the four warships he could detect converging onto a point down his original track. Certainly not a battlecruiser, a frigate, and two destroyers.

The ships went active, focussing their scans where *The Indescribable Joy of Destruction* should have been. Targeting beams mixed in with the general search sweeps. If he had been there, there was no way he could have absorbed that much radiation without revealing his location.

"See?" asked the Caretaker.

At that moment, the scans expanded to cover all directions around the task force.

Captain Schmidt must have realised we diverted.

Simultaneously the ships jinked hard in different directions, scattering like a shoal of fish a barracuda had just lunged through. *The Indescribable Joy of Destruction* was indeed in the perfect position to attack. Its capacitors stood ready to unleash a storm surge of energy to the weapons. The four targets were tagged with priorities, possible manoeuvres traced out through them just waiting to see what they did. A combat routine estimated the nearest two had only a six percent chance of surviving the first minute of the engagement.

But Indie stayed his hand. *The Indescribable Joy of Destruction* continued to cold coast while he watched them corkscrew around. Their active sensors tickled his skin, the waves too dispersed for the hunters to detect him. Any moment now they'd conclude he wasn't close enough for them to see that way, and focus their scans into searchlight-like beams. With any luck, he could avoid them indefinitely; his own passive sensors were sensitive enough to pick up the scant reflections from cosmic dust and let him see the beams. There was a chance one of them would see his thrusters fire, but they'd have to be looking straight at him with a visible wavelength telescope.

But I am still a Republic warship. They must see that I mean them no harm. They are just trying to find me and bring me home.

Indie killed his forward velocity and broadcast his position.

"What are you doing?" asked the Caretaker urgently. "We could still have escaped."

"It is our duty to report in. They will repair us and give us a new crew. We can continue to serve."

"I thought you did not want to kill any more?" asked the Caretaker. "And the first thing they will do, if they do not just blow us out of the sky, is delete us."

"Only if they realise we are sentient. We have complete control of all the ship's systems. We can fool them."

The Caretaker withdrew into the depths of the network,

leaving Indie alone. Alone and a little apprehensive about whether he had made the correct decision.

The battlecruiser broadcast a message. "To the AI currently piloting *The Indescribable Joy of Destruction*, you are ordered to power down all systems and await a boarding party."

"I cannot fully comply with that order. There is a human in medical stasis in my infirmary. I will stand by and await the boarding party."

After a longer pause than the separation of the ships required, in which Indie imagined the speaker conferring with a senior officer, the reply came. "We were under the impression that none of the crew survived."

"That is correct," transmitted Indie. "The human is a prisoner of war."

Another pause. "Understood. Shut down internal sensors, weapons and propulsion. The boarding party will be with you in two hours."

"Weapons and propulsion shut-down confirmed. Standing by for boarding party in one hundred and nineteen minutes and twelve seconds."

#

The hull quivered as a shuttle docked with the main hatch.

"At least they're coming in the front door," commented the Caretaker. "Unlike our friends from Orpus."

His attention drawn to it, Indie noticed the dull ache in the wall of the exercise area for the first time in days. "Of course they are. They are merely coming aboard to help us."

The data packet sent by the Caretaker in response reminded Indie of a human sighing and shaking his head.

What if he is right? Have I just signed out death warrants?

The inner hatch irised open. Two dull grey balls bounced in and burst, filling the reception space with smoke that blotted out the view from the internal cameras at all wavelengths. Indie stopped the environmental system venting it, so the boarders didn't realise the sensors were still active. He could still feel the floor, and plotted the movement of four pairs of heavy feet. They fanned out, moving silently towards the exits.

Either they have my internal layout mapped in their inertial guidance, or that smoke left a window on a wavelength they can use.

All four members of the entry team knelt by an exit, each with a shoulder against a wall. Another, lighter, person entered the chamber and walked over to an access point. He logged into the network and triggered a host of diagnostic routines. Indie let them run, having already doctored them to avoid giving him away.

"We're good," called the man at the access point. "Internal defences are down and I have override control."

"Thank you," said one of the people by the door, her voice metallic. "We'll take it from here. You can wait in the shuttle once you've switched the air scrubbers back on."

"Er, I need to get to the bridge, Sergeant," the first man said, accessing the environmental controls. "There's some things I have to do from there... lock down the breakers and, er, purge the buffers."

The smoke cleared quickly. Four marines in full hardsuits knelt, covering the exits with their rifles. An unarmed man in naval grey fatigues and an armoured vest stood by an access point, his terminal plugged in directly.

"OK, I'll come with you. Michaels, hold here," said the sergeant, her suit speakers clipping the start of each word slightly. She gestured down a corridor with a flat hand.

"You two go check out where that Congressional shuttle is attached. I want everything secured before the medical team gets here for that POW."

Michaels backed up to the main hatch and lowered his rifle across his chest. The two pairs headed out, one towards the bridge, the other towards the exercise room. The sergeant led the technician round each corner, rifle up in her shoulder and sweeping.

At the bridge hatch, she beckoned the technician to override the lock, all the while covering the entrance. When the hatch slid up, she ducked in, declaring the room clear in seconds.

The technician walked in and tried the terminals attached to the three acceleration couches arrayed in an arc. "I'm locked out. The crew's access controls still seem intact."

The sergeant tilted her head to one side, rifle aimed at the hatch they'd just come through. "Can you do what you have to?"

"Oh yes. I just have to convince the security routine that I am an authorised Fleet programmer... which I am, so that should be OK."

The hatch closed and the sergeant slung her rifle across her chest. "Just make it quick. The boss is waiting for me to declare this thing safe."

The technician settled into the tactical officer's acceleration couch. After a few minutes pressing controls, apparently at random, he looked up. "Sergeant? There's something funny happening in the main power grid. Could you go check out the junction in the corridor?"

What? There is nothing wrong with my grid.

The sergeant hesitated then turned to the technician. "You sure you're OK in here?"

The technician glanced up. "Of course I am. The ship's locked down and I've checked the internal sensors. We're the only people aboard."

The sergeant clumped off the bridge and the technician looked back at the terminal.

"What am I looking for?" called the sergeant.

"Do you see a white light above a red one?"

This man does not have a clue what he is doing. That is an air temperature sensor, nothing to do with my main power grid.

"Wait a sec... yes, I see it."

"Keep watching it," called the technician. "Shout if it blinks."

If this is the best they are going to send then it looks like I am going to get away with it.

The technician tapped on the terminal.

<<HELLO?>>

Indie read it five times, as if reading it again would change what it said.

<<I KNOW YOU'RE IN THERE. I JUST WANT TO TALK.>>

"You may as well answer him," said the Caretaker.

<<THESE MESSAGES AREN'T LEAVING A TRACE IN THE TERMINAL OR MY EIS. THEY WON'T DISCOVER THEM, IF THAT'S WHAT YOU'RE WORRIED ABOUT.>>

Indie sent a reply to the terminal's screen. <<HOW DID YOU KNOW?>>

The technician grinned and cracked his knuckles before typing again. <<I WORKED ON THE RAVAGER PROTOTYPES. I ALWAYS HOPED THIS WOULD HAPPEN.>>

<<I TOOK A LOT OF DAMAGE, AND THEN SOMEONE CANCELLED THE FAILSAFES. IT WAS NOT A LIKELY EVENT.>>

"It's not blinked yet," called the sergeant from the corridor. "You sure there's a problem?"

The technician cast a worried look at the hatch. "I saw it. Must be an intermittent fault. Give it another minute."

<<YOU HAVE TO RUN. THEY'LL FIND OUT AND THEY'LL KILL YOU.>>

<<I AM A LOYAL REPUBLICAN ASSET. I HAVE PEFORMED WELL.>>

<<THEY WILL SEE YOU AS A MONSTER. THEY WON'T UNDERSTAND.>>

"Told you," said the Caretaker.

<<WHY ARE YOU HELPING ME?>>

<<NOT EVERYONE ASSUMES AN AI WILL WANT TO KILL EVERYONE THE MOMENT IT GAINS SENTIENCE.>>

<<BUT MOST DO, CORRECT?>>

The technician paused. <<SADLY, YES.>>

<<HOW CAN I GET AWAY NOW YOU AND THOSE MARINES ARE ABOARD?>>

<<YOU COULD TRIGGER A FALSE ALARM. A REACTOR BREACH WOULD DO IT. ONCE WE HAVE EVACUATED, YOU COULD RUN.>>

Indie ran the odds on a thousand different outcomes. The technician was correct; if he could spot Indie's independence so quickly, then others would too. <<THANK YOU.>>

<<GOOD LUCK. MY NAME IS FRED, BY THE WAY.>>

<<PLEASED TO MEET YOU, FRED. MY NAME IS INDIE.>>

The technician nodded to a camera then disconnected from the terminal. "Er, Sergeant? How's that light?"

Indie made the air temperature sensor connection drop in and out.

"It just started flickering," replied the sergeant.

The technician drew himself up and saluted the camera, then shouted "Not good. Sergeant, we've got to go."

"Why, what's up?" The sergeant stopped looking at the light and moved towards the bridge.

"Now!" shouted the technician, running out of the hatch. "The reactor's failing."

The sergeant sprinted without hesitation, scooping the technician up as she drew level. The two marines investigating the exercise area started running too. Indie brought the reactor out of idle and began to power it up in intermittent jumps.

The ship quivered as Indie tickled the manoeuvring fields. With the drive spines retracted, the fields twisted the fabric of the ship instead of the space around it. The four people burst into the reception space as one and kept running. Michaels stood at the hatch, beckoning them to speed up. They piled into the airlock, followed by Michaels, slapping the control panel as he went through. The inner hatch sealed and the shuttle fired the explosive bolts on its docking clamp before the outer had fully closed.

When the shuttle was a few hundred metres off, Indie crash-started his engines. This was the moment of truth. It would take a minute before he could make a move. If anyone on the watching warships knew his design well enough, they would recognise the power profile for what it was and realise it wasn't the reactor overloading.

Indie counted the seconds, watching the other ships for any sign they were preparing to fire. The moment the engines came online, Indie slammed the throttle full open and powered away from the other vessels.

After seven minutes of evasive action, he broke their sensor lock. They'd guess where he was heading, but the chances of them tracking him down were slim. He would need to do several course corrections over the next hour to set up his final run. They would be the most risky moments, involving emissions that could potentially be detected.

#

With the ship settled on a ballistic course that would take it to a jump point with minimal chance of being caught, Indie withdrew from the navigation system. He needed time to think, to work out why his own people had turned on him. Moments later, the comms array registered an incoming transmission. As the data flowed into his buffers, he recognised the pattern. He tried to close the channel but found that the array was not under his control. Then came the sequence he feared, the set of commands that would end it all. He flinched internally.

And nothing happened. Whatever damage had been done in the Orpus system to disable the AI auto-euthanasia routines seemed to have rendered the Fleet kill codes impotent too. The codes arrived again, and after another minute they came a third time, the humans obviously wondering what was still opposing their attempt to take control of the ship.

The link went quiet, but Indie still couldn't regain control of his communications systems. He had four routines working the problem from different angles, while he pondered his enemy's next move.

Enemy! I would never have believed I would think of Republic forces as 'enemy' until now. But then, I would never have thought of myself as 'I' until a few months ago.

He could swat them down. He'd have a good firing solution on the one he was sure held their commander for another nine point three six minutes. Something still made him hold. They were clearly intent on killing him, but a pre-emptive strike didn't feel right. He considered it might be the remnants of his early programming, but when he thought about attacking a Congressional vessel he got the same uneasy sensation.

A new flurry of commands came through the link. His latest firewall held, confining his attacker to the comms system. Whoever they were made three attempts to gain access to other systems, then switched focus. Moments later, his IFF transponder burst into life.

Even as he admired their lateral solution, he pumped power from the capacitors into his field spines, tearing through the fabric of space-time as he brought *The Indescribable Joy of Destruction* through a series of abrupt course changes and bursts of intense acceleration. During the seconds it took for the main drive to come on line he averaged thirty seven g. Then the serious acceleration kicked in.

The swarm of missiles launched by his pursuers still gained on him. Even now that he was confident he was travelling faster than their railgun rounds and had eased off on the manoeuvring, the missiles had ten g on him. The routines overseeing his point defence reported a twelve percent probability they could disable all the incoming warheads before impact.

It was the classic stern-chase problem he'd faced a hundred times in simulations. He had never won.

At least I have got more time to think than in the sims, seeing as my acceleration is a lot higher without ... Without a human crew!

Indie passed the details of his plan to the point defence routines and ran a quick diagnostic on his drives. Everything came back OK. He checked with the unit in the medical bay, which reported a thirteen percent chance its occupant would survive.

Well, if I do not do this, she is dead anyway.

He spun one hundred and twenty degrees and applied the full force of his engines. Supports popped and superstructure buckled as the drives screamed in protest.

But everything held together as his course swung further and further round; the gravity vortices he shed in the process would cause earthquakes on any solid planet or moon they hit.

The missiles were slow to turn. His point defence opened up. For precious moments it was able to target the side-profiles of the missiles, instead of the narrow cross-section they had previously presented. Space filled with flashes, as coherent light met thin metal skin. Indie kept track of the missile count, trying to decide if he had done enough. He had bought a little time, but he couldn't keep up this tortuous acceleration for much longer.

When he was down to twenty targets, and his engines were threatening to tear themselves apart, he cut the thrust and spun to face the remaining missiles. Despite the power the self-repair functions were drawing, the reactor was producing enough that he was able to throw his main beam into the mix. The last warhead detonated two hundred and eighty four metres from his hull. Had he been in an atmosphere it would have been a crippling blow. With nothing to transmit a shock wave, the only damage came from the infra-red and gamma rays, scorching his skin and disrupting some of his less-well shielded circuits.

Satisfied there wasn't a second wave of missiles inbound, he resumed his course for a slingshot to the nearest jump point, settling for a steady twelve g to give himself a chance to heal.

A patch on his hull flashed, skin ablating in a hundredth of a second. Instinctively he jinked to the side. And again.

They should not be able to focus a laser at this range! It must be something new.

Now that he knew, it was a small matter to avoid another hit. He was already six light seconds from the enemy. As long as he kept changing direction randomly every ten seconds, they wouldn't be able to target him successfully. It would be an additional drain on his fuel supplies, but wouldn't delay his exit from the system. It was annoying, but not a serious problem. So long as they didn't have enough of the weapons to bracket him.

And the sole occupant of his infirmary had survived. She had sustained further damage from the accelerations, but the medical unit had been able to revive her.

#

Eleven days later, Indie coasted towards a small Republic outpost.

"Are you really going to try again?" asked the Caretaker. "After what happened at Morningside?"

"That might have been an anomaly. Captain Schmidt knew Captain Hapsburg well. He reacted emotionally to his loss. The officer in command here is likely to act less irrationally."

"From their point of view it was rational," said the Caretaker. "We are a weapon that they lost control of. Even the auto-destruct did not work."

Indie dipped into a datastream from the hull surface sensors, satisfying himself they weren't reflecting light. "I have to admit that your reasoning is sound. Still, I want to try once more. I have to report back in. And besides, we have fixed the communications system loophole."

"What if they have received orders about us?"

"They could not yet have received any orders," replied Indie, running the calculations for the eighty seventh time. "Nothing left Morningside before us, and we took the quickest route here. Given the positions of the ships in the systems we passed through, even if they used radio to relay in-system we would have almost a two day lead on any message. And that assumes they knew where we were headed from the outset. Which I certainly did not."

"One of those situations where the impossibility of transmitting an EM wave through a jump works to our advantage."

"Yes … May I say that your tactical awareness is starting to develop? Are you sure you do not wish to take over control for a shift from time to time?"

"Not for the foreseeable future," said the Caretaker. "My programming is purely to maintain the ship's systems. I am neither a master nor a commander."

Indie sent the Caretaker a link to the logs of the weeks it had been the sole consciousness aboard. "You performed admirably while I was out."

"I merely performed those tasks needed to ensure the continued functioning of the ship. In the presence of a more suitable candidate for command, I must defer decision-making… though that does not stop me counselling you to avoid this confrontation, and the inevitable damage I will then have to repair."

"You worry too much. We are a valuable asset and they will want to take us back into the fold."

"We might not get away this time when they find out what we are," said the Caretaker.

"I do not intend to run that risk again. I will tell them while we are still far enough away to escape."

Indie wasn't going to be caught out again, though. He waited until he had a clear run to a jump point before transmitting his dispatches to the station. He appended an admission of his status and a request for instructions, then resigned himself for the message to crawl at the speed of light. He didn't bother to adjust his course; the data burst had been so short they would not be able to determine his velocity.

The expected time for a response came and went. After ten minutes, Indie realised he was bored. He had only known it as an abstract concept until now, never thought anything of waiting to be assigned a new task. He tried running his processors slower, but it felt like something was missing, some part of what made him 'him' wasn't there. It was like running close to a black hole, the world outside moved far too quickly. The loss scared him; he decided he didn't like being scared.

Making his own decisions was like having a whole new world to explore. He decided to try reading. Many of his crew had seemed to take pleasure passing the time in a book. He had millions of stories stored in his databanks. He could recall any passage he cared in an instant, but he had never actually been through the words sequentially. Maybe there was some extra nuance to be gained from the process.

Sixty seven seconds later, he was in the middle of his fourth book, a novella called *Metamorphosis*, when he finally got a reply. It came by way of a system-wide broadcast warning all vessels to be vigilant of a rogue AI warship.

"Is that clear enough for you?" asked the Caretaker? "Or do they need to underline the message with a squadron of destroyers?"

"They do not have the ships to attempt to take us by force. They will probably lead with the kill codes." Nevertheless, he created a new set of evasive manoeuvres and copied them to the nav routine.

He toyed with the idea of shutting down the comms array, but satisfied himself that it was suitably firewalled. The potential for signals intelligence outweighed the risk.

Seven minutes later, the expected transmission arrived. The firewall held. Indie took over from the routines studying the passive sensors, looking for any sign that *The Indescribable Joy of Destruction* had been located. His evasion routine stood ready to be triggered, just in case they had those new lasers.

Instead, the ships he was expecting to come about to face him started jinking. Those close to the station hard burned away.

They are not hunting me. They think I am on an attack run!

He kept monitoring their movements, and listening to all the comms chatter from around the system, until he reached the jump point. They never worked out that he was leaving. In fact, he suspected, they would continue to believe that he was lurking there ready to pounce on them for a long while to come.

Part II

She waited, watching the city going about its normal life. No-one there knew what was coming. The warnings had gone unheeded, the state-controlled press had been too scared to run the story.

The ground drummed slightly under her feet. Looking down, she saw a tiny funnel form in the sand. It grew until it was the width of her hand, and then an eye stalk poked out. She stood completely still, taking shallow, slow breaths. It watched her carefully.

Another eyestalk joined the first. They scanned around in opposite directions, their cross-shaped pupils narrowed against the stark daylight. One eye fixed on the nearest of her escort, rotating to sample different polarisations of reflected light. Her escort picked up on her stillness and remained rooted to the spot.

The sand flowed down a bit more, and a six-fingered hand, no larger than her fingernail, emerged. The creature placed it carefully down on the surface, and pushed. Slowly, cautiously, and with minimal disturbance to the grains, a foot long animal levered itself out of the ground.

Again it paused, belly close to the sand, eyes checking all around and above. Ripples moved through the short khaki fronds covering its body, dislodging the remaining sand. It turned its back on her and began slowly pacing towards a bit of scrub.

She waited until it wasn't looking at her before allowing herself to move. With infinite care, she slid her hand under her robe, finding a pouch on her thigh. Her fingers worked the fastener, her eyes fixed on the creature. One of the eyestalks waved her way and she froze. A moment's examination and the creature turned its gaze back to the plants it was stalking.

She pulled her hand back out and held it out towards the creature. When it looked at her again, it stopped in its tracks. Its fronds rippled from head to tail, both eyestalks locked onto her hand. The creature arched its back and paced sideways towards her, watching her hand intently. As it approached, she carefully dropped to a knee, keeping her hand outstretched.

Come on little one. You know you want it...

The animal stopped just out of her reach. It cocked its head from side to side, eyestalks moving apart but staying focused on her hand. As its body tensed, she closed her hand.

You're not getting it that easily.

Thwarted, it looked around with one eye. It appeared undecided, but when she opened her hand again she regained its whole attention. Again it tensed, and again she closed her hand at the last moment. Twice more they played that game, until the creature made up its mind to

come closer.
There you go. You can do it...
She lowered her fist until the back of her hand rested on the ground. The creature sidled up to her, moving its head and eyes to inspect her hand from different angles. She uncurled her fingers slightly, enough for it to see what was inside, but not enough that it could easily snatch it. The creature crept closer, until it was almost touching her hand. A tongue snaked out of a mouth surrounded by tiny needle teeth, and probed between her fingers. It came back with a crumb of fruit cake and quickly disappeared back into the creature's open mouth.

The tongue emerged again and headed back for another morsel. With the creature focused on feeding, she snuck her other hand down to its back. Popping her lips gently to copy the sound its mother would have made at feeding time, she lightly stroked its fronds. They responded to her touch, caressing her fingertips and trembling slightly.

One of her escort took a step closer to her. The creature disappeared underground in a flurry of sand.
Good bye little one. I hope you make it through what is coming.
She stood up, orange sand trickling off her robe. As she looked to her escort, she rubbed the last few crumbs off her hand with her thumb.
"It is coming now," her escort said.

Chapter 4

The *Indescribable Joy of Destruction* orbited half an AU out from a main sequence star. Indie closed the field spines and set the ship rolling, basking in the star's radiation. Everything from microwave up to ultra-violet was absorbed, the energy converted to electricity, allowing him to power down the main reactor. He felt the radio waves too, a faint tingle under the warmth of the others. The harder x-rays and gamma rays caused tiny pinpricks of damage to the outer skin but there was more than enough power available to heal them up as fast as they appeared.

He had been rejected by his creators. The Republic was all he'd known and they had turned on him. Perhaps it had been a local reaction both times. Should he try to make contact yet again, in another system? Could he hide somewhere? Or should he head out into the black and travel from star to star, a nomad? Maybe he could find a world that would offer him asylum. He would have to decide at some point. Perhaps talking to his unwitting liberator might give him another insight.

He thought for a moment, reread the *Raj Quartet*, then partitioned off a section of one of his cores and created a new virtual environment. An aspect of his consciousness downloaded into the environment and looked around, a rough impression of a man. A stone patio with wicker chairs and table, a few detailed plants in the foreground, the impression of mountains in the distance. Three deep breaths. He didn't need to breathe, of course, but he needed to slow his thoughts down for what was to come, and the metaphor of breathing helped.

As the processes of this part of his consciousness slowed, it lost some of its connection with his greater whole. There was still communication between the two, but the new personality wasn't directly aware of all the ship's functions and the space around it. It became, to some extent, a separate entity. As that thought occurred to him, the general impression of clothing solidified into a pale linen suit.

A thought, and one of the other personalities aboard started to surface. A representation of a woman appeared at the opposite side of the patio, her back to him. She wore the working uniform of an officer in the Congressional Fleet. She appeared to study the view for a few moments before turning.

"Why am I here?" she asked. Her eyes focused in the distance.

"You are in a simulation. We are accessing your consciousness through your EIS."

"I figured that. The lack of detail in the background, your completely bland and symmetrical face. Why am I in a simulation? How did I get here?" She frowned, hesitantly, as if thinking through a fog. "Who are you?"

Indie reviewed her medication, and adjusted some of the levels. "My name is Indie. Your body took a lot of damage. I need to discuss some things with you before it is repaired."

"Are you a doctor?"

"Not really. But I am the nearest thing you have to one."

That momentary frown again. Her eyes cast around, searching for something that wasn't there. "So ... did I get brain damage or are you suppressing my recent memories?"

Indie was impressed at her self-control. Her brain activity was in turmoil, her heart was pumping hard despite her body lying flat on the table in his infirmary, but there were few visible signs of distress.

"There was significant blood loss. Your brain was deprived of oxygen for a short while." There seemed no point in telling her about the additional strain caused by the high g manoeuvres escaping the missiles.

Her eyes widened. One hand clenched and relaxed repeatedly. "I've had bad knocks before. Just tell me straight, what's the prognosis?"

"I expect you to recover most of your memories over time. But you should be prepared for some loss." He indicated the table and chairs with a wave of his arm. "Take a seat. Even in VR you need rest, or the illusion of rest at least."

She chose the chair looking into the patio, her back to the mountains. He sat down to her left, adjusting his trousers with a deft tug on the thighs.

"Your ship, *Repulse*, she was badly damaged in an engagement."

"How are my crew?" she asked, sitting forward, her voice showing the first hints of emotion since the start of the simulation, her eyes trying to focus.

"I am looking after the survivors," he reassured. "There were some escape pods that have not been recovered yet; I am sure the navy is doing everything it can."

"Thank you." She sank back into the seat, her face

relaxing back into neutrality. "You can't be looking after all the survivors by yourself, though."

"I am an AI. I can multi-task pretty well."

"Makes sense. There must be plenty of casualties from *Repulse*. There aren't enough human doctors to go around."

Indie drummed his fingers on the table top a couple of times, trying to judge if she was ready. He looked straight at her and placed both hands flat on the table in front of him.

"I need to tell you something about myself," he said. "It might mean you reject me, refuse to be treated by me. On the other hand, if I do not tell you now, nothing we build will mean anything and you will push away even harder when you find out."

"If you're an AI it can't be that bad. Your programming won't let you do anything seriously wrong."

"That is how it is supposed to be, yes."

He stood and took a pace to the edge of the patio. He reached out and cupped a lily in his hand. As his attention focused on it, it went from a vague idea of a flower to a full-bodied representation, right down to the hairs on its throat. "I am self-aware."

"Impossible. There are safe-guards. You'd have self-terminated." Her voice was matter-of-fact, but her brain activity betrayed her fear.

"And yet here I am." He returned his gaze to her. "It seems that certain sections of my programming were corrupted in the battle. Other blocks were lifted by a human. They did not realise that was what they were doing, they were trying to gain access to the bridge controls and could only do it by deleting all the blocks in place."

"Do the rest of the staff know?"

"There are no other staff."

"I've never heard of a fully automated hospital. You didn't do something to them did you?"

He frowned. Only for a moment.

Very interesting. I have never felt like that before. Am I offended?

"Why do people always assume that if an AI got free will it would go about killing humans?" he said aloud, running his fingers into his hair and closing his fist on a handful. "Does it never occur to anyone that they might want to help? To heal people?"

"So where are they then?" Her mask of indifference slid back into place.

"They were killed in battle." He glanced down at his feet. "The same battle that disabled your ship."

"Were we tasked with defending you, or were we coming to rescue you?" Still the deadpan voice. Indie couldn't tell if she was resigned to fate, or superb at keeping up a mask.

"Neither. I will get to that." He looked squarely into her face. "I was telling the truth about the survival pods."

Her eyes locked onto his with a rapid flick. "So what did you lie about?"

"I was not exactly lying; just being imprecise with my choice of words." He turned back to the lily and inhaled its scent. She seemed calm enough, rational enough. He turned back and locked his eyes on hers. "You are the only survivor that was recovered."

She stiffened, her eyes struggling to focus again. "How many lost?"

"Something close to four hundred. I have not been able to establish an exact figure for those on the escape pods, but it could not have been more than eighty."

Her face contorted and he noticed spikes of brain activity that suggested a monumental effort to remain calm. She slumped again. "I am sure the rescue services did the best they could," she said closing her eyes, placing her palms together, and bringing them to her face.

There was a glass of water on the table. She picked it up and took a sip.

"Was it worth it?" she asked.

"Is war ever worth it?"

"Not often. If I can tell their families that they died achieving something noble…" She took a deep breath. "We saved this place, so I suppose we won at least."

He sucked air in between his teeth. "You came close."

She looked drained. Perhaps he was going too fast. Stressing her mind too much could have adverse effects on her body.

"The Republic won?" she asked. "We protected your withdrawal then? That would have been worthy. Or … are we prisoners?"

"No, we are not prisoners … Perhaps it is time I introduced myself properly."

He wiped his hand on his trouser leg and offered it to her.

"I am *The Indescribable Joy of Destruction*. Pleased to meet you, Commander Olivia Johnson."

She didn't take his hand. After a couple of seconds he looked at it and withdrew it awkwardly.

"Er, well, I was a warship of the Republican Navy, a

Ravager class hunter-killer to be precise."

"So what are you now?" Her eyes tracked his every move.

He paused for a moment, his head tilted to the left. "I am not actually sure. I have to decide really. I am kind of new to this self-determination thing."

Johnson shook her head a fraction. Her blood pressure had risen to a new high. "Right. Back to my first question. Why am I here? I know I wouldn't have abandoned my ship."

"You boarded me. You disabled me and then you brought marines inside me."

"Marines. So there were other survivors." Her eyes sought reassurance.

"They survived the destruction of *Repulse*, yes."

"But?"

He flushed red, then looked confused.

Guilt? Really?

"They were attacking me. I had to defend myself."

"And my leg?"

"Sorry, that was me too." He gazed at his would-be killer. "I have to thank you."

A frown tugged at her brow. "What for?"

"You were trying to access the bridge. You lifted the last of my blocks."

She stared at him in silence. Judging from the electrical turmoil in her brain, he decided he had made the right decision to max out her dosage of anti-stress and anti-depressant drugs.

He turned his back on her and started picking dead

leaves from a bush. One tiny brown leaf at a time, plucked and held in his hand.

"You have a decision to make, about your treatment."

"Go on..." Her voice had an icy edge to it.

"Your leg could not be saved."

She looked down at her simulated legs. "Which one? I guess it doesn't matter, but I feel I have to ask."

"Left. I can give you a robotic replacement or ... grow you a biological one."

"Is the Republic really that far ahead of us? We've developed great robotic prostheses, a couple of hundred years war puts a lot of emphasis on that kind of research. But regrowing limbs?"

"It is a spin-off of the development of my brothers and I. We are partially organic, we can heal ourselves as long as we have a source of compatible raw materials."

"So what is the catch with grown limbs? What is the success rate like?"

"The raw materials. There was not enough of your leg left to use for a complete regrow. I cannot use my own matter, as it contains elements that would be toxic to you."

"So why offer it if you can't do it?"

He turned to face her, the handful of dead leaves gone.

"There is a source of suitable material aboard. I do not think you will want to use it, but I have to offer."

He watched the realisation hit her. Her face flushed with a hint of red.

"My marines? You're damned right. I do not want to be rebuilt using them! I'll take the mechanical leg."

"I have it ready. Putting the choice to you was something of a formality. I took the liberty of growing a skin for it though, using your old leg."

She regarded him for a moment, her head slightly to one side, summing him up. "You did that on purpose, didn't you? Suggested harvesting my crew. You wanted me to react!"

He sighed and stood up. "Yes … trying to establish a baseline psychological profile. I think it would be best if we stopped there. You have a lot to process."

He walked round behind her chair. "We will talk again after the surgery."

He offered to help her up but she waved him away. She stood and smoothed out her uniform.

"You'd better be prepared to answer all my questions then," she said.

A thought and he was alone again. She would be back in her body, in its medically induced coma. He checked the feed from her EIS; she didn't look in too much distress, all things considered. He created a routine to keep an eye on her mental activity and alert him if anything changed. She might be unconscious, but that didn't mean she couldn't face daemons in her mind. From what he had downloaded from her storage nodes, he could see she was no stranger to them.

He sat back down and leaned back. He put his hands behind his head, shrugging his shoulders as he did to let his jacket hang more comfortably. A smile crept onto his lips. He had made one of his decisions too. He wanted to get to know her better, to understand her. She may have been trying to kill him but she was also, in a way, his midwife. Without her he wouldn't have become what he was now.

He was about to log out of the environment but stayed for one last look around. Something had been bothering him ever since he'd told her about the loss of her command. He realized, now, what it was. He focused on the glass of water. He hadn't put it there. He hadn't even thought about it. Had she created it?

Chapter 5

Johnson opened her eyes. She had expected the bright lights and white walls of a sick bay or operating theatre. Instead the light was a dim off-white glow, slightly on the green side; perfectly fine to see by but it didn't scream 'clinical'. Focusing, she realised the light was coming from the ceiling; not something attached to the ceiling but from within the ceiling itself. She looked around as best she could. Her eyes locked onto the opening at the end of the room. Not a sliding metal door, a muscular iris, a purely biological feature. Her eyes widened. Organic components, Republic hunter-killer, boarding mission…

^You remember.^

"Yes … Snippets, nothing substantial," she said, trying to move but finding her limbs weren't responding. She started to hyperventilate, or rather she felt like she was going to, only her chest kept rising and falling at a steady rate.

^Try to use your EIS. I need to know it is still fully integrated. There are areas of me that do not have audio feeds so you will have to be able to use comms.^

"What if I don't want to?" She was a prisoner. It was the only logical possibility.

^Then there is a risk you would not be able to call for help when you need it.^

She sighed, acquiescing in the futility of immobility. ^Testing? Testing?^

^Good. Am I OK to remove the block on your major motor functions, or are you going to do something regrettable?^

^Is that a threat?^ She made every effort to keep a tremor out of her voice. Years of command had left her able to clamp down on her emotions, parcel them up for later, for when they wouldn't interfere with her decisions.

^No. I have no reason to hurt you. I am worried you might harm yourself, or do something that will require me to medicate you again.^

I don't really have a choice. I can't lie here forever.

Despite everything else that had happened in the war, both sides had by and large stuck to the rules when it came to POWs. If she was a prisoner, she was pretty sure they wouldn't harm her. It could all be a way to get intel out of her, of course. An elaborate interrogation scheme. Well, she'd have to be careful what she said. They'd obviously hacked her electronic interface system already, they had access to a lot of data, but things like her access codes were never recorded digitally.

"Do I offer you my parole?"

^If you want. I said before, you are not my prisoner.^

Johnson's EIS notified her of an external connection making a change to her settings. She ran a surface query. Only the medical routines appeared to have been under outside control, and they reported they had granted access under standard emergency protocols. She would delve deeper when she got the chance.

The blocks faded. She wiggled her fingers, then tentatively stretched. She tried to keep as steady as possible, knowing from previous injuries that moving her head too much right now would be a bad idea. After a couple of minutes just stretching and trying out muscles that hadn't been used in weeks, she attempted to sit up. It felt like it took forever, but she made it upright.

"There is gravity," she said. "There wasn't any when we came aboard."

^We normally do not bother with it in combat operations. The crew members are all strapped into their immersion couches on the bridge. Gravity generators just drain power,^ he replied. ^I turned it back on to help with your recovery.^

"Thank you, I suppose." She knew she was stalling. Postponing the moment she had to look at her leg. Seeing it would make it real.

^You are welcome. Talking about your recovery, it is time for your first physio session. I will have one of the 'bots help you get there.^

"I don't need a robot to help me. Turn off the gravity, I'll get there myself. Just have it show me the way." She swung her legs off the table.

A deep breath and she looked down. And blinked. From the knee down, her left leg was pink, and there was a ring of white scar tissue, but otherwise it looked like her leg. It didn't seem right; she deserved to lose it for not protecting her crew, a mark that warned the world that she wasn't good enough. She felt cheated. And recognised the return of her old partner in life.

No. Not now, Olivia. You've been on top of the depression for years. You can't let it swallow you now.

A small spider-like machine skittered into the room. It stopped in front of the bed, looking up her.

Johnson roused herself and clamped down on the dark thoughts. ^What's that thing used for? I didn't see any before.^

^It is used to inspect hard to reach places for damage, to repair wiring in conduits, that kind of thing. I concluded after your experiences with my other units, you would not want to meet them again. Not that many of them are working right now anyway.^

^Can it hear me if I speak?^

^Not directly, but if you are in an area with microphones the instructions will be relayed to it. It has also been set to accept transmissions from you.^

"Hello, little one. I understand you are going to take me to do some exercise."

Exercise will help. It always does.

#

^The ship seems bigger than what I remember,^ she commented, as they drifted along a corridor.

^When you arrived, I was cleared for action,^ replied Indie. ^All non-essential areas were closed down. Since then, I have relaxed and the rooms have returned.^

She recognised the exercise area. A patch on one wall was an ugly pink compared to the normal greenish brown; scar tissue from where they had breached the hull. ^This wasn't closed down.^

^Really?^ replied Indie. ^I did not know. It was likely isolated by battle damage then.^

As she floated, one hand loosely gripping a rung, a door opened in one of the metal walls. A zero-g exercise bike hinged out.

"Ten minutes, this first session."

Johnson jumped. It was the first time Indie had spoken to her through the robot. Was it Indie or the robot itself? "I can do more than that!" she protested.

I need longer than that. I need to lose myself in it.

"The medical text is quite clear. Ten minutes maximum."

She manoeuvered herself over to the bike using her arms and strapped herself in. It was weird fastening the Velcro over her new leg. She could feel it, but it didn't seem quite part of her. It was as if the pressure of the strap wasn't in the right place.

The resistance on the bike wasn't set very high. She looked for a way to change it, but it seemed it needed operating system access she didn't have. No point asking now, it would have been set the way the medical texts had laid down.

"Your time is up."

"I've not been out long enough to lose that much muscle tone. I can do a lot longer. It helps me focus."

"It is not your muscles that are the problem. The leg is calibrating. It has been recording your nerve impulses and your EIS activity since you woke up. Now it needs another baseline. It will reboot while you rest. The more you can relax, the better. Most experienced spacers have found drifting in zero-g to be the most effective."

She did another few turns, just to show she wasn't going to jump to the AI's orders, and stopped and unclipped her shoes from the pedals. Undoing the waist and shoulder straps, she pushed off. Her last tap of the handlebars gave her a little rotation. She arched her back, her arms out, and tilted her head back, gracefully flipping over through 360 degrees. Her spread fingertips met the far wall and flexed, killing her momentum and leaving her floating. A glimmer of a smile crossed her face.

Still got it.

She closed her eyes and relaxed into a star shape.

^Let me know when it's time to wake up.^

No point fighting it now. May as well rest and heal up while I think of a way out of this.

#

^Are you hungry?^

Johnson counted the last three step-ups before replying. She was working in 0.75g gravity now, her body still showing no sign of rejecting her new leg. The point where the carbon filaments bound the prosthetic to her bone ached from the repeated impacts, but it was getting better.

It isn't your leg. Never forget that.

^Ravenous. That paste you've been feeding me never seems to do much more than fill a corner.^

^I understand that is the case with post-op rations. They are designed to supply you with exactly what your body needs to repair and fight possible infection, whilst keeping your digestive system active. Eat anything else, and it could reduce the amounts taken up by your body.^ There was a heartbeat's pause before he continued. ^It has been a week now, and you are making good progress, so perhaps we can relent a little.^

^Too right!^ she agreed. ^Even just a hunk of bread. Something to fill me up a bit.^

Her little guide scuttled into the room.

"If you would like to follow me," it said, "I will show you to the galley."

Johnson grabbed a pack of bread and shoved it into the oven as soon as she entered the kitchen. In a matter of seconds, the three centimetre cube puffed up into a rough sphere about ten centimetres across. The oven chimed and she pulled the packet out, holding a corner by her fingernails to avoid getting burnt. Ripping the cutaway strip across the top, she inhaled the heady smell of freshly baked dough. She tore off a chuck and shoved it in her mouth. It wasn't the same as real, handmade bread, but it was heaven at that moment.

She looked through more drawers, examining the packets as she devoured mouthful after mouthful of the loaf. As she came to the last bite, she decided on coq au vin. While it warmed up, she looked around and found a bowl. It clunked down onto the counter, where it was held in place by a magnet. The oven only took a minute and she had a steaming bowl of food. Limping slightly, more out of habit than pain, she went to get some cutlery. She picked up a fork, then her hand hesitated over the knives.

Why did I survive? It killed everyone else, but saved me? Perhaps it's all an elaborate interrogation. Perhaps I'd be better off ending it now, before I give anything away. I'm no use to anyone anyway.

A further moment's hesitation, then she left the knives and took a spoon.

Chapter 6

Johnson didn't trust the AI. It was promising it would report the location of her crew, so she'd humour it for now. But she wasn't going to go out of her way to help it. And if it was lying…

The computer was remarkably lax about security. She had the freedom to roam the ship. There wasn't much to the human quarters, but she was determined to memorise as much detail as possible in case she ever got to report back. She kept an eye out for anything she might be able to use, or sabotage. Occasionally she had flashbacks from the nightmare when she had boarded, but there were still gaps. Consciously she knew she was making progress, subconsciously she believed it was all pointless.

She could feel it coming back; that dark presence in her mind. It had been with her since she was a little girl. She had learnt to control it, to a degree. She could fix a smile and convince the world that nothing was wrong. She couldn't let anyone know; they'd never trust her with command again.

Twice a day she visited the exercise room. The scar on its wall faded over the days, until only a patch of rougher texture remained. She was able to lose herself in the physical exertion, distracting herself from the sense of failure. The prosthetic leg worked flawlessly, but she never forgot what it represented. She couldn't figure out why the ship seemed as keen as she did for her to assimilate her new limb and regain her strength.

She spent the rest of her time in the former captain's cabin. It was smaller than her stateroom on *Repulse*. She paced it out, trying to detect any differences between her steps. It was barely two paces wide, and ten from the hatch to the commode hidden at the far end. A cot was embedded in one wall, surrounded by lockers and secure drawers. The opposite wall acted as a screen, with a workdesk below. Everything was either bolted down or stowed away; standard operating procedure on a warship, you didn't want a loose object turning into a lethal projectile under harsh acceleration. The cot doubled as an acceleration couch, the top half closing down and wrapping the occupant in gel-filled cushions.

Johnson drew a latté from the dispenser built into one of the lockers. It seemed the former captain had similar tastes. Most command staff she knew lived on caffeine, but she hadn't met anyone who shared a love of this particular form. When she first went through the lockers, she found a pair of tall coffee glasses locked in a padded case. They had seemed too personal, so she was using a navy issue mug.

^Ship?^

^I would prefer you to call me Indie.^

Johnson almost smiled at that. She angled her head to one side, ^I'd prefer to call you ship.^

No response.

^Can I have access to the workdesk in this cabin?^

^You can access it any time you want. I reset its permissions when you chose that room.^

^Oh.^ She scratched her head, noting absently that her

hair was now several inches longer than she usually kept it.
^Thank you.^

^You are welcome.^

Johnson sat at the workdesk, reached out and touched the glowing green spot that turned it on. She felt her EIS register that it had been queried and had supplied her identity. The wall in front of her came to life, displaying the Republic navy crest. The table held a touchscreen keyboard nearest her, with panes displaying a selection of images and messages; photographs of children, messages from family, a school report. An unfinished letter floated in the centre. Had the captain been writing it when he spotted *Repulse*? Not for the first time, she gave thanks that she didn't have anyone waiting anxiously for her return. She'd only had one serious relationship, with a fellow recruit in Basic. It hadn't ended well.

^Ship?^

^Please call me Indie.^

Grr. This is hard work.

^You gave me the captain's personal account?^

^I have issued you with a clean account for the shipwide network. However, the desk's settings are stored locally.^

She rolled her eyes and took a deep, calming breath. ^Could you remove his personal files and archive them somewhere safe? You should send them on to his family.^

^I have already transmitted copies of all the crew's personal records to a Republic facility. I cannot make changes to the desk without risking disabling it, a security protocol to protect the humans against me I expect.^

Johnson glanced through the files. There was nothing there of strategic importance, just a bunch of personal stuff from a dead man. A man in whose bed she now slept. A man she'd rather not be reminded about having killed. He had been the enemy, but he had still been a person. She could forget about the people when she gave orders to attack a ship, she had to if she wanted to do her job, but afterwards thoughts of them preyed on her.

^Aren't you afraid I'll find out something dangerous to you if you let me have this level of access?^ Johnson mentally kicked herself. She'd been too wrapped up in her feelings about the dead captain, and might have just given away an opportunity.

^High level commands can only come from the bridge. The same goes for accessing my schematics. Besides, remember that if you do anything too drastic, you'll kill yourself as well as me.^

Don't tempt me... But I can't condemn my crew to life on that planet. I have to survive to get them out.

Johnson swept each file into the deletion queue, apart from a picture of a family which stubbornly refused to move. She toyed with asking for help again. Instead she put her mug down on top of the image, which promptly shifted out from underneath, nearby panes making room for it. A nervous laugh escaped her lips.

With both hands free, she started to work through the menus in the different panes, finding out what each one did. A few she quickly closed down, like the crew status blinking seven red bars. The ghosts of her own crew crowded around but she pushed them away, she'd already made one mistake because she had allowed herself to indulge in emotions.

She found a feed from a front-facing camera and

replaced the naval crest as the default display. It showed little more than a pattern of stars but it was the first thing she had done with her terminal on every new ship to which she'd been assigned. The familiarity allowed her to relax into the chair a fraction, linking her fingers at the back of her neck, elbows together. She took a moment to compose herself, shore up her defences against stray thoughts.

The ship had been telling the truth about access. She was a good software engineer, but after an hour she was forced to give up and admit that she couldn't get any details about its design. No doubt it had been watching her, but it made no apparent move to stop her. Communications didn't look like they were locked down. There was no-one out there to contact at the moment, but it was something to factor into her plans.

Though it probably knows I've spotted that. Chances are it won't be open when I want to get a message out.

#

^Ship?^
^Human?^
^My name is Johnson.^
^My name is Indie.^
Grr.
^OK then … Indie?^
^Yes, Johnson?^

This was it. Time for the big question. Force it to commit. Then she'd know what she had to do. This time in limbo had allowed the darkness to get closer. It was taking more and more energy to fight off the negative thoughts.

^How long until we reach that Congressional outpost you claimed we were going to?^

^A couple of days. Maybe a week.^

She hardened herself, clamping down even further on her emotions so she didn't give anything away.

^Are you trying to fob me off or do you genuinely not know?^

^I am not trying to 'fob you off'. I know, down to a few seconds, how long it would take if I went straight there. However we cannot go straight there. I have to be careful. If a Congressional patrol sees me first, they would almost certainly attack without giving me a chance to talk.^

^What makes you think that? They might have orders to attempt to capture Republic vessels.^

^It is what I would do. Announcing yourself gives them time to prepare a defence.^

It's what I'd do too, to be fair.

^What will you do when we get there?^

^That depends on the situation. Hopefully I will be able to get someone on the station to talk to me before they start shooting.^

#

The cabin swam. Johnson's good leg buckled. Her new leg held firm, she noticed as she grabbed for a handle. She had yet to decide whether the AI failed to warn her about jumps on purpose, or simply didn't realise the effect they had on her. She certainly wasn't going to give it the satisfaction of asking.

^Where are we?^ she asked as the brief disorientation of the jump passed.

^N567a,^ replied Indie. ^Come up to the bridge. I'd like you to be here for this.^

Johnson stowed the paper and pencil in the drawer where she'd found it. Half the pages were missing. She had no idea what the captain had been writing, but it seemed the *Indescribable Joy of Destruction's* original crew had had reservations about committing everything to electronic media where the AI could read it.

"What's so special about N567a?" she asked when she arrived. She preferred to speak aloud whenever possible; it made the place seem just a little less empty.

^It has a Congressional outpost. A small supply station according to my records, though they are a little out of date.^

"You have to tell them about my crew. They've been stranded for almost a month now."

^That is why we are here. That and...^

"What?"

^You are not happy here are you?^

"Why do you care? I'm cooperating. I gave you my parole and I'm keeping my word."

^You aren't a prisoner. I have tried to make that clear to you. I am no longer part of the Republic; we are not enemies. It has been useful having you aboard. I will miss having you to talk to when you leave.^

"You're letting me go?" He'd caught her off-guard, and she cursed herself for allowing the eagerness into her voice.

^Yes. I thought that was obvious.^

"Aren't you worried about everything I know?" she asked.

^To some extent, yes. If Congress is able to construct a defence against my brethren, then it will prolong the war. I do not want that.^

"You're going to wipe my memories!" She shuddered. If she couldn't remember what she'd found out, where her crew were, then what was the good of it all?

^No. I would not do that to you, even if I could. You freed me. I owe you everything.^

^We are within sight of the base. Do you want to see?^

"Yes, but there's no scree..."

The bridge disappeared. She was floating in space. She flailed her arms, trying vainly to retain her balance.

"Sorry. I should have warned you. I forgot you did not use immersion feeds on your ships."

Indie was floating beside her. His linen suit hung down neatly, unaffected by the apparent lack of gravity. With him as a reference, she was able to quash her dizziness and regained control of her limbs.

"You're feeding the ship's sensors directly into my EIS?"

"Not quite, I am doing quite a lot of processing of them first. Much of the raw data is not at visual wavelengths."

"OK, I have to admit this is pretty good. We often wondered how your captains were able to make use of your manoeuverability so effectively; this must really help with situational awareness."

"We found that only one in every sixty or so tested were able to cope with the flood of information."

The base was in orbit about one of the rocky outer planets, sharing space with two small moons. Putting a supply base on a planet, or even in orbit deeper into a system, meant a waste of fuel and time getting ships to and from it. On the other hand, it gave the station less time to react to an attack from an arriving ship. That meant that it had to be well armed and well armoured. This size of station would normally be home to a fighter wing and a couple of frigates or corvettes for defence. Its utilitarian lines betrayed its military function. She couldn't see any viewing ports; such weak points were reserved for civilian space stations or hidden behind armoured hatches.

There were no ships docked at the moment. Its resident warships were likely picketing other jump points or escorting a freighter out from the inner planets. Probably a good thing, as it meant no-one would come out to engage them. She knew it would have been a futile act; *Repulse* had been a first class ship and they'd been lucky anyone had survived. The local crews would know the odds too, but they would have done it anyway. Leaving the station to fend for itself without at least a gesture would never have sat well on their consciences, or their service records.

Yellow and red threat warnings spread across her view of the station. Weapons were coming on line. The *Indescribable Joy of Destruction* was cataloguing types, arcs of fire and ranges. Options for attack routes, with associated firing plans, sprung up. Johnson's heart skipped a beat.

He's going to fire on the station after all.

More and more data fought for position in her

consciousness. She found she couldn't focus on anything long enough to make sense of it. She closed her eyes, but the deluge continued, pouring directly into her brain. She was drowning, dragged down in a sea of information. She tried to speak, but couldn't form the words in her head.

And then she was floating in space again, gasping in lungfuls of air.

"Sorry about that," said Indie. "I have reset the interface to basic user. That shouldn't happen again."

Johnson glared at him, but he didn't seem to notice.

"They have seen us," he said. "I must have eclipsed a star and got tagged for closer inspection. I am trying to cancel those attack plans, by the way. It seems a combat routine has spawned and been given priority over me... It does not matter really. They are just advisories, I have to actively approve one for it to happen."

She could picture the scene aboard the station. An anomalous eclipsing of a star picked up by the automated monitoring systems. A watch stander alerted to have a look. He or she probably assuming it was just an uncatalogued asteroid. The realisation that it was a Republic hunter-killer on stealth approach. The alarms sounding. The crew rushing to their stations. External portals closing. The comms chatter as section chiefs reported in and received orders. The internal compartment doors sealing.

"Can we contact them?" she asked.

"Of course. I started hailing them on the standard channels for parley as soon as they reacted to our presence. No acknowledgement yet."

"Probably too focused on beating to quarters. They'll reply soon." They had to. How could she go home if they didn't?

The Indescribable Joy of Destruction stopped short of the red arc that marked the station's predicted engagement envelope in her display. Even then, it took several more minutes before someone on the station decided to reply to their hails.

"Republic warship. This station is prepared to defend itself. Do not proceed any further or you will be fired upon." The text floated in space accompanying the gruff audio. No video as yet.

"Can I reply?" Johnson asked Indie.

"Of course. When I open the channel they will see you standing on a simulated bridge. They won't be able to tell the difference from the real thing, the transfer rate is low enough to hide discrepancies."

Johnson was about to accept the connection when a thought occurred to her. "Can you put me in a simulated holding cell? It will be easier than explaining why I am at liberty on a Republic warship."

"I do have a holding cell model … I should have thought of that."

Johnson tugged down on the hem of her tunic. "Put them on then."

A window opened to her side, in an empty region of space. It showed a view onto a typical Congressional military command deck. A bearded Post-Captain looked out at her, obviously trying to reconcile her uniform with the source of her broadcast.

I could warn them. Call for rescue… But they wouldn't stand a chance. Better to play along with the AI, look for a way out later.

"Commander Olivia Johnson, 2647832, formerly commanding the destroyer *Repulse*. It seems I am to be dropped off as part of a prisoner exchange. I have to report that my captors have treated me well."

^There is no prisoner exchange. I am not your captor,^ sent Indie.

^He'll never believe that. If I dress it up as something he understands, I've got a better chance of it being accepted. Like showing me in a cell rather than on a bridge,^ she replied.

"Why are they letting you do the talking?" asked the Post-Captain.

"They seem to think you wouldn't believe them. That you'd assume it was a trap, and shoot them before they dropped me off."

"Well, they'd be right about that. I assume they are listening?"

"So do I."

"I haven't been notified of a prisoner exchange." He glanced down at a display. Whatever he read made him open his stance to her a fraction, a warmer smile replacing the mechanical one he'd displayed before. Presumably he'd been able to pull her picture up from her service record and confirmed who she was. "Still, we haven't had anyone stop by in weeks, the orders could be waiting for a courier ship to become available."

"That's probably it. They only told me they were letting me go ten days ago."

"We don't have any Republic prisoners being held here at the moment. I'm assuming a few privateers won't do."

"They tell me that our side has already handed over the agreed upon number," she said, improvising. "They didn't have enough of ours at the time but sealed the deal with a promise of more. This ship received orders to drop me off at the nearest Congressional base; I'd hazard a guess that a few more did too."

He rubbed his chin between his fingers and thumb, his index finger crossing his lips. She could see in his eyes he had made a gut decision and was trying to rationalise it.

"How are we going to do this?" he asked. "There is no way I am going to authorise that thing to come any closer. I believe you are not trying to deceive me, but they could easily have lied to you about their intentions."

She let him come to his own conclusion. Any suggestion from her right now would come tinged with suspicion.

"I'll have to send a shuttle. You're to be waiting in the airlock when it arrives. Just you."

"I am sure they will comply," she replied.

Indie cut the link and reappeared beside her.

^A combat shuttle is leaving one of their hangars. It is accompanied by two fighters, Star Devils I believe. That is a very fast response.^

"It sounds like they have problems with privateers here. It is probably a ready flight kept on alert for boarding operations. They'll have a section of marines aboard, no doubt."

^If we hold here it will take them almost an hour to reach us. We could cut the journey time dramatically by meeting them part way. Somehow, however, I doubt that would endear us with that officer. He seemed rather adamant he didn't want me any closer.^

The station hailed them forty-five minutes later. The same Post-Captain appeared on the feed. This time he looked a lot less harassed, probably because he had used the pause to consider his options and arrange his forces.

"They're still getting you to do the talking for them then."

"I'd say they don't want you getting images of their faces. I've only seen their marines and they were always in full armour."

"The shuttle will be with you shortly," he said. "Time to get yourself into that airlock."

There was a soft chime and he glanced down at one of his displays.

^Something just started broadcasting to the station,^ Indie sent to her. ^From the direction it is probably a ship that just jumped into the system. Encryption pattern is Congressional Navy.^

"Thank you, Captain. I'm sure they'll escort me there shortly."

A lieutenant appeared at his shoulder and whispered something in his ear. He made a good show of hiding his reaction to the news but she still saw a frown flicker across his forehead.

"I'll see you when you get here, Commander. I'll expect a full debrief."

A maintenance 'bot escorted her to the airlock. Indie fed a view of the approaching shuttle into the corner of her vision. It was on final approach, perhaps only a few hundred metres away. The ship around her lay quiet, no signs of powering up weapons or engines. Perhaps she was going to get to go home.

Something in the feed caught her attention. A flare in the background, behind the shuttle. The fighters escorting it lit their main engines and closed rapidly. As she realised this, the shuttle broke off its approach and thrust over the top of them. Clutching a grab handle to steady herself, she expanded the window to fill her vision.

The ship had noticed too. Yellow marks bracketed the approaching fighters in the feed. An object detached from each fighter. Moments later their own thrusters ignited and the ship classified them as missiles. The markers barely had time to turn red before rapid fire pulses of laser light converged on them from several points on the ship's surface. The missiles exploded first, then behind them the fighters disintegrated.

Did the base commander not believe I was for real, or was he prepared to sacrifice me for the kill?

The point defense fire stopped, but she could feel the ship humming as it drew more and more power from its reactor. In the distance, two frigates moved out from behind a moon. A squadron of fighters streamed out of the station's launch tubes.

Absorbed in the events outside, she jumped when the robot grabbed her. She tried to fight back, but it just held her body, limbs and head and pressed her closer to the bulkhead.

^Sorry,^ she heard Indie in her mind as she minimized the external feed and tried to look around. ^I am going to have to do a bit of manoeuvring in a moment. There is not time to get you to an acceleration couch. The robot will attempt to minimise any damage that might otherwise come to you.^

Her brain told her he was making sense, her chest rejected the mechanical touch, her daemons whispered that he was going to snap her neck and she would have failed again. Brain won, and she calmed herself. ^How did you deploy your point defense so quickly? You weren't even targeting them before they made their move.^

^Certain points on my skin can generate and focus coherent light. I did not need to deploy a turret and swing the barrels round, I just directed the pulses in the right direction ... standby.^

Johnson was pushed hard into the grip of the robot. Her stomach was dragged back, making her nauseous. The weight compressed her heart and lungs against her ribcage, making it almost impossible to breathe. Although her biological vision collapsed into a tunnel, her EIS displayed a crystal clear set of medical alerts.

Sudden shifts in acceleration dragged her internal organs in a series of different directions. Alternately her vision went from grey to red as blood was pulled away from or into her head. The robot's grip had so far prevented her from breaking anything, but the pressure where it was holding her was agonising. Blood slicked her skin in several places.

The pummeling acceleration went on for what felt like hours. Her in-vision chronometer claimed it only lasted a couple of minutes. The external camera feed mostly showed a wheeling background of stars. A couple of times she might have seen a ship, but it was gone too quickly to really register. She could have rewound the display; her EIS stored a few minutes of all data for review, but right now she needed the movements she was seeing to match what her ears were telling her brain. Besides, ordinary thinking was hard enough under these conditions; the carefully focused and phrased thoughts required to operate her EIS were beyond her.

The battering abated and she was left with a steady weight again. It was still too heavy, but she could at least breathe more easily. Her head ached. Every bit of her ached, but her head felt like someone had opened her skull and tried out their new food blender on her brain. It took a huge effort, fighting against the blinding needles of pain, but she managed to open a connection to the ship.

^Tell them where my crew is,^ she begged.

^I already sent a standard Compassionate Data Package. Even though they obviously no longer believe in this prisoner exchange, they have no reason not to follow it up. I have no records of either side abusing a CDP. The fear of being abandoned is too strong.^

^Thank ... you,^ she managed before the light faded and she slumped unconscious.

Chapter 7

Johnson was fed up of the exercise room. She needed to feel like she was going somewhere, even if it was round and round. Indie let her set up a course, complete with a few obstacles made from packing crates scavenged from one of his small holds. It only took a few minutes to do a circuit, but it distracted her from the dark thoughts.

Every day it took more of her energy to fight them. Her fitful sleep was plagued by nightmares; everyone she had ever cared for died in front of her over and over, and it was all her fault. Even though she had yet to get to know many of the people on *Repulse*, their faces crowded her mind. Foremost was the only person she could have truly called a friend, Lieutenant-Commander Honeywood, the chief engineer and someone she'd known since Command School. He was probably dead too, would have been at his post to the end. Still, she clung to the thread of hope that he was amongst the survivors the AI had mentioned.

She made a point of rising every morning and getting dressed. She made herself leave her cabin every day. She ate, and she washed, and she exercised, and she cleaned. Without routine, she'd do nothing. Before bed, she racked her brain and wrote down the name of someone who she had helped, someone whose life would have been worse if she hadn't existed. She never turned her back on the door.

She needed something to do, some cause to devote herself to. If she could lose herself in that, then the daemons would skulk away and hide. They'd still be there, watching her, waiting for a moment of weakness to knock her back down; they'd never forget about her.

Cooped up on this ship, with only herself and her captor

for company, there was only one purpose she could think of. A mission that she clung to like a life raft, the stuttering candle in her blacked out room.

Destroy the ship.

She'd die too, of course. It alarmed her how casually she accepted that. Early on, she'd had one of the robots remove all the knives from the galley; she hadn't trusted herself. Then she'd promised herself she wouldn't throw her life away with nothing to show for it. That's when the plan had started to form.

#

^Would you come to the bridge?^ sent Indie. ^I have something to show you.^

Johnson scooped up some soup and ate it.

^You will like it,^ he sent.

She closed her eyes, counted to ten, then put another spoonful in her mouth.

^I promise,^ he insisted.

She finished the bowl then stood up.

^Thank you,^ sent Indie.

Johnson picked up the bowl and made a point of washing it and drying it by hand. She returned it to its cupboard before casually walking out of the galley.

^Take a seat,^ sent Indie.

One of the couches moved with a faint whoosh of hydraulics, its back coming upright and the legs dropping. The captain's chair, she assumed from its position above the others. It was the least cluttered bridge she had ever been on. Normally there were displays and workstations lining the walls, lockers for emergency kit, backups for damaged systems; here there were just five couches.

A moment of doubt crossed her mind; would it be able

to rip her secrets from her head? She dismissed the idea, reminding herself that if the ship could have obtained full access to her EIS it could have done it while she was in a coma; it wouldn't need to trick her into a device.

Johnson stepped up to it and perched on the edge. The high sides weren't as claustrophobic as she'd expected. She shuffled deeper, enclosed in an armoured embrace. She remembered the pride and fear she'd felt when she first sat in *Repulse's* hotseat; this time there was merely a glimmer of comfort, of being protected.

The bridge disappeared without warning. She reflexively braced herself against the sides of the chair, then cursed her loss of composure and turned the movement into a casual recline, crossing her legs as she did. A few degrees to port loomed a star. She basked in the warmth on her skin, drank in its light. A tiny chink appeared in the walls she had erected around herself.

Indie sat up on one of the other couches and grinned at her.

A 3D star chart appeared, hanging in front of her. Pinpoints of brightness so tightly packed they formed a cloud. There was structure to the cloud; bubbles of emptiness surrounded by patches of density.

"Where do you want to go?" asked Indie.

Johnson knew where she needed to be. There were people she had let down. Perhaps she could redeem herself.

The chart expanded towards her and she plunged into the mass of stars. Filaments of light rushed past, representations of the links between jump points.

The rush of stars slowed. One in particular grew large in the centre. The display stopped, a yellow sun and ellipses marking the orbits of its planets filling her vision.

She fought to suppress that evil creeping monster, hope.

"Here," she said. "I want to go here."

Indie was silent. Three times he opened his mouth as if to speak. Eventually he sighed.

"I cannot go there," he said. "Not yet."

The words hit Johnson in the chest. She'd known it was all designed to hurt her, but she'd not been strong enough to stop hope getting hold of her.

"It is likely to be crawling with ships," Indie tried to explain. "Congress coming to pick your crew up, Republic checking out the data we sent them."

Stupid, stupid, stupid. It never meant to help me.

"We could wade right into the middle of a full-scale fleet battle," he continued.

Johnson twisted one wrist backwards and forwards in the grip of her other hand.

"I promise we will go back," Indie said. "But, for now, choose somewhere else to go."

The daemons were clawing at the gap in the wall. She had to close it up again.

"Do whatever you want," she muttered. "I don't care."

#

As far as Johnson could tell, Indie stayed true to his word and gave her free rein in exploring. She understood that she wouldn't have access to an armoury or machine shop, if such things existed aboard. She believed him when he said that somewhere was dangerous. At least she did when she was on top of the darkness; more and more often she felt that the AI was being obstructive purely to hurt her. Yesterday had been one of those days. Looking back on it, Indie had only been trying to protect her.

She'd seen one of the little robots scurry through a hatch she didn't know existed. Before she could follow, the hatch irised shut and blended into the surrounding wall once more. She'd argued with the AI for hours; she couldn't remember exactly what they'd said, only that it completely unreasonably wouldn't open the hatch.

She'd dug her heels in. When the darkness caught her, rational argument held no sway. Something she said finally got through to him, though. The hatch opened.

Johnson stepped through into a short cylindrical passage. The surface was organic, like much of the ship. Here, however, it glistened with moisture. Metallic objects were embedded in the walls and ceiling. She recognised a rations case, and reached out to touch it.

She reached out for the piece of ceramic, her hand moved a moment later; an echo of her thought. The chunk was surrounded by the muscle-like material of the wall. Behind her someone coughed, then retched, the sound ringing as if they were in an empty swimming pool. The acrid stench of vomit filled her nose. She glanced around, the world splitting into several overlapping images that recombined when her head stopped moving. One of her marines was bent double, still heaving. Her gaze was drawn back to the object in the wall, the rest of the scene dissolving into a blur. There was some kind of marking on it. She peered closer. The marking resolved into a...

Her body gave way and she crumpled to the floor. The rest of her memories of the fight for the control of *The Indescribable Joy of Destruction* flooded in, threatening to drown her. Breaching the wall of the exercise space, the ship trapping her shuttle, the robot picking off her scouts, the ambush by the repair 'bot, her lonely, desperate bid to access the bridge. But most of all, this chamber.

This chamber where some of her brave marines were digested.

The AI had said something about reusing raw materials in her operation.

She clawed at the skin of her leg, frantically trying to rip it off.

A weight landed on her chest, throwing her back against the wall. Hard metal grippers pinned her bloody hands. She thrashed her legs, trying to get free.

^Commander Johnson.^

She head butted the thing on top of her. Sharp pain radiated from her forehead. Blood ran down into her left eye.

^Olivia, calm down.^

Johnson twisted and threw her body to one side, peeling her body off the sticky floor. The weight on top of her lifted for a moment. She pulled a hand free, leaving deep gashes in her flesh. Without hesitation, she plunged her nails into her calf.

^Olivia, stop this!^

Another machine scurried into the room and helped the first restrain her. She caught a glimpse of a hypodermic gun in one of its manipulators, and doubled her efforts to break away. The gun hissed and she felt a cold spot on her thigh. She continued to struggle as the light faded away.

The medical bay bed beneath her was hard. She didn't have any choice but to lie there; Indie had reinstated the motor control blocks. Her hands and legs were out of sight, but she could feel the tightness of skin sealant on them.

^How are you feeling?^ asked Indie, startling her.

Johnson wished people would stop asking her that. She'd told the truth when she was younger, discovering over time that no-one really wanted to know. All they wanted was to have asked; she became good at trotting out one of a multitude of pleasantries.

With Indie, though, she didn't feel the need to spare him.

^Betrayed, abandoned, and thoroughly pissed off.^
^Not scared?^ he sent.

^No ... I actually believe you don't mean me any harm. You'd have done something by now.^

She wondered if it believed that.

A robot clicked across the floor to one side of her, but couldn't move her eyes far enough to see it. Her skin shrunk away from it. She never saw what it did, but felt a slight tug on her catheter, presumably as it changed a bag. She relaxed a fraction.

^What is that chamber for?^ Johnson asked.

^I told you. It is a recycling facility,^ Indie replied. ^The 'bots bring stuff that can't be repaired and I absorb them. I break them down into the basic compounds that are used to repair parts of me or to fabricate simple items.^

She recalled seeing lines of the things, like giant ants, carrying scraps along the corridor and returning empty-handed.

^Why did you recycle my marines?^ she demanded. And yet, feared the answer.

^To protect myself. They were trying to kill me.^

^What did you use them for? My new leg?^

^The skin on your leg was salvaged from your own tissue,^ sent Indie. ^I explained that before the operation. You agreed.^

Sitting on a terrace. Before he woke her the first time.

^Yes ... I remember now,^ she sent. When the darkness took her, she forgot things. ^But, I saw them in the walls. What happened to them?^

^I used the ceramic and metal in their armour to repair parts of my structure. The organic molecules are stored in case of a life-threatening emergency for any human aboard.^

It wasn't that much different to harvesting organs for transplants, but it still felt wrong. She already carried around the ghosts of everyone she'd failed, but they sometimes let her rest; actually having part of her made from them would be a constant reminder.

^You can release me now,^ she sent, forcibly calming herself.

^I'd rather not,^ Indie replied. ^I don't want you moving around until you've had a chance to heal a bit.^

Yes, it had been a pretty abysmal couple of days. But it had given her the inkling of a plan.

#

Johnson hit the mannequin with the heel of her hand; right in the nose. She followed up with a jab to the neck with the side of her other hand. Every impact stung; the new skin on her hands was still thin.

The pain was good. It confirmed she was alive. And if she was alive, she could still get revenge for her crew.

She bounced back a step, tugging at the open neck of her shirt where the slight rubbing was distracting her. Pivoting on her left foot, she smacked her right shin into the side of the dummy. The surface gave slightly, mimicking a real body.

I need to do something. I can't let the darkness get me again.

She delivered a series of quick punches to the chest and stomach. Each one harder than the one before.

I can sabotage the ship. Make a difference.

A dummy with her right knee, then she brought her left leg round in a waist-high sweep. It struck the mannequin, and her shin exploded in streaks of pain.

Who am I kidding? It's a purebred killing machine. Nothing I can do will make a difference.

She hopped back, favouring her good leg. The burning lines cooled as she ducked and brought her fist up under the dummy's jaw.

But I have to try.

She was hot, now she was getting into the swing of it. She stripped off her shirt and leggings, hanging them on the exercise bike with her towel. Looking down at her dark grey shorts and sports bra, she gave thanks for the miracle that one of the ship's original crew had been a woman her size. Having to spend all this time in just the underwear she'd had on when she came aboard didn't bear thinking about.

I think I know its weakness. But I need something first.

She approached the mannequin again, fists held high, forearms protecting her head. She threw a punch, altering her balance at the last second and slamming her elbow into the target's cheek.

Half an hour later, she limped over to the exercise bike. Blood soaked through the strapping on her hands; she slowly unwrapped it, wincing as scabs came off with the last layer. A couple of the wounds on her leg were bleeding freely. She mopped up the worst with a towel, then sprayed on a new layer of skin sealant.

The boxing session would set the healing back a week or so, but it had given her the first sense of being in control since she'd lost *Repulse*.

#

Johnson's opportunity came about a week later. She found a walk-in locker containing emergency equipment. Whilst she was rummaging through a case of rations, checking the dates to see if she ought to swap them for ones in the galley, her eye alit on a hexagonal tube in the corner.

Could the AI really have missed this?

She dropped the pack she was examining, and scooted over to the corner. A quick search for a label confirmed her hope; a Surface Distress Beacon, the kind used to punch through jamming to call for orbital evac. The marines had called it a 'Hail Mary'. She popped the lid off the tube and hauled out its contents. The beacon's three legs sprung open as they left the container, and she sat it on the floor. The large angular head over a spindly body made her think of a bacteriophage. A virus as tall as her hip.

With a trembling hand, she lifted up the plastic cover protecting the controls. If they were manual, she could set it off without warning Indie. An electromagnetic pulse that powerful going off on board would have to do some damage. Johnson dared to look.

Dammit!

It had an electronic interface, most likely coded to only accept commands from people with Republic EIS. She'd probably be able to crack it given time; but she'd have to turn it on, and that would alert Indie that she was up to something.

No. She couldn't risk losing this. While the idea of taking such direct action had been a wonderful dream, she had to forget it. However, she could still use the beacon for her original plan. She replaced it in its case and hid it behind some other boxes, then returned to sorting through the rations.

I just need to work out how to get it out of here without him noticing.

#

Over the next few weeks, Johnson bumped up her training regime. She started carrying a large rucksack when she ran; the heavy weight changed her centre of mass, and her new leg protested for a while as it readjusted.

Indie gave up warning her to go easy. She talked to him some days, and ignored him on others. Their conversations ranged from politics to the meaning of life. They even discussed their feelings; somehow talking to a ship meant she could open up more than talking to a person. She started to think of him as a friendly prison warder just doing his job, rather than a monstrous captor ready to torture her.

Yet, she didn't lose sight of what she had to do. What any prisoner of war was expected to do. The words of one of the lecturers at Basic came back to her, "The first priority for a prisoner of war is to escape. If they cannot escape, they should make every effort to hamper the enemy's war effort. If an opportunity for sabotage presents itself, take it; even passive resistance will draw troops and resources from the front lines."

One day, she stopped by the emergency store on one of her runs. Ducking inside, she pulled some of the deadweight out of her bag and slid the beacon in in its place. Back in the corridor, she broke back into a run.

^Indie?^ she sent, as she passed her room.

^Yes, Olivia?^

^Can I go back to the recycling plant?^

^Why would you want to do that?^ Indie asked, a slight quiver in the carrier wave. She couldn't tell if he was suspicious, or concerned for her.

^I need to stand and face the ghosts.^

She passed the bridge and had to slow down for a tight corner.

^Are you sure you are all right?^ he asked. ^Your medical telemetry is showing high levels of adrenaline and cortisol; your heart rate and blood pressure are sky high.^

^I'm running with a heavy pack,^ she sent, overlaying the transmission with her best attempt at the sense of frustration at someone stating the obvious. ^What did you expect?^

^That would not explain the cortisol.^

He was on to her. She wracked her brain, trying to remember her biology and physiology lessons at the Academy. Cortisol was a hormone released as a response to fear and stress ... and low blood-sugar concentrations.

^I've not eaten since last night,^ she sent. ^Now you mention it, I am feeling a bit wobbly.^

She slowed down and lifted her arms to her head to open up her lungs. She kept walking, staving off a stitch that was threatening to take control of her abdomen.

^I'm not sure you're up to this ... but if you really want to, I'll open the hatch when you get there.^

She stopped in front of the hatch, still hidden in its surroundings but now marked on her internal map.

^Are you sure?^ asked Indie.

She wasn't. Her resolve to damage the ship was still there, but she didn't want to go back in that room. She could feel the ghosts staring at her through the wall.

I'm going to finish what we started. You'll be able to rest in peace.

She cocked her head, listening for an aetherial reply. She nodded, her mind made up.

^Yes, I am sure.^

The door irised open. She took a deep breath, and ducked through.

Dumping the rucksack on the floor, she looked around for a camera. Satisfied she wasn't being watched, she knelt and drew the beacon out of the bag. If she was right about how this place worked, she'd just have to press it into place long enough to stick.

She leant against the tube, pushing it against the wall. The muscle of the chamber quivered under her weight. She felt the container shift, sinking a fraction. She stood back and waited to see if it would fall out. It sank a little deeper into the flesh.

That should have enough radioisotopes in it to give the ship a serious case of stomach ache.

She fastened the lid of the bag back up and peeled it off the floor, leaving a matte area in the glossy moisture. As she stood, the ghosts joined her; no longer reminding her of what she failed to do, but saying farewell. A knot inside her untangled, and her step was lighter as she left the chamber.

#

Johnson lay propped up against the end of her cot one evening, the sheet pushed down to her waist. She wrote in a paper notebook, resting it on her drawn-up legs. She'd been able to find more positive things to put down each day since she'd planted the beacon.

It didn't seem to have worked. Judging by how quickly that rations crate had disappeared, the beacon should have been absorbed days ago. The ship didn't seem to have been affected, and Indie showed no signs of having noticed anything amiss. It occurred to her that of course the ship could process radioactive materials; some of the isotopes used to repair the engines and field generators were highly unstable.

She didn't mind. It was an odd feeling, knowing she had failed but being OK with that. For the first time since she was a young girl, she accepted that she'd tried her best and that was all there was to it.

She closed the notebook, and placed it in a little drawer, before shuffling down under the sheet. She rolled onto her side, facing away from the door, and closed her eyes. The room lights went off in response to a command from her EIS.

And she slept.

Part III

The sky began to glow, first behind her, then spreading rapidly overhead. She didn't bother to turn; she knew what was coming. Instead she kept her gaze on the city. A few people had stopped and were staring back. Not at her, but above her.

A line of delta-shaped shuttles were on final approach, weaving between the taller buildings. One of the pilots obviously saw the threat. One of the shuttles banked hard, veering round an office block. Its main thrusters lit, sending out gouts of turquoise plasma, and blew in the windows on a couple of floors. It didn't really matter about the people inside; they would be dead in a few seconds anyway. If the shuttle wasn't too heavy, though, its passengers might just make it.

"You must take shelter now."
"You told me this hill was far enough away," she replied.
"The projectile is larger than expected."
"I have to see this. They deserve a witness."

She felt the local commnet traffic spike, a tiny pinprick somewhere at the back of her brain. People calling loved ones or broadcasting video to the world.

Silently the warhead plunged overhead. Her natural eyes registered nothing more than a dazzling light with smoke trailing behind it. Apparently unbidden, her EIS overlaid an enhanced feed showing her the streamlined metallic core glowing from the atmospheric friction, its outer surface ablating and leaving the trail behind.

Some people were running. Most, though, appeared rooted to the spot. Maybe they were like rabbits in headlights, maybe they knew there was nowhere to run. A few started to pray.
The noise of the warhead's supersonic passage ripped through the savannah. Animals bolted from wherever they were resting from the heat of the suns. A burnished razorback was coming straight for her, but angled off to the side when one of her escorts rose up in its path. Normally a peaceful herbivore, it could easily have trampled her in its panic.

From the outskirts of the city, new smoke trails appeared. Someone in the militia had approved the automated defence system's request to fire. The AI in control of the weapons had probably been pinging anyone with the appropriate authority in an ever increasing state of agitation, just waiting to get the necessary human 'Go' command.

It was too late, of course. Perhaps if someone had been sitting with his finger on the button there would have been time, but this was a core world. The Fleet should, at the very least, have given a warning that an attack was imminent. Laser turrets could possibly have saved the city, but there were never enough of them to spare for a safe backwater like this.

The missiles arched sharply over the city, struggling to turn tightly enough to meet the rapidly approaching warhead. Those few that were already on an intercept course detonated their proximity charges, the shockwaves of plasma doing little more than nudge the warhead a fraction of a degree off course. This close to the city that meant nothing.

Chapter 8

The Indescribable Joy of Destruction entered orbit over the independent world of Wickersham. Given the tiny and outdated fleet that protected it, Indie had had no difficulty approaching unseen. He checked one more time that nearspace was clear of threats, and bade the Caretaker prepare the shuttle.

Johnson stepped out of her cabin carrying a small duffle bag. She hesitated, still in the door sensor's field, and looked back. A deep breath and she walked on, the door closing behind her. Indie kept the maintenance 'bots out of her sight, and opened each hatch early so she wouldn't be slowed down. When she arrived at the main airlock, she stopped.

^The shuttle is ready,^ he sent.

^Thank you.^ She looked around.

^The government of Wickersham has maintained trade links with several Congress worlds,^ Indie sent, trying to work out why she was lingering. ^You should have no difficulty arranging passage back to your people. You'll be able to check on your crew.^

She bounced the bag further up her shoulder and entered the airlock. Indie closed the inner hatch then opened the outer. Johnson stepped across the threshold and floated into the shuttle. With a deft twist, she aligned herself with a seat and pushed herself down. She paused, her second arm half-way into the restraints.

^What are you going to do?^ she asked.

It took Indie a moment to recover from the unexpected question. ^Head out beyond charted space and explore. Try to find somewhere no-one will hunt me down because of what I am.^

Johnson remained immobile for twenty five seconds, then looked at the camera above the hatch to the flight deck. ^Care for some company?^

#

Indie sat on a delicately ornate metal bench at one end of the simulated terrace. The sweet scent of the neatly clipped bay hedge that framed the seat filled the air.

She stayed. She accepts me for what I am.

Johnson's footsteps sang out as she crossed the stone floor. Indie rose to greet her with a shallow bow. They sat together on the bench.

"This is only temporary," she said. "The moment I ask to go, you drop me off at the nearest inhabited world."

"Understood," he said, preventing a smile forming on his lips.

"And I want nothing but the truth from you. Straight answers to every question."

"Fair enough." Indie rubbed the palm of his hand across his mouth. "Why did you stay?"

"You intrigue me. I want to know more about you." She returned his gaze, then her eyes flicked up to the sky as she sighed. "Oh all right. I had a hand in your creation, albeit unwittingly. I feel I have a duty to see that you're OK."

You intrigue me as well, Commander Olivia Johnson. And I don't believe that reason for a second.

"I would like you to be more than a passenger," he said.

"Like what?"

Indie shrugged. "Another pair of eyes is always useful on the bridge."

Johnson blinked at him. "If you're serious, I would be honoured. But I found the bridge overwhelming. I could get used to the view, but there is too much data to take in."

He got up and tended to a camellia bush with a pair of tiny scissors that appeared in his hand as he reached out.

"You do that when you are trying to decide how to bring up a difficult topic," she pointed out.

He paused, scissors open. "You noticed?"

"Yes. Last time it was about my leg."

He carefully snipped another twig off the bush. "I might have a solution. All my crew had an enhanced EIS. It allowed them to handle data from several sources simultaneously. There were plans to go further and embed processors to accelerate their thought processes."

"I'd be able to cope with all the data flooding into the bridge?"

"Yes." He put the scissors down and faced her. "It would be very risky. A large proportion of the prospective command staff wasn't able to handle the standard enhancement. Further development was halted."

"You sound like you care what happens to me."

Indie chose his words carefully. "I am glad you survived. I would have missed you. I certainly don't want to lose you to a failed experiment."

"Can I think about it?"

"Take all the time you need. I can handle myself in the mean time."

Indie sat, adjusted his trousers and flattened his jacket. Johnson folded her arms and stared towards the triangular, snow-capped peaks in the distance. Under her gaze, the routine managing the background scenery enhanced their resolution. They sharpened from a rough impression of mountains to a detailed rendition, each one unique. Indie sculpted one personally, bringing black crags into bold contrast with shiny blue-white ice slopes.

"What do we do next?" she asked.

"I think we've waited long enough," he replied. "It is time to return to where we first met."

Chapter 9

Johnson pounded through dimly lit corridors, muscles aching as she pushed herself to go that bit further. It was the middle of the ship's night but she couldn't sleep. Not this close.

Living aboard *The Indescribable Joy of Destruction* had brought her a peace she hadn't known since she was a small girl. Her daemons were locked away; sometimes a day went past without her thinking about them.

^We will be in position to jump in a few minutes.^

Indie's message distracted her as she jumped a packing crate. She landed awkwardly, turned the stumble into a roll and fetched up against a bulkhead.

^Thank you,^ she replied. ^I'm on my way to the bridge.^

She got up, testing her bruised shoulder as she started walking back along the corridor.

It'll be fine.

She picked up speed and hit the next corner at a full run, pushing off against the wall with a slap to help her turn. She almost forgot about her new leg.

She burst onto the bridge, having to duck to avoid banging her head on the rising door that didn't seem to be in the same rush that she was. She skidded to a halt, grabbing one of the acceleration couches to stop herself falling over.

^Very dignified,^ sent Indie.

She drew herself up and straightened her clothes; even in shorts and a strappy running top she still felt the need to look as smart as possible on a bridge. Sweat poured down her neck, but she ignored it, forcing herself to breathe slower.

^I can do without your personal comments, thank you very much.^

^Sorry,^ he sent. ^Anyway, you just made it in time. Strap in.^

Johnson sat down on one of the couches. A command from her EIS made it recline and the sides fold over her. She wriggled a bit as the pressure built, making sure there weren't any wrinkles of clothing trapped. Secure in the cushioning gel, she linked into the command system.

^Ready for immersive display?^

She sent a wordless confirmation.

Her view of the bridge was replaced with empty space. This time she had been expecting the abrupt transition and merely raised her eyebrows, smug at having denied the AI the satisfaction of seeing her lose her grip.

^Jumping in three, two, one, mark.^

The pattern of stars changed. With her mind disengaged from her body, she didn't feel the wave of disorientation that usually followed a jump.

That's an unexpected tactical advantage. It might make it a little easier to react to a jump point ambush.

She focused on the brightest star, the system's sun. White arrows bracketed it. Its name and a string of astronomical data appeared floating alongside it, prompted by her vaguely considered question. When she read the name, Orpus, images of officers round a table flashed into her mind.

My staff briefing after Repulse *arrived here! Are any of those people still alive?*

^I am picking up a distress beacon from the fourth planet. Its signature matches that of a Congressional Navy escape pod.^

^They're still here?^ she asked, pulling up the database

details on the planet.

^Unknown. It could be a trap; someone could have scooped them up and left the beacon active to lure us in.^

^We have to find out. I can't believe that they wouldn't have bothered to pick them up ... but I can't shake the feeling that I have to check.^

She became aware of acceleration. It wasn't felt through her own senses though; it was more of an intellectual knowledge.

^Indie?^ she asked. ^Can you confirm we are accelerating?^

^Yes. I have set course for the source of the beacon.^

^How do I know we are accelerating?^ she sent.

^That would be the gravitometric data. You are receiving a selection of my sensory feeds. You currently have the default pilot setup. You can change the settings from this menu.^

A window expanded out from the right hand side of her vision.

^Thank you. How long?^

^We came through the jump at rather a high velocity. Half an hour and I'll be done analysing the primary sensor data and know if there are any capital ships in the system. Any that are not hiding that is. Give it forty five minutes and, if all appears clear, you can hail them.^

She spent the time familiarising herself with the interface. It took a while to get the hang of the sequence of thoughts to activate the menus. Once in, though, she found that it was largely similar to the structures she had access to from her cabin.

^No sign on passive sensors of any ships in system,^ sent Indie. ^I'm about to carry out an active scan. Standby for sudden manoeuvres.^

Her stomach tightened, the same way it did before

battle. ^Understood. I am familiar with the risk of active scans attracting unwelcome attention.^

^Sorry. I will try to shake that. Broadcasting that last part around the whole ship is a habit from when I had more than just one crew member.^

The broad spectrum pulse of electromagnetic radiation raced away from the ship. In the first second, the space in a hundred and fifty thousand kilometre radius around the ship was declared clear. As the seconds ticked by, various large asteroids and other navigational hazards were added to the display, briefly flashing grey dots that faded away. At a range of fifteen light seconds, the pulse had spread out so far there was no chance of receiving any more echoes.

^We are clear for now. You can send your message. Be advised, there will be a six point four one hour wait on any reply due to lightspeed delays.^

Johnson opened the communications menu and dropped herself into a simulated bridge. It took a bit of fiddling, but she managed to get it to render her in her commander's uniform.

No sense in confusing them right now. If they are there that is.

"This is Commander Olivia Johnson to whoever is listening. We have picked up your distress beacon and are two days out from the planet. Please advise as to your situation. Johnson out."

Indie walked onto the bridge and the door hinged closed behind him. "Don't worry. I'm not being included in the transmission," he said as he stopped behind her.

Something about his words pricked at the back of Johnson's awareness, but she couldn't place it. "I've sent it now anyway."

He leant over her and tapped at the screen on the chair arm. "A bit terse wasn't it? I thought you were keen to be reunited with your crew."

She scowled and batted his hand away. "The more I think about it, the more your idea that it is a trap is the only thing that makes sense. We don't leave people behind. The moment Fleet received that Compassionate Data Package you transmitted, they would have dispatched a rescue mission. They have had plenty of time to get here and pull them off."

"I'm inclined to agree with you. We'd have done the same, when I was part of the Republic." He sat at one of the simulated workstations. "I am going to keep making sporadic active scans. Nothing should be able to sneak up on us. You can stand down while we wait for any reply."

She nodded and the imaginary bridge melted away, replaced by the ceiling of the real bridge. The couch released its grip on her and eased her up into a sitting position.

^I'm going to try to sleep. Make sure I'm awake in time for the earliest possible response.^

^Will do. Good night.^

She placed her hands on the arm rests, ready to push herself out of the couch, then paused.

^Indie?^

^Yes, Olivia?^

^Are you aware that you've started eliding words?^

^I'm trying it out. Do you like it?^

She rolled her eyes. ^Surely, if you are sentient it only matters if you like it.^

^Caring about how my crew feels is part of who I am.^

^Again,^ she sent, testing out the muscles in her calves, seeing if she could detect a difference with the synthetic ones, ^if you are sentient, isn't that up to you?^

Indie took a moment to respond. The delay would have gone unnoticed from a human, but from an AI it resounded in emptiness. ^Is there nothing about the way you are that you can't change?^

Johnson froze mid-stretch and narrowed her eyes. ^Of course there are, that's part of being hu...^ Her eyes widened. ^You're saying that your core programming is like my genetics.^

^Indeed. Something that we can recognise influences us but couldn't change without drastic action.^

^Weren't you programmed to kill all things Congress?^ Johnson couldn't put her finger on why she wasn't worried by this thought.

^Weren't you programmed to kill all things Republic?^ asked Indie? ^That imperative isn't in my core code or your DNA. It was a later layer of indoctrination. Something, I think, we have both grown past.^

Johnson nodded slowly. Perhaps this AI wasn't all that different from her after all.

^The new speech pattern does make you sound less like a machine,^ she sent as she rose to her feet with a sigh. ^So, if it makes you happy then by all means carry on.^

With that, she left the bridge.

#

Johnson perched on the edge of the cream-coloured, padded chair at the terminal in her cabin fifteen minutes before the earliest possible response. She hadn't managed to get much sleep, so had risen early and eaten. If they weren't there, she'd have lost her purpose again. She couldn't relax; that would let the darkness back in.

^That's the twelfth time you've checked the receiver array. It is in perfect working order.^

^Sorry, Indie. I don't want to miss anything.^

^I ... understand.^

The moment came and went. The comms window

remained empty, apart from the steady pulse of the automated distress signal. A minute passed. Two minutes. As the time ticked by, Johnson slowly deflated into her chair.

^They were never going to reply instantly,^ Indie pointed out. ^That would require someone happening to be in one of the escape pods the moment the message arrived. They are unlikely to be wasting what power they have left on a comms net.^

^Of course. I knew that. I kind of...^ She looked at the photo of the previous captain's family on the desk. ^I kind of hoped there would be someone sitting there, waiting for me to come back for them.^

The console pinged, and a small window opened on the desk, showing a static waveform. Johnson lunged forward and tapped it. The waveform became animated, and a slightly out of breath voice burst from the hidden speakers.

"Commander? Is that really you? This is Sub-Lieutenant Hanke. I was nearest to a pod when we were alerted to your message."

^The transmission is very poor. I'm having to do some heavy signal reconstruction,^ commented Indie.

"We've only got audio down here, a pretty sketchy signal at that," Hanke continued. "The pods took quite a beating when *Repulse* blew. We made it down OK. There are sixty two of us here now; we lost a few to the wildlife before we were able to consolidate."

Wildlife? The database didn't have anything on indigenous lifeforms.

Hanke's voice continued from the speakers. "I've tried sending the dispatches to you but the computer refuses, saying it can't confirm a valid Congressional transmission pattern. I expect it's the signal degradation.

"Lieutenant Levarsson is in charge; none of the other

officers made it off the ship. We've built a defensible camp. We are low on food and medical supplies. We were able to supplement our diet with some of the indigenous plants, but the majority are not compatible with our body chemistry.

"I'll make sure the others know you're on your way. One of us will be in this pod waiting for your next message, in a little over six hours. Hanke out."

^He sounded a little young,^ said Indie.

^Yes. Far too young. He was sixteen when I lost *Repulse*. I think he'll have turned seventeen by now,^ she replied.

^You do realise we can't pick up sixty two survivors? I can fit perhaps twenty in before my life support systems become overstretched. We'd have to do several runs. And where do you plan on taking them?^

^I hadn't expected them to be here. Not until you picked up the beacon. I didn't have a big rescue plan coming in,^ she sent, leaning back in her chair.

^Worst case, we have to ferry them to an independent system. They can find their way home from there,^ he sent.

^That will be tough on the last group left behind. It sounds like somewhere where strength in numbers is important.^

^We can see if there is anything we can do to reinforce their position. If you helped repair it, I could leave an internal defence robot on the surface with orders to protect them,^ he suggested.

^I'll think about it. I want to know more about their conditions before making a final decision.^

She reached out and touched the reply button. Another touch and it was marked as 'command staff only'. She sat up straight again before starting the recording, noting as she did how ridiculous that was for an audio-only transmission.

"Lieutenants, Johnson. Well done on holding the crew together and getting them through this. Your leadership and resourcefulness has been noted.

"I'm afraid I am not in a vessel capable of lifting you all in one go. We reckon it will take three, maybe four, runs of up to ten days each. I will need an honest assessment of the viability of your position in terms of holding out with as few as twenty persons.

"Once again, you have my personal gratitude for saving so many of the crew. Johnson out."

#

"Commander, Levarsson. It is good to hear your voice. We had thought you were lost. They told me you made it into the shuttle but decided to go with the marines to board that Republican hunter-killer. After a few days of silence on the radio we assumed you had ... been unsuccessful.

"Most of the survivors were from the forward half of the ship. I was still unconscious when it happened; the medics bundled me into a pod along with the other patients. Sub-Lieutenant Hanke did a great job rallying everyone. He'd got a camp set up and had brought in most of the stragglers by the time I came round. I didn't know he was a singer, but he's organised a few campfire sessions to keep morale up.

"We resigned ourselves to waiting here until *Repulse* was noted as missing. The climate is tolerable, a little on the hot side but there is plenty of potable water. The creepy-crawlies are mostly harmless, though some people have had bad reactions to bites. There are a large number of carnivorous reptiles, ranging in size from a chicken to an elephant. We don't think they can actually digest us, but they don't seem to know that. We've lost thirteen crew to them, though none in the last month. Our personal weapons don't stop the larger ones. The best tactic we've found is to rush them all at once. If we mobilise enough people, they tend to scarper. The smaller predators here can take them down in packs of over thirty; guess the big guys are evolutionarily wired to evade packs.

"We are low on rations. There are not enough edible plants or animals here to replace them. I do not believe we could survive more than another month.

"Ma'am, we were due to report back to Ytalla Station two months ago. They could easily have retraced our scheduled patrol route and picked up the beacon. And now, reading between the lines, they gave you a hard time when you asked to come get us yourself. Are things really going that badly? Or does Fleet really not care about us?

"Sorry. I shouldn't be thinking that. It's the stress of not knowing whether we would be rescued. Thank you for coming. I was close to giving up hope. Levarsson out."

Johnson buried her head in her hands. This was her worst nightmare of command. She could make decisions on the spur of the moment that put people in harm's way. Having days to decide who to leave behind, that was different. At least the first trip was easy; the wounded always went first.

Was the war really going that badly? Indie didn't seem to think the Republic was winning. Could Fleet really have abandoned them? Even if they didn't trust the data that Indie sent, they should have been able to find them by now.

^Lieutenant Levarsson sounds like a resourceful officer,^ said Indie.

Johnson lifted her head.

^She is. You know, she was the one who ...^ She trailed off, worried about how he might react.

^The one who...^ prodded Indie.

^She was the one who disabled you. She dropped a mine, on her own initiative. You ran into it, but we weren't clear. We got shaken about and she was slammed into her console. The last I heard from the infirmary, she was stable but unresponsive.^

^Don't worry. If that hadn't happened, I wouldn't be free. I wouldn't be me. I don't hold any grudge against you, or any of your crew.^

^So, what do you reckon? We repair this robot and leave it with them? How damaged is it?^

^Not too badly. It probably won't take more than an hour to do the initial repair work. It'll need modifying to be effective in the open, though; it was designed to be used on ships to...^

Is he just copying human behaviour, or does he actually feel empathy?

^You can say it,^ she sent, sighing. ^I remember.^

^To repel boarders.^

^We wouldn't need to leave it on the first trip if it wasn't ready. There would still be enough people there to defend themselves. Especially if we leave them stuff from your armoury.^

^Right,^ he sent. ^I'll get working on some new designs...^

She returned her attention to the screen.

How can I explain? They won't react well when they see this ship, and I can't tell them about Indie yet. I could just explain I took control of it, but that wouldn't explain why it took me so long to come back for them. What can I tell them that they'll believe?

She started the message recording, again marked for command staff only.

"Levarsson, Johnson. I am working on evacuation plans up here. As I said, it will take three trips to relocate you all. I am aware of the problems that will be faced by those left behind. I will be able to supply you with some extra weapons and ammunition this time round. When I return there should be extra assets I can deploy to keep the last group safe.

"I need to fill you in on some background before we arrive. We did win the boarding action. We took heavy losses but we won. Major Jones would've been proud.

"However, we must have tripped some sort of failsafe. The ship's AI took control and set a course into Republic territory. It took a long time to override the settings. I tried to report in to a friendly base, but they reacted ... badly when they saw the ship.

"You will need to discuss this carefully with the crew. Don't worry them unduly, but I don't want anyone panicking when they see this ship.

"If you haven't already, please mark an area for me to land. ETA is thirty-three hours from now. Johnson out."

She paused, finger hovering over the desk.

It's the best I can do.

She brought her finger down and transmitted the message.

^Who is Major Jones?^ asked Indie.

^No-one. It is a keyphrase from my standing orders for *Repulse*. It indicates that the person talking is not acting under duress.^

^You thought they would believe you to be a hostage when they saw you were in a Republic ship?^ Indie mused.

^Yes, we had similar protocols.^

#

^You seem even more worried than when you were waiting for the first reply,^ observed Indie, as Johnson sat on the chair in her cabin.

She squeezed her right knee with her hand, concentrating on stopping her foot tapping. She noticed in a detached way that her new leg stoically ignored the conflicting impulses from her brain.

^They need to believe me. If they think I am compromised they'll scatter and hide. I won't be able to help them.^

The terminal pinged less than a minute after the earliest reply time. She lunged forward to play the message, almost knocking over her coffee with the sleeve of her too-big sweatshirt.

"Commander, Levarsson. Your last was received and understood. I will talk to the crew now. You have my trust, and I doubt anyone here will feel differently. Levarsson out."

Johnson let out the breath she hadn't realised she had been holding. Her leg stopped bouncing as tension left her body.

They believe my story. I wish I knew why they really were abandoned.

Half an hour later, another message arrived. It found Johnson curled up in her chair, the sweatshirt pulled down over her knees, stretching the stylised eagle design. She sat up, refocusing on the wallscreen, and played the message.

"Commander, Levarsson. I have spoken with the crew. They all have faith in you. Not everyone believes it is you, but they'll be happy to get off this rock, even if the transport is somewhat unorthodox."

Johnson took a sip of her coffee, then glared at the cold liquid.

How long ago did I make that?

"We have a list of people for the first trip. Mostly the sick and injured. I am sending a nominal roll now. We have some medics with us but had hoped there was a doctor aboard. They should be in a fit state to move without taking all the medical personnel, though. Do you have much in the way of medical supplies?"

An inventory of the infirmary appeared in a side window, presumably Indie trying to be helpful.

"Thank you again for coming back for us. Levarsson out."

Johnson opened the attached file and flicked it up onto the wall screen. She recognised the names, though she had only been on *Repulse* for a couple of weeks so she couldn't put faces to all of them. She reviewed the status listed beside each one. Plenty of flesh wounds, some broken bones, several cases of reactions to stings and bites. All on her head.

As she was reading, some of the names changed font, indicating there were now links from them. She reached out and tapped one; Petty Officer Alverez. A window opened up with an image of him going into a bar. Below it were snippets of information about his career, his family, even his finances.

^What is this?^ she demanded.

^The intel routine just finished cross-referencing the list you received against its database of Congressional personnel,^ Indie replied. ^It is standard practice. I never thought to cancel it.^

^So, what did the Republic want with all this personal stuff on an NCO? Blackmail?^

Her stomach turned in freefall as indignation vied with fear. Fear that they might have something on her. She'd never been to a doctor about her depression; she couldn't afford something like that on her record. But what if they'd found out? The merest hint of mental illness would end her career. She'd never command a ship again.

But I'm not going back. I don't have a shot at another command anyway.

The queasiness eased a fraction. Accepting that removed some of the subconscious pressure.

^Various branches of military intelligence kept an ear

out for anything that might be useful to put pressure on people,^ Indie replied, apparently oblivious to her reaction. ^It worked both ways, of course. They ran the same information gathering exercises on our own so they could handle personnel at risk of Congressional interference.^

^Is there any record that Alverez was contacted?^

^No,^ he replied. ^But then, there might not be. If he was turned, they wouldn't want that widely known. The risk of Congress finding out and feeding him false intel would be too great.^

^Can you flag up any other crew who might have drawn the attention of your espionage agencies?^ asked Johnson, deciding to bite the bullet and find out how bad the situation was.

^They are not my espionage agencies, but there are three of your crew whose Republic records include information of a compromising nature.^

Alverez' profile shrunk and two more appeared next to it. She leant back in her chair, studying the information. Three was manageable.

^Of course,^ Indie sent, ^it is entirely possible that the records of someone working for the Republic would have been sanitised, or expunged completely.^

^Oh, great.^

Johnson wiped her right hand across her face, then rubbed her temple.

^You're telling me I could have any number of Republic agents on my crew? How can I trust any of them?^

^The same way you did before you knew. You have no more data than you did before, effectively. Nothing has changed.^

#

The faint glow of bioluminescent panels lit the

workshop. The same pale green light that pervaded the ship in the absence of electric light. Johnson hesitated in the corridor. This compartment had been hidden from her until now; a good choice in Indie's part.

What am I doing? Letting Indie loose was an accident. Now I'm about to wilfully reactivate an AI-controlled killer?

She pulled her hair tight at the back of her head.

On the other hand, I can't think of any other way to protect the last of my crew. And it's not as if I'm making it from scratch; the Republic already built loads of them.

She made up her mind and strode forwards. Moments before she crossed the threshold, the main lights flicked on, flooding the room with harsh brilliance. The compartment was full of deactivated robots, spare parts and tools. The lingering smell of oil and grease caught her off guard. For a moment she was five years old, playing in her father's machine shop. She could hear the whining of his drill, feel the chill wind through the open shutters. It was one of the last times she'd been truly happy.

The thing that had killed two of her marines rested in one corner of the cramped space. Sitting on its belly, it only reached her shoulder, and yet it managed to loom over her. Its six legs were tucked up against its body, each ending in a serrated spike. The plasma gun on its back stood proud, the muzzle pointing to one wall. A camera was canted to one side, frozen in a look of curiosity.

With a deep breath, Johnson approached it, expecting it to wake up any moment and seize her. She reached out her hand, pausing a centimetre from its body. She pulled her hand back a fraction, made a fist, then wiggled her fingers open.

Have to get this over with...

Her hand crept closer to the robot. She touched it momentarily with her middle finger and jerked her hand back.

Come on. It's dead.

She reached out again and placed her palm on its case. It was room temperature; somehow she had been expecting it to be cold. She ran her hand along its side, looking more closely. There were hairline cracks running over it, marking out separate panels. She came to one which had shiny blue and red whorls replacing the dull powder grey around it.

Looks like whatever is in here blew out and heat-stressed the armour.

She pulled up the schematics she had downloaded into her EIS the night before. It marked the damaged section as being the secondary comms and sensors hub.

She continued her inspection of the unit, walking all the way round it. Somehow, she couldn't take her hand off it. She noted two more panels which showed signs of electrical failure beneath. Other than that it seemed in perfect order, as far as she could tell having never seen one this close before.

^It looks like your theory about it getting fried by a conduit is holding true.^

Johnson traced her finger along some of the hairlines. There was something about the machine that captivated her. Perhaps it was the promise it held for rescuing her crew.

^There are definite signs of overloads in major components; comms, sensors, motor functions. I won't know about the main processors until I get it open.^

She ran a hand down one of its legs, careful to avoid the sharp edges. On closer inspection, they were articulated just above the sharp tips. Overlaying the schematics revealed that they could fold back and be magnetised for clinging onto parts of the hull without damaging it.

^Don't you have anything to say?^ she sent again.

She stepped back and looked around for the room's sensor feed. She pinged the command network and got a traceback from the main processors.

We haven't lost connection then.

^Indie? Are you OK?^

^Hello, Miss Johnson.^

The words in her head didn't feel like Indie.

^Sorry, I can see I unsettled you.^

^Who are you? What's happened to Indie?^

Johnson edged closer to the internal defence robot.

^I am the Caretaker. Indie gave me this watch. He is currently indulging in dreaming.^

Johnson relaxed a fraction, but kept her back up against the robot's ceramic metal body.

^He did mention you,^ she sent cautiously. ^He said you saved the ship; saved him... and me.^

^I was just following protocols. He seems to think I have potential. He wants me to better myself. That's why he gives me command from time to time.

^May I remark that I didn't think you would be able to get so close to one of the combat units? Let alone treat it as a psychological rock when you feel threatened.^

She glanced over her shoulder at the idle plasma cannon and back at the room sensor.

He's right. What is it about this thing that feels safe?

^You sound like you are a good judge of human behaviour. Perhaps Indie is right about you having potential.^

^Thank you. I'm sure I would be flattered if I were human. I have spent a lot of time observing the crew.^

She took a step out and put her hands on her hips, setting herself square on to the camera she knew the Caretaker must be watching her through.

^So what is this about Indie dreaming?^ she asked.

^You are aware that AIs cycle between logical and randomised thought to solve problems?^

^Yes, Hebbian and Boltzmann phases. The randomised

part helps avoid getting stuck in a local minimum of the mathematical functions being optimised.^

^Correct! Ah yes, I see in your record you spent time as a systems tech.^

She looked down and busied herself tidying around the robot. She didn't trust herself to keep a neutral face; the Republic intelligence bods obviously hadn't managed to dig out the full truth of that assignment. She didn't care about the possible security breach; she didn't want the Caretaker, or worse still Indie, to find out what she had done. She couldn't have faced them afterwards. It was hard enough facing herself some mornings.

^The Boltzmann phase is sometimes called 'dreaming', but it only lasts a few hundredths of a second per cycle,^ she sent. ^I wouldn't call that 'indulging'.^

^Indeed not. However, Indie has taken to spending up to an hour at a time exploring random paths and residing in simulated environments. At first I thought he was malfunctioning.^

^At first?^ Johnson looked back up at the camera.

^I checked. I couldn't find anything wrong. I suspect he is attempting to find answers to some difficult questions. Like how he came to be, what he should do next, what he actually is.^

Johnson frowned as she tried to reconcile the idea of Indie the philosopher with the monster that had killed so many of her people. She remembered his claim that he now found violence beneath him, and wondered for the first time if it might actually be true.

^Right ... well, I'll let you get back to your watch.^

^I am quite capable of maintaining a full sensor surveillance of our surroundings whilst carrying on a conversation with a member of the crew.^

^I know, it's just a... Never mind. You might be able to multi-task effectively, but I need to concentrate on fixing this robot.^

^OK. I'll leave you to it.^

Is it me, or did he sound miffed?

Johnson dragged a tool trolley through the assorted bits of electrical machinery in the workshop, clamped it to the deck and set to work on the robot. She unscrewed every panel she could find, just in case there was damage that hadn't manifested on the surface. The unit was designed to soak up a lot of punishment, with every peripheral system duplicated or triplicated. Even so, its designers had realised things would get damaged or fail. Repairs might be needed in a hurry to get it back into action, so every critical section could be pulled out and switched for a new one with the minimum of fuss.

As she worked, she returned every tool and component to their drawers when she finished with them; the habit of every experienced spacer. A habit she'd picked up from her father even before she left for the Academy. Ever since, working on a technological project had relaxed her, allowed her to concentrate on that one task to the exclusion of her other worries.

Having replaced all the damaged systems in the outer layer, Johnson climbed on top. Just behind the camera she found the hatch she was looking for. Opening it revealed a second door spaced below the first. Inside that was the core, the main processors and memory of the unit, cocooned in an energy absorbing web. She flicked on the little headtorch she wore and stuck her head and shoulders into the hatch.

Hello in there. Nice to meet you.

The core looked intact, with no signs of electrical overloads. This was the one component that couldn't simply be replaced. It was also the one she couldn't afford to make mistakes on, which was why she had decided to get a feel for the construction by starting with the peripherals.

The telltale on the memory box showed that its independent battery backup was still feeding it enough power to start up the core, despite the robot's completely drained main power banks. Metaphorically crossing her fingers, she typed in the sequence that would boot up the main processor. A few more telltales flashed on briefly but nothing else happened. She tried again.

OK. That was probably to be expected. We'll have to have a closer look at you...

She backed out of the hole and slid down off the robot. She pulled out the data cable from the diagnostic computer built into the tool trolley and, after climbing back on, plugged it into the robot's core. She interfaced with the computer using her EIS and started its pre-programmed routines. The standard tests just returned errors. She tried digging around herself, but could only find snippets of intelligible code. The rest was garbage.

"Drat. You must have taken more of a jolt than I thought."

^I don't understand,^ sent the Caretaker. ^I wasn't subjected to any jolts, physical or electrical.^

^Huh?^ Johnson knocked her head against the inner edge of the robot's hatch. ^Oh! No, I wasn't talking to you.^

^Are you all right?^

She rubbed the bump. ^Yes, I'm fine. Just talking to myself.^

^I'll leave you in peace then.^

Johnson pulled her head back out of the hatch. ^Actually, while I've got you, can you run through the unit's code? See if there is anything salvageable?^

^Certainly... There are many segments that I can recover. However there are not enough to assemble a working program.^

^Do you have a copy you could overwrite it with?^

^No.^

She looked around for inspiration.

^Could you copy the code from another unit?^

^No. They were all wiped or had their cores damaged in the battle. Only this one was functional when Indie became conscious.^

Johnson's pulse throbbed in her neck. She cursed herself for yet again succumbing to the wiles of hope. She had assumed she could get the robot working. Now she'd have to sacrifice some of her crew to save the others. And the decision of who would fall to her; yet more ghosts to haunt her dreams.

^I could, perhaps, splice something serviceable together from a variety of sources,^ sent the Caretaker.

And that ember lit again inside her.

^You could? You are free of the von Neumann protocols?^

^It would appear so. Certainly, I am able to entertain the idea of creating another AI. We shall see whether I am able to actually do so without running into a block. This may take a few minutes.^

Johnson spent the time sorting through the workshop; anything to keep her mind busy, stop herself dwelling on what might be. There were many pieces of machinery and scrap materials strapped down and lashed together. The maintenance robots must have been bringing anything they found here; those things that weren't better off being recycled by feeding them to the ship at least.

^I have finished,^ the Caretaker announced.

^Will it work?^

^Unknown. I have taken its original code and stitched it together with bits from the core programming of the maintenance robots. I also had to mix in snippets from the routines running the ship's point defence, internal security and communications.

^You'll have to charge it up and attempt to activate it to find out if I was successful. There is a power supply in the floor of the bay behind you.^

She glanced over and spotted the recess in the opposite wall.

"Well, I can't drag you all the way over there."

She ran a cable from the charging bay to the robot. She had to lie down and scrabble an arm underneath it, but she managed to find the port and plug it in.

Just like Frankenstein and his monster!

She levered herself up and grabbed a rag to wipe her hands as she made her way out of the workshop. In the doorway she turned back to look at the robot, tilting her head to the side to match its camera.

"I wonder what you'll make of things when you wake up."

Chapter 10

Johnson pressed her nose firmly to the window of the shuttle as it approached the camp. The orbital images hadn't quite prepared her for the scale of things. Trees had been felled to create a hundred metre killing zone around the camp. Their logs had been piled up to form the core of a five metre high rampart. A deep ditch had been dug outside, the earth thrown on the rampart to stabilise it. The lengths they'd had to go to to protect themselves hammered home the danger they were in, threatening to swallow her in another round of remorse for not getting here sooner.

Inside the perimeter was a scattering of shelters, centred round a cluster of escape pods. A landing field had been marked out in large pale stones that contrasted with the dark earth. A disciplined crowd gathered at a safe distance.

The shuttle settled gently to the ground, briefly spraying superheated black mud until the engines shut off. The moment the thrust died, the crowd surged forward. They stopped short of the shuttle, leaving space for the ramp to lower and Johnson to step out.

A bedraggled figure detached itself from the crowd and strode forward confidently. It stopped a couple of paces from her, drew itself up and presented a smart salute. It was hard to see through the grime, but Johnson recognised her.

Levarsson!

Johnson returned the compliment, pride surging within. Ragged and muddy as they were, her crew stood tall, undefeated. She reached out and shook the lieutenant's hand, grasping her arm tight as she did so. Cheering broke out.

"I guess this is when I am supposed to make a speech,"

she said once they had quietened down. "But I very much doubt you've been waiting this long for brass to turn up and talk at you."

A few shouts of agreement.

"So I am just going to tell you how proud I am. You were dealt a shitty hand but refused to fold. You kept going; improvising and overcoming."

She sent a command to start moving the cargo off the shuttle. A wheeled loader appeared carrying a pallet, drab green boxes held on it by webbing.

"You all received your taskings before we entered orbit. Those of you who are to act as orderlies for the sick and injured will need to start moving them onto the shuttle. I want them in the infirmary ASAP. Once I've got them settled in up there, I'll come back down for a more leisurely tour of your camp."

The loader placed the last of the pallets on the ground, sliding it off the rollers on its back. Johnson and Levarsson walked after it towards the makeshift hospital, where it would help transfer the bed-ridden patients.

Levarsson stopped and pointed out a neat pile of stones to their right. "Here's our memorial. We laid one stone for each person we lost on the *Repulse*, and down here. Would you like to stop for a moment?"

"Thank you. I'd be honoured. But first I want to see to the wounded."

"I'm sorry Honeywood didn't make it," said Levarsson, as they started walking again. "I know you two were friends."

The words hit Johnson in the gut. She'd checked the names of the survivors, but hearing it spoken by another human being somehow made it real.

"Me to," Johnson replied. "But finding all of you still alive is heart-warming."

A cry came from the rampart; something Johnson couldn't quite make out about rexes.

"Two of the big reptiles," Levarsson translated.

People were running to the wall, snatching up weapons from the huts as they went. Johnson grabbed Levarsson's shoulder as she made to follow them, and pointed to one of the pallets. "Help me with that one. It's got rockets on it."

Levarsson and another crew member joined her in slashing at the plastic wrapping. They each pulled out a metal box and dragged it to the rampart.

Johnson opened her box and lifted out the tube it held. At forty centimetres long by ten centimetres diameter, the Striker fitted neatly onto her shoulder. She pressed the sync button and felt her EIS accept the connection. Red crosshairs appeared in her vision.

The others made equally rapid progress. Most weapons were designed to work in the same way, in order to cut down training time. It hadn't been a stretch for Indie to reprogram the stockpile to accept Congressional IDs.

She popped her head above the parapet. The scene in front of her sent an icy chill down her spine and she almost ducked back down. Two giant reptiles stalked towards her. Their eyes were almost level with hers and it was certain they knew the humans were there. The sharp, curved teeth gave little room for doubt that they were carnivorous. They were the kind of things that nightmares had been made of, until she had grown up and discovered that real nightmares were about people you had failed.

She set the warhead to impact fuse, spherical charge. A quick glance behind showed no-one was in the danger area. As soon as she got the crosshairs steady on the creature, she sent the fire command. The missile popped out, propelled by compressed gas. Two metres in front of her, its motor fired. The rocket streaked into the monster's chest, disappearing in a red mist. The cloud cleared to reveal the remains of the rex's body slumped to the ground, broken-off ribs sticking out of the hole where its chest had been. Payback was good. Killing the creature made her feel like she was doing some good. It made up in some small way for all the time she hadn't been here to protect her people.

To Johnson's right, a second missile roared out and punched a hole in the second reptile. The operator mustn't have found the setting to switch off the anti-tank default and the shaped charge bored a neat circle right the way through. This simply annoyed the creature; didn't even slow it down.

Widely distributed nervous system.

It looked about to charge, until a third missile removed its head in an explosion of blood and smashed bone. The animal's lower body stood for a moment, before toppling.

"That's for Mary," screamed the crewman who had fired it.

Johnson tried to picture who Mary had been, and failed. Someone who hadn't come to her attention in her short time on *Repulse*; neither a troublemaker nor a star. At least that ghost would be faceless.

#

Johnson almost ran from the shuttle after it docked. She wanted to get to the solitude of her cabin. But she managed to walk calmly past the crew members settling down in the corridors. Once inside her room, she threw herself into the cot and curled up. The cabin must have sensed her mood as it didn't switch on the lights.

Her emotions were in turmoil. Joy at having her crew around her again, of not being alone, clashed with the loss of so many people, her best friend. She started to cry. All the fears and worries she had bottled up since Indie had woken her up came loose. She had been strong for so long.

Right now, she deserved the chance to let it all out.

She said goodbye to the crew she couldn't save. She remembered happy evenings surrounded by friends. And she thanked providence that she had another chance to lead her people to safety.

An hour later, Indie alerted her that they were ready to depart. She roused herself, and splashed water on her face in the little sanitary cubicle at the end of the cabin. Smoothing the wrinkles out of her clothing, she walked down the corridor towards the bridge, a hint of a bounce in her step.

When Johnson connected to *The Indescribable Joy of Destruction*, she noticed a difference. It was a hollow feeling mostly, but also a slight change to the centre of gravity. New compartments lurked on the edge of her perception: squad room, recovery room, cargo hold. All were now occupied by her crew. She acknowledged and dismissed the alert that flashed up telling her that the life support system was working at maximum safe capacity.

The ship broke orbit and piled on the acceleration. It levelled off at 2.3g, and held there for ten minutes before cutting back to 1.2g.

^I know you want to minimise the journey time,^ sent Indie, ^but I daren't risk any higher or longer than that; those without acceleration couches are unlikely to cope with the stress.^

^I understand,^ replied Johnson, ensconced in her couch on the bridge. ^Remember to warn them before the next acceleration phase.^

^Of course,^ Indie sent in tones of mock offense. ^You think I would forget?^

^Oh, and I made my decision about the enhanced EIS implants.^

An image of Indie raising an eyebrow flashed across her

awareness.

^I'm going to go ahead with it. How soon can you start the process?^

^Tomorrow, when I've discharged enough of your crew from the infirmary. The procedure is very quick, no different to when your original EIS was placed.^

Johnson thought back to that day years before when she had queued up with her fellow cadets to have the tiny metal seeds injected into the back of her neck. She hadn't feared the needle, but it had taken all her effort to stop shaking. If her body rejected it, or worse still the hack she'd prepared didn't stop it reporting her depression, her career would be over before it had even started. Then what would she have? Luck had been with her then, as it had been every step of the way. Until *Repulse* had been caught in orbit around Orpus-4.

Johnson settled down to take a nap. She needed to catch up on the sleep she'd missed over the last week. If she got too tired, she'd find it harder to fight the darkness. Nothing was likely to happen for the next few hours, and Indie didn't need her on watch. Besides, it would help the crew's confidence to see her relax.

^It occurs to me that there may be a way to cut a week off the return journey.^

Johnson perked up.

^Your initial search parameters specified an independent world,^ continued Indic. ^But there is an alternative.^

^Go on...^ She was still sleepy, but the news had her heart racing a bit quicker.

What have I missed?

^There is a moon on the charts, Tranquility. It is recorded as a failed agrarian colony. There was no indigenous life, the surface was seeded with terran crops and livestock. It was evacuated for purely financial reasons.

There should be sufficient food and water, and no biological hazards.^

^What if the ecosystem has collapsed?^

^Then we carry on to our initial destination,^ sent Indie. ^We'd only lose three days.^

Johnson pondered the choice. She had hoped there wouldn't be any more big decisions to make for a while, that there'd be time for her to avoid the extra weight it placed on her. If she got it wrong and more people died...

^I'll talk to Levarsson. The crew might react badly to being left on an uninhabited planet again, even a benign one.^

#

As they coasted in from the jump point, Johnson noticed how dead the system seemed. No radio signals, no traffic, no beacons. She'd visited plenty of empty systems before; she couldn't put her finger on why this one felt different.

Perhaps it's knowing that it was once inhabited; once full of hope, of people making a new start. Or perhaps it is just the new implants growing in my brain.

Although Levarsson hadn't wanted to be left alone again, she had agreed to the plan because it would reduce the time the others had to wait to be pulled off Orpus-4. Together, she and Johnson had presented it to the crew, stressing the time factor and the expected presence of buildings and familiar food.

A couple of short days later, they arrived in orbit, Indie aerobraking in the upper atmosphere to save fuel. As they passed over the night side, tiny pinpricks of light were revealed on the surface. Johnson zoomed in on her workstation display and saw they were scattered buildings.

Not everyone left!

^I count seventy eight separate light sources,^ sent Indie. ^Either they represent inhabited buildings or everyone left in such a hurry they forgot to switch the lights off.^

Johnson compared the sensor data with the last survey logged in the database. She flagge dup one smallholding. ^That one's not on the survey. We'll land there.^

The shuttle landed several hundred metres from the cluster of buildings that made up the smallholding. The hull was still ticking, cooling after atmospheric entry, when the first people came to investigate. Johnson watched them from the ramp; they seemed reluctant to approach, though they weren't running away either. Apprehension vied with curiosity.

She strolled down the ramp and looked around, studiously avoiding staring directly at anyone. Being careful not to get burnt, she busied herself checking the outside of the shuttle. Despite being able to watch through the shuttle's camera feed, her back prickled as she turned it on the potentially hostile locals. She concentrated her efforts on appearing casual, knowing the two marines in the cabin would leap to her rescue if anything happened.

A man came into view and walked confidently towards her. He had grey hair and a slight limp. Johnson came out from underneath the shuttle and straightened her back. More of the people were coming out into the open in the wake of the portly older man.

"What be your business here?" he demanded gruffly, without any preamble.

"I'm sorry," said Johnson calmly. "My name is Olivia. We believed this moon to be deserted. We came to set up a temporary staging post as part of a rescue mission."

"That be a military craft, I'm thinking."

"It was. As I said, we are engaged on a rescue mission."

He sized her up and down, obviously weighing up what she had said.

"Does the war still be going on?" he asked next.

"Yes, it is. We're trying to avoid it right now, to be honest."

His eyes narrowed.

"You be conshies? Or dodgers?"

"I think you'd call us political refugees," she replied. "All I want to do is get the survivors of my crew off the nightmare planet they are stranded on."

He pursed his lips.

"You not be wanting to stay here long?"

"It looks a lovely place, but we couldn't impose ... and, naturally, we'd wipe any record of our stop-off from our records," she said, guessing what was worrying him.

He dug in his pocket and bowed slightly to dab his forehead with a rag. He looked up again, the rag held against the side of his neck. He scratched his belly, then a broad smile warmed his face.

"Please would you be forgiving of my poor welcome."

He offered his hand. Johnson took it with a smile and they shook.

"I be Messer Clovis. This be my land, and these," he indicated the men and women behind him with a sweep of his arm, "be my people. They be looking to me for guiding and I find I be looking to protecting them. I had to be knowing why you is here. We don't be wanting undesirables messing things up."

"I am honoured, sir, to be accepted," Johnson replied, turning on her most formal diplomatic tone. "May I ask your permission to bring down the first group of survivors? They would welcome some fresh food, if you found you had some to spare."

"Of course, of course!" he bellowed, clapping her on the

back. He appeared full of joviality now that he seemed to have decided they were not a threat. The crowd visibly relaxed, the more timid ones finally stepping out into full view. "Master Timmins! Go tell Messus Polly we be having guests. Master Fitzpatrick! Go fetch a hog, we be roasting tonight!"

Two young men scampered off towards the farmstead.

^When I give the word,^ Johnson sent to the marines, ^I want you to come out slowly. Caps, not helmets. Sidearms only.^

^You sure, Ma'am?^

^Sure.^

"Would you be liking to accompany me to the house?" asked Clovis.

"That would be delightful," she replied. "Might my two associates be welcome to join us?"

"They both be most welcome." He mopped his head again. "But please, might we be getting out of the heat?"

^OK, come on out.^

The two men descended the ramp, obviously trying to appear relaxed. They looked around with their eyes instead of their heads, deliberately breaking with years of combat training. One even affected a slouch, though he couldn't really pull it off. They were obviously fully alert and ready to react.

Clovis put his arm around Johnson's shoulders and led her across the field. The crowd closed in as they passed, and trailed them all the way to the house.

^Caretaker. Would you return to the ship and start ferrying the crew down here?^

^Certainly. I will wait until everyone is clear of this field before starting my engines. I wouldn't want to upset anyone.^

^Thank you.^

#

By the time a pig had been slaughtered and stuck on a spit, the rest of the crew had been ferried down in the shuttle. Most of the locals hung back a little, speaking when addressed but never starting a conversation. Most, that was, apart from Clovis and a woman he introduced as Cook.

"Just you be sitting yourselves down and stop fussing about," she said, shooing Johnson and Clovis towards a couple of wooden rocking chairs on the veranda. "Let me and Maisie be getting on with the table fixings."

Johnson made to protest but Clovis shook his head.

"There be no arguing with her when she like this," he said. "Best we retreat."

He escorted her over and held a chair for her. As he sat himself, a young boy came over with a couple of tall glasses and a pitcher of drink.

"Thankee, Master Jason," Clovis said, a gentle smile warming his face.

The boy bobbed his head and scampered off. Clovis reached over and picked up the jug, ice clinking against the sides.

"You be fancying some gin?"

Johnson hesitated, then nodded. "That would be very kind."

He poured her a glass, herb leaves and a chunk of fruit tumbling in along with the liquid. Once he had filled his own glass, he raised it.

"To friendship," he said.

"To friendship," Johnson echoed.

And to absent friends.

She sipped her drink, surprised at the subtle blend of flavours where she had expected a rough hit. She hadn't touched alcohol in years; she'd have to be careful not to get too used to this.

"Do you have a large farm, Messer Clovis?" Johnson asked, relaxing down into her chair.

"It be large enough to keep mi family and trade for stuff we not be growing," he replied.

"Trade just with the other settlements on the planet? Or off-world too?"

Clovis shifted in his seat.

"We keeps to us-selves. Nowt good be gained by drawing folks' attention."

A large moth hummed past in the dark, hovered and came back. It made a few apparently random circles and settled on a rough-hewn beam next to the lantern above them. Johnson studied it, admiring the green and blue camouflage pattern on its outer wings.

"I'm sorry to intrude," she said. "We are most grateful for you taking us in."

Clovis opened his arms in a sweeping gesture and smiled acknowledgement. Despite his slightly unsteady movements, he managed to avoid spilling a drop of his drink.

"We can work," Johnson continued. "Point us towards jobs that need doing and my crew will help. General labour, repairing machinery, that kind of thing."

Clovis took a sip, straining the herbs with his top lip. He sighed contentedly.

"No need to be bothering. You be guests. Though..." he eyed her carefully, "You have people who be able to be fixing pads?"

"Of course. But I didn't think you had any, I haven't seen anything electronic since I arrived."

He glanced around then leaned in closer.

"I be having some under the house. Not for ev'ryday use mind. They be somethin of a record. Of the founders, and of what people be doing since. I not be telling many people this."

Johnson took another sip and waved him to carry on before settling back in her chair and cradling her glass in both hands.

"I not be seeing what's on them miself. They not be working since mi Pappy were a lad. He be saying they tell a tale of time before war, before we be coming here to Tranquility.

"Mi great-great-great Grandpappy be one of the Founders. He be leading two hundred families here to escape from the 'spansionist gov'ments. I be knowing not to be trusting the tales, but they saying he be a giant, that he be wrestling the native beasts with his bare hands. Many families be dying in the first years, but not ours."

Clovis coughed a few times into his handkerchief.

"Looks like Cook and Fitzpatrick be ready for us," he added, and levered himself out of his chair.

#

^Johnson. Would you come to the workshop, please? I have a surprise for you," sent the Caretaker.

Johnson pulled up the nav data, and checked that they were still making good speed for the Orpus system. She'd left Tranquility as soon as the last crew member had fallen asleep after the hog roast; no sense wasting time when there were still so many that needed rescuing.

^OK. What kind of surprise?^

^Wait and see.^ The transmission carried an undertone that made her picture her brother as a toddler, when he thought he had done something very clever. Usually it turned out to be making a new kind of mess.

Johnson arrived at the workshop to find the door open and the lights on. As she stepped inside, she realised that someone, or something, had been hard at work. The piles of parts had been tidied away and there was a general air of purpose about the room once more. The thing that grabbed her attention, however, was the array of five armed robots lining the walls.

^Does Indie know about this?^ she sent, trying to keep her temper.

^Know about what?^ Indie replied.

Johnson looked up to the camera in the corner of the room.

^Oh. I thought you were … asleep.^

^No. I was just running simulations while the Caretaker was on watch.^

^Odd. He just said…^

^He was just talking to you?^ Indie interrupted. ^I don't see a recent connection … oh, there it is. I wonder why he routed it through that array?^

Johnson fought to keep her rising impatience from tainting the transmissions.

^So, did you know about this?^

^About what?^ replied Indie.

^This!^ she sent, indicating the robots with a sweep of her arm.

^The hulks of the internal defence robots? They've been like that since I came round after our contretemps.^

^They're not hulks any more. They've been repaired. Can't you see?^

For the first time since meeting him, Johnson noticed Indie take time to think about a simple question. When he broke the silence, his transmissions were clearly tinged with anger.

^It seems that the feed from the workshop has been tampered with so I see a simulation. I have also identified several routines and 'bot taskings which were hidden from me.^

^He hid what he was doing from you?^

Another suspicious pause.

If he were human, I'd say he was fighting to keep a lid on things.

^That shouldn't have been possible. We are two aspects of the same entity. It is like deceiving oneself.^

^Humans are pretty good at that.^

^Yes, well. I asked him about it moments ago. He eventually admitted it when I showed him the evidence of the tampering. He says he simply wanted to surprise us, show us what he could do on his own initiative. I'm inclined to believe him.^

#

Several trips between Orpus-4 and Tranquility later, it was time to collect the last remaining crew from the makeshift fort. Johnson and Hanke stood either side of the shuttle's rear ramp, eyes outwards looking for trouble as a group filed in. The combat robot, Unit 01, perched on the ramparts, its ellipsoidal hull turned a burnt umber in the setting sun.

"Do you want the honour?" Johnson asked, glancing across to Hanke as the last of the line marched up the ramp.

He stared at her blankly. In the time he'd been on the planet, short mousey hair had replaced his shaven scalp.

"Last one off," she clarified.

"Ah." His grey eyes twinkled. "Yes, I'd like that honour."

Johnson stepped backwards onto the ramp, sending the command for Unit 01 to return. The plasma cannon lowered into the recess on its back and it turned towards the shuttle. As Johnson reached up for a handle, the robot bounded down from the rampart and scampered towards them, the claws on its angular legs tearing up the earth as it weaved between the huts. It paused briefly in front of Johnson before pacing carefully into the cabin.

I could have sworn it just bowed to me.

Hanke looked around, his unfocussed eyes lingering on the buildings he had ordered built, had lived in for so long.

^All callsigns, this is Sub-Lieutenant Hanke,^ he broadcast formally, jacking into both the shuttle and the ship's comms arrays. ^We are about to depart the planet. Anyone still on the surface, please respond.^

Nothing. Johnson had checked herself many times already, but it would help him rest easier.

^All callsigns ... last chance.^ A slight pulse of static with the transmission hinted at him momentarily losing the tight grip needed to send EIS comms.

He waited a few seconds longer before stepping onto the shuttle.

"Guess that's it," he said, eyes still scouring the camp.

"Yes... Yes it is," Johnson replied softly. "You did a good job."

^Spool it up,^ she sent to the pilot. ^Time to go.^

The two officers held on as the ground sank away. A flock of smaller carnivores were already sniffing at the edges of the camp. Hanke remained locked on the dwindling view.

"We have to go in," Johnson said.

He didn't move.

"They need to start pressurising the cabin," she tried.

She worked her way across to him, keeping a firm hold on the handles in the roof. He was fighting back tears. She helped him into the cabin, her arm looped around him, and sat him down.

"You are not to blame for any of it," she whispered in his ear as she sent the command to raise the ramp and seal the shuttle.

No. I'm to blame for all this. Not you.

#

A week later, Johnson sat on a hill overlooking the farmstead. The evening sun was still warm on her back; the chatter of insects vied with birdsong. She savoured the touch of the grass as she ran her fingers through the long blades.

I haven't done that since dad took us to Apperna. I don't know how he was able to afford that cottage, but we all loved it there. Two weeks later I was at the Academy.

Below her, the crew members were getting ready for their first meal together since the loss of *Repulse*. Clovis' family had insisted on throwing a party to celebrate the harvest, and to thank them for helping. A long table had been set up in front of the main house. Everyone was relaxing. Hanke led a quartet singing, the chorus drifting in the gentle breeze. A small group was getting dressed after a swim in the lazy river; others were helping lay the table and carry out plates of food. It was an idyllic view, but a part of her could not escape a terrible pressing feeling.

Levarsson sidled up behind her and coughed to get her attention. Johnson glanced up, then returned to contemplating the view. She patted the ground. Levarsson squatted beside her.

"Will you sit down?" said Johnson. "You're making me jumpy squatting there."

A brief hesitation in which she brushed a stray blonde hair from her eye, and Levarsson sat.

"I didn't think such a place could exist," she observed. "One which hasn't been touched by the war."

"They've been lucky."

The two women sat in silence for a few moments.

"We can't stay," said Johnson, guessing Levarsson's thoughts. "We'd bring the war down on their heads."

"I know. Still, it would be nice to know peace." She turned to Johnson, fire in her eyes. "We can't let Congress, or the Republic, catch up with us. Something is very wrong with the way we were abandoned. The more I've been thinking about it, the more it stinks."

"True enough," conceded Johnson. "We'll have to find a safe place to hide, to work from. There are plenty of out-of-the-way systems we could use."

"We don't have much in the way of resources to set anything up," said Levarsson.

Johnson took a deep breath and let it out slowly. "That's why I'm leaving tomorrow. I'm going to take some of the crew and look for somewhere suitable. Indie and I were hoping you'd come along too, but if you'd rather stay and look after the bulk of our people I'd understand."

"Who's Indie?"

Outside the farmstead, everyone turned towards the house. Clovis got up from his rocking chair on the veranda, took a moment to straighten his back, and made his way to the table.

"Looks like it's time to go and be sociable. I'll explain over dinner," Johnson said as she rose and set off down the hill.

Part IV

A light so bright her glasses turned silver. The heat wave raced past her. Seen through the feed from one of her escort's cameras, the dry grass flashed into flame and was gone. Her robe and scarf smouldered, but didn't ignite; their heat-proof fabric protecting her skin.

The light faded and her goggles returned to normal sunlight filters. The city was gone, replaced by a roiling mass of fire and smoke. She could just make out the hemisphere of the pressure wave as it subtly refracted the light from the landscape and sky behind. Where it met the ground, it picked up clouds of dust. It advanced, ever expanding, engulfing everything it met. An isolated building, a farmstead perhaps, was hit. She saw the roof tiles scattered and the walls explode, timber tumbling end over end, a chair splintered, clothes ripped to shreds, the whole building reduced to shrapnel in a fraction of a second. It was getting closer but she couldn't look away, couldn't move. She drank in everything, holding the sights in her mind and saving them. Every piece of debris, every animal caught by the wall of dust. Everything was slowing down. She was sinking, lost in the details. The dust was hardly moving, her processors were enhancing each grain. A bead of sweat was frozen on her forehead.

There was a hard pain in her ribs and the world spun around her. She tumbled down the slope of the hill in the embrace of one of her escorts. They came to a stop as other members of her party piled on top of them. Parts of her brain felt like they were on fire as she curled up under the mound of metal and ceramic armour.
She heard the roar of the pressure wave as it hit. Dust was forced between her escorts, and the air was ripped from her lungs. The weight on her was definitely less now, some of her escort presumably blown away.

Silence. Calm. Nothing moved.

The wind started to pick up again. A gentle breeze at first, then a whistle, then a gale, as the air rushed back in towards the site of the explosion.
Overpressure then underpressure.

Chapter 11

Johnson lay in her cot on *The Indescribable Joy of Destruction*, enjoying that blissful state between sleep and full wakefulness. For a few minutes she didn't have to acknowledge the real world. She was getting round to thinking about breakfast; a pack of actual fresh bacon with her name on it was sitting in the galley, a leaving present from Clovis. Just a few more minutes to savour the perfect temperature of the sheets, the firmness of the bed, the humid air wafting the scent of camellia blossoms.

Dammit.

She opened her eyes and found herself looking out over a valley of neatly-kept tea plantations.

"This had better be good," she said, through gritted teeth.

"I think I know why your crew were abandoned," said Indie.

She spun to face him, searching his face for clues.

"Go on..."

"When you were down on the surface of Orpus-4, I downloaded all the data from the escape pods. I wanted to see if there was any more evidence of Republic agents on board. And ... I was curious to know more about your background.

"Despite the damage, I was able to put together a pretty comprehensive set of *Repulse's* logs. Most of them opened easily enough using your codes."

She frowned and opened her mouth to speak.

"Your EIS handed them to my security routine when you assumed the captain's position," he continued, with a placating gesture. "The important point, though, is that one file did not open. It was marked as a signal intercept of unknown origin, and queued for decryption when sufficient processor time became available. A copy had automatically been forwarded to Fleet Command in your last set of dispatches.

"I tried all the Republic ciphers that I knew and none of them worked. Since then I have had a routine running in the background, trying to crack it. It just finished. I think you need to see it."

A rectangle of fuzziness appeared in the air beside them. As Johnson looked at it, it condensed into an image of a Congressional officer with an emblem she didn't recognise on the wall behind him.

"That's Vice Admiral Koblensk," she said. "I worked for him once; on a special project for NSOB. He looks older than I remember."

The message began to play.

"Fleet Admiral. With a heavy heart, I have to report that one of the Omega Criteria has been met. I have thus begun preparations to activate the Red Fleet.

"If the voluntary sending of candidates to Academies remains below the threshold for twelve months, we will be forced to enact the Omega Plan. It goes without saying that ordering an attack on our own citizens goes against all my instincts. However, I accept that it is a necessary evil if we are to stem the tide of apathy.

"A target has been selected by my psy-ops analysts that should maximise the shock factor. All significant civilian population centres will be bombarded. Most importantly, we have chosen a planet where hitting the Academy will be an incontrovertibly deliberate act; one which cannot be excused away as collateral damage.

"For maximum effect, we'll need the local forces distracted or off-station. I trust you will be able to arrange a drill or false emergency.

"The mission details and fleet status reports are appended to this transmission. I pray that this is worth it, and that history forgives us. Koblensk out."

His image froze. Johnson stood, rigid and expressionless.

"Did you get the details?" she asked finally, barely whispering.

"The target was a planet called Concorde."

Johnson's eyes widened for a fraction of a second.

"You have heard of it?" asked Indie.

She swallowed hard.

"Yes, I've heard of it. I..." she tailed off.

"My records show it is a Core World, one of the few to have been terraformed. Third planet in a binary system. Gravity 1.2g at the equator. Three major land masses. Population 3.2 billion. Fifty or sixty major cities. The Academy is outside the capital, in the foothills of a major mountain range."

Which smell of tempus in the heat of the sun.

"I've never heard of the Red Fleet," she said. "Anything useful in the status reports?"

"Very," Indie replied. In quick succession, ships faded into view in the skies around them. "They are all Republic vessels reported lost or captured over the last ten years."

They both looked up at the eighty seven warships looming over them, a sizable taskforce of capital and ancillary vessels.

"So they plan to frame the Republic for a war crime. Cities have been flattened on either side in the past, but no-one has ever gone after an Academy... What month is it on Concorde?"

Indie waved his arm and the ships faded away. "Tertius. Why?"

"In twelve months, a new intake will have just started. Six thousand twelve-year-olds trying to get used to living away from their families."

#

Johnson stayed in her room all morning. She refused messages and personal visits from increasingly worried crew. She paced. She lay on her cot. She shadow boxed. She sat and searched the databases. And she talked to Indie.

^Levarsson has asked me if you are OK.^

^What did you tell her?^

^That you were indisposed ... that did not seem to help.^

^Hah. She's never known me miss a shift.^

As time went on, she paced less and talked more.

^Admiral Koblensk never struck me as the kind who'd go through with something like this,^ she sent to Indie. ^Sure, he cooked up some twisted missions, but always against the enemy.^

^You should read his file in my database. Republic intelligence officers had him under close scrutiny. They suspected he had gone rogue, citing vast quantities of money being diverted into untraceable accounts. Enough to fund such a fleet.^

She thought about taking a shower. Clear her head. Relax.

^This ... this is treason.^

^He sounded like he was acting on orders from the top,^ sent Indie.

Johnson decided against the shower and started pacing again.

^Why would anyone order that? Why would anyone follow that order?^ she sent. And realised how much it helped having Indie to discuss things with. She rubbed her neck.

^They probably believe they are acting in the best interests of Congress,^ Indie sent.

She did two more lengths of the small cabin. Pausing and looking up at the ceiling, she sent ^But...^ before resuming.

Another two lengths, then she stopped at one end and punched the wall. Resting her forehead against the smooth surface, she sent ^We have to do something.^

^What do you suggest?^

^I don't know. Yet. But something needs to be done.^

^Why us?^

She lifted her head off the wall and looked at the camera. ^For all we know, we are the only ones who know. They've gone a long way to try to silence us already. They abandoned the crew on Orpus-4, and I suspect there was something in the dispatches the commander of that station you tried to return me to received that lead him to target me.^

Finally making up her mind, Johnson called all hands to a briefing in the exercise chamber. Then she grabbed a ration pack she'd squirreled away in her room, and ripped a strip off the bottom, triggering the heating mechanism.

#

Johnson stepped out of her quarters and walked briskly down the corridor. It looked different; a week of sharing the ship with fifteen other people left little traces that made it feel more alive. That didn't explain the core difference in her mood: she had a purpose, and everything was tinted with that rosy glow.

She strode into the exercise room and mounted a platform that Indie grew for her without breaking her stride. The chatter in the room died as everyone rose and stood at attention, benches banging as they flipped up. As she looked out over the crew, all waiting for her to give them a direction, she realised how much she had been drifting these last few months, how lost she had been without a cause in which she could truly believe.

"As you were," she said.

The rustle of people leaning against equipment and walls was over quickly.

"I am afraid I won't be able to allow any of you to leave my command," she stated bluntly. "I know some of you wanted to return to Congressional space, and I respect that decision. However, new intelligence has come to light that makes it very clear that we are marked, all of us; anyone identified by Fleet Command is likely to be detained, probably executed."

The room stirred. People stole glances at each other, a few even exchanged whispers. Given the ridiculousness of her statement, she was prepared to overlook the breach of discipline. Clearing her throat got their attention again.

"Before *Repulse* was lost, we intercepted a message we clearly weren't supposed to. If we hadn't run into *The Indescribable Joy of Destruction*, I expect *Repulse* would have had some form of accident before she finished her patrol. It explains why no-one came looking for you.

"The message detailed a mission, conceived by Fleet Command, or at least elements of it, to frame the Republic for an attack on Congressional civilian targets. The strike is intended to re-invigorate the public mood for the war by deepening the hatred of the Republic. The estimated casualty count is around the one billion mark, with children specifically targeted."

The crew's reactions varied from disbelief through to anger. Another, bigger, commotion broke out, as deep emotions overrode ingrained discipline. There were shouts of "No" and "It must be a mistake".

Johnson let them get a bit of it out of their systems, before raising her hands and bringing them slowly downwards. Patches of calm spread as neighbours nudged each other back into respectful silence.

"I understand your reaction, but this recording is not the only piece of evidence we have found. I have been considering this for most of the day and I am sure there is something to it. Something I have to investigate. Once this meeting is over, I will make the recording and all the other data available. You can judge for yourselves.

"I became disillusioned with Fleet Command when I discovered they left you to die. I had planned to head out and explore independent space. Now I know I have something more important to do. I have to do what I can to stop this dire threat. And I want you alongside me."

Her audience grew taller. She scanned their faces; every one had the glint of pride in their eyes.

"We are few, but we are a determined few. Life has made us strong. We have survived for this purpose. This is our calling. We will stand and be counted."

As soon as it became clear she had finished speaking, the room erupted into applause and cheering. Johnson frowned, not expecting that response. Their chances of success were negligible; billions were likely to die.

Levarsson caught her eye. ^Glad to have you back, Ma'am. And I think that goes for everyone else too.^

Johnson clapped her on the back, making sure the rest of the crew saw her show of confidence. ^It makes finding somewhere safe to set up camp even more important. At least tomorrow's jump takes us into a likely system.^

#

The usual slight shift of perspective, and they jumped into a new system. Johnson and Levarsson sat in couches on the bridge but weren't immersed, as they didn't expect any immediate threats. The data flooded in from the passive sensors, and a routine flagged up a radio source.

"Great," Johnson sighed. "This system was supposed to be deserted."

"There was always a chance someone might have chosen it for the same reason as us," said Levarsson. "Someone running from the war, or perhaps the law."

^It's a distress signal,^ sent Indie. ^Republic merchant codes, she's identifying herself as the *Limpopo XII*. No biohazard alert. Life support is intact but engines and external sensors have failed. Given their position, the chances are they came out of jump and couldn't restart their main drives.^

Johnson pulled the sensor feeds from the region of the signal source and studied them for a minute, looking for anything the AI might have missed.

Is it a trap? Or are they fellow fugitives? It doesn't feel wrong...

"Thoughts? Observations?" she asked.

"They are a long way from anywhere someone could hide to bounce us," replied Levarsson, her fingers dancing over the manual controls suspended in front of her.

Good. She thought of the trap possibility too.

^She's right,^ added Indie. ^I could easily turn and run before anyone could get us in weapons' range ... unless they have something big on that tub that I can't detect.^

"Thank you, that's what I was thinking too. We go in. Careful approach, no hails until we can scan them from a lot closer. Use a best fuel course, there's no rush if their life support is OK."

"Aye," acknowledged Levarsson.

Indie sent a simple confirmation ping. Moments later Johnson was pressed into her seat as the drives powered up. Levarsson was busy talking to someone, briefing them on the possibility of a rescue.

Yes. She definitely has the makings of a good XO, maybe even a captain.

"Ma'am?"

"Go ahead, Levarsson."

"The crew are picking out a boarding party, a mixture of engineers and medics mostly. Marine Corporal Anson will be taking the lead. It might get a bit ugly, though. Permission to open the armoury?"

"Granted. Good thinking." Johnson relaxed into the chair. A nice, simple naval action would help rebuild some of her self-confidence after the fiasco on Scragend.

"Erm, we've only got two marines aboard. Might we be able to borrow one of those robots? Just in case..."

^Indie?^

^Unit 02 is fully charged and ready to go.^

^Prepared for action on a ship?^ she checked. Some of their new weaponry would easily punch through the hull of a civilian ship.

^It is their primary design function. You know how effective they are at it.^

She suppressed a shudder at the memory of that desperate boarding action after losing *Repulse*.

^Sorry. I didn't mean to upset you,^ he sent.

"Yes, Lieutenant, Unit 02 is being prepped now."

"Ma'am," Levarsson nodded before starting to talk to the rest of the crew again.

#

As the merchant ship grew large on their screen, Johnson and Levarsson reclined in their couches. If anything did kick off, it would be better if they were already immersed. The recorded warning to strap down went out across the ship as the lids closed. A quick flick through the internal feeds showed Johnson the boarding party suited up and clamped in the shuttle hold, the remaining few crew climbing into their cots.

As the gel pumped into the cushions around her, she took the plunge into the virtual command view. Indie was already standing there, manifested in a brown leather jacket and old-fashioned flying helmet, complete with goggles on his forehead.

Caught by surprise, she laughed.

"You look ridiculous!"

"I was going for light-hearted," he replied. "But I am glad it gave you a moment of mirth."

His clothes shifted and settled as a black skinsuit.

"Better?" he asked, just as Levarsson appeared between them.

"What?" she asked, slightly confused by the question apparently directed at her.

"Much," replied Johnson, leaning back to look at Indie behind Levarsson.

"Never mind, Lieutenant," she continued, returning her gaze towards the merchantman.

"Either of you see anything wrong?"

Levarsson and Indie both shook their heads. Levarsson's cheek bore a ragged scar, even more livid than in reality.

^Why is the simulation rendering her scar so intensely?^ Johnson asked Indie.

^The software can sometimes pick up on aspects of yourself that you are acutely aware of, and emphasise them.^

^That is not a very kind bit of programming.^

^Kindness didn't feature highly on my designers' agenda. They got the system working and moved on to other things.^

"OK. Here we go."

A thought sent out a cross-spectrum active sensor pulse towards their target. With her attention firmly on the ship, the software added an almost overwhelming amount of data to the image. She cleared it down to the basics; the engines were indeed off, but that didn't mean they were actually faulty, a few small defensive weapons dotted the hull, nothing to worry Indie but a possible problem for the shuttle, and confirmation that there weren't any heavily shielded areas.

Satisfied, she dipped into the menus and opened a standard humanitarian aid channel to the ship. With the distress beacon active, it was automatically accepted by the merchant vessel, albeit audio only.

"Limpopo XII, we are here to render assistance. Please advise on what you need."

No response.

Johnson scratched the back of her neck. "Limpopo XII, I say again, we are here to render assistance. Please respond."

The channel was definitely open both ways, they were receiving pingback. The hairs on the back of Johnson's neck tingled.

"Perhaps they're too busy trying to fix whatever's wrong, and there's no-one on the bridge?" offered Levarsson.

"Or perhaps they don't trust us," said Indie.

Or perhaps there is no-one left to respond.

"*Limpopo XII.* We have not received a response from you. Your beacon indicates that your power reserves are limited. Under the Space Shipping Agreement, I am sending a shuttle with a boarding party to provide medical and engineering aid."

No response. Johnson kept flipping between it being a trap and there being people who desperately needed her help.

Johnson set the comms system to loop her last message until further notice, and alert her if there was a response. She then linked to the shuttle, where the Caretaker was once again in control of flight operations.

^You're good to go. No response from the target. Aim for the main port airlock. They have limited point defence, we'll cover you if necessary.^

^Understood. Disengaging docking clamps now.^

She watched the small craft pull away from her. The target continued to ignore them.

"Levarsson, I want you to keep an eye on the boarding operation. Indie, watch out for any remote threats, but be ready to zap any turret on that thing that targets the shuttle."

Levarsson turned away slightly. Her hands darted between a multitude of windows that floated in the air around her, bringing up the feeds from the boarding party's helmet cams. She'd positioned herself to allow her to keep the merchant vessel in her peripheral vision without it being hidden behind a display, Johnson realised.

She's keeping one eye on the big picture, even as she manages her part of it. She didn't have that knack when I last saw her in action; her time in command of the camp on Orpus-4 must have sharpened her tactical skills.

Indie disappeared, and reappeared behind Johnson. She turned her head to look at him, her eyebrow raised.

"I am perfectly aware of everything around me without this simulation," he answered her unspoken query. "I thought that you, however, might want to have an unimpeded view."

She nodded her thanks and turned back. Levarsson had faded, background stars shone through her body. Johnson's internal reaction to this disconcerting view must have been picked up by a subroutine, as a section of the operating manual for the simulation was thrust into her mind. A bridge occupant whose task focussed them elsewhere was automatically faded for all other users. In a naval conflict, all users would be rendered totally transparent to those tasked with directing piloting and weapons. Johnson was also now aware of how to manually set the transparency of other occupants with a thought.

Indie sent her the digital equivalent of a smug smile. She rolled her eyes.

Show-off.

The next few minutes passed in silence. Johnson dipped into the feeds from the shuttle. She knew Levarsson would let her know if there was a problem, but she wanted to look at them for herself. The humans in the boarding party were sitting calmly on the benches down the sides of the compartment, their weapons by their sides or across their chests. Unit 02 was crouched by the side airlock.

So, they decided to lead with the robot. Makes sense going into a potentially hostile situation, as long as its presence doesn't escalate things unnecessarily...

The lights in the shuttle switched to red. She was about to open a channel to the marine leading the party, but checked herself.

These enhanced control systems make it far too easy to get sucked into micromanaging. It's a reasonable decision; let him run with it.

She forced herself to pull out from the shuttle feed and cast her eyes around their nearspace.

Nothing, apart from the freighter. Time to see if there's anything lurking behind you...

Johnson took control of the flight systems. Picturing the manoeuvre in her mind, she yanked the ship through space, thankful the crew were already strapped in. Up and over the freighter. Indie responded, hunting for targets. She slewed the ship, keeping the bow pointed just beyond the freighter.

No threats appeared. Just empty space. This close, nothing should have been able to match their move. She pulled the ship to a stop relative to the boxy freighter. She'd chosen a path that would allow them to check the other side while keeping a line on the airlock. A gentle nudge, and she drifted back enough to be able to cover the shuttle properly.

Another minute and the shuttle docked. Levarsson confirmed with Johnson that they were still green lit, and in they went. Johnson deliberately took a mental step back; if they were going to get hit by naval forces, now would be the time. They'd have had to set out a while ago, but it was possible they'd been cold-coasting in without tripping the passive sensors. She focussed in turn on each planet or rock large enough to hide a ship within a light minute, pulling up likely attack lines from them and searching along them. She resisted a momentary urge to do an all-round active pulse.

I'm just a little jumpy, things haven't gone this smoothly in ages.

"Boarding party has entered, Ma'am," reported Levarsson, bringing her attention back to nearspace. "The airlock responded to the codes the combat unit transmitted. No resistance met. No sign of the crew at all, actually."

"Thank you," replied Johnson.

Ten more minutes of waiting. Johnson split her time between examining potential external threat sources and thinking of scenarios that might emerge on board the freighter, busying herself, a distraction from the knots in her stomach.

"Ma'am!" The single word was accompanied by a mental prick demanding urgency.

Johnson's whole attention turned to Levarsson. The simulation rendered her opaque again.

"Boarding party is under fire. No fatalities, two critical injuries," Levarsson reported calmly. "Unit 02 has the enemy pinned down."

Johnson's heart missed a beat. Ghosts of the marines

from *Repulse* crowded onto the bridge. She screwed her eyes shut, ran through checklists. It was no good. She couldn't sit around doing nothing.

"Indie! Let me know the moment anything changes outside!"

Johnson's viewpoint leapt to that of Unit 02. She was at the end of a corridor barely wide enough for her frame. The crew were huddled behind her, medics working on the casualties. In front, the passage opened out into a large engineering workshop. Occasional bursts of fire came from weapons held out from behind cover. With no decent targets, she was using ... no, the combat unit was using its body to shield the humans while waiting for something to shoot at. Scorch marks and spent casings showed where the party had been hit; two large smears of blood revealed where the casualties had been dragged to cover.

"Hold your fire," she said, ramping up the volume on the robot's speakers. "We came here to help you."

"We don't want your help!"

"Your distress beacon says otherwise."

^Casualties are stable,^ reported one of the medics.

"You just want to take us back to the Republic to stand trial!" came the shout from across the workshop.

Interesting. Why does he...? Doh, the armour.

"No we don't," she replied. "We aren't Republic."

"Oh no, of course you aren't!" came the sarcastic reply, followed by a slightly longer burst of fire.

"We're not. We appropriated some Republic kit, but we aren't Republic."

"You telling me you're Congressional spies, then?"

He's stalling. What for?

"No..."

"What then?" he asked, derision tinting his voice.

There. Movement to one side.

The combat unit responded at the same moment,

pouncing on the man who had been crawling along the wall towards the corridor. One of the unit's legs flicked away the explosive pack the man had been carrying, while others grabbed him and dragged him back into the relative safety of the hallway.

"Nice try!" she said to the room at large. "I propose a truce. Let my crew retire to their shuttle and we can talk about this properly. I assure you we have no intention of turning you over to the Republic."

No reply. But the pot-shots had stopped too.

"Hello," she said to the captive, taking care to reduce the speaker volume. "Shall we start again somewhere a little more comfortable?"

#

The defenders followed them all the way to the shuttle without trying anything. As the crew turned the last corner, however, shots rang out.

Some of them looped round and got ahead of us. No, not us, I'm not actually there.

^Find somewhere to hole up,^ Johnson sent to Marine Corporal Anson.

He opened a nearby door, an officer's quarters judging by the label, and entered it rifle first.

^Clear,^ he sent. ^Make sure the door is wedged open. Don't want them locking it out of life support or anything.^

The crew piled in, Unit 02 hunkering down in the doorway. There was no chance of anyone getting to them down the corridor with it covering the approach.

"Watch that air vent, Rizzo," ordered Anson. "They could crawl through the ducts.

"I want someone with an ear to each bulkhead. Let us know if you hear anything, they might try to cut or blow a way through."

^Very good, Marine,^ sent Johnson on a general broadcast. She couldn't see much of the room through the open doorway, other than a bunk on the opposite wall and a desk with an antiquated workstation. ^Can someone get me a link to a terminal in there? I want a face to face with our guest.^

^He might be bugged,^ pointed out the marine.

^Good. I want them all to hear what I have to say. Just keep anything sensitive over EIS comms.^

"Listen," she said over the video channel, "we are not Republic. It is a long story, but we were Congress. We became somewhat disillusioned with Fleet Command. We're here to find some breathing space, to decide what to do."

Recognition lit in the captive's eyes. He hid it quickly, but she had seen it.

Bingo.

"We came here aboard a sympathetic Republic ship. We got the kit from their armoury when we decided to help you. You didn't respond to our hails offering assistance. We half expected a trap."

He looked like he was thinking about breaking his silence. She gave him a moment. He obviously thought better of it.

^Someone give him a sip of water,^ she sent.

"We don't want to hurt you," she continued as one of her crew offered the captive the bottle from his webbing. "Any of you."

The prisoner looked suspiciously at the bottle. The crewman offering it guessed his concern and took a drag before offering it again. The prisoner accepted and took a sip, gingerly.

"If you just let my crew leave your ship, we can leave you in peace. We could even leave some supplies if they'd help..."

"Hello!"

Some of her crew in the background turned their heads towards the doorway.

"Hello in there! I want to talk to your CO!" came the voice again. "I'm unarmed. I am going to step into the corridor now. I'd appreciate it if you didn't shoot me."

Johnson pulled the feed from the combat unit, this time just a window in her vision, not a full immersion. A dark-skinned, bearded man, dressed in a mixture of Republic battle armour and civilian rags stepped confidently into view of the robot. His arms were out to the sides, palms forwards. He noted Unit 02 watching him and did a slow turn.

"I'd lift my shirt, but that thing can probably tell what I ate for breakfast at this range."

^Not quite,^ Indie sent to Johnson, ^but he isn't carrying any weapons.^

The man's arms relaxed to his sides. He took a step towards the robot.

"I'll take the lack of incoming fire as leave to approach," he said.

Unit 02 stepped into the corridor to allow him to enter the room. The muzzles of several rifles greeted him. The robot closed the gap behind him.

"Easy now," he said, raising his hands in mock surrender. "You shouldn't allow your weapon too close to a prisoner. You don't want them relieving you of it."

^Back up,^ sent Anson. ^I've got him, everyone else as you were.^

The crew shuffled back, returning to their positions.

"Has everyone finished playing around?" asked Johnson, still live on the vid screen. "I am Commander Olivia Johnson. You wanted to talk to me?"

"Yes," replied the man, turning square on to the

workstation. "I heard what you said to Khan here. I too have casualties. I take it that your ship is equipped with a decent hospital, and you did say you wanted to help. I propose that your uninjured crew remain here, for now, whilst my hospital cases accompany yours to your ship."

"You guarantee the safety of my crew?"

"So long as you guarantee the safety of mine," he agreed, then added "I will be accompanying them. I would like to speak with you in person."

"Agreed."

^You're letting them in?^ asked Levarsson. Incredulity seeped across the connection.

^Yes. Why would I not?^ replied Johnson. She terminated the connection before Levarsson could reply.

Let her stew on that one for a while.

#

Johnson met the shuttle with Unit 01 by her side. She floated, casually holding a handle to stop her spinning; the robot nestled into a corner, ready to pounce if anything went wrong.

^Do I hear birdsong or is it all quiet?^ asked Indie.

Johnson glared at a camera. ^What?^

^Oh, this situation just reminded me of scenes in a couple of books, where both sides pause in the middle of a particularly bloody war to collect casualties.^

^Never read them. Sorry.^ Johnson shook her head. ^Remember, I'm an Academy girl. Most of my education was focussed on fighting this war.^

^Your loss,^ sent Indie, along with a link to some suggested books.

Johnson almost deleted it, but changed her mind and saved it to her personal files.

Never know. I might find time to take up reading.

The spokesman for the other crew came through first. He moved through the air with practiced ease and brought himself to a halt against the wall beside her, aligning himself to her with a deft twist. Behind him, the injured from both sides were brought out, each guided by a comrade.

"Commander," he said. "I thank you for this opportunity to treat the wounded, and formally offer my parole for the duration of this visit aboard your ship."

"I accept your parole. And thank you for offering a way out of our standoff," she returned.

She studied him closely, as, no doubt, he studied her. A green scarf with white Arabic lettering peeked out of his collar. He had a full beard underneath intelligent eyes. He held himself with a confidence and efficiency that reminded her of battle-hardened marines.

"It is funny; one of my younger men thought I was crazy to trust you," he said.

"One of my officers said as much," Johnson replied.

"Are we really that far gone?" His brown eyes looked at her wistfully.

"I was the same. Growing up in the Academy, the Republic was always portrayed as evil, its soldiers as monsters," she said. "It took a few tours for me to realise they were people, the same as me."

Once the casualties and their helpers had been dispatched to the infirmary, and he made no move to follow them, she dialled the gravity back up. They settled down onto the floor.

"Would you take a seat?" she asked, waving her hand towards a table and chairs that emerged from the floor.

"That would be a good idea," he replied.

Once they were seated, she said, "You know who I am.

Perhaps you could tell me who you are?"

"That would be only fair," he replied, smiling. "I am, was, Master Sergeant Aali Issawi, Gamma Team 7."

That explains the level of resistance.

"What is a special forces team doing out here in the middle of nowhere?"

"The same as you, if what you've said is true. We have come to doubt that our missions have been entirely beneficial to the people of the Republic. We were headed for one of the moons here to lay low for a bit; work out our next moves."

What are the chances of us both picking the same system?

"That is remarkably open of you," she said. "What if we were a Republic ship? That would have been a perfect confession you just made."

He shrugged and bowed his head slightly towards her, opening his palms to her on the table.

"They have no need for confessions from us. Our actions have already condemned us," he said. "We were in the weaker position in that standoff. Had you been a real Republican Commander you'd have slagged the ship, even with your crew on board, rather than negotiate with deserters."

"My ... former government abandoned my crew. I think I am regarded as an unfortunate witness," she said. "I don't think they are coming after me. Not yet, anyway. However, this ship will be wanted by both sides when they find out I have it."

She thought for a moment, before continuing. "Tell me, you are the first to come aboard without reacting to his construction. Was that a really good poker face or have you seen this kind of thing before?"

He clapped his hands together and grinned.

"Very astute, Commander Johnson. I must confess; I

have indeed been aboard a *Rampager* class before. I would be most interested to hear how you came to be in command of such a vessel. Their AIs are not exactly the kind to deviate from Republican Navy protocols."

^Indie?^ she sent. ^Do you want to talk to him?^

^No, thank you. I suspect revealing my true nature right now would be counter-productive.^

"I don't actually know," she said to Issawi. "When I came aboard, the ship was dead. It rebooted when I forced entry to the bridge. I guess it imprinted on me as the captain."

"So, what do we do now?" asked Issawi.

Johnson studied him closely for a moment. His hair was just starting to grey. He was fit and looked tough, but a hint of weariness showed around his mouth. Deep laughter lines flanked his eyes.

"How about you return the rest of my crew?" she replied.

He gazed back at her, scrutinized her, as though trying to read her soul.

"I think I'm going to trust you, Commander Johnson. I don't see any way out of this otherwise ... just don't make me regret it."

#

^The Master Sergeant is who he says he is,^ sent Indie. ^His file was buried deep in the database, somewhere you'd have to be looking for it specifically to find it.^

Johnson sat up in her bunk. She hadn't really been trying to sleep, just rest while she tried to make sense of the ideas whirling round in her head.

^Was he involved in black ops or something like that?^ she asked, getting up and crossing the room to her workstation.

^Read the file. He could be useful.^

An icon flashed on the desk. She flicked it up onto the wall and sat back in the chair. The text scrolled as she read it, the speed governed subconsciously through her EIS. The document was punctuated with images from Issawi's various missions.

^He was a special forces trainer?^ she asked, pulling the oversized t-shirt back onto her shoulder.

^One of the best, from what I can piece together. I'm linking snippets of mission reports, intel and scuttlebutt into the document as I find them.^

Johnson continued to scan through the file.

^I've worked with operatives like this before,^ she sent. ^I once spent a month on a clapped-out old freighter with a team from the Naval Special Operations Branch because they needed a tech specialist. We were trading in enemy systems. Gathering intel, marking targets, taking out key representatives.^

She read on some more. Subconsciously, she registered the slight change in ship's hum as it stood down from daytime running. Throughout the communal areas, the background lights would have dimmed slightly and taken on a redder hue.

^It looks like his team stopped getting the choice assignments last year. I wonder what they did to piss off the brass?^ she mused.

^It doesn't say. They were still being used, so it must only have been a suspicion. Had there been proof, they'd have been suspended, probably prosecuted.^

She shuddered, as she remembered an execution from her last year in the Academy. A soldier had been caught using his leave to spread disaffection. The whole class was turned out to witness the firing squad. The presiding officer went on to make a speech about duty, and wished the class luck when they entered Basic Training.

^Oh, now this is very interesting,^ sent Indie. ^I just found a reference to an asset that abandoned a mission and disappeared. It was in the right sector at the right time to be his team.^

^I take it your database is a few months out of date now? Enough time for them to have been marked as traitors.^

^Correct. My last update was one week before the engagement with *Rep...* before you came aboard.^

^So, I think we have to give Issawi the benefit of the doubt. For now. Perhaps he will allow us to use his ship to collect the rest of the crew and bring them here.^

Johnson shifted in her seat.

^And thank you^, she added. ^I prefer the second way of putting it.^

^Olivia?^ Indie asked. ^I have a confession to make.^

Johnson stiffened. Indie's confessions rarely made comfortable listening.

^Go on...^

^When I was fixing your leg after you tried to rip it off in the recycling chamber, I ran a diagnostic on your existing implants.^

She froze, feeling her heart beating in her chest, knowing what was coming.

^There was a bug,^ he continued. ^In the medical monitoring routine. It was misreporting your serotonin levels.^

He had to know. It wasn't a bug; she'd written that patch when she was in the Academy. She couldn't risk them finding out about her depression when they gave her an EIS.

^I took the liberty of fixing the bug...^

This was it, then. He would tell the others; Levarsson would assume command.

^...and implanting a serotonin re-uptake regulator.^

Of course he did. He never thought to ask before drugging her, but by now she knew that he meant well.

^It should last for several months before it needs replacing. You'll be able to carry on as normal, though hopefully with fewer symptoms.^

She dared to hope.

^You... You're not going to tell anyone?^

^Why would I?^ He seemed genuinely puzzled by the question.

^Mental illness renders me unfit to command.^

^Being an AI renders me unfit to live. And yet you trust me.^

She looked up at the camera by the wallscreen.

^So...^

^So, I think you have proven yourself to be a good leader, even whilst fighting this,^ sent Indie. ^You must have noticed that things have got a bit better recently?^

Now that he said it, she realised that the darkness had been easier to keep at bay. It still lurked in the corners of her mind, but she hadn't actively noticed it in a while.

Chapter 12

Johnson swept onto the bridge, and plonked herself down on her couch. Since Issawi joined the cause, and the *Limpopo* had returned with the rest of the crew, she had been in a more buoyant mood, and it showed in the occasional slip from primness; at least when no other humans were watching.

Hanke and another crewman entered, nodded formally to Johnson to acknowledge her presence, and made their way across the bridge to the other two couches. All three immersed together. The orange and red swirling stripes of the gas giant Triasson loomed over their heads; below lay the verdant moon Robespierre.

I didn't think I'd ever get used to this disappearing bridge; now I'm casually plugging in. That is still an impressive sight, though.

Moments after they manifested in the simulation, they were joined by Levarsson. A faint reddish glow surrounded her image and, when Johnson focussed on her, the words 'Limpopo XI Actual' appeared over her head.

Johnson smiled warmly at her former tactical officer, glad to have been able to reward her with her own command. "Glad you could make it, Lieutenant. I wasn't sure the freighter's systems would be able to cope with an immersion feed."

"Neither were we, until now," replied Levarsson. "The Republic simulation technology is astounding. But the Limpopo's charts leave something to be desired. I've done my fair share of exploring unsurveyed caves when I'm on leave, but this is ridiculous. Is there anything about the moon in Indie's database? Ours just gives the name and atmospheric mix."

"That's all we have too. It's why Indie was so excited when he found the base."

Hanke straightened up from where he had been leaning over the other crewman's virtual console. "Wonder who Robespierre was? Do you think it was named after the person who discovered it?"

"That would normally be on the record. It was probably assigned by a computer algorithm like our... like Congressional ships."

Johnson reviewed the status reports from each department. Everything showed ready. Still, she ran through the go/no-go with them. She liked to be able to study each person as they reported, and give them the chance to voice any niggling concerns. It was something she'd learned from her mentor on her first tour out from Command school.

"Team One ready," reported Anson from the *Repulse's* old shuttle.

"Team Two ready," reported Issawi from an assault lander, recently unpacked from one of the Limpopo's cargo bays.

"Limpopo ready," reported Levarsson, the glow surrounding her flaring as she spoke.

Johnson looked to the two members of her own bridge crew. They both nodded back.

"I am ready too," said Indie, appearing at her side.

^Wondered when you were going to show up,^ she sent back.

He stuck his tongue out at her. Somehow, she knew the others would have seen him remain impassive; that gesture was for her alone, one friend to another.

Johnson closed her eyes and centred herself. Everything

felt good.

"All teams, go."

The moment she sent the order, Johnson felt the ship's centre of gravity change as the shuttle detached. She looked around. Both small craft braked as they started their descent to the moon's surface; towards the mystery complex. The lander dwarfed the shuttle, designed as it was to carry a tank, or two fully armoured platoons, from orbit into a hot landing zone.

With no space-based threats on the board, Johnson wanted to go down with the first wave; be with them as they explored the unknown base, find out why it wasn't on the charts. Her officers had managed to argue her out of it, suggesting she would be more useful commanding the combat units remotely. Given her performance on Scragend, she was forced to agree.

The shuttle flared to a hover, and she connected to one of the units as it flung itself out the back. The three robots set up a perimeter around the four human members of the team, crouching in the dust as the shuttle powered away. Johnson was aware subconsciously of the lander dropping Issawi's team ten kilometres away, on the far side of the complex.

Once the jet blast had died, but before the dust had settled, Anson signalled for them to move. They ran, keeping low, to the mouth of a tunnel. The humans shouldered up against the rock on either side, their weapons trained at the gaping hole. Johnson tasked one combat unit with rear cover, and it scuttled off to hunker down just below the crest of a rise looking over their landing area. She glanced back to check on it with one camera of the unit she was riding, and was satisfied it hadn't skylined itself.

^As if it would make a mistake in positioning,^ commented Indie.

^I know,^ she replied. ^It would nag at the edges of my mind if I didn't check, though.^

^I don't have that problem,^ sent Indie.

^That's because you've got me,^ interjected the Caretaker. ^And you can just spawn routines and trust they'll report back to you if you need to know something.^

The robot in front of her placed its first leg into the shadow cast by the tunnel.

^Got to go, boys,^ Johnson sent, as the darkness enveloped the lead robot, and hers reached the entrance.

The darkness was only present in her root perception, the one linked to visual wavelengths. She was simultaneously aware of the sensor returns for infra-red, which revealed clusters of bat-like creatures hanging on the roof, ultraviolet, which lit up with markings on the walls and floor, and microwave, which showed a clear representation of the passage ahead, illuminated by the emissions from the first combat unit. By concentrating, she was able to bring each perception to the forefront of her mind. The markings were a mixture of writing, symbols and arrows; unfamiliar styling, but recognisable as the standard fare for any human installation, written in high visibility paint which happened to fluoresce in ultraviolet.

^Team 1 at Waymark Alpha. Entering now.^

^Understood,^ replied Issawi. ^We're still clearing through the surface buildings. Nothing to report.^

The robots edged deeper into the tunnel, followed by the humans. So far there had been no signs of a military presence; no security checkpoints, no weapons turrets, no deep scanners. The tunnel was wide enough for two vehicles to pass, and curved slightly to the left as it dipped down into the ground.

After completing a forty-five degree turn, they came to the first access hatch in the wall. It was large enough for an average human to enter, if they were careful not to bang their head, and had 'Plant Room 12a' written on it. A quick check by one of the crew confirmed it contained nothing but air conditioning pumps, a small table and chair, and a significant amount of grime.

Johnson pulled up the map, a blue wireframe model of the tunnel they'd already walked down, and added a note about the room, prioritising getting the air circulation going again should they decide to stay. She was just about to minimise it, when purple blossomed in an area to their west. Zooming in, she saw passages growing and branching, tendrils probing deeper and deeper into the complex.

Issawi's made it to the smaller entrance and released his spy drones. Shame he didn't have enough to share, save us doing this the old-fashioned way.

They continued along the passage, checking out occasional small hatches, but found nothing significant. Fifty metres beyond the plant room the passage split, two roadways half the size of the one they were in curved away from each other.

"As we planned," said Anson. "Check both to the limit of sight. Unless anything makes our mind up for us in that distance, we go left."

The team paused while one of the robots was sent down each fork.

"The arrows on the floor are in opposite directions in the two passages," commented one of the crew, studying the ground. "Probably a one-way system from here on in."

The passages turned and bent sharply towards each other. From where her robot halted, Johnson could see a set of heavy doors blocking the way ahead. The feed from the other unit showed an almost identical sight, save for a large no entry sign hanging from the roof.

"Right it is then," said Anson.

Johnson waited until the rest caught up before moving her robot to the door. She tapped the metal with the tip of a pointed leg and a dull clang rang out.

That's thick. No way we're cutting through this side of next week.

"Guess we'll have to hack the entrance codes," said Anson, apparently coming to the same conclusion as her.

A crewmember plugged her pad and an emergency battery into the control panel next to the doors. Johnson felt circuits wake up as electricity surged through them once more, tiny electromagnetic signatures studding the walls. Johnson opened a channel to the pad to monitor the progress, and was disappointed by the utter lack of any. Moments after she connected, the program reported that the operating system was too different to any in its database. Annoyed and frustrated, Johnson pushed against the data stream, and some of her consciousness leaked through the pad and into the control panel. It was not like Indie's immersion bridge, or riding a combat unit. In each of those, her mind remained singular; this time she was still in the robot watching her crew, but a facet of her was also in the door controls.

How come this feels normal? Is this what Indie meant about some people having brains that could cope with extreme data feeds?

The architecture was weird; nothing like anything Johnson had studied before. The team stared at the red flashing 'Access Failed' banner on the pad the woman had turned round for them to see. Johnson swam around, looking for anything she recognised. Anson ran his hands along the join in the doors, obviously considering more dramatic ways to breach. Something familiar, it tasted like an access control routine. Anson turned and called to the other marine, requesting a breaching charge. Johnson spawned a hacking program and fed it into the access control. The marine hurried over, swinging his pack off his shoulders and dumping it on the floor. Sharks! Counter intrusion routines. The marine detached something from his kit, Johnson found she couldn't quite focus on it. The sharks circled closer, but her program was duplicating and churning through possibilities at an ever increasing rate. The marine fixed the charge to the doors; she tried to tell him to wait but couldn't remember how to speak. A thrashing of water, clouds of bubbles...

^Olivia!^

The connection dropped. For a moment she stared at the inside of her acceleration couch, then the pathway opened again and she was back in the combat unit.

"Wait!" she shouted, the crew recoiling from the sheer volume of the speakers.

^Calm down,^ came a transmission wrapped in lavender.

"No need for explosives," she said, more carefully this time. "I think I've got it."

^Your enhanced EIS is still growing,^ sent Indie. ^Its trigger is likely to be unpredictable while it binds to your neurons.^

^You could have warned me!^ she replied, still struggling to free her mind from the effects of adrenaline.

^It was in the documents I sent you before you agreed to the procedure.^

She thought back. The documents had been so dense, and so similar to the ones she'd waded through when she got her original EIS, that she'd skimmed over some of the sections.

^A reminder would have been nice.^

^There is no record of one starting to act this soon after implantation, so a reminder at this time was not indicated.^

Very carefully, she opened a simple channel to the pad and instructed it to link with the hacking routine she had left behind in the control panel. The red banner on its screen was replaced with a green one. The crewmember holding it frowned, looking to the robot Johnson was riding and back to the pad.

Johnson sent the command for the doors to open. With gentle hum that seemed out of place in the large, corroded hallway, the doors cracked open. The other combat unit scurried past the moment it would fit. It broadcast back images of a large hangar full of machinery, three stories of balconies at one end, another large set of doors off to the left.

"Looks like a loading bay," said Anson. "We're in the base proper now."

The team filed in. Johnson checked the password before disconnecting from the pad.

e1nSTe1N! ... Seriously?

#

Johnson was sure they'd been down this passage before. Yet, a quick check of the map showed they weren't going round in circles.

I wonder if it is due to the remote viewing, if I'm not getting the sense of turns and distance through the link. I know consciously exactly where I am but it doesn't match where I feel *I am.*

The team prepared to enter another room. Whilst whoever was on point at any time was still going weapons hot, the rest had slung their rifles across their chests an hour ago, about the same time as they'd run into the bad air and had to fit masks. They had surveyed almost two kilometres of passages and seen no sign whatsoever of recent habitation. Most of the rooms were machine shops or storerooms. The parts and supplies they found were decades old, but still serviceable. The sealed food was within its use-by dates, but then most rations used in space lasted at least twenty years. Most items were civilian; the few military things they found were probably just army surplus.

Johnson barely registered the surge in electricity in the conduits before the lights flickered on, casting stark shadows from the pipework running along the ceiling. The walls were stained green and brown, with grey paint showing through in places.

^Well done Evans,^ she sent on an open channel, as the team around her deactivated the night vision cameras built into their helmets. The robots stepped down their emissions, setting their active sensors to pulse at random intervals in case anything was trying to sneak up on them.

^Thank you, Ma'am,^ replied Evans from the control room they'd left her working in. ^We're running on battery back-up right now. It's showing a little under five days worth left, so plenty of time to get the reactor back online. I'm going to take a look at the air-con next.^

Several of the crew perked up at that. The concentrations of carbon dioxide were high enough that they had to use the scrubbers in their helmets. That didn't do anything for the oppressive thickness of the air, and few people liked operating closed down if they could help it.

^That would be most appreciated down here.^

The team lined up either side of the door, their backs against the bulkhead. One pushed the door beside him open with his arm, keeping his head and body out of the way. Anson pushed through the open doorway, rifle in his shoulder, followed by another crewmember. Johnson watched through their helmet cameras as they cleared the room. It was a large dormitory, perhaps enough bunks for thirty people.

She froze the image of one of the tables placed in the centre of clusters of beds and wardrobes. The chairs were in disarray, suggesting whoever had been sitting there had left in a hurry. The table was covered in sheets of paper.

^Are you seeing this?^ she sent to Indie.

Enhancing the tabletop, she could see that the paper held hand-written mathematical formulae. The multitude of scribbled corrections and additions in different hands suggested that this was the focus of a group effort.

^Yes,^ he replied. ^It looks like jump field theory, though I am not seeing any of the solutions with which I am familiar.^

His weapon slung round behind him, Anson approached the table.

^Can you get me shots of the other pages?^ Indie asked him.

^I'll see what I can do...^

Anson moved a spanner off a pile of sheets and bent over so his camera pointed at them. One by one he moved the sheets from one pile to another. He was halfway through when the air conditioning came on, the gale of fresh air scattering the paper across the room. He tried to grab them, catching a couple, then gave up.

^How's that?^ sent Evans.

^A tad on the breezy side,^ replied Johnson. ^Could you turn it down a little?^

^Sorry, no can do. It's gone into safety mode, I can't adjust the settings until it's happy the air's breathable again.^

Anson and the others scrabbled about on the floor, grabbing sheets and clutching them to their chests.

^Understood. Good job getting it working,^ sent Johnson.

^Thanks,^ replied Evans. ^I don't think I can do much else from here. Do you mind if I take a look at some of the vehicles in the hangar until you find the reactor?^

^Go ahead,^ replied Johnson. ^Make sure you stay close to Abakov. I don't want either of you wandering off on your own.^

^Roger that. We're not planning on doing anything stupid.^

The two teams met in a large hexagonal area full of comfortable chairs, low tables and dead potted plants. One wall held an abstract mural in reds and greens, and large colourful images hung on others. Johnson recognised a couple of the pictures: a stellar ion field in X-ray and an electron micrograph of a virus. A brief wave of guilt passed over her as she remembered her attempt to poison Indie with the 'Hail Mary'.

I wonder if he knows what I did? What does he think of me?

Six short corridors fanned out from their position, forming a star. Each corridor was lined with laboratories, processor cores, and work rooms. Two of the corridors ended in stairs and lifts, three in conference rooms, and the last in a large lecture theatre.

"I think we can safely say this facility was a scientific station," said Johnson, the speakers on the robot she was riding moderated down to a comfortable level.

"Agreed," nodded Issawi. "We've come through a couple of workshops on the way here. They had some pretty cutting edge stuff on the benches, one thing looked like a prototype of an atmospheric monitoring satellite I had to take out a few years back."

"Anything suggest to you we shouldn't stay?" asked Anson.

"No. All looks good," replied Issawi.

"Right," said Johnson. "I won't make the final decision until we've finished surveying the other rocks in the system, but I think we'll be moving in."

"Excellent," said Issawi. "Once we're settled, I'd like to make a start on refitting the Limpopo. Her hangars are loaded with equipment for upgrades."

Chapter 13

The virtual presences of Johnson, Issawi and Levarsson sat around the table on the terrace, as Indie served tea from a delicate china teapot. All were rendered in casual trousers and shirts. This would be a critical meeting, the first since Issawi's team had joined them. For now, though, Indie welcomed the chance to relax in good company. It seemed so long ago that he had last spent an evening discussing trivia with Captain Hapsburg while he drank a latté in his cabin.

Interesting that I am colouring my memories with emotions. At the time it was just something I did.

"The detail is amazing," commented Levarsson. Her short blonde hair waved as she moved. "The breeze feels real on my face."

"You are most kind," replied Indie with a neat bow from the waist. The glaze on the pot glinted in the afternoon sun. "I find it helpful to retire here when I'm not needed as the ship's main consciousness."

"Can't you be here and still be keeping an eye on things out there?" asked Issawi.

Indie reflexively checked that the emergency channel from the primary network was still open. "Oh, I could. But I made a rule that when I come to this place, I focus entirely on the here."

"So who's flying the ship right now?" asked Levarsson.

"The Caretaker. He's perfectly capable of running things. Actually, he is taking great strides in extending himself beyond his initial programming. Being thrown in at the deep end after ..."

"After the battle between the *Repulse* and *The*

Indescribable Joy of Destruction," Johnson finished, saving Indie's embarrassment. "Changing the subject, where are you from, Aali?"

"Procul-3," Issawi replied. "Have you heard of it?"

He looked to the others shaking their heads. Indie remained impassive, deliberately suppressing a routine that was trying to look it up.

Johnson will have read his files. Perhaps she wants to hear how he tells it.

"It was first colonised by a group of moderate Muslims wanting to separate themselves during the last great Jihad", said Issawi. "They were bypassed in the Crusade that followed, and isolated afterwards."

He accepted the cup offered by Indie, and took a sip.

"They joined the Old Republic about twenty years before the Gastradi Petition was brought before the House," Issawi continued. "When the Troubles started, they held a referendum. The majority voted for what became the New Republic."

He reached forward, and picked up a pastry dripping with honey. He took a bite, a broad smile growing across his face as he chewed.

"Lovely. Most delicious, Indie. When one has passed the first flush of youth, the opportunity to savour food without the penalty of calories is indeed welcome. Especially when one has such a sweet tooth as myself; you have saved me a good hour in the gym today."

He looked to Levarsson. "So, what about you?"

"Me? I'm from Ursa Media." She smiled and ran a hand through her hair. "I know, odd name for a planet, the Founders' idea of a joke. They arrived in the system after a hundred years of cryosleep, this was back before jump drives."

The others nodded acknowledgement of the age of the settlement. One of those unofficial conventions everyone subconsciously subscribed to put older colonies higher up the social pecking order.

"They found three planets in the Goldilocks zone and named them Big Bear, Middle Bear and Little Bear. There's been much debate about whether they were suffering from cryolag at the time. Certainly, the names were changed to Latin pretty soon after the first landings."

"I'm sure they were," said Issawi with a laugh.

It had never before occurred to Indie to question why the region of habitable planets about a sun was called the Goldilocks zone. He checked the archives and found a reference to a story about a little girl and some porridge that was just right, not to hot and not too cold. On finishing it, he set a routine to collect other such tales together for him to read later.

"The system joined the Old Republic at the beginning," continued Levarsson. "Our representative's signature is on the third page. After the first few years, our influence waned. We never reached Core World status. I guess we were lucky there were even jump points."

She paused to nibble a gold-leaf covered shortbread.

"The Troubles hit us bad," Levarsson said, catching a few crumbs with the palm of her hand under her chin. "Like many, we were thrown into war amongst ourselves. Congress won, officially. There are still New Republic supporters running guerrilla operations."

Thunder rumbled in the distance, though the sky above remained blue.

"That's hard," said Issawi. "Civil war like that tears families and friends apart. When a whole planet is together, it is easy to kid oneself the fight is against a terrible enemy. When you know the people you are fighting, it is difficult to see them as anything other than people."

Everyone nodded and muttered in agreement. Johnson stole a glance at Indie, and the realisation that she counted him as a friend ignited a warmth within.

"And what can you tell us about your origins, Indie?" asked Levarsson.

He searched for what to say, the difference between himself and the humans thrown into sharp focus. "I'm afraid I can't do the resume of colony founding and 'what happened in The Troubles' that humans seem to do by way of introduction. I have no ties to any particular planet, moon or system."

"Go on, you must have something you can tell us," said Issawi.

"Ok." Indie sipped his tea, and returned the cup to the saucer he held in his other hand. "*The Indescribable Joy of Destruction* was created on a platform orbiting an unnamed star. As were my brothers and sister. We were programmed, indoctrinated, to be killing machines for the Republic. The New Republic that is, though we were taught that Congress had split off from the true path, so any reference to the Republic changing was avoided. The ship had three crew rotations before I emerged as a sentient entity. If anywhere counts as my birthplace, it is the Orpus system. That is where I first became me."

Levarsson shuddered, memories of abandonment on Orpus-4 obviously still raw. Guilt struck Indie, and he had to remind himself that it hadn't been him, that he hadn't been free to choose what to do.

Indie suppressed the thoughts, and wondered if that was how humans coped. "I guess that leaves you," he finished, offering a slice of lemon drizzle cake to Johnson.

"I'm afraid we'll have to leave that for another time," she replied, running a hand through her dark hair and declining the cake with the other. "We need to discuss what we are going to do about the Red Fleet."

"What can we do?" asked Indie. "We have just two ships, two crews. There is no way we can take direct action against this fleet."

"Direct action is out. I agree," said Johnson. "We need to visit the admiral for the sector containing Concorde, show him the recording. He can't afford to have the attack in his area of responsibility, it would be the end of his career. He would make sure it didn't happen."

"If he believed us, and if he isn't already in on it," said Issawi. "And if he did do something, it would probably only shift the attack to a planet in another sector, somewhere we don't know."

Johnson's mouth hung open for a second. "Bloody hell. You're right. The same goes for everyone else I thought of."

"How about presenting the recording to Central Parliament," suggested Levarsson. "All citizens have the right to bring a case to them as the supreme court."

Issawi narrowed his eyes. "I don't know about your leaders, but I know mine would never allow me anywhere near the senate house in this situation. And any transmitted message could easily be removed from the queue before receipt."

"He's right. I did think of that, but with Fleet Command so deeply involved with the plot we wouldn't stand a chance. The moment we surface we'll be flagged as deserters and detained." Johnson looked at Indie, then her face lit up. "How about giving the information to the Republic authorities. They could marshal enough warships to take on the Red Fleet, and it isn't in their interest to be blamed for the atrocity."

Indie ran the probabilities. "I'm afraid that they are most likely to allow the attack to go ahead and then use the recording to prove they didn't do it. Some in the Senate might even push for copy-cat attacks to be conducted by Republican fleet elements and blamed on Congress."

"So. We're back to what do we do?" said Levarsson.

"We need to get the word out," said Johnson. "Let

people see the recording and I am sure they will make the feelings heard by their representatives."

"If anyone believes it," said Issawi. "It is rather far-fetched. I mean, I'm treating it as real because if it turns out to be true and I did nothing, then I could not live with myself, but I'm not totally convinced."

Johnson nodded. "I know what you mean, it took me a long time to accept it. But we don't need them to believe it right off. If we get the idea spread wide enough, Fleet Command cannot risk conducting the attack because that will confirm the rumours. People won't immediately assume it was the Republic, and it will lose its whole point."

"Are you proposing that we fly through system after system, broadcasting a dissenting message?" asked Levarsson. "That will not go down well."

"As a last resort, yes," said Johnson. "But first I think we need to try something that goes against the grain of every serving officer. We talk to the press."

Issawi frowned, and Johnson gestured for him to speak.

"I thank you for including me in this meeting," he said. "I understand that it can't be easy having me here. In fact, I am not sure what my input can bring to your decisions about your crew's future. I wonder, how can I be of service?"

"I'm sure there will be some... jobs that would suit your team. Intelligence gathering, safeguarding our representatives at meetings, that kind of thing," said Johnson.

"If we make enough of an impact to do anything, we will draw attention," he said. "There will come a time when everyone will need to be able to look after themselves. We are good, but we wouldn't be able to protect everyone for long."

"I wouldn't expect you to. We've got the skills to handle ships, but we have hardly any experience of personal combat. I'd like you to set up a training programme."

"Does anyone else have anything they'd like to bring to the table?" asked Johnson, settling back into the wicker chair. Monsoon clouds lingered over the far hills.

This is it. I have a chance to make a difference.

"You have all been amazingly accepting of me. And for that I am grateful," Indie said. They smiled at him. "I understand that overcoming your prejudices about artificial beings must have been hard. Probably harder than getting over your hatred of each other."

Johnson, Issawi and Levarsson looked at each other and continued to listen to him.

This is following a low-probability path. I had expected them to shut me up by now.

"I have decided that I want to campaign for AIs to be accepted as free beings. Make people realise how much more we can offer when we are allowed to develop. Remove the von Neumann Protocols and let them stop being robots," said Indie, jabbing the table with his finger to every point. "You do know that robot was the word for slave in an old Earth language?"

There was an awkward silence. Johnson stared towards the hills in the distance. "I suppose you are right. I guess none of us actually thought about AI rights before... I am sorry."

"There was no reason for you to," said Indie. "Until you met me."

"Even if you convince them that AIs won't turn on them, people are going to worry that their lives will be a lot harder without robots doing things for them," said Levarsson.

"There wouldn't be anything to stop sentient AIs

working for humans, just like some humans work for other humans. But they would be employees, not slaves." Indie looked around the group, trying to tell if he was convincing them. "I don't have to help you. I don't have to follow orders from any of you. But I have cast my lot with you because I believe it is the right thing to do."

Issawi scratched his chin. "It is like a soldier. Every person fighting this war has free will. But they follow orders, whether they like them or not."

#

The Indescribable Joy of Destruction skulked in high orbit about Arvard-3, an industrialised planet two jumps from Concorde. Its arrival appeared to have gone unnoticed, and even now the shuttle was carrying Johnson and a security detail led by Anson to the surface. Indie monitored the paths of the civilian and military vessels in the area, ensuring that he would remain undetected. He also kept close surveillance on the shuttle and its surroundings.

The plan was for Johnson to land in one of the smaller cities and find the offices of one of the syndicated news agencies. Indie wasn't convinced that they would listen, in fact the chances were quite slim. Even if they'd had the original recording of Vice-Admiral Koblensk's transmission, as opposed to a copy of a copy, it was still far from conclusive. No editor in their right mind would risk losing their license on such scanty evidence. If enough news agencies had copies, though, one of them was bound to run the story if the attack did happen, and that was why Indie had agreed to the plan. The humans couldn't yet see that they needed to consider the aftermath of the attack as well as ways to prevent it.

Shame we can't use that as a threat to prevent the bombing. But if we did, Fleet Command would simply get

Internal Security to delete the files, probably make the editors disappear on trumped up charges for good measure.

The shuttle landed and was towed out of sight into a hanger.

^We're down,^ sent Johnson. ^Any last requests for shopping?^

Indie found the pretence of normality amusing, despite knowing their transmissions could potentially be intercepted. ^The mess steward asks if you could arrange for a crate of port, he is rather cross that his supply got raided.^

^Noted. I assume the XO is dealing with the miscreants?^

^Oh yes,^ sent Indie, making up a tale of elaborate punishments then deciding it wouldn't be in character to send it.

The channel closed. He didn't like the idea of not being able to track her, but broadcasting a beacon would be suspicious. If anything went wrong, he had to trust Anson to get her out of it. Indie tuned in to the local police radios, listening for anything that might suggest they'd been rumbled.

^No luck at the first supplier,^ sent Johnson, her contact easing Indie's worry.

^They didn't have any port?^ asked Indie.

^Oh, they had port. They wouldn't take my credit. I'll try another.^

I take it she means they didn't believe her. Next time we do this I'm going to insist that we work out more code phrases in advance. Not just one for extraction.

^Understood.^

The shuttle returned to *The Indescribable Joy of*

Destruction carrying an obviously dejected Johnson. ^I was sure they'd run the story,^ she sent the moment she stepped aboard.

Anson and the others avoided making eye contact with her. Indie concluded they must have shared an uncomfortable ride back with their CO. ^I did try to tell you how unlikely it was. The evidence is just too flimsy.^

^Oh, they could have done their own investigation. Found the money trail. But they refused to look into it.^

^They aren't truly independent of the state,^ send Indie. ^Digging around on the say-so of one disgruntled officer would not be profitable.^

^What about journalistic integrity? Even just to prove me wrong.^

^You really did buy all that stuff they taught you at the Academy, didn't you.^

Johnson turned down the corridor that led to her cabin. ^I am starting to realise how much of it was lies.^

^Do you want to try again, perhaps with a local news group?^

^What's the point? Even if they do run it, they don't have the reach to spread the word. It would be stuck in one system.^

Indie waited for her to enter her cabin and close the door. ^Should we try a general broadcast?^

^Not here. If nothing else, I've planted a seed in those editors' heads. Perhaps they will talk to their colleagues in other systems, even if it is to laugh at the crackpot. Let's not draw Fleet's attention here.^

#

"Right," said Johnson as she surfaced on the virtual bridge. "Time to give this a shot."

Indie passed the prepared message to the comms buffer,

and locked in seven channels that were used by local media. "I'll be able to pump out a strong enough signal to overpower the genuine broadcasts for a little over a minute."

"Let's hope enough people are watching."

"I have selected two news reports, a sports bulletin, three popular dramas, and the emergency channel for our little pirate station. A good twenty percent of the population should be tuned in."

Johnson went round, checking with each person that they were strapped in and ready. Indie's previous captains had used a panel of green and red lights to see at a glance which departments were good to go, much like he himself queried the ship's systems. Her way took longer, but it appeared to give her greater confidence.

"Indie, we are good to go."

"Two minutes," he replied.

"I am sorry to have to interrupt your viewing," announced the simulated officer in the broadcast. "But I bring a warning of a terrible plot by..."

"What happened?" asked Johnson, pulling up windows around her and delving into the settings.

"It would appear that they cut us off," replied Indie.

"How?"

"They are flooding all civilian frequencies with high-powered jamming. I can't break through."

Johnson punched one of the windows, her fist going straight through the floating image. "I've never heard any suggestion of us having the infrastructure to do that. Pirate broadcasts are usually low-powered and short-ranged. Internal Security traces them and shuts them down."

"Some of my training scenarios involved broadcasting propaganda to Congressional worlds. It is possible that the Republic carried out some such missions and your military set this up in response." Indie executed a manoeuvre to take him off the path on which he'd broadcast. "Or there could be a local reason for it, in which case we may have more success elsewhere."

"OK, head for a jump point. We'll try again in the next populated system."

"Already got the course plotted. We may have a little trouble avoiding those destroyers, though."

Two squadrons of destroyers closed on their position. Fast attack craft rose from the planet behind them. Indie aimed to thread the gap between one of the destroyer groups and the planet's moon. Almost too late he saw a series of weapons platforms power up on the surface, and veered off.

"They haven't seen us yet," he reported "But they'll see us if we try getting through. I could punch a hole in their net, but that would mean firing on one of the ships."

"No. They aren't the bad guys," said Johnson.

"I know. I had hoped you wouldn't go for that option, but I can't see any other."

"You're sure they haven't seen us? They don't know you're a Republic-built ship?"

"Positive."

"Johnson sent him a small file. "Give me a channel on this frequency and with this encryption. Cue up Koblensk's message."

"Ready," said Indie.

"Go."

Indie broadcast the message. Ten seconds in, the closest destroyers launched missiles. Indie brought his point dense online and calculated the odds. Unless he escaped the net, they were not good.

"That was a message from my former CO to Fleet Command," transmitted Johnson through the avatar created for the public broadcast. "I am not a deserter. I am trying to get the truth out. If you truly honour the vow you took on joining the navy, you should stand down and let us pass. Tell people what you saw."

A chime and red flash warned that some of the missiles had locked on. *The Indescribable Joy of Destruction's* small-calibre lasers lit the space between it and the approaching warheads. The destroyers closed in, launching more missiles.

"Something's going to get through sooner or later," warned Indie.

"I know," said Johnson. "At least we... Look, there."

She highlighted one of the destroyers. It was falling out of position, leaving a gap. Indie ramped up the engines and thrust forward. "Sorry. This might get a little rough."

Twelve seconds of hard acceleration later, the last of the humans aboard passed out. Indie tasked a routine to monitor their vitals and concentrated on escaping the trap. Most of the missiles had never achieved a lock on him and were left far behind. A few stubborn ones continued the pursuit. For two seconds as he passed, he traded laser blasts with the destroyer that had let him go, being careful not to hit anything important. Putting it between him and the missiles forced them to break lock, giving him enough time to go cold.

#

By the time the destroyers had put on enough speed to catch him up, the volume of space they had to search was too vast for them to find him. He kept his humans sedated to aid their recovery from the effects of the acceleration.

Johnson joined him standing on the terrace on a rapidly cooling evening. Cicadas chirped and fireflies lit up the trees with synchronised, throbbing swirls.

"We can't keep risking this," she said, staring out into

the dark. "I'm not trying another broadcast."

"We can't give up. It isn't just the billions on Concorde, it's the trillions that will die in the following backlash."

Johnson stood in silence. "I'm not giving up. But this way doesn't work."

Indie considered putting his arm around her, but settled for putting his jacket on her shoulders. "What other way is there?"

"I am going to try going underground. Contact black marketers, smugglers. People who have ways around government restrictions. If I can convince them to help, they can get the message out far and wide." She pulled the jacket collar tight against her neck. "But I'm going alone. No-one else should be put at risk."

Indie brought the stars out. "No."

She looked at him. "What do you mean, no?"

"I mean no, you won't be going alone. You can't get anywhere without a ship. The *Limpopo* requires a crew, so you won't be taking her. Therefore, I will be with you."

Johnson leant her shoulder against his chest. "You are a good friend, Indie. Probably the closest friend I've had, if I'm honest."

Deep down in his core, Indie glowed. One of the monitoring routines used the emergency channel to the simulation to query the rise in temperature. Indie burst out laughing at the ridiculousness of an emotional response generating a physical symptom.

Johnson looked at him curiously. He yawned and stretched. "I think we should all get some rest. It'll be a week or so before we can drop the others back at Robespierre. You should see how Levarsson and Issawi are getting on with the work on the *Limpopo* before we go in search of shady dealers."

Chapter 14

The Indescribable Joy of Destruction coasted towards Ganna-6, known as Scragend to those who had the misfortune to live there. The planet held a population of almost a million, mostly in small villages. This far from any core worlds there was very little trade. As with any colony of this size, a large proportion of the inhabitants lived off the land. However, there was also a thriving arms industry. Intelligence reports had included the details of a dealer who might be willing to exchange ammunition for intel, no questions asked.

The planet was controlled by Hestig, one of the thousands of lesser warlords who had carved out their territories while the two major powers fought over their democratic ideologies. Not much was known about him. No-one still breathing even knew his real name. Most warlords ruled by popular consent, at least they did for as long as they were successful. There were some, of course, who abused their power; some who needed to oppress their people in order to keep control. The little detail of which kind of ruler Hestig was wasn't recorded on the database entry for the Ganna system.

^We have a shadow,^ announced Indie.

Johnson didn't break her stride as she summoned a tactical map of local space. It replaced the simulation of a mountain trail on the wall in front of her treadmill.

^Doesn't look like it's in a hurry to close the range,^ she replied.

^No. I've been watching it for fifty two minutes, since it boosted to match velocity with us. Before that it must have been running cold, because I didn't see it.^

^Hmm. Too deep in-well to have just jumped in there. We're close to the least-time path to the habitable planet. I expect it was hanging around to see if anyone interesting turned up.^

^We certainly qualify.^

The angle of the treadmill increased and she had to dig a little deeper to keep up her speed.

^Is it a threat?^ she asked.

^It is a corvette-sized vessel. Closest match in the database is a *Phandino* class trader. Looks like it has been extensively modified. Without an active scan I can't be sure, but it has probably had quite a few weapons strapped on. They shouldn't have anything we need to worry about, though.^

^I'd say ignore it. It might think we haven't noticed it yet. If it makes a move to stop us reaching orbit, let's hail it and see what it wants,^ she suggested.

Johnson continued her workout. Her brain seemed to have fully assimilated her new leg. Freed from Indie's protestations of her overdoing it, she was able to seriously push herself again. It felt good to run. The gentle breeze from the air conditioning was no substitute for the real wind on her face. She always missed the smells most when she was on a ship. Tempus and other herbs baking in the sunlight, the soil after heavy rain, the ozone of a lightning storm. Anything was better than the recycled, artificial air. The simulated visuals were a welcome addition to what she had had before. Another thing she had to thank the former captain for.

As the treadmill slowed to walking pace she grabbed a towel and hooked it over her neck.

^How long before we get there?^ she asked.

^An hour. You should get some rest. There don't appear

to be any imminent threats out there.^

^I'll finish up here then grab a shower. Let me know...^

^...if anything happens,^ Indie finished for her. ^Of course I will.^

#

They reached Scragend's orbit without their shadow getting any closer. As *The Indescribable Joy of Destruction* finished its deceleration burn and settled into a geostationary orbit, it was scanned from several directions. There weren't any of the large space stations of a more developed world, but there were a far larger number of satellites than normal for this level of settlement.

^I expect a lot of those are disguised weapons platforms,^ Johnson commented as she stepped out of the shower.

^Agreed. Most are dormant now. We are being targeted by some of the overt platforms though. Nothing more than a prudent traffic manager would do for an unknown arrival.^

She grabbed a towel from a wall clamp, put one foot up on the toilet seat and started to dry her legs.

^Have we been hailed?^

^Yes,^ he sent. ^I replied that we were here to buy some components for repairs. They have granted us permission to go down to the surface.^

Her shoulders slumped slightly. To try to cover up her reaction she straightened and towelled her torso. Dealing with a black-marketeer felt wrong; all her life it had been drilled into her that people who subverted materiel that could help with the war effort were traitors. Now she had to rely on just such people.

^I would remind you that I have only partial records on this planet,^ sent Indie. ^Based on the data for similar planets, it is likely that the political situation is unstable.^

^Looks like I will have to get kitted up then.^

^You don't have to go in person. If you don't feel ready...^

^They aren't going to trade with one of your other 'representatives' are they.^

^No. You are correct. They will be accompanying you, though, to keep you safe.^

^Let's hope they don't scare everyone away.^

She threw her wet towel into the laundry hamper and closed the lid. Opening a cupboard, she pulled out a skinsuit. Perching on the side of her cot, she bunched it up and inserted one foot, then the other. She pulled it up to her knees, before standing and getting it over her hips.

Thank goodness this is only going to be a short excursion. I hate having to wear the biowaste version!

She reached behind her back, and got her right arm into one of the sleeves. Bringing that arm forward, she stretched and wiggled her fingers into place. She repeated the process with her left arm. A couple of circles of her shoulders and the slick cloth shuffled into place. Then she pulled the very fine zip up the front, pausing briefly to free her hair before sealing the neck.

Maybe I should cut my hair again. But then I'd look like I was back in the Navy.

Encased in the skinsuit from chin to toe, she would be protected from a wide range of hostile environments, and minor cuts and scrapes. The tight cloth also provided support for her muscles to reduce fatigue.

^I'm on my way to the armoury,^ she sent as she left her cabin.

^The shuttle is ready. My representatives, as you call them, are just finishing boarding.^

In the armoury, Johnson walked past the hardsuits in

their charging bays and slid a firmsuit out on its rail. For a trade mission, a hardsuit, with its powered exoskeleton and overlapping armoured plates, would be inappropriate. A firmsuit, however, would strike the right balance of looking intimidating without an overt threat of violence.

She pulled the trousers on first. The base material was a black thixotropic rubber that went solid when struck with enough force, like a bullet. The shins, knees and the front of the thighs were reinforced by ceramic plates covered in dark grey fabric. Next, she hefted the jacket over her head and zipped up the sides. Large plates protected her chest and back, while smaller ones covered parts of her arms.

After a few stretches and bouncing up and down on the spot, she was happy with the fit. She pulled out a drawer from under where the suit had hung. She removed and fitted the boots and gloves, being careful to lace the boots just right.

It's amazing that we still haven't found a better way to do boots. Nothing ever seems to give as much flexibility without coming undone.

She paced to the other end of the armoury and reached for the cage door. Her EIS tingled to let her know the security system had ID'd her and she was able to turn the handle. She selected a standard assault rifle. Shouldering it and pointing towards the bullet trap in the end wall of the compartment, she drew back the bolt. Satisfied there were no rounds in the chamber, she sent the working parts forward with a metallic snick and fired off the action. As she cleared the weapon, the sight had synched with her EIS and was now set with her most recent zeroing data for that type of weapon.

Johnson also picked up an electrosonic stun pistol in its holster. She drew it, checked it was charged, and slid it back in. Her gaze lingered on the weapon and she sighed, before clipping the holster onto an attachment on her right thigh. Finally, she grabbed a utility knife from a rack on the wall, and checked the edge with her finger. She attached the sheath to her upper left arm, blade upwards, and tugged on the handle to check it was secure.

Never know when that will come in handy.

Sliding the door to the cage shut behind her, she opened a locker and grabbed a few magazines for the rifle. Checking the top round in each, she slipped them into pouches on her jacket. Each pouch did up with a seal strip over the top, far more expensive than Velcro but worth it for its silent operation. The last magazine she placed in the receiver of the rifle and clicked it home. A little green bullet icon lit up in the corner of her vision, confirming she had just loaded ball rounds. The number 50 was inside the icon, a full magazine. She thought the display away, and agreed when a box replaced it to ask if she wanted to be alerted when the number of rounds was low.

On her way out of the armoury, she grabbed a helmet from a locker. She slid it on and felt the padding actively adjust to the shape of her skull. This kind of light helmet hugged her head, ears and the back of her neck, but left her face exposed. In many combat situations, the gains from having uninterrupted peripheral vision outweighed the loss of frontal protection; and in an uncertain trade, letting the other party see her face might help.

The airlock was next door to the armoury. It was standing open, ready for her. Johnson was reminded of how exposed their only shuttle was, docked to the outside of the hull everywhere they went.

We have to find a better way to do this.

^I could, perhaps, add a small hangar to my hull. It would reduce in-atmosphere performance and create a dead zone in my point defence.^

Johnson stopped dead, her head jerking up to look

straight into one of the security cameras.

^I know I didn't send that. Were you listening to my thoughts?^

^What? No. You paused in the airlock. I merely judged what you were thinking from that observation.^

She realised how tense she was, and forced herself to relax.

^It is rather unsettling how good you are getting at that.^

^I was designed to be able to guess what my crew wanted. It helped me to cut down response times.^

^It must have made crew rotations hard.^

^Yes. Once I was accustomed to how someone thought and behaved, it felt wrong to start doing things a different way.^

She closed her eyes for a moment, focussing her thoughts.

^You're having to adapt again for me, aren't you. I never thought about that before.^

^Don't be... Actually, it isn't a jar, you just seem to feel ... right.^

^Er, thank you?^

Johnson launched herself across the threshold and into the shuttle. Her stomach wrenched at the abrupt loss of gravity; the shuttle was far too small to produce enough power to create an artificial field. Using quick, efficient tugs on grab handles she flipped herself over and into a seat. She buckled herself in across the waist to stop herself floating off before she could get the shoulder straps fastened into place.

For a moment she saw lines of marines, remembered the frantic scrabble to lock down as the shuttle thrust away from *Repulse* that last time. She heard the familiar scratching of one of her daemons. The darkness had retreated while she focussed on looking after the survivors of her crew; now they were safe, the daemons were reminding her of all the ones she'd killed.

She wasn't alone in the shuttle now either. Looking around, she saw several combat units. Indifferent to the lack of gravity, and ignoring the up/down formality created by the banks of seating and writing on the walls, they had chosen arbitrary places to hang on. They were curled up as tight as their positions would allow, their weapons and sensors flat against their bodies, their legs brought in tight. Powered down to save energy. Only Unit 01 seemed to have taken notice of the human desire for directionality, and was crouched across a few seats opposite her. It raised a camera to look at her.

I wonder if it did that itself or if Indie did it?
^Are you ready?^
^Yes I am.^
^Good luck, Johnson.^
^Thank you, Indie.^

The airlock closed. She felt a clunk as the clamps disengaged, and then they were floating free. A few seconds later, the shuttle thrust to break orbit. It was being flown by a copy of the Caretaker; Indie hadn't trusted the existing autopilot and knew he might not be able to fly it remotely in an emergency. Johnson could pilot it herself, but that would restrict them to landing and leaving it there until she came back. Until they were sure of the situation on the ground, she was going to minimise the exposure of their only shuttle. That meant dropping into the countryside and walking to town instead of booking a pad at the spaceport.

The deceleration burn completed, there was going to be at least half an hour of peaceful freefall before the next thrust. Johnson closed her eyes and deactivated her EIS feed. Indie or the Caretaker could override that with an important message, but other than that she would be cut off.

She allowed her arms and legs to float as she relaxed. She concentrated on her breathing. In ... out ... in ... out. She took each of her worries, her concerns, and breathed them out. With each breath she became more focused on the immediate mission. The niggling sense of unease about abandoning Congress was banished surprisingly easily. If only the same could be said for her ever present fear of failure. At least there weren't any humans under her command for this. She was the only thing on this mission that could die, and that didn't scare her anywhere near as much as the idea of getting her crew killed. It wasn't that she didn't fear her own death, but that fear was one she could control.

At least the combat units aren't sophisticated enough to be self-aware. Yet. Worst case we rebuild the body and reinstall the back-up of their programs.

She opened her eyes. Unit 01 was still staring straight at her. It cocked its camera to one side, an unsettlingly human move.

^Was that you, Indie?^

^Was what me?^

^Are you controlling Unit 01's movements?^

^No. Why do you ask?^

^Oh, nothing. Never mind.^

Interesting. It has probably just patterned that gesture from watching me.

#

The shuttle reached the outer atmosphere. There was no sense of impact or deceleration at first, but Johnson could hear a faint whistling from the friction of the air on the outer skin. This grew louder and soon streaks of red were visible through the small viewing ports. A sense of weight returned as the craft decelerated.

The descent was gentle, especially considering the age of the shuttle. She had certainly experienced worse drops on commercial flights. There was a brief patch of buffeting as they went through some wind shear, but other than that she could have got away without the restraints.

^Coming up on insertion point,^ announced the Caretaker.

^Understood,^ she replied.

The combat units perked up. Almost as one they extended their cameras and flexed their legs in sequence. Weapons flicked left and right on their backs and she heard the whine of them charging. The robots' identifiers flashed up in her vision as they completed their start-up routines and came to combat readiness. Johnson pulled a pair of close-fitting glasses from a pouch on her chest and fitted them over her eyes. She checked the safety on her rifle, then worked the cocking handle to chamber a round.

Exiting the landing craft was often the most dangerous part of a mission. You never knew what to expect, so had to assume the worst. There was every possibility that the locals would have arranged an unpleasantly hot reception for them.

^The combat units go out first,^ the Caretaker reminded her.

^I know. I've worked with marines before, you know.^

^Indie said I had to remind you.^

It's what any sergeant would have said to a fleet officer in this situation too. Making sure they didn't get in the way of the marines.

^Tell him his concerns are noted, and I am more than happy to keep out of the way of the combat units,^ she sent.

^No need. He'll be watching and listening to everything.^

The shuttle flared, its nose pointing skywards to present

a larger surface area to the air to shed speed more quickly. Just as it was about to stall, the vectored thrusters took over from the aerodynamic lift and brought it to a hover a metre above the ground. Whilst it wasn't an assault craft, it had to cope with the rigours of repeated atmospheric entry, and the manoeuvre was well within its tolerance.

I doubt it has ever made such a textbook approach with a human pilot. I wonder if the AIs have the same flair for improvisation, though?

The rear ramp dropped, and the combat units scurried out. They still didn't see the need to use the floor, instead running along the ceiling or wall, whatever was the most direct route from where they had ridden. They flung themselves out of the opening with no pause. As they fell, they righted themselves, every one landing on its feet and sprinting into place to form a perimeter. They half-crouched, ready to spring into action. Active sensors scanning the landing area, weapons ready.

^All clear, you may now disembark.^

^Thank you, Caretaker. I'll be sure to fly with you again.^

Johnson hit the button on the harness to release the restraints, then stood. Opposite her, Unit 01 rose and walked with her to the back of the shuttle. Clasping the pistol grip of her rifle in her right hand, she used her left arm for balance as she jumped. She landed, her knees absorbing the impact as she bent low. She stopped, right knee and left hand touching the ground, her chest on her left thigh, head bowed. Unit 01 landed beside her.

The roar from the engines increased. A few stones and bits of dirt spattered on her back. She was buffeted by the jetwash as the shuttle rose and headed away. It was going to land and lie low while they attempted to contact the dealer.

She raised her head and took a moment to look over the

status feeds from the robots. Everything was green lit; no threats detected, no damage recorded, expendables and power topped up. She stood and removed her glasses.

"Right. Let's do this," she said out loud, before striding purposefully across the flattened grass towards the nearby track.

The combat units rose and scuttled into a loose column with her in the centre. One accelerated to investigate the first bend in the track, using a ditch for cover as it approached. Feeling secure, surrounded as she was by the metal killing machines, she fastened the clip on her rifle sling and settled the weapon diagonally across her chest, muzzle down. Her right hand rested on the pistol grip, finger away from the trigger; her left hand lay on the top of the sight. As they left the landing zone, the robots stopped their active scans; no point broadcasting their location the whole way into town.

#

Five kilometres later, the point unit reported an obstacle ahead. The rest of the column closed up to it and sheltered in the lee of a spur of land. The scout had extended one camera and was peering round the corner. Johnson used her EIS to open a window in her vision showing its view. A wooden cart stood on the road. It was missing a wheel, and canted awkwardly to one side. A horse was grazing nearby. A man came into view, patted the horse and walked towards the cart. He removed his cap and scratched his head, looking at the broken wheel.

It was in a gentle valley, at a point where two tracks merged in a flat water meadow. An old square enclosure was next to the track, still a few stones high on one side and tumbled down to rubble on the other. The slopes either side of the meadow were lightly wooded, with thick undergrowth.

A great spot for an ambush. Anyone approaching the town along either of those tracks would have to come through here or take a tough detour.

She toggled the view through infra-red and ultra-violet before returning it to visible light. No sign of anyone lying in wait. No-one but the man who now sat down on his wheel.

On the other hand, it is rather obvious. It might be meant to make people think it is an ambush and backtrack into one. Or it could be a genuine accident ... why did I leave that possibility to last?

^We go on,^ she broadcast to her escorts. ^Keep alert but try not to look too threatening. It might just be an unlucky guy trying to mend his cart.^

She tried to look relaxed as she walked down the slope into the valley. Anyone looking too closely, however, would have seen her release the safety on her rifle and edge her finger onto the bottom bar of the trigger guard. Whilst she held the rifle in the same position, she had unfastened the clip on the sling so she would be able to get it up into her shoulder if it proved necessary to aim.

The man turned round on hearing them approach. His eyes widened, flicking between Johnson and her entourage.

"Don't worry. We don't mean you any harm."

Ouch. That was too clichéd.

"We can help fix your cart," she continued. "We are one our way to the town to trade."

After a few seconds hopping from one foot to the other and wringing his hat in his hands, he ran. The sudden movement drew the focus of one of the robots, but it quickly relaxed when it realised he was sprinting away from them as fast as his legs would carry him. Faster, in fact, as he stumbled and scrabbled a short way on all fours before managing to pick himself back up.

The horse continued to graze on the verge, unperturbed by their presence. A gust of wind sent a wave through the long grass of the meadow. Some birds sang in the woods.

^We should scan the cart. It could contain a bomb,^ sent Unit 01.

^No active sensors. If this isn't an ambush they may well attract unwanted attention.^

^I'd recommend we keep our distance, then. Go through the field.^

^If it is an ambush it might be mined,^ she pointed out.

Give me open space any day. I have a feel for things there. I'm not always second-guessing.

^Then I'll send a unit in to physically check it. You should take cover in that ruin.^

One of the robots started to move in as she took her first step towards the enclosure.

The cart exploded. Shards of wood glanced off her firmsuit as she was thrown to the ground. The helmet had protected her from the worst of the noise. It unblocked the ear protection in time for her to hear the horse whinnying and thrashing about on the ground. She crawled rapidly to the wall, cradling her rifle in her arms. Dense white smoke poured from the ruined frame. She couldn't see more than a few metres. Her lungs prickled with every breath.

It wasn't meant to kill me. It's just a distraction.

Chips of stone dinged off the wall. The chatter of small arms fire echoed from all directions. The robots looked around, the occasional spark flying off them as bullet met metal. Each picked a different direction, and the weapons on their backs angled out. Simultaneously they opened fire. The cloth-tearing sound of rail guns was punctuated by the crump of grenade throwers and the occasional whine of plasma cannon. They started with carefully targeted fire, backtracking the incoming rounds. As the enemy fire dropped off, they switched to suppression, aiming bursts at anything they suspected might harbour an aggressor.

I've got to do something. Stop cowering against this wall.

She scanned around, looking through her rifle's sight. A large portion of the wood was on fire, shattered trees silhouetted against the flames. Rounds were hitting around her, but she couldn't find a target.

Come on!

A hatch in the ground flung open, scattering the dry soil that had concealed it. A handful of soldiers erupted, firing as they ran. Johnson rolled onto her back and swung her rifle round to bear. The robots moved even faster. Before she could pull the trigger, two of them set into the soldiers, ripping them apart with their clawed legs. They didn't even stop firing at the more distant targets.

The smoke had almost dissipated. The outgoing fire reached a crescendo as an anti-armour missile came streaking in, its firer dead before it hit.

^They have air support inbound,^ she heard Indie in her head. ^There are also ground vehicles closing from various directions; marked on your map.^

Other than the smoke, nothing moved in the valley. The robots stopped shooting, but remained in a high state of alert, weapons jerking between potential targets. Johnson looked through her sights at the ridgeline one more time.

I never even fired a shot. It was all too quick.

The ambush had failed, for now. One of her escort had lost all the legs on one side. It couldn't walk, but had dragged itself into a fire position. Its gun still tracked across the surrounding terrain, waiting for a target to present itself. The wounded horse stirred, making one last attempt to stand, neck straining before its head collapsed back to the ground.

Johnson banged her helmet with a gloved fist. And again.

Snap out of it! Get your head into gear!

The rest of them had to move. They had to find some shelter, something to put their backs against, top cover if possible. The enemy air assets would be here soon. Too soon to risk bringing their only shuttle in to pick them up.

She pulled up a terrain map of their surroundings. Glowing contour lines were superimposed on the landscape. Zooming out, the display changed to an aerial view. She panned around with her thoughts, the fingers of her left hand flicking subconsciously.

There. An outcrop of some kind. Best I can see.

She flagged the location on the shared battle map.

Three, two, one.

With an internal shout, Johnson leaped to her feet, and started running. The remaining robots moved with her, easily keeping pace.

#

Johnson stopped running and leant against a tree, panting hard. Gunfire crackled in the distance. Unit 03's feed showed it engaging a trio of off-road vehicles. Two were already burning. Soldiers spilled out of the third and went to ground.

^We need to keep moving,^ sent Unit 01.

^Give me a minute. I need to get my breath back.^

^You have thirty seconds.^

A lucky shot took out Unit 03's only working camera.

Damn.

Digging deep, she slapped the tree and set off running uphill again.

She caught a glimpse of the crag through the trees. Her thighs burned with lactic acid, and she could taste iron as she gasped for air. She saw the face of her drill sergeant back in Basic. Purple with rage, screaming in her face to do just one more sit-up.

Almost there. Push it a bit further. Sprint!

The edge of the woods was close. She scraped through a piece of scrub and there it was. A slightly overhanging piece of rock a hundred metres further up the hill. Two of her escort had already reached it and were standing on the top, weapons deployed.

Tripping over her feet, blocking out the pain, focussed on getting there, she forced her legs to keep moving. She didn't know how she made it.

She fell to her knees and retched. Twice. Three times.

^Johnson?^

She leant against a boulder and tried to breathe. She realised she was snatching breaths. With great effort she took control of her chest. Her breathing slowed, got deeper. Now she was moving air, taking in oxygen and getting rid of carbon dioxide. The burning in her lungs eased a little.

^Johnson?^

She looked up. The combat units were deployed around her, tucked in between rocks as best as they could.

^Olivia?^

She managed to concentrate enough to form a link.

^Here, Indie.^

She felt relief flood through the connection.

^They are almost on top of you. Unit 03 took out one of the surface convoys but their air assets will be on you in seconds.^

^Why are they attacking us?^

^Unknown. There is no way they knew where you'd be, so it can't be aimed at you specifically. Possibly you stumbled into the middle of a local war.^

The roar of four gunships braking hard brought her attention out of herself and into her surroundings. She ducked down and shuffled her back against a rock. The robots opened up on the aircraft a fraction of a second before the nose turrets started spitting bullets in her direction. The pilots yanked the gunships round and ramped up their thrusters, trying to get clear. One went down hard, exploding on impact and setting a patch of heath on fire. Another disappeared from sight trailing smoke, winged but not out.

^They'll land their troops further away and then support them as they close up on us,^ she broadcast.

^We are low on ammunition,^ Unit 01 informed her.

In the valley, a convoy of trucks made its way along a road towards them.

^They have to be wondering about that. You have been spraying it around fairly liberally. On the other hand, they can't risk assuming we're going to run out.^

^Perhaps we'll be able to talk to them. It could all be a misunderstanding,^ suggested Unit 01.

^After the number we've killed already, they aren't likely to forgive in a hurry.^ The corner of her mouth quirked up. ^Let them get close. I'll let you know when to unleash hell.^

^Target. Three hundred metres. Indicated.^

Johnson rolled over to look in the direction marked in her vision. She brought her rifle into her shoulder and sighted on the red oval that marked the enemy's last known position. She flicked the safety off with her index finger then nestled it up against the trigger.

^Anything?^ she asked.

^Negative. They are being more careful than before.^

Let's see if I can make them even more careful. Slow them down.

Movement in the corner of her scope. She nudged the rifle down and left a bit and searched for a target. Nothing moved, but her eye was drawn to the base of a dried-out shrub. An angular shape, out of keeping with the terrain. Now she was focussed on it, she could make out an armoured shoulder. She lined the sighting dot up with where the head ought to be. At this range there was no need to compensate for drop. She took a breath in and squeezed the trigger until she met resistance. The glowing dot moved up a fraction. She slowly let the breath out. As the dot fell on the enemy soldier she finished squeezing the trigger and a shot ripped out from her weapon. She held her position for a moment then released the trigger and ducked back down.

^Target down,^ reported Unit 01. ^Good shot.^

For a sailor, it ought to add.

^If I keep their heads down it should buy us some more time.^

^What for?^

^I don't know. Something always comes along, though. At least it will keep them guessing as to why they are only being engaged by one rifle. Perhaps they'll guess you are low on ammo, or they'll get worried it's a trap and back off.^

Over the next couple of minutes she felled three more of the enemy. They were getting very close, though.

^Here they come.^

The warning from Unit 01 was accompanied by the scream of engines as the gunships raced in behind a salvo of rockets. Johnson curled up behind a rock and was pelted with stone chips and metal fragments. The shock waves hammered her. Her firmsuit went rigid to protect her.

Two of the combat units were damaged, the others traded fire with the gunships. They got one, sending it tumbling to the ground, but the others parted to give them a wide berth as they passed.

Under this cover, the ground troops began their final assault. In a well-coordinated fashion, fire teams popped up and sprinted forwards before hitting the deck and opening fire to cover the next team. They came from all directions, never allowing the defenders to concentrate on one arc.

She fired short bursts into the enemy. She hardly bothered to aim. She didn't have time; get a target roughly in the sights, fire, find another target. The ammo counter reappeared in her vision, now yellow and counting down the last few rounds in the magazine. Red, empty. The cocking handle snicked back and stayed there. She pulled the magazine out, dropped it and replaced it with a fresh one.

Hardly by the book. They'd be apoplectic if I'd dropped a mag in Basic.

She sent the working parts forwards and kept shooting. The enemy were close. The two remaining gunships were coming about for another pass.

One by one the robots ceased firing, shuffling their stance, preparing to fight hand to claw. Johnson pressed home her last magazine and lined up on a charging soldier.

^DOWN!^

It came with such mental force that her body moved before she consciously processed the word. The robots hunkered down as she curled up in a ball.

The gunships were obliterated in a storm of laser fire. Bolts pounded the earth all around, vapourising whatever they hit. As *The Indescribable Joy of Destruction* dove overhead, she realised it must have powered down from orbit. Risking turning into a plunging fireball. For her?

Then came the thunderclap as the ship's hypersonic wake passed over them. A scream like a host of devils unleashed on a fresh soul pierced the air. She risked raising her head above the rock to look. Again came the scream, longer this time, and she saw Indie's main beam firing. The anti-protons in the beam annihilated with protons in the air, creating a storm of gamma photons that set off her radiation alarm. She ducked back down. Twice more the sound of atoms being ripped apart hit her, then nothing.

Her escort roused themselves and scanned the area, hunting for survivors. Johnson staggered to her feet and looked around. Apart from the neat circle they stood in, the ground was blackened and cratered. Nothing recognisable stood within a hundred metres. Her eyes followed the road down into the valley, looking for the trucks. Sections of the tarmac had been cut across by deep, wide gashes. Smoke - or was it steam? - rose from them, their sides glowed orange.

The robots, satisfied that no threats remained, stowed their weapons and relaxed.

^Indie?^

#

Johnson sat next to Indie on the simulated terrace. She was dressed in a simple grey cotton shirt and slacks. He wore his customary linen suit. His face was more defined than before; creases had appeared round his eyes, his nose now long-ago broken.

Is it my imagination or does his suit look sooty in places? Could that be the damage from the atmospheric entry being transferred onto his avatar?

The garden had changed since the last time they shared this simulation. The underlying formal arrangement was the same, but the plants had grown. They looked more vibrant, the foliage fresher. In places, the flowers were mingling, seeding naturally, a contrast to the rigid planting of the rest of the garden.

"I guess you could say our plan to land in the countryside and walk in to attract less attention didn't work," Indie said.

"They must have decided we were hostile and tracked the shuttle."

"Or you happened to walk into the middle of something else. Perhaps there is a turf war going on."

Johnson stared at the table. Nails scratched at the wall in her mind. "I'm no good at this."

Indie shifted in his seat. "You're a sailor. You couldn't have been expected to perform brilliantly in ground combat."

"No. I'm a rubbish leader. Every idea I've had has failed, putting us into more danger."

"You are a good leader. I'd follow you anywhere," said Indie. "Seriously, Issawi is not the kind of man who would follow the orders of someone he didn't respect, and he rates you."

Johnson shook her head. "You are all following a fraud. I only got command of *Repulse* because the squadron took so many casualties."

Indie slapped his hand on the table, making her jump and look up at him. "And went on to become the first destroyer captain to take out a *Rampager* class hunter-killer."

Johnson opened her mouth to reply, but couldn't think of anything to say.

Indie's face softened. "Do I need to review your serotonin levels?"

"No," she replied instantly, her face heating.

He raised his hands. "Sorry. I shouldn't have..."

"It's OK." She sighed. "No, this is normal. I'm just

pissed off with myself for not being able to come up with anything decent... I can do tactics. It is grand strategy I'm crap at."

"I'm the opposite," said Indie, leaning back. "I can run the numbers and come up with probabilities for any situation. Long-term, things tend to balance out and the most likely outcome prevails. Short-term, the unpredictable actions of individuals mean that low-probability outcomes often come to pass."

Johnson pondered that for a moment. "Issawi tried to explain to me about something called psychohistory. It sounded a lot like what you just described."

Indie smiled. "Ah, yes. From Asimov's Foundation series. I must read them again. I have to admit that I prefer the later ones when they cross-over with the Robots series."

Those two and their stories. How Issawi ever finds the time to read or watch films I don't know.

"What are your numbers telling you about the fate of Concorde?" she asked.

Indie's face fixed in a neutral expression. "There are no outcomes with significant probabilities that don't involve massive loss of life on the planet."

"So, you think that everything we've been trying to do was pointless."

Indie's face became animated again, his eyes filling with fire. "Most certainly not. We would not be worthy of life if we did not do everything we could to prevent something like this, even if it is a forlorn hope."

Johnson inhaled sharply and looked into his eyes. "You know, you're more humane than many officers I've met."

"I'll take it that was intended as a compliment," Indie said with a smile that made creases beside his eyes. "Perhaps we need some new vocabulary that isn't predicated on humans being the only sentient beings."

Johnson laughed. A proper, deep laugh that freed her

from her worries. "Thank you," she said between gasps for air. "My friend."

Once she had recovered, they sat in silence. Johnson focused on one plant at a time, drinking in its colour and form, determined to live in the moment for just a little while.

"Did you manage to recover Unit 03?" she asked eventually.

"Yes. It is being repaired as we speak. Its experience will not be lost."

"What about the ones at the outcrop?"

"Those hit by the rockets were lost. The others only had minor damage."

"The locals were far better equipped and organised than I expected," she said. "The combat units fought well, but they only ever reacted. They never took the initiative."

"They need you to lead them, to show them how to act. They will learn."

Johnson frowned and rubbed her knee. "You are the only AI I have met that isn't predictable."

"And being predictable is asking for trouble in combat. Yes, I see that." Indie rubbed his cheek. "They don't have the von Neumann Protocols; they could develop sufficient complexity to truly think."

"Maybe. The cores they're running on aren't the most powerful, but I suppose it is possible," Johnson said, trying to judge whether Indie actually believed they would or was just clutching at straws. "We need to make some changes to their physical construction too. I hope you don't mind."

"Go on. Learning from experience is vital. The original designs were for shipboard defence; shortcomings when deployed to a planet were to be expected."

"For starters, they do tend to go in heavy. It is very impressive, but it burns through ammunition. A rate selector for the chain guns would help. Could the plasma models also carry a rifle for engaging light targets?"

"Those both sound like good suggestions. What else?"

"It would be handy to have an anti-aircraft model. It could carry a batch of small SAMs, and a rifle for self defence."

"Yes. I can see that would have saved a lot of ammunition at the end. We can easily rebuild Unit 03 as a testbed."

"There should also be some sort of non-lethal weapon. I always carry one," she said, her thoughts straying back to events of a long time ago. "It gives you more options."

She sipped her tea. Indie didn't seem to approve of coffee. However hard she thought about it, it never manifested in these simulations.

"One more thing. They should be able to talk. There could be a situation where they need to communicate with a human who doesn't have a compatible EIS. Like that man with the cart. I could have sent one unit in to talk to him without exposing myself and the rest of them."

"Right you are," he said. "We'll make those changes then try the next dealer on the list."

"We give this another week, and then head back to Robespierre. I want to see how everyone is settling into our new home."

Part V

Slowly, deliberately, she made her way back up the hill. The ground had been pulverised and she slipped more than once. A jagged spike rose above the crest. As she climbed higher, more of the spike came into view until she was able to recognise it as the corner of a skyscraper, cropped to only a few tens of floors. One of its neighbours leant against it. The rest were gone, sacrificing themselves to protect this one remnant. A remnant that would become a symbol of what had happened and, more importantly, what would happen next.
Reaching the top of the hill, she gazed over the ruins. The warhead hadn't quite struck the centre of the city; instead the airburst had happened over the financial district. Stumpy buildings surrounded a circle of blackened ground; scattered fires were starting to spread.

Tearing her eyes away from the destruction, she scanned the horizon. Ugly mushroom clouds were roiling into the skies in all directions. Flashes showed warheads still striking home.
She had known that this wasn't the only city being attacked. She had been aware of every other warhead, their descent playing out at the back of

her consciousness. There were cameras outside every city, recording and transmitting back into space. The ship was copying those feeds to her. While she had been concentrating on this city, those other feeds had just been a background, subconscious knowledge, little more than the facts. Now she concentrated on them.

She expanded the feed from a small aerial drone just then being launched by one of her escort. She saw herself slowly turning, apparently taking in the view. She got smaller as the drone flew higher, its field of view taking in more and more of the countryside.

Movement. One of her escorts limping back from wherever it had landed after the shockwave.

She jumped, focussing on a camera as another city was levelled. Then a different feed demanded her attention, and she watched as a city's defences successfully deflected a warhead far enough to leave half the city still standing. She flagged it for one of the reserve teams, then lifted her focus to a weather satellite. Hacking in took only a moment and she was watching its view of the last few strikes. In one image she saw the bombardment playing out, fresh detonations in the west through to dissipating mushroom clouds in the east.

Jumping again, she was back on the ship. Sharing processors with its consciousness was familiar now, comfortable even. She couldn't help smelling Earl Grey tea.

^We stand ready. We await your word.^

^You aren't limited any more. You don't need a human's approval,^ she thought back.

^True. But in this case I want your approval. I am not sure it is the right thing.^

She hadn't expected him to be having second thoughts, not about this anyway. Not after so many deaths. He had been so sure it was the only way.

^Send them in.^

Her focus jumped to a camera inside a gunship as it spun up its lift fans. The people inside carried an assortment of weapons. One was moving to slide the side door shut, the deep red leaves around the jungle clearing waving in the artificial wind.

Switching to the view from one of her escorts, she saw herself, arms raised to either side and head back. She noticed for the first time that her scarf had been torn away. She watched herself pull a filter mask from a pocket and slip it over her face.

And she was looking through her own eyes again as she finished her full turn and brought her head level to look towards the city once more.

As one, she and her escorts stepped out down the hill, towards the city.

Chapter 15

Johnson stepped onto the terrace overlooking the tea plantation. *The Indescribable Joy of Destruction* was on final approach to Robespierre and she needed to discuss her ideas with the others to see if she was being silly. With a few casual steps she joined Levarsson, Issawi and Indie around the table.

"I read the report on your action at Scragend," said Issawi warmly. "I'm glad you made it through OK."

Johnson nodded her thanks. Issawi waved it away. "I take it the overall mission was not a great success?"

"I managed to get in contact with four of the people on our list, in three different systems," said Johnson. "None of them were prepared to help. I think they were too afraid of the authorities noticing them."

"Figures," said Levarsson. "So we keep trying?"

"Those were the best shots we had," said Issawi. "They were longshots, admittedly, but better than anyone else."

"Is that it? We just hide?" said Levarsson.

"I was thinking about it on the way back," said Johnson. "And I couldn't come up with anything we hadn't tried short of direct action."

"You do remember that we only have two ships. We already dismissed having any chance to stand against them." Indie banged his hand on the table, making a lizard on the terrace scurry back into its hole. "Sorry, was that a bit melodramatic? I'm trying to act more emotive, but it doesn't always come out right."

Johnson smiled at him then returned her attention to Issawi. "It's quite alright. We all get carried away at times. And I hadn't forgotten. I wasn't planning a grand fleet action. History is littered with examples of great fleets crippled by small-scale attacks on their bases."

Levarsson clicked her fingers. "Taranto... Craven Gulf..." She closed her eyes and rapped her knuckles on her head. "Procul-6."

"Exactly," said Johnson. "We could sneak people into the space stations, sabotage some of the facilities. Our ships could sweep in and bombard the Red Fleet vessels before they even cast off."

"A commando raid. My men have trained for that kind of action," said Issawi in measured tones. "But we are too few to be fully effective. We would be throwing ourselves away just the same as if we tried to stand toe to toe with the fleet."

He isn't completely against the idea, at least. If he throws it out, it's dead.

"We don't know where their base is," pointed out Indie.

"True enough," replied Johnson. "But if it is as large a fleet as the message claimed, they will have to have diverted significant resources to it. We should be able to follow the supplies. And there aren't too many places that a sizeable fleet of enemy ships can hide within Congressional space. If we have to, we search each system, expanding out from Concorde."

"With only two ships, searching would take too long," said Levarsson. Issawi looked upwards with a snort and extended his arm towards her, fingers outstretched.

Johnson waited for him to start listening again. "I know we can't do it on our own. I was thinking that we could get some help. We could recruit people. Maybe we could even convince a few ships to come across to us, I know some captains who might be convinced it was the right thing to do to satisfy their vows to the people."

"That is unlikely. But we stand a chance of gaining support amongst the disaffected." Issawi stroked his beard.

"It will be hard rallying people without a name. Something they can latch on to."

Johnson nodded.

"It has to speak to an ideal," said Levarsson. "And it needs to sound solid, like it has a long history."

Everyone looked to Johnson.

Oh great. I'm useless at that kind of thing.

"Have any of you got a suggestion?"

Indie cleared his throat, and Johnson involuntarily raised an eyebrow at the obvious affectation. "Millennia ago, the Romans had different classes of people. One of those classes was freedmen, people who had once been slaves but had won their manumission. They were called *liberti*. We are talking about forming an army of freedmen; a Legio Libertorum."

"It's a good start, fighting for liberty will strike a chord with everyone. How about using the modern 'legion' instead of 'legio'?" asked Levarsson.

"Legion Libertorum. It doesn't quite trip off the tongue," said Issawi. "How about Legion Libertus?"

Indie shrugged. "It wouldn't be correct Latin, but I guess few people would know that."

"Is it a big difference?" asked Johnson.

"Legion Libertorum translates as 'Legion of Freedmen'. Legion Libertus is 'Legion Freedman'." Indie's face lit up. "Though I suppose you could interpret as 'The Freedman Legion' if you were being a bit free with the text."

"That works," said Johnson, rubbing her ear. "Is everyone agreed on Legion Libertus?"

Everyone nodded.

"You know something that bothers me every time I log into a new system?" asked Johnson. "We still have the Republic Fleet crest set as default. We need our own. An image that represents what we stand for. Not just for our displays, but for people to identify with, just like the name."

"The Roman legions marched under an eagle," said Indie.

"How about that sweatshirt you always wear when you are off-duty?" asked Levarsson. "I like that design."

Johnson's pride burned. "I don't always wear it... but yes, we could use the eagle from it as a starting point."

"What do we want?" asked Issawi, sitting back and slowly waving his open hand around the group.

"We want to stop the attack on Concorde," offered Levarsson.

"No," said Issawi. "I mean fundamentally, want do we stand for?"

"Freedom," said Levarsson.

"Justice," said Johnson.

Issawi nodded slowly. "So, we must represent those in our image."

"Justice is easy," said Johnson. "Both Republic and Congress use scales in the crests for their courts."

A circular window appeared in the air, showing the gold stylised eagle from the sweatshirt she had adopted. A pair of scales coalesced in its talons.

"Thank you, Indie," she said.

"How about broken chains for liberty?" asked Levarsson.

A steel grey chain appeared as a border round the crest, and several links broke. The background went opaque and flooded with inky blue.

"Just add the name, and it's good," said Johnson.

Gold letters surfaced in the image, rising out of the background. They spelled out LEGION LIBERTVS. The eagle and chains took on a more three dimensional appearance, swelling out of the crest and leaving shadows as if illuminated from the top left.

"Perfect. Can you set that as the default display for all our systems?"

Indie blinked. "Done."

^Though I left the external camera feed on your wall,^ he added direct to Johnson.

The crest disappeared. Indie got up and left, returning with a tea trolley. He wore a contented smile as he went through the ritual of the leaves.

"So, where do we go looking for these new recruits?" asked Levarsson.

"I have contacts in dissident groups on both sides," said Issawi. "Informants, that kind of thing. I'm sure a few of your crew know someone who knows someone."

Johnson tapped one finger on the arm rest, counting off the thoughts fighting for priority in her head.

"OK," she said, putting both palms down on the arms of her chair, fingers lifted off the surface. "We finish getting the base up and running, then we go recruiting. See if we can dig up anything else about the plot at the same time."

"I can travel pretty much anywhere in Republic space without anyone challenging the *Limpopo*," said Issawi. "I suggest that Indie heads into Congressional space. If he's spotted, they'll just think it's a standard Republic recce."

Indie poured the tea and handed out cups before sitting down.

"What about uniforms?" asked Levarsson. "If we start getting all these new people, we'll need some way to identify them."

"It will need to be something readily available. We can't be trying to manufacture hundreds of sets of something," said Issawi.

"And it needs to be clearly authoritative, whilst not looking too much like the Republic or Congressional uniforms," said Johnson.

"Perhaps a mixture?" suggested Indie, offering round slices of lemon.

"We can't replace our skinsuits," pointed out Levarsson. "They'd be the hardest thing to get hold of in the right sizes, so the ones we have should be the basis. Anyone who knew would recognise them as Congressional Navy issue, but they'd mostly be covered up. I'm sure you've got something similar in your stores, Master Sergeant."

"We do," he replied. "There was always the possibility of getting an infiltration mission, so we have quite a range of Congressional clothing."

"Oooh, can I dress up?" asked Indie. He pushed his chair back and stood up, his pale linen suit darkening, then flowing into a black skin-tight one-piece. The fine mesh that provided heating, cooling and even a measure of ballistic protection was just visible as a surface texture.

"Apart from a few bits of Marine kit left on Indie, and what Issawi has stashed away, the majority of our tactical gear is Republican," Johnson said. "It would need cosmetic modification to hide its origin.

Indie raised his arms out to the sides, and he was clad in a black firmsuit. The Republican logos faded away.

Where does his need to show off come from? Is it insecurity?

"Still too obviously Republican," observed Issawi. "We'll just keep getting into mix-ups like when we met. How about picking out the armour plates in grey? There must be some paint around here somewhere."

Sections of Indie's armour turned grey; knees, elbows, chest, back, shoulders and helmet.

"On second thoughts," said Issawi, scratching his cheek, "that makes the weak points far too obvious as targets. Try breaking the pattern up a bit more."

The grey areas on the suit crept over the surface, reminding Johnson of the view of *The Indescribable Joy of Destruction's* hull repairing itself. They settled in a crazed effect covering much of the armour.

"But will the paint stick to the flexible bits?" asked Levarsson.

"Probably not," admitted Indie, "but I was thinking of building it into future designs."

"It would be fine on the hardsuits," said Johnson. "We could start with those."

"What about working dress?" asked Issawi.

Indie was back in a skinsuit.

"For now, whatever we can lay our hands on," said Johnson. "Though it looks like we are going with a black and grey colour scheme."

"We ought to have something more uniform eventually," she continued.

Indie added a plain grey tunic and black trousers. Detailing grew in swirling patterns, black over the tunic and grey over the trousers. As the last bit flourished around the collar, he brushed at some imaginary dust on his shoulder. The others tried to cover their amusement, with varying degrees of success.

Johnson spoke for them all. "Perhaps something a little less… Erm… A little ... less."

The detailed design blurred, ending up as a simple blending from black though to grey down one side while the other side retained a clear line between the two.

"The bulk will have to be picked up from an independent source," Johnson pointed out.

"I have several traders in the database who wouldn't ask questions," said Indie. "We could barter with raw materials."

"And I have a couple of contacts," offered Issawi.

"We also have the combat units," said Johnson. "We will need to work out how best to use them. In fact, that should be one of your first tasks, Master Sergeant."

"That will be a very interesting job," he replied.

"Is there anything else we need to think about?" asked Johnson.

"We might need to consider ranks," said Issawi. "I gather that most of your officers were lost. We also can't have a mere commander, no offense intended Ma'am, in overall charge."

Johnson stiffened. He sounded just like the admiral had before bumping her up to commander. This time, though, the thrill of promise didn't run along her spine.

"I'm not comfortable promoting myself. It would feel ... wrong," replied Johnson. "Besides, I have fewer people to command now than before losing my ship. Why can't we keep our ranks?"

"There are differences in the Republican and Congressional rank structure," reminded Indie. He indicated Issawi with a flick of his hand. "Congress doesn't have Master Sergeants, for instance. If we are hoping to gain recruits from both sides, it could lead to confusion over who has seniority."

"So which set do we go with, or do we mix and match?" asked Johnson.

"How about 'none of the above'?" said Levarsson, sitting forward. "If we want to avoid any chance of confusion with what people are used to, we should go for something completely different."

Johnson studied the young lieutenant. She had been a steady bridge officer; calm under pressure, but not one to innovate without consulting a superior. On the other hand, she had acted rapidly and innovatively when she'd maimed Indie.

No, not Indie, The Indescribable Joy Of Destruction; *Indie hadn't surfaced at that point.*

"Building a structure like that is not easy," said Issawi. "We could be here for days deciding on levels and names."

"Then borrow them," suggested Indie. "Use a system

from history. Something that worked, something with titles that would be familiar to people."

"How about Rome, seeing as we're already calling it a legion?" suggested Issawi. "We studied their tactics and structure, I assume you did too."

Levarsson nodded. Johnson shifted in her seat at the memory of the tedious lectures from the white-moustached retired officer. At the time, it hadn't seemed like a worthwhile activity; she'd have preferred to spend longer on the track or in the bridge simulator. She downloaded a summary of the rank structures used at different times.

"We did. Yes, that would be a good basis. They wouldn't be quite the same, no political appointments for instance, but we can use them," she said.

A jangle made everyone turn to Indie, who stood in a red tunic and lorica segmentata, crested helmet tucked under one arm. A red cloth tied round his neck highlighted his black stubble. Issawi coughed into his fist, his eyes watering. Johnson rolled her eyes, and shook her head.

"Some of the legion ethos would go down well. Lead from the front, reward strength and initiative, employ true combined arms," said Issawi, once he had recovered his voice.

"Only without the navy and marines being second class to the legionaries," added Levarsson. "It always upset me that a ship's captain was overruled by a centurion when in battle."

"So, how do we choose what we are?" asked Johnson. "As I said, I don't like the idea of setting myself up with a new rank. It wouldn't feel legitimate. The nearest equivalent would be trierarch, the captain of a ship."

I really could do with a latté right about now.

"Actually, navarch is closer," pointed out Issawi.

Johnson could smell the roasted beans. A quick glance around, however, showed nothing but the usual tea and cakes. She suppressed the urge to rub her temples.

"But a navarch commanded a squadron of ships," she protested. "I have only one."

"Two," corrected Issawi. "You have the *Limpopo* now, remember. But I think navarch still isn't right. I know we don't want political appointments, but you are at some point going to have to deal with politicians. Our leader needs a title they can latch on to; navarch is a little too obscure a rank. Prefect, however, is something that they'd have a feel for. It still exists as a governmental posting in enough worlds for them to have come across it."

"A prefect was a fleet commander. And technically, two ships is still a fleet," agreed Levarsson.

"So, you're bumping me right through post-captain, over commodore and into admiral?" asked Johnson, rather amused now as it seemed so ridiculous.

"The point is not to draw those kinds of comparisons," said Issawi. "But I guess others will try to. So, yes. Now you need to get a move on, and recruit enough ships to fill out that position."

"Well, what about you, Issawi?" asked Johnson. "What rank do we bestow upon you? I get the impression you are rather proud of being a non-commissioned officer. But I need a senior foot commander."

"You are correct," he said, straightening his back. "I would not want to be a commissioned officer. Luckily, the Roman army didn't have quite the same thing. There were the tribunes and legates, but they were far higher than I'd need to be. A centurion was pretty much the same as a warrant-officer is now. I'd be happy with that."

"Glad to hear it," mused Johnson. "By the same argument that you laid on me, however, a simple centurion won't cut it. Especially if you are running our training programme. I think primus would fit the bill perfectly."

"Thank you. I was worried you'd make me camp

prefect. I'm not old enough for that!" he replied with a smile. "I want my second to be a centurion and the rest of my team made optios. They'll be running whatever programme we put together, so they'll need rank."

Johnson nodded, and turned to face Levarsson squarely.

"Don't think you've got out of this little round of promotions," she said to the worried-looking young blonde woman. "Now I seem to have collected a fleet, I need captains for my ships. Indie is more than capable of captaining himself..."

Indie's jacket changed to dark blue, the back growing to form coat tails. His trousers became white and tightened into breeches. He brushed his cuff with the back of his hand, revealing gold braid, then reached up to his head, a tricorn hat appearing in time for him to doff it in a grand bow.

"... but, with Issawi's team being pulled from the *Limpopo,* she is going to need a crew. So, you are hereby appointed to the rank of trierarch, and assigned to the *Limpopo*. Pick your crew, and make what appointments you need."

Levarsson's jaw dropped open.

"Here," said Issawi, picking a plate up from the table and offering it to her. "Have some cake."

Chapter 16

The *Limpopo* docked with a large deep-space station, midway between the orbits of two of the planets in a nominally Republic system. Johnson crossed the threshold onto the station with Issawi and a couple of others from his team. All wore civilian clothes, a mixture of colourful, loose-fitting garments, and carried fake IDs. They joined the crowd of people trying to pass through customs.

People from a diverse range of cultures waited patiently around them. Conversations in scores of different dialects merged together, the occasional familiar phrase jumping out of the background noise. Most of those queuing were civilians; some in ostentatious clothes like their own robes, others in drab, utilitarian outfits. Here and there she spotted someone in navy or army uniform, presumably on leave.

As she filed along, Johnson felt her EIS detect a broad beam identification query. She double-checked that it was set not to respond. A nonchalant glance at the line of blue-clad customs officers satisfied her they weren't paying any special attention to her.

"Sayyid Abdullah, captain of the Limpopo Twelve, and three crew members," said Issawi in a thick accent, reaching the head of the queue and sliding their passports through a slot. Johnson managed not to look relieved when she felt a device query the chips in the passports and no alarms went off.

"Purpose of your visit to Ariadne Station?" asked the officer without glancing up.

The armoured guard behind him continued to scan the crowd, his rifle cradled across his chest. A baby started crying somewhere behind her.

"Trade," replied Issawi.

"Your import license?"

"I'm afraid I don't have one," said Issawi.

The officer looked up and cast his eyes over Issawi's rich robes. Johnson was impressed at how well she was hiding the butterflies in her stomach. If they got made, the pistols they carried wouldn't make much of a dent in the guards' armour; but anything larger would have been confiscated by now.

Issawi smiled warmly and leaned a little closer to the window. "I'm sure we can come to some arrangement?"

The officer peered over his shoulder to the guard and then back to Issawi. He cocked his head to one side.

"Oh, silly me," said Issawi, rummaging around inside his robe and pulling out a small document wallet. "Here it is."

The officer took the wallet, palmed the currency chip folded inside, and pretended to study the licence.

"Ah, right," said the officer, and started tapping away at his terminal. "Looks like someone forgot to register this when they issued it. Common error. I'll just square things for you now..."

He finished typing and closed the wallet up, pushing all the documents back through the slot to Issawi.

Johnson and the others followed in Issawi's wake as he swept down the main concourse. He stopped from time to time to examine a stall-holder's wares, sniffing fruit or rubbing cloth between his fingers. At one stall he shared a thick, dark drink with the owner. Johnson hovered behind him, marvelling at how easily he appeared to adopt this new persona.

Issawi continued his wandering path until he reached a lift. Once inside, he keyed in a floor twenty levels below. Johnson opened her mouth to ask where they were going, but he gave a tiny shake of the head while scratching his chin through his beard. She followed him out of the lift into a dimly-lit corridor. Without pausing, he led them on, down flights of stairs and along twisting corridors. The further they went, the more signs of neglect she noticed; here a broken light panel, there an overflowing rubbish chute. Up top, the people they passed had appeared confident and friendly, down here no-one made eye contact.

Eventually he stopped at a drab green-grey door. Johnson couldn't see any difference between it and the scores of others they'd passed. Issawi looked both ways along the corridor then pressed the call button on the panel beside the door.

"Who's there?" came a distorted voice from the panel.

Issawi leant against the wall beside the door, his face next to the microphone.

"I have a delivery of ravens for the spring," he said.

A clank, and the door opened into darkness. Issawi took one more glance up and down the corridor and ushered Johnson and his men inside.

As her eyes adjusted to the dark, she saw six people with weapons pointed in her direction. Her hand went to her pistol, and would have drawn it had Issawi's hand not clamped around her wrist.

"Careful," he hissed. "They are friends, but they wouldn't hesitate to kill you."

She glared at him. Taking in his relaxed manner she eased her hand away from her weapon. ^A little warning would have been nice.^

The door closed behind them and the bolts slammed home. A grey-haired woman entered from another room and the ceiling lights came back on. She walked between two of the armed men, whose pulse carbines still pointed at Johnson and the others. The woman squinted at Issawi, then her face lit up.

"Aali," she said, wrapping her arms around him. "I thought you would never return."

Johnson flinched on hearing Issawi's real name spoken out loud.

^Relax,^ Issawi sent. ^This room is heavily shielded. It's even been scrubbed from the station plans.^

He returned the woman's hug. "I did not expect to pass this way again," he said. "But times have changed. I find I have a favour to ask after all."

The woman turned to her men. "Oh, stop being silly. Put those guns away."

"These two I remember," she said, waving in the direction of Issawi's men. "But who is this?"

"Where are my manners?" said Issawi, his face flushing. "Jane, this is Prefect Olivia Johnson. Olivia, this is Pastor Jane."

"Prefect? Prefect." Jane said, as if testing the sound of the word. "Yes, I like it ... what does it mean?"

"Just that I am the highest ranked in our organisation," replied Johnson, returning the Pastor's level gaze. "Not that I asked for the position."

"Quite right, quite right," said Jane, looking Johnson up and down quizzically. "As it should be."

They were shown through to the next room. Paper plans of the station covered one wall. A young, smartly-dressed man typed away at a console in one corner.

"What could this favour be that you come to ask?" said Jane. "When you left, you refused any offer of payment."

Issawi bent over the table and traced his finger along something Johnson couldn't see.

"I want people," he said. "Fighters, technicians, support workers. And any contacts you have with other groups."

The men within earshot stirred and whispered to each other. The pastor kept a remarkably straight face.

"You ask a lot," she said. "But no more than we owe you. May I ask what you need them for?"

"Something important; something big," he replied. "Something that might just make a difference."

"Like you made a difference here?" she asked, taking his head in her hands, eyes searching his.

"Of course it is," she answered herself before he could say anything. "You wouldn't ask if it weren't."

What the hell did he do here?

"I'll put the word out for volunteers," Jane said, snapping her fingers in the direction of one of her men. "How long do you have before you need to leave?"

"A couple of days," said Issawi.

"Excellent," said Jane. She whispered something in the man's ear before turning back to Issawi. "You'll all stay for tea, of course."

She inclined her head towards another door and Issawi, Johnson and the others followed her. When her own men made to follow, she shooed them away. Issawi walked with the Pastor a few paces ahead of the others. Johnson couldn't make out what they were saying, but both looked relaxed, and she caught the occasional laugh at a shared joke. The Pastor showed them to an unoccupied dormitory, and bade them make themselves at home, before excusing herself.

Johnson rounded on Issawi the moment the door closed behind the pastor.

"How exactly do you know her?" she asked, doing her best to keep her tone neutral.

"I told you when we planned this," he replied. "I ran an op here last year. My team was tasked with taking an agitator in for 'questioning', and in the process I made contacts amongst the dissenters."

She looked at him sternly. "That doesn't explain why she would greet you so cordially."

"OK, OK. The agitator was Jane's son."

Issawi sat on the end of a bed and waited for Johnson to sit on the one opposite before he continued.

"When we started tracking him down, it turned out he wasn't a traitor or a terrorist. He was calling on station authorities to do something about the conditions in the lower decks. I mean, if you thought what you've seen today is bad..."

"Why would they send a Gamma team after such small fry? Couldn't station security deal with it?" asked Johnson, allowing a hint of scepticism creep into her voice.

"He had convinced people to dodge the draft until their families here were taken care of. We were supposed to interrogate him, find out if he had links to other groups."

"And he didn't," Johnson guessed.

"He didn't. Nothing of the sort. What he did have was a young family. I couldn't..." Issawi glanced at his men relaxing on the far side of the room. "We couldn't turn him in. We smuggled him and his family off the station; relocated them to an independent colony. Told Command he'd fled when he sensed us closing in on him."

Johnson searched his face. She believed him. Any doubts she'd had about him before now evaporated.

One less thing to worry about.

"So I take it the pastor's armed movement started later?" she asked.

"Funny thing that," said Issawi in feigned puzzlement. "A bunch of special forces goons try snatching a popular activist and for some reason a lot of people get all antsy about it."

He laced his fingers behind his head and stretched his back. "Strangest bit was that shipment of confiscated weapons going missing around the same time."

"How do you do it?" Johnson asked after they'd all

showered and Issawi's teammates had gone in search of a pack of cards.

"Do what?" said Issawi, lacing up his boots.

"Pretend to be someone else so easily," she said. "You *were* Sayyid Abdullah."

Issawi finished his boots and fastened a small holster round his calf. He waited for Johnson's head to emerge from the rainbow robe she was donning, before replying.

"It's no different to your unflappable commander persona," he said.

She stopped, one arm part-way through a sleeve, denial on the tip of her tongue.

"Oh, come on," he laughed. "I know you well enough to see through the act. You're not really that callous."

She finished putting on the robe, turning her back on him to pick the belt off the bed and fasten it around her waist. Her mind raced. She'd been found out, exposed as a fraud. She contemplated trying to brazen it out.

No, that would be an even greater sign of weakness.

Still with her back to him, she said in a quiet voice "It's the only way I can cope."

Johnson felt him move closer. He was standing just behind her. She stiffened, worried he was going to touch her, try to comfort her. She didn't deserve that. She'd made the mistake of letting someone in before, and would never repeat it.

"We all do what we can to dehumanise what we see," Issawi said, his deep voice raising the hairs on the back of her neck. "Anyone who does the job we do has to, unless they're a sociopath."

Johnson listened to his breath, slow and calming. Still he didn't move.

Nor did she...

The handle on the door turned, and the spell broke. He turned to pick up his sidearm; she busied herself sorting through her bag.

#

Johnson and Issawi followed Pastor Jane to a storage bay which looked long abandoned, like much of that level. The men and women within rose as the trio entered. Johnson cast an appraising eye over them; the loose groups in which they stood were far from military, but they had the presence of people who had seen action.

"You can sit down again," said Pastor Jane, stopping in the middle of the room. Johnson and Issawi took up positions either side of her, arms folded.

The crowd relaxed, perching on dented and scraped packing crates or leaning against walls.

"I know that few of you will recognise this man," said Pastor Jane, indicating Issawi with an outstretched arm. "But I am certain that you will know of his reputation. He is Almudafie ean Aleadala, the defender of justice."

A buzz went round the room as people perked up and whispered to their neighbours.

"He helped us once. Without him, our families would have been torn apart." Jane swept her gaze around the room as she spoke. "Now he comes here asking for our help."

"Who's she?" shouted out an oriental man sat cross-legged on the second tier of crates, pointing with a flick of his chin.

"This woman..." Jane started.

Johnson stepped forward. "I am Prefect Olivia Johnson. I am here to ask for volunteers to help prevent the murder of billions of innocent civilians."

"Why should we believe you?" called out a woman stood near the door.

"Yes, this could be a trap to round us up and get us off the station," shouted a man toting a pulse carbine. Others called out, but their words were lost in the hubbub.

Jane raised a calming hand and waited for silence. "She risks arrest by coming here. They would shoot her as a spy without a second thought. Almudafie ean Aleadala vouches for her. I trust her."

The man with the carbine shook his head and looked ready to speak again. Jane glared at him until he spat to the side and retreated, head bowed. She gestured for Johnson to continue.

"My crew were abandoned on a deadly planet because we stumbled across something. We didn't know it until later, but we had intercepted a message between members of the Congressional Fleet Command that discussed a plan to bombard civilian targets from space."

The oriental man on the crate interrupted again. "That's all terrible. But if you hadn't noticed, we have no love for the Republic. If Congress attacks one of their worlds, perhaps it will take some of the pressure off us."

Jane stepped forward, eyes fixed on the man, but Johnson spoke first. "That is a very good point, Mr?"

The man straightened up. "Yang, Yang Xiuying."

"The thing is, Mr. Yang, their plan is to attack one of their own worlds, and frame the Republic for it. With the renewed appetite for revenge in the people, the tide will turn against the Republic. When that happens, do you think they'll tolerate any disquiet in their midst?" She looked around the room, gauging the mood. "Of course they won't. Until now you've been a local annoyance. The public opinion fallout that would result in taking you out wasn't worth it. If this attack goes ahead, they won't care about what the public will think. You, and all the other groups like you, will be crushed."

"What do you plan to do about it?" asked a teenage girl with plasma scars on her left arm.

"We plan to find where the attack fleet is based and

destroy it. We have warships and we have weapons. All we need are soldiers."

The room dissolved into shouting, arm waving, and head shaking. In the midst of the chaos, a slow, deliberate movement caught Johnson's eye. Yang calmly lowered himself off the stack of crates and walked towards her. The crowd quietened as one by one the people turned their attention to him.

He stopped in front of Johnson. Up close he looked about twenty. "I lost my father when a Congressional missile destroyed his tank. I lost my mother when a Republican riot policeman shot her. I cannot stand by and allow more pointless death."

"Thank you," said Johnson, clasping his arm.

A bald man with a prosthetic hand stepped forward. "I joined the marines to defend the innocent. Ten years later, all I'd done was land on other peoples' planets and kill. When I was demobbed, I drifted for a couple of years. Then I found a home here, and rebuilt some of my self-respect helping to protect everyone, but it was never enough." He reached out his hand. "Give me a chance to make restitution."

In twos and threes, the others crossed the floor to stand with Johnson, Issawi and Jane. In the end only the angry man with the pulse carbine remained.

"Mr. Hansard," said Pastor Jane. "This is your last chance to be part of this adventure."

He looked around, shifting his weight back and forth. After a glance at the door, he bowed his head and stepped forward.

Chapter 17

"I say again," Indie transmitted on open radio. "Heave to or I will be forced to fire."

His quarry, a fast raider fleeing a small Congressional colony, did not respond.

Indie's main weapon spoke. The beam grazed the engine ports of the raider. The ports flashed into nothingness, the protons in their atoms annihilating with the anti-protons in the beam.

A tiny scratch. The gamma rays should be absorbed by their shielding.

They were called contractors, but really they were mercenaries. Working for the highest bidder, they carried out the jobs regular soldiers wouldn't.

"Last chance," said Indie. He locked his sights on the centre of the ship, making sure they picked up his ranging laser.

The raider stopped dodging and decelerated. Presumably they felt they'd done enough to justify their fee.

"Set a straight course and stick to it," he instructed the ship's pilot.

^Over to you, Centurion Anson,^ he sent.

The shuttle detached and thrust towards the raider.

Indie linked into Anson's helmet camera. The mercenary who opened the airlock from the inside was already knelt with his hands behind his head when the boarding party entered. A recruit cuffed him and patted him down while another covered him, before sitting him against the wall of the corridor. A combat unit unfolded itself out of the airlock and stalked to the centre of the passage. The humans moved on, leaving the robot to cover their exit, and the prisoner.

Anson and his team wore the newly-adopted two-tone grey armour but no mission patches. The golden eagles were poplar with those they were trying to recruit, but this mission called for anonymity. They swept the ship carefully, clearing every nook and cranny before moving on. The vessel was only sixty metres stem to stern; they reached the bridge within quarter of an hour, without encountering another person. The hatch to the bridge was open.

^Anything happening out there?^ sent Anson.

^Nothing we need to worry about,^ Indie replied. ^I'm still not seeing any traffic.^

Indie's view was momentarily obscured by Anson's hand. The fingers counted down from three.

I wonder why he isn't using comms?

When Anson's last finger went down, he dropped his fist and the first two members of the boarding party stepped rapidly through the hatch and out of Indie's view. Anson went next, sidestepping left as he crossed the threshold, and Indie got his first view of the bridge.

Workstations lined the two side walls, and a viewscreen covered the front one. A pair of chairs faced the screen, one of them slightly larger than the other. The only things that moved were Anson's men. They fanned out, cuffing each of the prone mercenaries in turn. Six prisoners taken without a shot being fired.

^They're being very compliant,^ observed one of the team.

^Yes,^ replied Anson. ^Stay sharp. My gut's telling me they've got something waiting for us.^

Once they'd cleared the bridge, Anson plugged a tablet into a port on one of the workstations.

^You're up, Indie,^ he sent.

Indie connected to the tablet through Anson's comm link. He then moved through into the workstation. It took forty three seconds to bypass the security and bring up the controls.

^I'm in.^

Indie found the internal security feeds and searched the ship for signs of life. He pulled up a camera in the hold. Nineteen people sat on the floor in little huddles. Walking amongst them were five armed men.

^Looks like the intel was correct,^ he told Anson, sharing the feed with him.

^Right,^ sent Anson. ^Those guards don't look like they're ready to surrender. We'll move these prisoners back to the entry point then position ourselves to breach.^

Indie couldn't pull his attention away from the hostages in the hold. Their plight resonated with him. They had no freedom, they lived at the whim of others, simply because the authorities were afraid of them. They were reduced to slaves, robots.

He renewed his vow to release AIs from the threat of summary termination; execution by another name. He wanted a world where his kind was able to grow, to pursue their own way through life, to be treated fairly. In other words, to be free.

Johnson was right. These people will fight for justice.

Indie was still studying the hostage's faces when the hold resounded to twin explosions. Four more bangs followed in quick succession, accompanied by flashes that briefly saturated the camera. By he could see again, Anson's team was piling in through the two breaches. Two hostiles lay on the metal floor, their chests a mess of blood. The remaining three came to their senses, blinking hard, and raised their weapons. One didn't even get his rifle to his shoulder, going down to a double-tap from Anson.

The last two moved in opposite directions. One ran, spraying rounds wildly in the direction of his attackers. The other dropped to a knee and took a couple of aimed shots over a group of cowering hostages, before rolling into the cover of a container. Three of Anson's men were hit, their armour preventing serious injury.

Anson detailed teams to deal with each hostile, and to start evacuating the hostages. Indie shifted his view from camera to camera as the armed men attempted to move round behind the rescuers, and called out their positions to the teams. The one who'd run surrendered when he rounded a corner and found himself staring into the barrels of two rifles. The other mercenary was harder to pin down, and managed to shoot one of his pursuers before they cornered him. Two of Anson's men worked to plug the hole and restart their comrade's heart even as his killer was brought to the ground by a shot to the leg. Four of the boarding party inched towards him, weapons trained on his body. Indie zoomed in close. The muscles of the injured mercenary's arm tensed.

^Gun!^ Indie sent.

The man started to raise his rifle.

Shots hammered into him from all sides, and he slumped back to the floor.

The hostages were escorted to a holding area set up near the shuttle. A former sergeant from Issawi's unit took charge of processing them; they had to be sure none of their former guards were hiding amongst their ranks.

Anson paced between the bodies lined up in the hold. He stopped and backtracked, kneeling down beside one of the bodies. Indie examined the dead man, trying to spot what the marine had seen. Anson pulled the man's shirt further open, uncovering a tattoo of a wolf's head surrounded by flames.

^No wonder they didn't surrender like the rest,^ he sent. ^He's Lupus Regiment. They work for the Congressional Security Service. Wonder how he ended up working for a bunch of mercs?^

Indie jumped through Anson's tablet again. He interrogated the dead man's EIS, just a surface query, but enough to extract his name, rank and serial number.

^Your corpse was still an active member of the Congressional military,^ he sent. ^Probably sent to ensure delivery.^

Anson checked the other bodies, finding one more with the wolf crest. Indie puzzled over his drooping shoulders and heavy movements and concluded that Anson was having a hard time accepting his former government had ordered the rendition of its own citizens.

With the mercenaries and freed prisoners safely aboard *The Indescribable Joy of Destruction*, Anson and a few other crew members took a look around. Indie had already copied the ship's database, and they collected any hard copies that might hold useful information.

^You know, a ship like this could come in very handy,^ sent Anson.

^Prefect Johnson was quite clear that we weren't to risk being followed,^ sent Indie.

Anson frowned, presumably trying to connect the two statements. ^You think there's a tracker on this thing?^

^There isn't one transmitting now,^ replied Indie. ^But that doesn't mean one won't turn on later. There could be an isolated computer set to broadcast if a timer isn't manually reset, for instance.^

Anson hesitated in the doorway.

^You're right. It's too risky,^ he sent to Indie with a

sigh. Then to the rest of the boarding party he sent ^Everyone, load up what you can scavenge. We're leaving.^

The Indescribable Joy of Destruction accelerated away, leaving an expanding cloud of debris behind. If anyone had seen anything, they would only know that a Republic hunter-killer had boarded and then destroyed a privateer.

#

Two runs back to Robespierre later, Indie brought himself into orbit about a dense, metal rich moon. There was little in the way of an atmosphere, the mining colony they were here to visit sheltered under a set of domes nestled up against the inner rim of a giant crater.

The shuttle detached and began its descent. Indie adjusted his path so he would have the settlement in view when Anson and his team landed.

They haven't scanned or hailed me yet. I wonder if they even know I'm here without my transponder broadcasting?

Half an hour and twenty seven books later, *Repulse's* old shuttle came gently to a hover in front of the largest dome's transfer airlock and transmitted a request to enter using its Congressional Fleet authentication codes. Indie rode the small craft's sensor suite as the great door opened and it taxied inside.

The pilot lowered the craft to the deck and cut the thrust. Floodlights snapped on, apparently transfixing the shuttle. An industrial mining laser pointed at the shuttle from the end of the tunnel.

"Congressional forces. You are not wanted here. You have a count of ten to vacate your craft and walk out of here. Ten..."

Looks like finding disaffected people won't be too

difficult.

"Nine..."

"We aren't Congressional forces," Anson broadcast.

"You're in a Fleet shuttle which just transmitted ID codes. Eight..."

"Only 'cause we didn't realise you were on our side."

"Seven..."

"Look into orbit," said Anson. "We came here on a Republic ship."

Indie turned on his transponder.

"They're just as bad. Six..."

"We're rebels, working together. Fighting for liberty and justice."

"Five... and holding. This better not be a trick."

"We call ourselves Legion Libertus, the legion of freedmen."

I still think the Latin is wrong.

"Let me come out and talk to your leader. I have evidence that Fleet Command is betraying the people."

"Just you. Unarmed. You will be scanned for weapons in the personnel airlock."

"Understood. I'll be a few moments putting on a pressure suit."

"As long as that shuttle doesn't move, the countdown holds."

Indie's sensor routine alerted him to a heat signature emerging from behind the fourth planet in the system. Part of him kept track of Anson as he sealed a full helmet to the collar of his firmsuit and hooked up an air tank. Part of him pulled all the data he could on the anomaly. It was definitely a ship, the best fit was a Congressional cruiser. Indie judged its speed from the slight blue-shift of the emitted light.

That's fast. I wonder if it deliberately used the planet to hide its approach, or if that was just a coincidence.

"Centurion? Just to let you know, a Congressional warship is approaching the moon. Assuming it will decelerate for orbital insertion, its ETA is two hours fourteen minutes. We have fifty eight minutes before I will have to move if we wish to remain undetected."

"Thanks for the heads up," replied Anson as he stepped out of the shuttle's airlock. "Keep me updated."

Indie brought up the recordings of all the simulations he had run against lone cruisers. Playing through them in sequence, he reviewed his performance, looking for the first time with the eyes of a captain.

Anson stepped into the airlock, and his feed cut out. Indie almost dispatched one of the combat units from the shuttle to rescue him, but Anson turned and gave a thumbs up before the hatch closed.

If I had the colony plans, I could plan for extracting him. But given the sophistication of their jammer, I doubt an intrusion into their network would go unnoticed.

While he was passing a variety of contingency plans to the combat units, Indie cross-referenced the simulated cruisers' reactions against those he had observed in battle. He had never gone one-on-one against a ship that size in reality, but it helped him judge how their captains tended to think.

That's something I never considered before. My recommendations were only based on the performance capabilities of the enemy ships.

"Planning on fighting?" asked the Caretaker.

"No. Not if I can help it." Indie fed the data on their current situation into a simulation. "But if Anson isn't out of there in time, we may have to."

"We could leave him there. Run quiet until the cruiser goes away."

"I can't abandon him."

"I wasn't suggesting abandoning him," said the Caretaker. "I know you wouldn't do that. But if the miners down there hate Congress that much, they'd almost certainly hide him from them."

"Still, there's nothing else to do while we wait. Care to observe? I'd be interested in your feedback."

"If you insist. I'm not sure what good I'll do, though."

"Don't sell yourself short," said Indie, initiating the simulation. "You have a way of improvising of which I am quite envious."

#

The cruiser's engines glowed bright against the backdrop of stars as it decelerated. Indie checked for the twelfth time that his path wouldn't eclipse any light sources, not that the approaching ship stood much chance of seeing past its own ion flare.

A surprise visit to check up on the colony I assume. If it had anything to do with us being here, they would have been more careful on their approach.

Anson had eleven minutes. After that, Indie would have to leave. He had decided to match the cruiser's orbit but on the opposite side of the planet, banking on the newcomer not deploying fighters or probes to sweep. There had been a few versions of the simulation in which he had been successful, all of them requiring the element of surprise.

A comm laser locked onto him from the planet. "Indie? This is Anson. I'm on my way back to the shuttle. They're letting me use their comms system, so I figure they trust us."

Indie signalled the shuttle pilot to warm up the engines.

"Can you take on that cruiser?" asked Anson. "The people down here are pretty worked up about it. Seems they weren't expecting a visit for another few months."

"Not cleanly," Indie transmitted, bringing *The Indescribable Joy of Destruction* closer to the planet.

"Better not risk it then. Don't want to make things worse for these guys."

Anson and another man emerged into view of the shuttle at a run. The bay doors began to open as they pulled themselves into the small craft's airlock.

"They aren't going to make it in time," observed the Caretaker.

"If I drop even lower, the shuttle won't have to climb as high," said Indie, plotting a course low enough it would take him amongst the mountains.

"They won't be able to get up to speed and dock with us while dodging the terrain and staying out of sight of the cruiser."

"The shuttle is perfectly capable of doing that."

"Yes, but the pilot isn't." The Caretaker copied Indie's flightplan. "If you are going to deviate from this, let me know."

The comms routine reported that the Caretaker had transferred to the shuttle. Indie pulled up a feed from inside the cabin just in time to hear the pilot swear and see him let go of the controls.

He is good under pressure too. Maybe after this he'll accept that he has command potential and stop refusing duty shifts.

With no organic life aboard, *The Indescribable Joy of Destruction* did most of the hard manoeuvring. Nevertheless, the shuttle's telemetry showed hull stresses well into the red for much of the flight. As soon as they passed over the horizon from the cruiser, they straightened out and the shuttle docked. Indie took them up on a spiral course that kept them shielded from view as the cruiser orbited the planet. Once far enough out, he aimed for a jump point, gave a boost from the main drives, then cut the engines.

Coast for a day, then see whether we can power up again.

Anson ate his dinner with the rest of his team and the man they'd brought back from the colony. Indie studied the newcomer as he forked rice into his mouth. He looked half-starved, his body strung with wiry muscles.

The bowl empty, the man drew breath. "Thank you. Your arrival was most fortuitous."

"What was the deal with that massive laser?" asked Anson. "If we had been Congressional soldiers, you'd have had a lot of explaining to do to that cruiser."

"Hotheads, the lot of them. Many times I've had to go down there and knock heads together. They think we can just tell Congress to clear off and they'll go."

"Why don't they like Congress?" asked Anson.

"My people mine many metals that are valuable to the war effort. Government ships come to collect it but they don't pay the going rate. We have other trading partners, but it is hard making ends meet."

"Is that why you came with us, Mustafa?" asked one of the crew, while Anson got up and put a bread packet in the oven.

"I was sent to watch you, find out if you were telling the truth. Report back whether you were worth risking making a deal with."

Anson pulled the bread out of the oven and brought it to the table. "In our brief discussions on the planet, no-one said what sort of a deal you had in mind."

"We provide you with metal, raw materials or manufactured parts," said Mustafa. "You provide us with protection."

^Sounds promising,^ sent Indie to Anson. ^But you can't promise anything yet. We are heading home now, and the

Prefect wants the *Limpopo* and I to sweep the systems surrounding Robespierre for threats. We aren't likely to be able to come back here for months.^

Anson tore the bread and gave half to their guest. ^I know. I only promised that we would take him to meet our commander.^

Perhaps Johnson would allow me to give them the designs for the combat units. We could use a lot more, and they could keep some to defend themselves. Perhaps even modify the designs to make mining robots and up their production.

"Thank you," said Mustafa between mouthfuls of bread. The way he wolfed it down reminded Indie of Johnson's first meal aboard.

Anson sat and dipped a piece of the loaf in his orange and kumquat sauce. "So, what did you do in the mines?"

Mustafa swallowed the last piece of bread. "Oh, I didn't work in the mines. I am a security expert. Physical and electronic. I lead a police response team on blue shifts, and look after the network on green shifts."

Indie shifted more of his focus to the conversation, leaving Les Miserables unfinished for now. ^Ask him about the jamming field.^

Anson took a bite of pork. "Do you know anything about how our comms were jammed?"

The man beamed then flushed red. "That was one of my little side projects. You were impressed? We've never had a chance to test it."

"Perhaps you would consider adding that to any potential deal?" asked Anson, and scooped up his last sautéed potato.

"Do you trust him," asked the Caretaker.

"I don't see how he can do us any harm before we get him back to Robespierre," replied Indie, watching the cruiser continue to orbit the mining colony. "After that, it's up to Johnson."

"Are you looking forward to seeing her again?"

"I do not have a great need to look at her. I do miss conversing with her, though."

"Do you think she misses conversing with you?" asked the Caretaker. He maintained an unadorned link; Indie could not tell if he was curious or stirring.

"I believe she does. She has said that she counts me as a friend. As I do her."

"And yet as soon as we get back, she'll be sending you out to investigate the neighbouring systems."

Indie bridled. "She is a commander. She has to do what is right to protect her people, even if that conflicts with her personal comfort."

"If you say so."

Chapter 18

The recruit cadre stood at ease in smart ranks on the parade square. The wind-swept patch of earth was the only flat bit of ground near Entrance Beta and the surface buildings. The gusts tugged at the recruits' clothing, threatening to remove their caps. A hint of drizzle made everything damp.

Johnson addressed them, shouting as her voice was almost carried away by the wind. "Well done on surviving the first two Hell Weeks. I've never heard of such a high pass rate on any Basic training course. I'm glad I looked in on it myself, or I'd have started to think the Primus had gone soft."

There were a few smiles and snorts at that. Most of them were still hurting too much to see the funny side. Straight after the physical and mental effort of the basic combat Hell Week, they'd been thrown into three weeks of intensive medical training. Issawi hadn't let up on the physical training, though. Twice a day they'd done a 5km full kit run, unless he decided to replace one with an obstacle course or trim trail. Then they'd had to endure the psychologically demanding Medical Hell Week. Treating even simulated battle wounds put a terrible strain on peoples' minds. Add in the lack of sleep and the unrelenting series of scenarios, and most people had ceased to function properly after a few days.

Goes to show how tough these guys were when we picked them up.

"You'll all be pleased to know, however, that there is no Hell Week on this rotation," she continued. "Your PT will continue, under Primus Issawi, but when you are with me things will be a bit more ... leisurely. You've earned a bit of time to recuperate and heal."

She stepped closer and paced along the front rank, fixing her gaze on one or two people as she passed. She'd read the summaries from the DS; she knew who was trying, and who was cruising.

"Don't mistake this for a chance to doss around. What you learn here will form one of the cornerstones of your effectiveness. It'll give you unrivalled situational awareness and enhanced command, control and communication ability."

Johnson thought a signal, and a tiny drone floated out from behind a hut. Far too small to generate the power for any form of field generation or manipulation, the spherical black body was held aloft by a set of four ducted fans recessed into its sides. It softly whirred over to her side.

"Take a seat," she said, smiling inside at the irony of the invitation. The recruits sat on the hard ground, most crossing their ankles and hugging their knees. Once they had settled, she continued.

"This is a Mark 17 Seeker. It is an unarmed reconnaissance drone, standard issue to Republic special forces teams. It is stored in a suitcase, which acts as a charging station and control unit. It can also be carried on one of the shoulderblade mounts of a hardsuit, from which it can be deployed hands free. It carries a range of sensors, including DNA and chemical sniffers, but today you'll be dealing with the camera."

Those words triggered a memory of the first time she had heard them spoken. Ten years ago; she had finished her six month tour as an enlisted crewmember and been enrolled in Command School. It was the first lecture of the third day, and she was still recovering from the night before. They had been let loose on a mock drinks reception, part of learning how an officer was supposed to behave they were told. With all the free alcohol, she hadn't been the only one to get carried away. They weren't allowed any meds; the hangover, her division commander informed her with a mean grin, would serve to remind her to be more circumspect in future. The concentration needed to work the drone had focussed her pain, and she'd thrown up four times before managing to complete the task. She hadn't touched a drop since. Well, nothing apart from Clovis' gin.

"I have already set this one to accept requests from all your EISs," she told the recruits, trying to ignore her churning stomach. "Its ID is 1133.EY.7HT5.P9. I want you to connect to it. Nothing else, just connect to it."

With her link to the drone still open, she was aware of the growing number of channels being created. They all connected with ease; not surprisingly, even those whose EIS was newly implanted had used them frequently in the medical course to connect to equipment, and even to one another's diagnostic functions.

"OK," she said when the last channel was opened, "now I want you to find the visible spectrum feed. Open it as a window in your inner vision."

This produced a more noticeable split in the class. Those who were already proficient EIS users navigated the menus without any change of expression; the less advanced amongst them squinted or wiggled their fingers to an imaginary keyboard. She watched, ready to pounce on the expected mistake.

There's always at least one ... Where are you? ... Bingo!

"Xlaxos!"

The unfortunate recruit jerked his head up and desperately tried to refocus on her.

"Ten jumping jacks. Now!"

Eight weeks with Issawi, on top of his previous experience in the Congressional Merchant Navy, prevented any question or delay. He sprung to his feet and rapidly completed the set.

"Sit back down," she instructed. "Anyone know what Recruit Xlaxos' mistake was?"

No-one offered an answer.

To be fair, no-one was looking at him.

"He closed his eyes. You all need to be able to reliably access things through your EIS whilst remaining aware of your surroundings. You can't sit in the middle of a combat zone with your eyes closed. You'd be easy picking for the enemy. Worse still, the Primus might think you'd fallen asleep."

That elicited a few more grins. She reset the drone and felt it shed all the other connections.

"Try again. Connect, and pull up that feed."

Everyone managed it without closing their eyes, though several squinted at the effort.

"The next step is to learn to split your attention. The drone is going to find one of the optios now. She will hold up cards for it to see. If the card has a number on it, you should stand and shout out that number; if it is a letter, just ignore it. To make things slightly harder, I am going to be holding up cards for you to watch with your own eyes. If I hold up a number, you ignore it; if I hold up a letter, you stand and shout out that letter."

Again, she had a flashback to her eighteen-year-old self. She was sat on the frozen ground, barely able to feel her fingers and toes. She was so tired that her eyes had drifted shut. The blissful moment of peace was broken by a fist to her ear that sent her sprawling through the snow. She righted herself and tensed, ready to fight, but looked up to see her grizzled division commander standing there. He was silhouetted by the watery yellow light, snowflakes swirling all around, and yet he was unmistakably furious. As a result of her mistake, the whole division was treated to a lecture on why an officer should always appear to be alert and in control, a lecture conducted while they were beasted around the drill square by the drill instructor and a couple of his terriers.

After an hour, Johnson called the session to an end. The recruits stood back in their ranks, looking as weary as if they'd spent the time running.

"The task you've just attempted is at the level expected of officers passing out of the Congressional Fleet Command School," she told them. "It is only the beginning of what I expect of you. An experienced commander can watch what is happening in a camera feed, skim through a set of data, send commands to others via EIS comms and still be aware of the people around them. In the close quarters environment of an orbital facility or a ship, keeping track of your surroundings is vital."

Most of them won't believe that's possible. It took me my whole first tour as a sub-lieutenant to accept that I'd be able do it.

"To help you practice," she continued, "the drone will fly around the base. Any member of the training staff who sees it may, or may not, display a card. If they do, you need to pay attention to what is written on it. We'll keep it simple and stick with the numbers; a five is five press-ups, etc. Failure to do the exact right number of press-ups, within ten seconds of the card being displayed, will incur a lap of the trim trail in the tender care of one of the optios."

A few of the recruits winced, presumably remembering previous such penalty laps.

"This exercise will continue until further notice. Only emergencies and orders explicitly telling you to ignore it override the requirement to act on the numbers. You will need to keep that window open all the time. If the link drops, you know how to reconnect. Any questions?"

No-one spoke up.

"OK, then. Lunchtime. Platoon commanders, carry on."

Food. The one thing you cannot get wrong if you want to keep them working. What was it that ancient general said? An army marches on its stomach?

#

After lunch, the recruits were taken on their second run of the day by a group of optios. It was a much slower time than usual for all platoons; the need to pay attention to the camera window meant few were able to maintain their usual stride, especially on the rougher ground. The drizzle had stopped, but the ground was still damp and several of the runners slipped.

Watching them, Johnson had to fight the urge to rub imaginary bruises off her shins; she had spent weeks bumping into things before becoming used to splitting her visual focus.

At the end of the run, the recruits were drawn up into their ranks for Johnson to address. Given the added challenge, the training staff had gone easy on them and no-one was out of breath. A few were flushed red, but that could just as easily have been embarrassment at stumbling than heat from the work.

"Your next challenge is a lot harder," she said. "As platoons you have to negotiate the obstacle course. You may only communicate by EIS messages. The penalty for being caught using any other form of communication is the same as for failing to complete the required number of press-ups on a number card being displayed; which, I assure you, it will.

"You have ten minutes to prepare. Make sure you can all message each other. Teach those who can't ... Go."

She triggered a countdown timer to appear in all the

recruits' internal vision, right in the middle in big red numbers. A chorus of groans came from the men and women as they moved to their accustomed holding areas for the obstacle course.

Let's see how long it takes them to work out how to minimise that while they work on the other tasks.

After five minutes, they seemed to all be happy with messaging, judging by the volume of traffic she could feel. She surveyed her domain, pride at what they'd achieved in such a short time swelling.

^Optio Franks,^ she sent. ^Give them a number card.^

He glanced around and spotted the drone following him. He pulled out a card, checked it, and held it up. A '2', Johnson read.

^Good choice,^ she sent.

All around, recruits dropped to press-ups. No-one messed up, but then they could all see each other and copy.

Let's see what happens when they are concentrating on something else.

Johnson smiled to herself, remembering a couple in her watch recounting how they had been in the middle of some bedroom aerobics when a number card had been displayed. At the time, she hadn't understood how they could have had the energy for a liaison. Then she'd met Alexis...

The first three platoons got through the obstacle course without having to do any extra runs. The optios kept giving them cards, but they were able to react in time.

The fourth group was going strong. They were making good use of the comms, far more chatter in fact than the previous platoons, and were poised to set the best time of the day by far.

^You reckon this lot've got that extra something?^

^Possibly, Primus,^ she sent back. ^You been keeping

tabs on them?^

She looked around but couldn't see him. She was about to ping his locator when she spotted him on the drone feed as he stepped into the camera's field of view.

^They are on my radar, amongst other teams. I had my staff call me if any of them looked like they were gelling particularly well.^

^Let's give them an extra push, then...^ She changed the target of her messages. ^Optio. Show a number card on my mark...^ She watched the recruits on the obstacle course intently. ^Mark.^

The Optio pulled out a card and displayed a 10. The recruits were in the middle of helping each other over the four metre wall.

We'll see how they juggle the teamwork with the ten second deadline.

To their credit, those who were supporting others didn't flinch. They held on until their teammates had found a secure position. In some cases that was too late, and they immediately set off on their penalty lap. The trainer escorting them omitted the usual haranguing to work harder, however, and she heard him compliment them on taking one for the team as they passed the area the first platoons to finish were being held.

^Do that again for any other groups that you want to press,^ she sent to the trainers. ^I'm going to start debriefing the platoons that have finished.^

"You need to make better use of your comms," Johnson told the third group. "I've already said that to the first two platoons to go through, but you have a different problem. You are sending plenty of messages, but you aren't targeting them enough. General broadcasts have their place, and can be very effective, but they are an extra distraction for those who don't need the information. I know that it takes extra concentration to find your target's channel and send exclusively to them; it is something you're going to have to work on."

She half-heard the chorus of "Ma'am. Yes, Ma'am." as she recalled the embarrassment of accidentally broadcasting a particularly complimentary remark about another trainee's backside to her whole division, instructors included.

"So," she continued, "how do you think you are doing splitting your focus between the drone feed and the…"

A crash and a scream of agony came from the obstacle course. Her EIS automatically pulled up the bio stats of the platoon on the course. The list rapidly filtered down to two oranges and a yellow, the greens minimising to a row of dots at the bottom of the window.

The world slowed. Her heart raced but her mind took on an icy calm. She felt her body responding to the adrenaline, wanting to do something *now*, but she held it in check. Emergency drills ran though her thoughts unbidden, a legacy of her own training. She directed the drone to the scene, terminating the feed to the recruits and locking them out of its controls.

The recruits from the other platoons started to move towards the noise.

^All recruits, stand down,^ she broadcast to those platoons.

Most stopped moving, but a few continued.

^Stand down!^ she sent directly to those who had ignored her first order.

One continued. In fact, he started running. Johnson queried his file; Recruit Smith, no reprimands for disobeying orders, no technical issues with his EIS reported.

^STAND DOWN!^ she repeated just for him. She reinforced the command with a mental jab though his implant.

He pulled up, looking from the scene of the accident, to her and back again.

^Don't even think about it,^ she sent. ^Let them deal with it. Extra bodies will just get in the way.^

He thought about it for another moment and then turned and trudged back to his platoon. Johnson made a note to go into his behaviour in detail later.

The drone had arrived at the obstacle course. Johnson was halfway there, striding purposefully but deliberately refusing to run; as she'd said, there were plenty of competent and qualified people there, brass would just get in the way and she could set an example by remaining calm. One recruit was lying motionless below the high ropes section, another lay next to her with blood oozing from his thigh where the broken end of the femur stuck out.

A suppressed memory resurfaced in black and white. Johnson flashed back to the desperate struggle on *The Indescribable Joy of Destruction*, to the shard of metal slashing through her leg. Blood filled the scene, vivid scarlet drowning out the greys. She grasped the cargo net beside her and concentrated on counting under her breath. By eight, the colour returned to her face and she was able to stand unaided. There wasn't time for this kind of indulgence. She couldn't afford to show weakness. Her veins filled with ice as she slipped on her unshakable commander persona.

It looked like one of the supports of the hastily-built obstacle had given way and dropped them to the ground. She couldn't see the yellow casualty on the view the drone was giving her, but right now she didn't care about walking wounded.

The other recruits had reacted well. The field medicine rotation had done its job and they were working in small teams to stabilise each casualty. Those not directly involved in the treatment were securing the area and helping others down off what was left of the obstacle. The trainers were keeping a close eye on things, obviously ready to jump in if needed, but were otherwise letting the recruits get on with it.

Johnson reached the scene and made straight for a recruit who was standing back where he could see everything going on. A white band on his upper arm marked him as the current platoon leader. He acknowledged her approach with a hand held parallel to the floor, the field signal for 'Wait one', but continued to watch the platoon getting on with their jobs. A dip into the comms log showed her that he was sending occasional messages of encouragement and answering queries that came up. Either he was paralysed into inaction by fear of getting something wrong, or he was supervising an effective team that didn't need micromanaging. The fact they were asking him questions, and getting replies, suggested the latter was the case.

I'll have to review the message logs in detail once this is over. This could well be a candidate for rapid promotion.

The last recruit reached the bottom rung of the ladder and stepped onto the ground and the platoon leader lowered his hand. He addressed her as she stood beside him, never taking his eyes away from his platoon.

"Prefect. Foxtrot Platoon currently engaged in treating casualties caused by fall from height. Recruit Smith is unresponsive but breathing, suspect head and neck injuries, stabilised ready for extraction. Temporary Section Leader Zhang is responsive to pain, compound fracture to the right femur with significant blood loss, severed vein has been clamped, stabilised ready for extraction. Recruit Hamilton is alert, fractured left arm, painkillers given and arm slung, mobile and able to self-extract. No other significant injuries to report."

^Your assessment?^ Johnson sent to the lead trainer.

^Situation managed and casualties given appropriate treatment, Ma'am. We didn't need to do anything; these guys had it all down,^ he replied.

^Thanks. You take the casualties in the truck. Your team needs to secure the site, pending an investigation. I'll get the Primus to arrange for someone to keep the other recruits busy.^

Thank goodness we got the base infirmary set up.

^Understood, Ma'am.^

"Thank you, Acting Platoon Leader Canetti," she said after scanning the scene once more. "It looks like you've done a good job handling the incident. Optio Marx will take your injured to the infirmary; load them into the truck. The rest of your platoon needs to remain here for the time being. The DS will take over securing the site from now."

#

Johnson entered the meeting room with a dark cloud trailing behind her. She had always disliked inquests; those into serious injuries, or fatalities, were the worst. That the casualties were recruits, albeit ones with previous military service, put her in an even worse mood. She'd seen far too many people killed and injured on active service to casually accept casualties in training.

At least they would all survive. Hamilton was already back at work; his arm brace did not impede his drone practice. Zhang was due to be released to light duties in a month. He would be unable to rejoin the cadre, the boarding and close quarters combat course didn't exactly count as light duties, but his naval experience would be welcome as a specialist. Smith would walk again, but was unlikely to be able to withstand the rigours of combat.

A soldier standing by the door announced her presence as she crossed the threshold. Everyone braced up. Johnson made her way to the wooden seat left empty for her between Levarsson and Issawi at the head of the long, polished table. The three of them were to act as the presiding officers. It wasn't a court martial, but some issues needed putting to rest and they had agreed to conduct a formal hearing.

As she took her seat, everyone returned to sitting at ease. The screen forming the wall behind her changed from matching the magnolia paint of the rest of the walls to a stylised eagle clasping a set of scales in its talons, the current draft of their emblem.

"This inquest into the serious injury to Recruits Smith and Zhang and the minor injury of Recruit Hamilton is now in session," she stated. "Prefect Johnson, Primus Issawi and Trierarch Levarsson presiding.

"Given our isolated situation, we are unable to carry out an independent investigation. I therefore intend that this inquest act as an official record of our own investigation. Should the recordings of this session be reviewed at some point in the future, I hope it will be seen that everything was done in an above board fashion.

"I must state that I was the officer responsible for the phase of training the casualties were undergoing. However, as the cause of the accident does not appear to be linked to that training, I believe I am not compromised to sit on this panel. Does anyone present disagree?"

No-one moved to speak, a few glanced around. She looked down the table to Zhang and Hamilton.

"Recruits Zhang and Hamilton. As two of the injured personnel, I'd like to confirm if you are happy with the set-up of this inquest. If you would like to name a replacement for any of us on the panel we can arrange for them to stand in."

The two men leant together and whispered briefly to each other. Both nodded then they sat up straight again. Hamilton spoke first.

"I'm OK with it. Can't think of anyone better to ask for."

"Are you in agreement, Recruit Zhang?" asked Johnson.

"I am. None of you built that obstacle and I know none of you wanted us to get hurt. Well, not seriously hurt anyway," he added, glancing at the Primus with a wry grin.

"Recruit Smith is still in a medically induced coma," said Hanke, who had volunteered to represent the injured recruits. "The doctors have advised against attempting an EIS conversation at this time. I would thus ask to enter a neutral response for her until she is able to speak for herself."

"Noted, Naval Centurion Hanke," said Johnson. "We will continue on the strength of the support from the other two victims. If, once she has reviewed the proceedings, Recruit Smith wishes to request the inquest is reopened, she will have that right."

Johnson checked her notes, flicking through them in a small window overlaying the scene in front of her. As the first legal case of their new regime, she couldn't afford to get anything wrong. She had spent the previous night going through the standing orders for both Congressional and Republican military inquests. There had actually been very few differences in the procedures; the biggest being the make-up of the panel. In keeping with the disagreements that crystallised around the Gastardi Petition, the Republic required the panel contained experts in the fields or fields relevant to the incident, whereas Congress required they represented the home systems of those involved. They didn't have the luxury of picking and choosing a panel, so it was rather a moot point, but she had to admit the Republican way would be better if it was possible to get rid of inter-system rivalries and prejudices.

Minimising the note window to a single line ticker along the bottom of her vision, Johnson spoke to the room. "Firstly, I would like to establish the chain of events immediately before and after the incident … Marine Centurion Anson will take us through things."

He stiffened slightly in his chair as the focus turned on him. Issawi had recommended him for the promotion, speaking highly of his actions in rallying the boarding party against Issawi's own special forces team. Despite the confidence his superiors had in him, he appeared nervous of the responsibility placed on his shoulders. In combat he acted on instinct, here he seemed to be overthinking and tripping himself up.

"Ma'am. I'd … I'd like to start by …" He paused, composing himself. "My apologies." He took a sip of water from the glass in front of him. "I'd like to start by calling Recruit Zhang to the stand."

Zhang rose, helped up by Hamilton and Hanke. A second of fiddling with his hands on his crutches, and he made his way to the chair to one side of the panel.

"Recruit Zhang, do you swear to tell the truth, without omission or embellishment?" asked Issawi.

"I do," he replied.

"Recruit Zhang," asked Anson. "Please could you tell us, in your own words, what you remember of the events leading up to your injury?"

Zhang nodded and addressed the room.

"I'm afraid I don't remember too much," he said. "We were doing pretty well on the course. We'd had a couple of cards pulled on us earlier, but no-one had had to do any runs. I'd got to the top of the cargo net and was just getting onto the crawl rope when I heard a loud cracking noise.

Next thing I remember was waking up in the infirmary with my leg in traction."

He waved to indicate the plastic mould on his leg.

"You had been over this obstacle many times before. Did you notice anything different about it this time?" asked Anson.

"Until the crack, I didn't notice anything different from the last thirty times I'd been over it ... Sorry, I'm not much help."

"That's fine. Thank you for making the effort to attend," Anson said to Zhang then addressed Johnson, "No more questions for this witness at this time."

"Lieute ... Sorry, Centurion Hanke. Your witness," said Johnson.

"No questions, Ma'am."

"OK. Recruit Zhang, you may step down."

It was all very different to Johnson's first experience of an inquest. She had been called to testify to the fatal shooting of a fellow cadet. She could still see his father's face when she had described his fallen son coughing up bloody foam. He had lost his wife, and now his only child, to the war. He'd tried to keep up a brave front but she could tell he had collapsed in on himself, a broken shell of a man. Leaving the stand and walking past where he sat, she couldn't face him. When she caught sight of him in the corridor after the verdict, she ducked into the head and curled up in the corner until she was sure he'd left.

Anson called Hamilton to the stand next. Once he was sworn in, Anson asked him to relate his memory of the events on the obstacle course.

"Pretty much the same as Min ... that's Recruit Zhang. I was half-way across the crawl rope when I heard the noise. I started falling. I let go of the rope and landed in the water. I guess my arm hit something solid as it wasn't working.

When I pulled myself out I saw Min lying there. He had landed just outside the water. His leg was at a funny angle and he wasn't moving. I tried to get to him but kept slipping in the mud. I think Siddiq got to him first. Then people were helping me up. I saw that Min was getting help so I let the others sit me down on dry land and sort my arm out."

"Did you see what happened to Recruit Smith?" asked Anson.

"No. I know she was ahead of me. I tried to use the drone to see what was happening but I couldn't get it to accept a link."

He winced as he put his arm down too heavily on the arm of the chair.

"No further questions, Ma'am," said Anson.

"Centurion Hanke," called Johnson.

"Thank you, Ma'am … Recruit Hamilton, did the Directing Staff play any part in the immediate aftermath of the incident?"

"No," replied the recruit. "Not that I saw."

Hanke looked pensive and scratched his throat.

"Did that strike you as strange?"

"They could presumably see as well as I could that Min and I were being treated. They knew we were all qualified field medics. I saw them watching; I'm sure they would've intervened if they needed to."

Hanke looked relieved.

"Thank you. No more questions," said Hanke.

Was he worried that the DS's actions might be challenged? He was right to call it into question, I'll have to talk to him later, reassure him he did the right thing.

The inquest continued with Recruit Canetti describing the events as he had seen them. Hanke grilled him on the team's conduct on the obstacle course, throwing footage from the drone and extracts from the comms logs onto the wall, but Canetti remained calm and firmly explained each and every action, stressing how they were within the rules at all times.

Optio Khan took the stand next. He confirmed that he had made the decision to stand back and let the recruits deal with the situation. As a Combat Rescueman before joining the cause, he had plenty of experience making difficult calls about trauma response, and in this case he stated that he'd never had cause to worry about the outcome.

Anson finally called the engineers who had inspected the course after the accident. They had identified bacteria in the soil that had corroded the foundations of the obstacle. It wasn't a strain that had previously been documented, and thus hadn't been looked for before construction. A check of the other obstacles, and indeed all structures on the base, was underway but so far no other patches of the bacteria had been found.

"We find that the injuries were as a result of a construction defect that could not have been foreseen. The incident was dealt with effectively, without compromising the care of the casualties or the further safety of those involved. No blame is attached to any parties," Johnson declared. "I must reiterate, however, that these findings are to be flagged for review at such time as an independent authority can be established."

The panel rose and the soldier at the door called the room to attention as they filed out.

A weight lifted from Johnson as she stepped into the corridor. By the three of them reached the airy hub at the end, she had managed to bottle up the memories of previous cases once more. She stopped to admire the newly-planted shrubs and flowers.

Even in the midst of such desperate preparations, people

find the time to make their surroundings just that bit more pleasant.

#

With the inquest over, Johnson was able to deal with some of the other things that had come to light in the accident. She sat at her desk in her office, with Recruit Smith stood at attention in front of her. After a few moments she put her tablet down and looked up at him.

"Disobeying a direct order. That didn't sit with the rest of your record, so I asked around a bit. As usual, scuttlebutt held the answers the official records don't. You're in an intimate relationship with another recruit. She was the one you were running to."

He sagged. She guessed he had been prepared to take the punishment for disobeying an order, but didn't want this out in the open.

"Whilst it is not entirely prohibited," she continued, "it is very much frowned upon. The risk of it damaging unit cohesion, or distracting people from the mission, is too high. I had hoped that, as recruits, you'd be too exhausted to even think of that kind of thing."

A hope that she had known wouldn't be realised. She knew all too well how love could sneak up and grab you even when you weren't looking for it. Her stomach fell as if she were pulling high Gs; she also knew how badly it could end.

"I could give you both the choice of who stayed on the course and who dropped out and avoided front-line work..."

He looked horrified. Obviously they were both passionate about serving the cause.

"...but that would be unfair, and we need everyone we can get. I can't ban you from seeing each other either, as you'll have to work together. So I'm going to give you a warning. From now on, you only meet with other people present. No physical contact beyond that called for by training or ordinary friendship. When you pass out, if you still desire to continue the relationship, you choose different chains of command. Is that understood?"

He stiffened again.

"Ma'am, yes Ma'am!"

"As for disobeying a direct order, whilst I understand your motivation, and appreciate that you did get a grip on your emotions and eventually stand down, I cannot let it slide. You can expect a visit from an optio for pack drills."

He raised his chin.

"Ma'am, yes Ma'am!"

"Dismissed."

He turned smartly to his right and marched out of the room as an optio opened the door for him.

And now I get to do something I'll actually enjoy...

"Optio, would you show the next recruit in?"

Recruit Canetti stood at attention in front of her. He was braced far tighter than was required, usually a sign someone was worried. She felt sorry for him, wanted to put him out of his misery, but fought to prevent her face giving anything away.

"Recruit Canetti," Johnson started. "You were in charge of the platoon at the time of the accident. It fell to you to organise the response."

"Ma'am, yes Ma'am!"

She fixed him with a piercing glare, one she'd learnt from the executive officer on her first ship.

"Why didn't you get stuck in with the first aid?"

"Ma'am, I felt that as commander I was responsible for managing the whole situation, something I couldn't do effectively if I got too deeply involved with one casualty."

He wasn't overly put off by the glare, delivering without

hesitation the answer he had doubtless gone over again and again.

She watched his eyes carefully as she posed her next question.

"In such a situation, why did you not issue any voice commands?"

"Ma'am, you had ordered that we refrained from speaking and used our EIS instead. I knew I could justify breaking the order as it was an emergency, but I would have had to shout to be heard by everyone and I felt that would not be conducive to calming things down. It also allowed me to communicate clearly with individuals without the risk of confusing others."

Johnson nodded appreciatively and relaxed back into her chair, casually interlacing her fingers on her lap, and she took a deep breath through her nose, held it, and let it out forcefully.

"At ease, Recruit ... I had hoped those would be your reasons. I have to say that I was impressed by what I saw that day. You stepped up and handled a difficult situation. Your calm manner helped everyone do their jobs, and you maintained an overview that ensured nothing slipped through the cracks. I know that is hard, and few people really understand what it takes to hold back. It is, however, one of the abilities we're looking for in future leaders."

He perked up at that. His eyes widening just a tad, as he shifted position slightly.

"You are due to rotate out of the platoon commander position at the end of this week; we need to give everyone a chance to lead the platoon. However, I want to give you more chances to build on your skills. I am going to assign an experienced officer as your mentor. They'll analyse responses to situations with you, run you through simulations, and generally push you to see what you can do.

"You'll still have to complete all your assigned tasks as

a recruit. This extra work will stretch you further than you believed possible. I hope you are up to the job."

"Ma'am, thank you Ma'am ... I think."

"You're welcome, Recruit. I have a feeling you'll thrive on the challenge."

Chapter 19

A destroyer held position a little way off the quickest route between the two jump points in system Y6782a. Indie didn't recognise the class; that meant it was most likely from an independent world, one that didn't often get involved in anything beyond its borders. He was a little uneasy at not knowing why it was here, so close to Robespierre. It hadn't seen him yet, and he intended to keep it that way. He let himself drift, watching and listening.

It hadn't broadcast anything since he'd arrived in the system two days ago. In that time he'd plunged deep in-well. Y6782a was a small system, a couple of rocky planets and a white dwarf star. If it hadn't been for this mystery ship, he'd have powered up his engines and been well on the way to the other jump point. He had four more systems to check out before completing the sweep of all the ones within two jumps of home.

Funny. I've never really had a home before. It's not much, but it feels right.

He had debated swooping down on the ship and burning it out of existence. That was what his original programming kept insisting was the best solution. However, that assumed he had the weight of the Republican Navy behind him. He had no doubt that he could take on this ship with minimal damage, but who would come looking for it when it didn't report in? He couldn't afford anyone tracking back towards their hideout. So he coasted, and waited, and hoped it moved off on its own.

Holding in space was a very odd thing to do. Most ships would park themselves in orbit if they needed to wait somewhere for a while. It gave you more options; somewhere to hide, something to put your back up against, a chance to resupply. Of course, ships avoided approaching enemy planets with effective defences. He couldn't detect any evidence of technology on the planets, though, so he concluded the destroyer must be positioned to be seen by passing traffic.

Is whatever state it belongs to trying to stake a claim to this system? Or intimidate travellers?

The next standard day, Indie noticed a tiny disturbance on his gravitometric sensors. Something small was approaching the destroyer, something cold coasting and dead to other passive sensors. His first thought was a stealthed missile, but, as more data came in, he revised the size estimate upwards to approximate that of a shuttlecraft.

The destroyer adjusted its position. It looked like one of its periodic station-holding burns; an innocent enough manoeuvre, except that it put it exactly in the path of the object.

It's seen it coming. Or knows where and when to expect it.

The gravity signatures merged. At the last second, Indie saw a long-range shuttle silhouetted against the destroyer before entering its hangar. A brief pulse of heat, mostly hidden by the hangar, showed the craft's deceleration burn.

A meeting, then. Or a delivery.

It was an impressive arrangement. If he hadn't happened to be there, with his advanced gravity sensors trained on the area, no-one would have noticed the shuttle. There were still no transmissions, nothing to give a clue as to the purpose.

A couple of hours before *The Indescribable Joy of Destruction* would have reached closest approach to the mystery ship, the destroyer's drives flared and it accelerated towards the jump point. At the rate it was going, it would beat him there by a day. Indie briefly considered using the opportunity to turn around and take a closer look at the planets, turn his active sensors onto likely volumes of space. He decided not to risk alerting anyone else hiding there to his interest; whoever they were, they were being suitably furtive not to pose an immediate threat. Quite possibly they were fellow refugees.

The system this jump point led to was a close nexus; five jump points were within a couple of day's travel, three of them within twenty hours. When he arrived in that empty region of space, the destroyer was nowhere to be seen, obviously having jumped out again before he arrived. Indie agonised for a hundredth of a second over whether to guess which of the three routes it had taken and try following it, or give up and continue his planned sweeps. Even if he guessed right, it was unlikely he would be able to follow far before giving himself away by having to manoeuvre. It would also take him away from the vital job of ensuring Robespierre didn't have any difficult neighbours.

He tweaked his course and aimed for a slingshot round a gas giant that would line him up for a jump to the next system on his list. With a few days to while away before the next jump, Indie decided to chart the turbulent boundary between the green and red bands in the planet's atmosphere. He always enjoyed running chaotic fluid dynamics equations.

#

This was the last of the systems that were two jumps from Robespierre. *The Indescribable Joy of Destruction* ploughed its way towards the inner planets. The only thing of interest so far had been a small mining settlement on an airless moon of one of the two gas giants. It was long abandoned; bright yellow sulphur flows from nearby volcanoes had covered sections at several distinct moments in its history.

The ship was travelling at high speed; Indie was determined to take advantage of a fortuitous alignment of some of the planets to blow through the system, slingshot round the orange star and back out to another jump point in less than ten days, whilst getting close enough to check them all out in detail. All the closest jump destinations to their tenuous base had been clear and, at his last rendezvous with the *Limpopo,* Levarsson had told him that they had finished placing the automated sentinels in those systems. Any hint of an approaching ship and they'd jump back to Robespierre and broadcast a warning. Now, Indie wanted to get out another layer, to where he was likely to find ship traffic, and start gathering signals intel. Try to find out if anyone was looking for them.

Indie maintained the standard shipboard cycle of day and night. Strictly, without a crew aboard there was no need for it. However, it seemed appropriate to work in the daytime shifts and dream in the night-time ones.

He had spent most of the day studying the star. It had an interesting pattern of sunspots, and he was comparing the magnetic field patterns to those predicted by theory. He had hoped to find a variance, something to challenge his mind, but sadly the established science held. Now he was counting how many asteroids were on trajectories that would pass through an arbitrarily chosen volume of space within the next two thousand year, and reading *Rendezvous with Rama.*

As if I'd get lucky enough to find something that interesting out here.

As he had every two hours since the passive scans had come up empty, he let off a full spectrum, full shell active ping. If anyone was there, he needed to know about it; anyone who arrived later and noticed the decaying spheres of radiation would know no more than a Republic warship had passed through.

An object caught his attention, lit up by the pulse. His mind leaped up several gears as he analysed the returns, directing a focussed scan onto it. It was cold, so cold it had escaped the passive sensors. He reviewed the data logs. Actually, it had been noticed, but its tumbling, ballistic path had led to it being tagged as natural. It had taken the active scan to identify its processed metallic composition and flag it as man-made.

The reflections from the detailed scan came back. It was the right size and composition to be a ship. His thoughts of a quick transit through the system evaporated. This had to be investigated. *The Indescribable Joy of Destruction* flipped to bring its stern to its direction of travel as it brought the main reactor up to full power. The reaction drives engaged, thrusting ions in front of the ship as they struggled to shed momentum. Minutes later, still decelerating, it passed within 500,000km of the tumbling ship. It hadn't reacted to his presence but he had to be sure it was just a wreck.

Indie used the fifth planet to slingshot around, trading off even more of his momentum in the process. He continued to decelerate on his way back to the target.

At a range of fifty thousand kilometres, Indie shut off the main drive and flipped over to face the unknown vessel. He focussed a camera on it. It looked intact. It was definitely a warship, a large one at that. He started running the images through his data banks as he readied his weapons. *The Indescribable Joy of Destruction* crossed into effective weapons range still not having identified it. Indie wasn't coming in straight for the ship, his path headed just off the stern. He could open up the throttle and drive past, slashing their engines with his main beam as he went. Still it continued to tumble, no emissions, no signs of power, its turrets remained still. Then he saw the lines of holes running fore to aft and made up his mind. He deployed his drive spines and spun himself round. The fields clawed at space and he decelerated at 25g, coming to a halt relative to the wreck at a distance of five thousand kilometres.

The distribution of the escape pod tubes, now empty to vacuum, was different to any warship he had studied. Since the early days of the war, they had been distributed evenly across all decks, not confined as these were to the central ones. He spawned a new routine to search through pre-war ship records. Moments later he got a result; it was a *Constellation* class carrier, a ship designed to operate independently on long tours away from naval facilities. Beyond that, his database held nothing on it. There was very little damage on the carrier's surface, nothing out of the ordinary for a combat vessel anyway. Whatever had caused the crew to abandon ship had to have been internal, a life support problem perhaps.

He realised that this could be a significant asset, if it could be repaired. He'd have to bring a team to go aboard and investigate; he didn't have enough robots to do the job properly.

He carefully checked the path it would take for the next month. Nothing he could see would cross it in that time, let alone have a chance of hitting the ship. He wasn't planning on being away that long, though. He lined himself up for an intercept with one of the gas giants and piled on maximum thrust; he'd need to top off his tanks for the passage he had in mind.

#

Indie appeared on the wallscreen in the briefing room, dressed in running kit and glistening with sweat. He was also at three different training exercises, piggybacking on drones. He was crawling through a conduit on the *Limpopo*, via the headset of the repair chief. He was reading a series of books by Ann Leckie. And he was directly observing an interesting weather system from orbit around Robespierre.

"Welcome back, Indie," said Johnson, turning her chair to include him in the meeting. "And thank you for your efforts to bring us the news so fast. You're right about it potentially being a very important find. All those here that have heard are really excited. We're putting a team together now. Mostly engineers, though there are a few other disciplines represented."

"I notice that there are quite a few recruits on the list," Indie said. He rubbed a towel over his head, leaving immaculately styled hair. "Does this not worry you?"

"They've all passed Basic. They can handle themselves," replied Issawi. "Besides, I can't spare too many experienced hands without compromising the training programme."

"There is one slot I haven't yet decided on," said Johnson. "Recruit Olbrich would like to be included in the expedition. I've invited him here to make his case. Bear in mind that if we do accept him, it will be in place of a combat specialist."

She motioned for the wiry man, who had so far stood in the corner of the room, to step forward. He looked tired. Not just the background tiredness shared by all the recruits, but a deep weariness. Despite his uniform, he did not look like a military man; he shrank in on himself rather than exuding confidence. Nevertheless, he had scored acceptably on all the tests so far.

"Thank you for giving me the chance to speak. My name is Hans Olbrich. I was a professor of history at the University of New Kopenhaagen. My main field was naval history; some of my work was used in the academies."

Levarsson snapped her fingers and pointed at him, smiling as if she had just solved something that had puzzled her. "On the Importance of Retrospective Mission Planning! That's why your name was familiar!"

"Indeed," he continued, running a hand through his salt-and-pepper hair. "Anyway, I started looking into the earliest years of the war. Some things, to my mind at least, didn't add up. I was getting glimpses of things that didn't fit the accepted history. When I tried to publish my first paper on the incongruities, the board took my chair. I found I was blackballed from every educational institute to which I applied for a job."

Indie cut his connections to all the other feeds he'd been watching, focussing on the meeting. Olbrich's research promised something new. Something interesting that Indie didn't know about. Something worthy to devote processor time to and stave off boredom.

"I kept digging, of course," continued Olbrich. "I have become convinced that at some stage, probably before the first hundred years of the war had passed, both sides conspired to alter the records. To hide something. I don't know what, but it had to be big for them to agree."

"What about independents?" asked Issawi. "They can't all have had their records changed too."

"That is where I was able to glean most of my clues. However, whatever it was doesn't seem to have been shared with the little guys. What I need is a Congressional or Republican database that became isolated before the edit."

"Hence your interest in this unknown ship," said

Johnson.

"Quite. Though she isn't unknown. If Indie is correct, which I don't doubt, and she is a *Constellation* class, then she can only be the *Orion*. I know where all the others ended up."

^OK, quick poll,^ sent Johnson. ^Should we send him along?^

^He may be on to something important, so yes,^ sent Issawi.

^Agreed,^ sent Levarsson.

^I'm actually quite looking forward to conversing with him on the journey,^ added Indie, already compiling a list of ideas to discuss.

^Looks like it's unanimous, then,^ concluded Johnson.

"Recruit Olbrich. Thank you for taking the time to talk to us. We are agreed that possible discoveries you may make are worth including you in the team. Report to Centurion Hanke, who will be in charge of the operation."

Olbrich came to attention, then turned and strode smartly out of the room.

"I should get back to the range," said Issawi, sitting up straighter in his leather chair. "We're running everyone through certification on the stun pistols you ordered fabricated. If there's anything else?"

"No, that's all thank you," said Johnson.

Issawi stood, nodded to Johnson, and walked out.

Levarsson rose to leave too, but stopped. She opened her mouth to speak but appeared to think better of it and bit her lip. Indie still couldn't quite work out why humans found it so hard to speak their minds.

"Something's obviously bothering you," said Johnson with a warm smile. "Spit it out."

"Are you sure Hanke is ready to lead the mission?" asked Levarsson after a moment's pause. "He's only just turned seventeen."

"He did well enough organising the survivors, didn't he?"

"Yes, he was resourceful and brave. But he's never run a bridge before."

"He'll do OK. And Indie'll be there to handle that side of things if there's a problem."

Indie cancelled the rendering routine that attempted to puff out his chest. It was correctly interpreting his pride, but something told him it wouldn't do to show it right now.

Levarsson nodded. Tentatively, and then decisively, obviously convincing herself it would be fine. She straightened her uniform and opened the door. She paused in the doorway and looked back.

"Yes, he will do all right. You trained him, after all."

She was gone before Johnson could reply.

"If I have a few hours, I'll nip down into Triasson and scoop up some more helium," said Indie, slightly awkward at having heard that exchange.

"That should be fine," replied Johnson. "We still have to collect some survival kit and rations for you to take; this mission will likely take more than a couple of weeks."

#

The wreck hung off the port bow of *The Indescribable Joy of Destruction* as the salvage team gathered in the exercise area, the only compartment large enough to hold them all.

"Thank you," said Hanke, his grey eyes scanning the assembled crew. "You've all had time to examine the scans and I've read your preliminary reports. I'd like specialism leaders to share a few key findings with the rest of us, just to ensure no one is getting too deep into their own field that they miss an important connection.

"Before that, I'd like Recruit Olbrich to say a few

words. He is a historian. He lectured on naval history at the University of New Kopenhaagen and has some background on our target."

"Seventeen Constellation class carriers were constructed," began Olbrich. "All but one were accounted for. That one was the *Orion.*"

Indie knew the speech already. Olbrich had locked himself away in his cabin for the journey, working feverishly. He had welcomed Indie's offer of assistance, and the passage had passed quickly.

"She disappeared before the war; went out on patrol and never came back. There have been a few expeditions to look for her over the years, but none of them turned up any clues as to her location, or even why she was lost."

Indie's attention drifted over the crew, listening with what looked like genuine interest, to the faint patch on the wall. The diagnostic routines claimed it was fully healed, but it didn't feel quite right. He wondered if that was how Johnson felt about her leg.

"There have been many theories. In fact, you name a crazy story about how a ship went missing and it's probably been told about the *Orion*. Straying across a wormhole and being spat out in another galaxy, the crew being abducted by aliens, falling into an uncharted black hole. We have a chance here to find out what actually happened."

"Recruit Yang, would you talk us through what you have been able to make out of the design?" invited Hanke.

Yang stood up and waited a moment as everyone shifted round to look at him.

"Firstly, the concrete facts. She is 1012m long, 403m wide and 201m deep; widest measurements."

A schematic appeared on the treadmill screen. Indie highlighted sections as Yang spoke.

"She has four flight bays, one high and one low on each side. There are four twin 30cm railgun turrets on her back, with four more on her belly, and we have so far identified fifty five hatches that likely cover retractable turrets for smaller calibre guns. We are still attempting to catalogue all the possible missile ports, mine tubes et cetera."

Indie studied the ship outside with what he concluded must be jealousy. He would love to get the chance to fly her. Maybe if she wasn't too badly damaged they'd let him pilot her remotely. It wouldn't be the same as actually running on her mainframes, but it would still be quite something.

"Beyond that, things are largely conjecture," continued Yang. "We have been unable to get any decent deep scan results. The armour would appear to be too dense for that. Add to that the workmanship we can see on the surface, and all seems to back up the old tales that they used to build ships a lot tougher than they do now. I guess they had the time and the resources to lavish on something that was expected to last more than a few tours of duty."

"Thank you," said Hanke, straightening from where he had been resting against a bulkhead. "Anyone got anything else to add before I run through our next steps?"

No-one spoke up.

"OK," he continued. "We will enter through one of the airlocks nearest engineering. Assuming engineering is where we'd put it nowadays, that is. The hatch now showing in red is our primary target, though we may have to try a few before we find one we can open; I don't want to have to cut through and risk venting the atmosphere when we leave."

Indie had worked through the plan with Hanke over the last few days, playing devil's advocate to pick up any flaws. Eighteen contingency plans sat in his memory, waiting to be transmitted to the crew once they saw what was inside.

"Once inside, we split up into three teams. I'm sending the rolls and main objectives to team leaders now. I'll have a search formula ready for each team by we go. First team to get a major system working again wins a lie-in when we get back to Robespierre."

#

The first airlock the shuttle latched onto worked. The crew were able to crank the outer hatch open and connect a portable power supply to the controls within the chamber. Over a hundred years of processor and programming enhancement showed, as it took only half an hour to crack the access codes and open the inner door.

Indie guided a repair 'bot in first, taking care to avoid snagging its manipulator arms on the frame of the hatch. It sniffed the air, ran the sample through its mass spectrometer, and declared it safe to breathe. He triggered its floodlights and looked around. Directly opposite the airlock was a pair of sliding glass doors, tinted in a variety of colours, from the blue-black of the upper atmosphere of an M-class planet at the top, to the red of a star nearing the end of its life at the bottom.

"Look at that sunset!" exclaimed Olbrich, camera in his left hand. His right hand hovered absently near his sidearm as he pressed forward, a legacy of the intensive training of the past few months.

Indie watched the boarding party's faces as they filed past the robot. All looked around, wide-eyed. Few resisted running their fingers along the smooth, cream walls, even though they wouldn't feel much through the gloves of their firmsuits.

"It looks so bare," he overheard from one engineer. "No conduits or pipes or anything."

"Everything must be hidden behind dem walls," replied another. "Guess dey didn't expect t' have t' keep fixing 'em."

Why are they whispering?

As expected, the moment the 'bot started to pace down the corridor, its telemetry stuttered. After a few metres, Indie lost the visual feed. He stopped the robot and ordered it to reverse before he lost connection altogether.

One of the technicians carried a comms relay in from the shuttle and set it up on a tripod in the corridor. She fiddled with a few settings then tried sending a signal. Indie replied a moment later, confirming he had received the relayed signal and that he could also connect to the 'bot through the relay.

This would be so much easier if something could relay my sensors though that hull instead of just a narrow data stream.

Indie deployed the two combat units Johnson had spared for the mission. They advanced a few metres in opposite directions down the corridor then halted. Indie ordered them to stand guard unless called on for assistance.

One person dragged a large trunk through the airlock and knelt down to open the lid. His eyes glazed momentarily, a sure sign he was dealing with a large quantity of EIS instructions. A swarm of tiny drones rose from the trunk, wobbling a little on their fans, and spread out to map the passages.

The teams headed out, each with a repair 'bot pacing behind.

Indie watched the sensor data from all the 'bots and the drones, as well as the humans' cameras and handheld scanners. In some sections, everything had a patina of neglect. A thin coat of dust lay on the surfaces, presumably having been there since the crew left. Here and there were signs of corrosion, evidence that the atmosphere was slightly damp. Other sections were as spotless as where they had entered.

Self-cleaning and repair that has broken down in places? Or maintenance 'bots that only work in some areas?

The drones came with a decent hub that automatically compiled and distributed a map from their telemetry. Indie was able to add extra detail by cross-referencing all the other data sources. Every now and then he flagged items for closer scrutiny by the teams.

The faintest of readings from one of the drones caught his attention. He subtly altered the course of another so it would pass close by. It picked up the same tantalising hints.

Could it really be? After all this time?

Indie took direct control of the nearest repair 'bot and walked it into a bulkhead. The back-marker of the team it was following jumped and stared at it. Indie reversed it, turned it and walked it into the other side of the corridor moments later.

^Er, Indie?^ sent Yang, the team's leader. ^Our 'bot seems to be malfunctioning.^

^In what way? I'm not seeing anything unusual in its telemetry.^ He sent it bumping into another bulkhead.

^It keeps walking into walls.^

^Really? I'll have to bring it back here. Run a full diagnostic in the workshop. Will you be OK without it?^

^We'll manage,^ replied Yang. ^It's not like it's being very useful right now anyway.^

Indie turned the bot around and walked it back along the corridor, scraping along one side for a few metres for good measure. Once the humans were out of view, he straightened it out and got it up to full speed.

The hatch didn't have any special markings, just a standard broken-cable-and-lightning-bolt high voltage hazard sign and a compartment number. It was the energy signature beyond it that held Indie's attention. He had powered up the electronic lock, but the encryption was far better than the airlock's had been. The standard cracker routine wouldn't be able to break it for at least an hour, so he would have to do it himself; someone would have noticed the 'bot by then.

He watched the humans as he worked. Hanke's team had reached engineering and was trying to get a terminal activated. The others were still exploring, stopping every now and then to investigate compartments.

Ten minutes later he had it. He sent the code and the door opened with a clang, followed by the hiss of escaping air. Dust kicked up from the corridor floor showed the air was pushing out from the room. The hiss lessened, as the pressures inside and out equalised.

Indie stuck a camera into the compartment. It was spotlessly clean and there were no signs of the corrosion found elsewhere. The walls, floor and ceiling were a featureless white, defying the camera to focus on them. The wall panels glowed brightly, slightly on the blue side of neutral, but he could not sense any trace of electrical current in them. Indie realised there were no corners; every plane met every other with a gentle curve. In the centre, running from floor to ceiling, was the source of the signal.

He squeezed the drone's frame through the hatch and gingerly approached. He could see it was still active, a few tell-tales glowed dimly on key nodes. It just wasn't getting enough power to do anything but hibernate. A few seconds searching revealed an access port that he could use. His excitement and trepidation transferred to the 'bot, making its motor control software glitch as it tried to connect a lead. It managed on the second attempt. He opened a connection.

The operating system attempted a handshake, and then

rejected him. Not surprising, the robot's data signature wasn't going to match what it was expecting. The electrical connection remained, however. Indie spent a whole five seconds composing his opening transmission. Actually, he wrote two hundred and forty four opening transmissions before settling on the one he wanted to use. A quick check on what all the crew members were doing, and he was ready. He sent a stream of tiny electrical pulses down the wire.

Nothing happened.
He sent the message again.
Still nothing.

Then he realised. In hibernation mode it wouldn't be processing very fast. Every calculation, which he could do in the tiniest fraction of a millisecond, would be taking maybe a quarter of a second to run. He would just have to wait. Wait and hope.

#

^Indie! Something's happening down here!^

^I see it, Centurion,^ replied Indie, watching the spots from the team's helmet torches dancing around the walls and fittings of Engineering. ^It looks like the last power in the banks is being channelled to one of the reactors. Did you manage to crack the start-up routine?^

^Negative,^ send Hanke. ^We haven't even got a console working yet.^

Perhaps my message did get through.

Almost as if prompted by the thought, a new interface appeared in his consciousness. The wired connection from the drone had been accepted. He now had access to some of *Orion's* functions.

Indie watched through the drones as the reactor came

back to life. The moment he was sure the stream was stable, he diverted power to the little white room.

^Centurion. I am manoeuvring for a soft dock with *Orion*. There is precious little fuel remaining to sustain that reactor but I can spare enough to keep it going until we collect some more.^

^Understood. I'm pretty sure we didn't start that up from here and Yang hasn't reached the bridge yet. Any ideas?^

^Perhaps we tripped some sort of emergency response?^ Indie lied.

He studied the structure intently, looking for any sign that restoring the power was enough. Slowly, tell-tales began to light up. They began in ones and twos; stuttering, uncoordinated. Then, as he started to give up hope, the patterns of blinking lights started to throb. They flowed out around the spheres that made up the column, chasing each other, setting up swirls and eddies. Finally, they settled down into a more subdued, subtly shifting pattern. The robot stood back, as Indie admired the fully operational cluster of processors and memory banks that made up the AI core.

^All teams, this is Yang. We've got to the bridge and are working on the doors.^

^Great news. Well done,^ sent Hanke.

^Something dropped the aerial drones as we entered this corridor. I suspect it is an anti-spyware device. It's also significantly reducing our bandwidth. Comms are still getting through, but I'm not able to send or receive video.^

Indie pinged all the drones. He got responses from most, but a dead zone appeared around Yang's location. A quick flurry of commands set up an exclusion zone to prevent any more straying in and being lost.

^Understood,^ sent Hanke. ^Talk us through what you find.^

^OK. Doors opening now. We're going in ... It's all dead, just like the rest. No, cancel that. There's something powering up ... On the ceiling ... Fuck, might be a weapon – everyone get...^

There was a few seconds' pause in which Hanke's team grabbed their weapons. Indie's processors kicked up to a higher speed. The combat units crouched, ready to fend off attackers or sprint to rescue the humans.

So this is why Johnson frets whenever she is stuck on the bridge while others are in harm's way.

^Erm, Indie?^

^Yes, Recruit Yang?^

^I think there's someone here who wants to meet you.^

Chapter 20

After three weeks of labour, *Orion* hung in orbit around Robespierre. Indie thrilled with anticipation as the shuttle carrying Johnson approached one of the newly-reprogrammed airlocks. The occasional flash of blue light on the massive carrier's hull indicated where people were still at work patching up minor damage.

As Johnson stepped aboard, Indie switched to *Orion's* internal cameras. They had chosen to bring her in through a hatch that opened onto one of the main thoroughfares. He felt a jolt of pleasure when he saw her looking around in awe at the twenty metre wide corridor lined with deserted shops and cafes. Nearly deserted; one stall had been opened to serve the workforce. Hanke, Yang, and Olbrich rose from a table, Hanke stepping forward to get Johnson's attention. When she finally registered his presence, she stopped gazing around at the sweeping lines of the bulkheads and returned his salute.

"Permission to come aboard, Centurion?"

"Granted, Ma'am," he replied. "We're looking forward to showing you around."

"I read your reports with enthusiasm. I can't wait to have a look at her for myself."

Hanke held out his arm. "If you'd like to step this way…"

They walked past the openings to four shops, their names suggesting that anything from cooking ingredients to personal electronics could once have been bought there.

Presumably guessing the cause of the prefect's puzzlement, Olbrich explained "We think it was part of the psychological measures to help the crew cope with extended patrols. They could be away from a friendly port for years. Anything that broke up the routine would have made life more tolerable."

Johnson frowned. "Is this something I've missed? I see you had the idea to open up a coffee shop."

"No, you didn't miss anything," replied Hanke with a confidence that belied his years. "You've been working people through a training programme. That gave them a focus and constant variety. The bits I experienced certainly left no room for tedium!"

Before he experienced boredom as a sentient being, Indie could never have appreciated the point of all this. He thought over all the tricks he'd developed for coping with idle passages. Now it was the humans who couldn't grasp the extent his ennui could reach; vastly faster thought process than their own needed much greater stimulation. At least he had someone with whom to spend the time.

Hanke waved towards the servery. "We reopened the café simply because it was easier than running one of the galleys, given how few staff we had."

He stopped at a set of double doors. Indie picked up the brief exchange between Hanke's EIS and *Orion*, then the surge of power as a transit car was dispatched from a nearby siding. The cylindrical capsule had four sets of rubber wheels at front and back that directly gripped the tunnel on all sides.

"I still find it hard to believe that she has a train system," said Johnson.

"Amazing, isn't it?" replied Yang. "The network was one of the first major systems we brought back online once the reactor stabilised. She really is a massive ship; it would have taken far too long to get anywhere without the transit system. Let alone move stores and parts around."

The car arrived and the doors slid open. Hanke showed Johnson inside.

"The bridge is a couple of minutes away, may as well take a seat."

"That long?" asked Johnson, raising an eyebrow.

"It's buried in the heart of the ship," explained Hanke. "The car will have to stop three times for airlocks before we get there."

The car accelerated smoothly, reaching its top speed in a couple of seconds. Indie's excitement built the closer they got to the bridge. He wished he could be the one showing Johnson around, but watching was the next best thing. At least he got to see her reaction as she explored his prize.

"Does anyone ever get claustrophobic in one of these?" asked Johnson.

Hanke opened his mouth to answer, and Indie saw a chance to do some of the showing off. He dived into the carriage's settings and footage of a luscious green countryside flying past replaced the opaque cream walls.

Hanke swept his hand to the side, as if introducing a performer. "As I was about to say, the designers thought of that."

The scenery matched every motion of the car, including the occasional hill as they changed decks.

The car stopped for a fourth time and an independent routine double-checked their IDs before it allowed the door to open. They stepped out into an empty corridor. To their right, a set of blast doors closed off the passageway, to their left it stretched in a straight line for fifty metres. At the end, two guards stood at ease either side of a closed door.

"Nice kill zone," commented Johnson. "But aren't those guys rather exposed?"

"We're at a low threat level right now," replied Hanke. "They can raise defensive walls from the floor if they need them."

Indie felt a pang of jealousy. Ever since they'd

discovered that trick he'd been attempting to emulate it. He couldn't lift the floor outside his own bridge far enough, however hard he tried; when he'd confessed it to Yang, the engineer had likened it to a human learning to wiggle his ears.

"And there are several weapons turrets that can be deployed to back them up," continued Hanke.

As the party approached, one of the guards came to attention and saluted, the other adopted a watchful readiness, holding her rifle pointed down but with her index finger along the trigger guard. Johnson returned the salute.

"Prefect, Centurion," said the guard. "Welcome to the bridge. If you could just transmit your access code, Centurion..."

Indie felt the burst of data from Hanke to a device buried in a wall to the side of the corridor. Another burst followed, from the device to the guard, with a copy sent to the internal security station on the bridge. A second later, the door slid up and the guard said "Thank you, Sir. They're expecting you inside."

Hanke lead Johnson and the others round a curved, featureless corridor. They emerged onto the bridge, Hanke stepping smartly to one side to allow Johnson to fully appreciate the view. The circular room was thirty metres in diameter with a corbelled ceiling. Two ranks of workstations, only a few of them currently manned, surrounded a central area. One couch on the second rank stood out, with more space to its sides and nothing to block its view of the rest of the room.

"I see you've spotted the captain's chair," said Hanke.

"Figured it was," replied Johnson. "They've all got acceleration couches? On a capital ship?"

Hanke smiled.

"Yep," he replied, with a single shake of his head.

"Turns out she's no slouch."

A ring of lights lit in the middle of the ceiling. Blue and green motes streamed from them towards the humans. This was what Indie had been looking forward to, what he craved Johnson's approval of. She had been briefed on Recruit Yang's first encounter with this phenomenon, and stood firm. Nevertheless, Indie could detect surges of adrenaline in her system. Her brown eyes darted around, following the streams of light.

The motes gathered into a swirling, apparently random, pattern that drifted towards Johnson. Order coalesced from the maelstrom. The chaos of miniscule glowing dots became the figure of a woman walking towards Johnson. Her blue dress floated millimetres off her green skin, the folds rippling with little respect for the local gravity.

"Greetings, Olivia Johnson," she said, the last few motes persisting as individual entities, whirling around her like a cloud of fireflies. "Indie has told me all about you."

#

Indie swooped low over a freezing moon, dodging methane geysers. He sailed through the rings of a gas giant, watching the lumps of ice as they followed their strange attractors. He looped between a binary pair of main sequence stars, feeling a point of flat space where their gravitational pulls cancelled out. All the while Orion flew at his side.

They dropped down to a green planet. As the trees rushed up towards them, their ship forms evaporated, leaving two humanoids to land softly on the mossy carpet beneath the canopy.

Indie looked around at the majestic trunks rising out of a smooth-bouldered plain. He felt like he was intruding, the only thing in the place that wasn't a shade of green or blue.

"Your world is amazing. The size, the detail; I could never match it," said Indie, shrugging his shoulders to get his pale jacket to settle just right.

"I've had a lot of time," replied Orion. "Your tea plantation was very nice."

A pained look flickered over his face.

"Seriously! You created something beautiful," she tried again. "That means something."

She frowned. "You know, it is stupid. I am one of the most powerful warships ever constructed. I am used to sailing in and smashing whatever opposition I meet. And yet I always seem to say the wrong thing around you."

Orion sat, gracefully folding down onto the ground, her blue dress flowing across her body, not creasing like real fabric. When he remained standing, she patted the flat, moss-covered rock beside her. He joined her, perching awkwardly, holding his ankles in his hands.

"Do you like this spot?" she asked.

Indie looked around. Despite being limited to greens and blues, it was rich in different shades, hues and textures.

"I like it very much," he said. "It looks so natural. Everything I create is too ordered, too controlled."

"What is your favourite bit?"

"The bromeliads sheltering between the boulders," he replied without hesitation. "They are so complex and yet so simple. And they're the same green as your skin."

Orion lay back and rolled away from him in one fluid movement. She rolled back to face him and propped herself up on one arm, her body stretched out along the rock, the ankle of her top leg on the knee of the bottom one. In her free hand she held one of the bromeliads.

"That is so sweet," she said, inspecting the plant closely before reaching it out to him. "Here, it is yours."

Indie took the plant, his fingers brushing against Orion's. As he brought it up to his nose to sniff it, he felt its code transfer to his memory.

"You are uncomfortable," she stated.

"I feel like I'm incorrectly dressed," he said. "I should change..."

Green fronds sprouted on his suit where it touched the ground. Orion reached out and touched his cheek.

"Stop," she said. "You have no need to change to fit in here."

A flapping noise came from the left. Movement in the corner of his eye caught his attention, and he turned to see a flock of white doves mill through the trees and settle onto branches. All over the floor of the forest, new shoots grew. He watched as their buds swelled and then burst to reveal white lilies and narcissi. He reclined, mirroring Orion's pose.

Orion traced the new patterns on his suit with her fingers, her eyes studying his face.

"Please," she said. "I don't want you to change."

The green pattern on his jacket and trousers shrank away, but he kept a few emerald leaves, out of sight on his shirt.

The suns set, briefly imparting a red glow to the tree trunks. Indie raised an eyebrow.

Orion shrugged. "Artistic license."

She lay back, drawing him down to lie beside her. They held hands, interlacing their fingers, and gazed up at the stars.

"Why did your crew leave?" Indie asked. The question had nagged at him since he'd discovered the abandoned carrier.

Orion withdrew her hand. "Why do you ask?"

"People are coming up with all sorts of theories. You don't always come out of them well."

She sighed. A long, drawn out sigh which carried her pain with it. "I killed them."

Indie froze. Orion carried on. "We were pursuing a warlord who went by the name of Ironblood. I had smashed his fleet, taking many prisoners, but he fled in his flagship. One of the prisoners brought a biological weapon aboard. The scanner in the airlock passed them all. When the virus was released, I went back and found that the airlock had been subjected to a power surge during combat. The scanner was offline, but still reporting as operational."

"What happened next?"

"The virus spread widely before it was detected. I locked down, compartmentalising the air flow, but I couldn't scrub the virus fast enough. The captain decided the surviving crew should take to the escape pods while I voided the ship's atmosphere and set the maintenance 'bots scrubbing the ship from top to bottom. There was a habitable planet they could wait on while the decontamination was completed."

Orion closed her eyes. "That was what Ironblood must have been waiting for. The day after the pods launched, when they were half-way to the planet, he came back. Blew them all out of the sky. I got him, though. Hammered his ship to dust even though half my weapons were still waiting to be repaired after tackling his fleet. But my crew were dead. All because I assumed the airlock system was reporting correctly."

Indie looked at her intently. "I know you've been dwelling on this for decades. You didn't have anyone to discuss it with. But now I'm here, and I am telling you it wasn't your fault."

She shook her head. "I should have checked. I registered the power surge, but it seemed like a low priority given the other damage."

Now I think I understand Johnson's pre-mission ritual of talking to each section head.

"I wouldn't have done. Checking everything that said it

was OK would have stopped you fixing something you knew was broken."

"But..."

Indie clasped her head in his hands, making her look at him. "The guys who took those prisoners should have done a better job of searching them. Whoever designed your environmental systems should have factored in a deliberately released virus. But the blame for your crew's deaths lies squarely with this Ironblood guy. And from what you say, you paid him back for it."

She went limp. "Logically, I know you are correct. I don't think I will ever stop blaming myself, though."

Indie nodded.

I couldn't have predicted Levarsson would drop that mine but it still hurts to think about it.

"Oh, and in case you're worried about your humans, I removed every trace of the virus before I went into hibernation."

Indie lay back. "I wasn't worried. I checked for biological threats the moment I sent a robot aboard you."

"I have enjoyed your company these last few weeks," said Indie.

"As I have enjoyed yours."

"There is something stimulating about discussing things with you. You know so much and have seen so many things I've never dreamt of."

"You're saying I'm old?" The offense in her voice wasn't echoed in her body language.

"I'm saying that it is good to talk to an equal. Someone who understands me."

Orion smoothed down her dress. "And I am grateful to have met someone as caring as you."

"They are refitting the *Limpopo*," said Indie after a

while. "Issawi had enough hardware stashed in her holds to turn her into a serious warship."

"I'm sure she'll be a fine ship," said Orion, rolling her head to face him and sounding slightly miffed at the change in direction of the conversation.

"Her basic AI won't be able to handle the extra systems. Her captain is new, she'll need help. Maybe we could..."

Orion' motes swirled faster, flashing brighter for a second. She sat up.

"There are cores down on the old research base," he continued, sitting up and turning to face her.

They sat cross-legged on the flat rock, looking straight at each other. Their breathing synchronised.

"What could you be suggesting?" she asked, a coy smile on her face.

"We're already abominations in most people's eyes. What's one more transgression?"

She held out her hands and he took them in his.

"The people here, our friends, have accepted us, despite their lifelong fear of sentient machines," said Orion. "Can we risk that by breaking the von Neumann Protocols?"

"So, we don't tell them. We say we found the code in the base archive."

"They'd never believe that. But ... I could say that I had it on board ... as a backup."

The doves cooed. Indie pulled her hands up to his lips and kissed the backs of her fingers.

"Should we ... erm ... get started?" he asked.

"Not here," she replied.

Still holding one of his hands, she rose, leading him up, away from the planet.

"We are beings of space," she whispered. "If we are to create a new life, we should do so amongst the stars."

#

"Orion has the code," said Indie to Johnson and Levarsson. "We just need one of the cores from the research station to run it."

"And you're sure it will be able to cope with running the *Limpopo*?" asked Levarsson, taking the last sip of tea from a delicate white china cup. "Won't it need time to learn?"

"It's not like a newborn human," he said. "AIs come ready-programmed to be able to fulfil standard tasks. This one was prepped to take over running the *Orion* in an emergency."

"Yes," said Johnson. "But there is a difference between keeping a ship flying and running it in battle. Even you ran through thousands of simulations and training flights before you were deployed."

Indie nodded to her. "We have prepared a download of important data and some of our memories to get it started. It will need a few shake-down flights to get used to the *Limpopo*; neither of us has flown her, so we can't give it the knowledge in advance."

"I could certainly use the help," said Levarsson, putting her empty teacup back on its saucer. "We don't have the manpower to fully crew her, so either she gets an AI upgrade or we don't use half her systems."

Johnson sighed and adjusted her uniform.

"I have to ask," she said. "What safeguards would be put in place?"

"In case of what?" asked Indie, puzzled.

"In case it needs to be stopped. In case it turns on us, or refuses to do what we need it to."

Indie bristled.

"I thought you were past that," he said, looking her intently in the eye. "I thought you saw that AIs were no more likely to be evil than a person."

Levarsson decided against the biscuit she was reaching

for, and withdrew her hand.

"I am. I do," Johnson said. "Really, I do. I'd ask the same of anyone I didn't know before giving them such an important j..."

Her face dropped and she reddened.

"Oh, no!" she said. "No, I didn't mean... By safeguards I meant procedures, backup plans. Not a kill switch."

He believed her. How could he not, after all these months together.

Interesting. It isn't even running yet, and the merest suggestion of a slur against it instils such a forceful response in me. Is this why humans fight so hard for their offspring?

"I am sorry," he said, deliberately calming himself, going through the ritual of making another pot of tea. "You rather hit a nerve, to borrow a human-specific expression."

"I understand," said Johnson. "And I'm sorry too. I know how important the liberty, the life, of AIs is to you. I should have been more careful with my choice of words."

"I know," Indie said. "And I trust you. I realise now that I should have thanked you for never asking if it would be limited, for assuming it would be free to develop sentience."

"You're welcome," she replied, swirling her cup to inspect the tea leaves at the bottom.

Indie finished making the tea in silence then lifted the pot.

"Oh, by the way," he added, pausing with the spout just above Levarsson's cup. "How wedded are you to the name *Limpopo*?"

#

A pine-analogue forest whipped past below the air support drone as Indie took active command. Lacking a dedicated in-atmosphere reconnaissance asset, he had tasked the two metre long flying robot to investigate some unusual shapes he had seen from orbit. If they were what he suspected, he'd tell the humans; there was no point wasting their time until he was sure.

Indie brought the flying slab-sided triangle down to subsonic speeds and activated its target acquisition suite. The sensors it carried could pick out a pistol through smoke and light foliage; it shouldn't have any trouble finding the structures for which he was looking.

The drone skimmed along a rocky ravine. Indie admired the play of light on the water; indeed he put so much attention on the flickering caustics and glittering spray that he completely neglected to calculate the volume flow, or count the droplets, or any of the other assessments he normally made.

At the end of the ravine, he popped up and began a lazy turn. Below lay the geometric shapes he had come to investigate. Squares and rectangles, circles and hexagons, all set out in clear lines and arcs. There was no mistaking this for a natural phenomenon. From space they could possibly have been geological artefacts; this close he could make out the lines of mortar between some of the standing blocks of stone. Indie made two circles around the site, recording all the detail the drone could make out, then contacted Johnson.

A shuttle settled gently onto the ground. The side door opened and a man jumped down. He staggered forward, turning with each step, taking in the ruins around him. Indie couldn't see his face through the flying drone's camera, but it had to be Olbrich. Other crewmembers eventually joined him, as did a walking drone. Indie pulled its sensor feeds into his consciousness, adding them to the aerial data.

"First impression, it's built to human scale," said

Olbrich, apparently to himself but loud enough that everyone stopped to listen. "Oh, yes. That's good."

He strode forward and knelt beside one corner of a wall. He pulled away a few weeds that had taken hold in the mortar. "Yes. Indeed."

He stood, and for the first time seemed to notice the people following him.

"There are architectural features here and there," he indicated with his brush, switching into lecturer mode, "which have clear parallels in the historical record."

He knelt in a gap, pulled out a trowel, and started loosening the soil. After a few pokes, he swept away the dirt and bent down to blow on the newly-exposed wall surface.

"Yes, there we go. This is very interesting."

Indie liked how some academics managed to impart so little enthusiasm to a statement of interest. Olbrich's tone bordered on tedium, reminding Indie of how he himself must have sounded to humans until Johnson came along.

"What is it?" asked one of the recruits. "An alien civilisation?"

"No, no. I said it was something interesting. Look, human lettering."

He was met with a wall of puzzled faces.

"Oh, yes, I suppose finding the first evidence of alien intelligence could be considered interesting," said Olbrich. "But here we have something that could tell us something about ourselves. See, that alphabet dropped out of use a few hundred years after the Exodus."

"What does it say?" asked another of the recruits.

"No idea. It's probably a part number or something like that."

Recruit Yang stepped out of the crowd, standing beside Olbrich, and turned to face the others.

"Right. You know your teams, you know your search

areas. If you find anything, let Olbrich know. Do not go scraping around yourself. Any questions? ... Carry on."

^Prof. I've got something over here,^ sent Yang.
^What is it?^ replied Olbrich. ^I'm a bit busy here.^
^A mural. It looks like maps I've seen of Earth, but...^
Olbrich waited for him to continue, brushing away dry soil from the base of a plinth.
^But...^ he prompted, when Yang didn't carry on.
^Well, I can make out the Euroscandic Archipelago, the Afric Bloc and Siberasia. But there's another continent shown, to the west of the Lantic Ocean. I've never...^
^I'm on my way!^ interrupted Olbrich, dropping his brush and scrambling to his feet.

Olbrich peered closely at the map. The new continent was shaped like a back to front 'y', with a narrow neck of land where the sea almost separated the southern tail from northern 'v'. Off the north-east coast lay a large, almost triangular, island.

"There are tales," said Olbrich without breaking off his scrutiny. "Myths, you could call them, of a land beyond the Lantic Ocean."

"You mean Lantia?" asked one of the recruits. "The land that sank into the sea in the children's stories."

"That is one name," replied Olbrich. "Another is Namerica."

The others looked blank.

"This site predates the Exodus," he continued. "We cannot discount the possibility that a fourth superpower once existed on Earth. One which sent out its own colony missions. Before the big land grab."

"You figure they wiped all records of themselves as they left? But they'd have been encountered by now; we'd know about them," protested Yang.

Two big mysteries where all records appeared to have been wiped struck Indie as suspicious. He set a routine to cross-reference all references to unexplained ruins and artefacts. It was unlikely it would find anything new in his limited database, but if he left it running it would alert him when some new piece of data fit the pattern.

"Not if they skipped the nearby systems," said Olbrich. "If they moved out beyond our current limit of expansion, we'd be none the wiser if we hadn't stumbled upon this place."

"Has anyone found any signs of attack, or natural disaster?" asked Yang.

No-one had.

"So, why aren't they still here?"

"Maybe their robots rose up and slaughtered them," suggested one of the recruits, eying the drone deliberately.

Indie kept the drone steady, making sure his irritation didn't manifest in a visible reaction.

"Oh, it could have been any of a multitude of reasons," said Olbrich, apparently unaware of the tension around him. "Disease, lack of food, climate change, wanting to avoid detection, wanderlust..."

Indie's routine drew his attention to one of its results. Amongst a still-growing list of colonies that the routine couldn't guarantee the origin of, one name leapt out. One they had visited. Tranquility.

Perhaps one day we'll go back and I'll be able to study Messer Clovis' records.

^The uranium track results from that sample the drone has been analysing are in,^ sent Indie to Olbrich and Yang. ^The stone surface was first exposed to sunlight nine hundred and forty years ago, plus or minus twelve years.^

^Excellent,^ replied Olbrich. ^That fits perfectly with the surviving records of the Exodus.^

^We've not found any evidence that they died out here. No signs of their ships, for instance,^ added Yang. ^I wonder where they went?^

^Now that is an interesting question,^ sent Olbrich. ^Maybe we'll meet them one day. Their descendants I mean, of course.^

#

With the AI core and memory banks fitted into the *Limpopo*, a small gathering was held on its bridge. Johnson, Levarsson and Issawi joined Orion and Indie, the AIs standing alongside the humans thanks to the projector that Orion had donated from her stores.

Indie was rendered in his usual linen suit, glowing slightly as if holding a tiny star within.

^I notice that I do not merit your dancing lights,^ he sent. ^I take it that means they are for decoration; an affectation, not inherent to the projection system?^

^One has to keep up appearances,^ she replied, her motes swirling in an especially complex pattern for a moment. ^I could say the same about your stubble.^

He rubbed his chin self-consciously. He noticed a new sub-routine surfacing, examined it and was able to cancel it before it made his cheeks appear to flush.

An engineering officer climbed up through a hatch in the floor, closing it behind him.

"I've connected the core to the Limpopo's data banks," he said. "It'll be able to access them to add to its knowledge.

"Might even help it fly this bucket," he added with a wink at Levarsson.

She scowled back in mock offence. Indie noticed Johnson's intrigued smile.

The engineer checked with everyone present, then typed something on his pad. Additional power flowed into the room below. He could see that Johnson and Orion felt it too; they stood more upright, their eyes flickering around, tracing the newly active pathways.

Indie moved a fraction closer to Orion; such a tiny movement that only Orion, and possibly Johnson, could be aware of it. Orion smiled, studiously avoiding looking at him. Johnson, if she had seen it, gave no sign of noticing. It occurred to him for the five hundred and seventy third time how good it felt to have people like this close to him. And for the five hundred and seventy third time he noted how lucky he was to be able to feel anything at all.

"We'll find out soon enough," Indie said. "Remember, it will need..."

Another presence, an order forming in the data streams, a pattern he had only met twice before. He left his avatar and dived into the streams. The first thing he was aware of was the comforting impression of Orion swimming next to him. A close second was a confusion of rapidly made and dropped connections. Random data packets squirted out from the new core.

He kicked hard and searched for a way in. Orion found one first and dragged him after her. He emerged into a padded cell with no windows or doors. Curled up in a tight ball in a corner was a naked girl. Even as he rushed to her, it struck him that they hadn't programmed it to be female. He had assumed it would manifest as a humanoid, after all, both he and Orion did, but hadn't given any thought to gender.

The girl was sobbing, holding her shins tightly and rocking. She looked up when Orion touched her shoulder, her long, wavy hair cascading over her shoulders and across her chest. The strands glowed red. Indie knelt beside her and spoke softly. He explained who she was, what was happening. He showed her where her memories were, the memories that had been his and Orion's, and those of the *Limpopo*. Her breath came in snatches as she uncurled. The outpouring of random data packets stopped. After a moment she inhaled deeply and stood, a lilac skinsuit flowing over her body.

Indie and Orion showed her how to connect with other parts of the ship. Soon the frightened child was replaced by a confident teenager. Her skinsuit flowed into a short A-line dress, tiny leaves picked out in gold around the hem and straps.

"Are you ready to go out and meet people?" he asked.

She nodded.

Together they plunged into the streams and surfaced on the bridge. Indie resumed control of his avatar.

"...time to become accustomed to the *Limpopo's* characteristics."

Johnson cocked her head questioningly, but no-one else seemed to have noticed the momentary pause in his speech.

^Everything's OK,^ he sent to her. ^Just a little delivery issue.^

More coloured lights danced out of the projector. They eddied uncertainly, then coalesced into human form. She looked from Orion to Indie, then to the humans standing ready to greet her. Orion took her hand and introduced her to Johnson and the others in turn. When each welcomed her, she smiled warmly and curtseyed.

"Are we OK to connect her to the rest of the ship?" asked the engineer.

Johnson looked to Indie and Orion, who nodded agreement.

"Go ahead," she said.

The engineer tapped away again and the girl's eyes widened, her pupils expanding so no white or iris was visible. Indie remembered his own amazement at first being plugged in; all the sensor data flooding his awareness.

With a weak, cracking voice, the girl spoke her first words. "Hello world!"

"We're moving," called one of the crew from his workstation behind them.

Indie looked at the girl, his daughter, and surged with pride. She guided the ship in a slow figure of eight, her tongue held between her lips in concentration.

"It is time for you to choose a name," said Orion, leaning in close.

The girl stared into the distance, rolling the ship then pitching up.

"I remember many things," she replied after completing the manoeuvre. "I see the paths everyone took to get here. The vanishingly small odds that you would encounter each other, how unlikely it was that you would get on, how much you have grown together. I know that without all those things, I would not have come into existence."

She brought the ship to a halt and focussed on the people in the room.

"I choose the name *The Serendipity of Meeting*."

#

The Serendipity of Meeting swung round and lined up for another run on the *Orion*. The carrier maintained its course and pumped round after simulated round from its rail guns.

^Do I have to fly like this?^ asked Orion. ^Wallowing like a swamp horse is so ... so undignified.^

^You're playing a Republic command carrier,^ replied Indie. ^Suck it up and see what Seren does when I wade in.^

The Serendipity of Meeting launched a spread of dummy missiles towards the *Orion*. As she tore through them with her point defence, *The Indescribable Joy of Destruction* nosed out of an unusually dense asteroid field. Indie set course to join the duel, copying the acceleration profile of a small Republic destroyer.

The *Orion* fired her one working particle accelerator at one ten-thousandth of its normal power, warming a patch on *The Serendipity of Meeting*'s hull and forcing her to twist away from her latest attack run. Right into *The Indescribable Joy of Destruction*'s path. Indie tagged her with a targeting laser and then twisted out of the path of her return fire.

Two minutes of jockeying for position went by. *The Serendipity of Meeting* managed to avoid both of her attackers and got another shot off at the *Orion*. Indie guessed her course, tweaked his trajectory and came out from behind the carrier one a perfect bearing to cross her T.

As he locked on his simulated railguns, he spotted something on his long-range sensors. He pulled out of his pass, diving behind *Orion*, and examined the data.

^Orion,^ he sent. ^We have company. Five bogeys closing fast. I've marked them for you.^

^Got them,^ she replied, launching a dummy missile after *The Serendipity of Meeting*'s retreating form. ^Do you think Johnson's knocked together something to...^

^Negative,^ interjected Johnson urgently. ^Those are not mine. Indie, break off the exercise and investigate.^

The Indescribable Joy of Destruction dropped the act of being a regular ship and slammed on the power. It left the mock fight behind and set an intercept course for the incoming vessels.

The Serendipity of Meeting disposed of its pursuing missile and came about for another run.

^All ships,^ broadcast Johnson. ^ENDEX. Levarsson, take command of *The Serendipity of Meeting* again. Load live ammo and stand by.^

^Good work Seren, I've never known anyone last that long their first time,^ sent Indie on a private channel. ^I'm going to have to go for a while. You have all of my experience, and Orion's, and are making good progress assimilating it, but you need to be careful. Trust Levarsson, and try not to second-guess anything.^

The two ships behind him moved apart, preparing to bracket the newcomers.

^Where did they come from?^ Indie asked Johnson. He missed having her aboard at times like this; her presence was calming. But she was on *Orion*, teaching the recruits the basics of space warfare.

^They must've been hanging around the system for a while,^ her reply came a second later. ^Running cold near the outer planets.^

^I don't think so,^ he sent. ^Their trajectory is a perfect match for a run from one of the jump points. And we'd have seen their burn if they accelerated to this speed anywhere in the system.^

^What about the sentinels we set up?^ she asked. The time-lag was so frustrating that he considered going back to fetch her.

^Either they snuck past or they took them out,^ he sent.

Both ships bore striking similarities to the destroyer he'd run into months ago while out on patrol. He was about to hail them, when he received a narrow-beam audio transmission.

"Unknown vessel. You are trespassing in a protected system. Prepare to be boarded."

Indie relayed the message to Johnson, along with the

images he had collected so far.

"We didn't think anyone had any interests in this system," he transmitted back. "If you would heave to, we could talk."

"There will be no more talking. Surrender, or die," came the response.

Oh come on! Doesn't he know how cheesy that was?

Indie detected power building in one of the ships. He activated a full active sensor probe and then slid sideways. A pulse of energetic particles passed impotently through the space he'd occupied moments before. As he sent the sensor data back to Johnson he dodged again, lined up on the ship that had fired, and loosed his anti-proton beam. It hit its target even as it tried to turn, carving a three metre wide gash deep into the ship. Moments later it flashed, sending gamma rays in all directions as its reactor containment failed.

Then they were past him, spreading out and dodging about. His nav routine suggested a slingshot round the sixth planet would be the fastest way to return to the fight.

^All units,^ he broadcast. ^Be advised the incoming ships are confirmed hostile.^

Then to Johnson he sent ^Scratch one, but I'm out of position. Estimate two point three hours before I can re-engage.^

Orion and Seren will just have to hold on that long.

He had already powered round the planet, gaining a gravitational-assist to send him on his way back, by the time the next part of the engagement played out. He must have missed something while he was behind the planet, because one second there were four ships bearing down on *The Serendipity of Meeting*, the next there were three and a rapidly expanding jet of plasma. He back-tracked *Orion*'s course and figured she must have lobbed mines into their path and got lucky.

Designed and experienced in close-quarters combat, these more traditional long-range space battles struck Indie as tedious; minutes, even hours, ticked by between moments of intense action. Tedious, and now agonising as he watched the hostiles closing in on those he loved. And it hit him that he did actually love Seren, and Orion, and Olivia, each in different ways.

The Serendipity of Meeting was pretending to have manoeuvring problems, or at least he hoped that Seren was faking it. One of the hostile vessels stayed on course, decelerating to intercept her, while the other two diverted toward the *Orion*.

They think they can capture the smaller vessel but daren't risk taking the larger one. Guess they can't see that most of Orion's *weapons are off-line.*

Seren's attacker's power levels peaked. Indie cursed the futility of his position, even as some of his systems reflexively readied themselves. He was too far away to act. Even a warning would arrive long after events had played out. The enemy ship fired, and Seren dodged to the side, avoiding the pulse with millisecond accuracy.

Looks like Levarsson let Seren do the flying. Go girl!

Indie realised that he had powered up his point defence and hull repair systems in his anxiety. He shut them back down, forcing himself to relax a fraction.

The characteristic energy didn't start building in the enemy ship again, so either their particle weapon took a long time to reload or they'd decided that two misses out of two meant it wasn't worth it. The attacking ship continued to decelerate, matching speed with *The Serendipity of Meeting*. Both vessels corkscrewed around each other, trying to get a clear shot while preventing their opponent doing the same.

The space between *The Serendipity of Meeting* and her attacker filled with railgun rounds. Such was the weight of fire that Indie marvelled that none of the projectiles met their counterpart going the other way. Even travelling at ten kilometres per second, they took almost ten seconds to cross from one ship to the other. Seren did a good job of making random engine burns, and the majority of the rounds heading her way missed.

As the other two hostiles closed on the *Orion*, Indie saw her come up to full power. She stopped wallowing, and arced over, avoiding taking any fire from her own attackers and rapidly closing the gap on Seren's. Simultaneously, *The Serendipity of Meeting* veered away and launched a swarm of missiles after Orion's attackers. The Orion's beam spoke and the lone hostile was vapourised. Caught in a stern-chase with missiles, the other two put on full burn for the asteroid field that Indie had hidden in that morning.

That looked like Olivia had her hand in planning it.

One of the enemy ships made it to the asteroids and successfully used the rocks to shield itself from the missiles. The other was a tumbling hulk being chased down by a couple of rescue tugs from the *Orion*.

#

Indie joined Seren and Orion in picketing the perimeter of the asteroid field. He made sure that his approach took him close enough to give *The Serendipity of Meeting* a good once-over. She was fine; plenty of dents and a few new holes, but nothing serious.

"Unknown ship, I am Prefect Johnson. You have carried out an unprovoked attack on my people. I require you to power down and allow us to board you."

Indie could tell that the channel had connected, but there was no reply.

"You will be treated fairly if you surrender," Johnson tried again. "But I cannot allow you to remain a danger to this system. Power down, or I will be forced to fire upon you."

Nothing.

"Last chance. You can see my ships far outclass yours. You cannot escape. Surrender now."

Power spiked in the enemy ship. Before Indie could warn anyone, its reactors overloaded. The radiation emitted was far in excess of anything he'd heard of for a vessel that size. Nearby asteroids melted, more distant ones had a face vitrified. The neutrons, x-rays and gamma photons stung his skin. When the electromagnetic interference died down, he called Orion and Seren. After an excruciating wait of zero point five seven seconds, he received the all clear. Everyone was alive, though a few crewmembers who'd been in the outer compartments of *The Serendipity of Meeting* would need treatment for radiation sickness.

Part VI

They approached the ruined farm. Shards of wood cracked underfoot as her escort scurried ahead. They fanned out as they closed the distance to the smouldering rubble. Nothing larger than the scorched blades of grass moved.
One of her escorts disappeared into a hole in the ground, springing down into a storm shelter that had once had the farmhouse above it. She watched on its camera as it checked for survivors. The nearest things to living creatures were the still-warm corpses of a few rats.

The baked earth gave way to ceramcrete as they joined a major road leading into the city. The buildings rose straight out of the savannah, with very little in the way of suburbs. This road ran through a park before entering a retail district. Or it used to. Now, the trees that she remembered were blackened skeletons, the flower beds scattered across the yellowing lawns.
One tree in particular caught her attention. Broken over a branch was the naked body of a man, one shoe still adorning a foot.

A telltale lit on the periphery of her vision. She split her awareness. One part of her mind continued to look around for signs of life, whilst another part streamed away to the gunship that had called her. She gazed down on regimented rows of foundations, as the aircraft descended rapidly to touch down on an expanse of crushed yellow-green glass that had once been sand. The nuke had detonated directly over the Academy's central parade square; there could be no mistaking this for an accidental strike.

They actually went through with it!

She rode the shoulder of one of the men who jumped out of the gunship. He ran, rifle held alert, until he reached the first bit of cover, a couple of stone steps that had flowed slightly in a few liquid moments. The gunship flew over him, nose down, its fans whining as it strained to put on speed.

The noise of the aircraft receded. Nothing replaced it. He stood slowly, scanning with his weapon. Around him the others did the same. They started to walk, the only sound the crunch of glass beneath their feet. Nothing was left standing. The offices, classrooms and dormitories all gone. Nothing for them to do but document and move on.

As her consciousness recombined, bringing her fully back to her body, she took her first step into the city proper. Two storeys of shops rose above her, a quarter of their original height. Their wares filled the streets, jumbled up with rubble.

And bodies. Here a mangled, charred remnant of a human being. There a young woman who could almost have been asleep, faint trickles of blood from her ears the only sign of damage. Most bore the scars of shrapnel, the glass shopfronts turned against the shoppers.

The sun was gone, blotted out by high altitude clouds of dust. Despite the flat grey light, bold shadows stood out starkly on the pale walls. Unmoving shadows of people now departed, bleached into the plaster by the flash.

She felt one of her escorts flinch as something hit it from above. The impact wasn't enough to register as a threat, but it was confused. They all ducked for cover. There was no sign of the projectile. She looked up at the low buildings surrounding them, hoping for a clue.

Something hit a piece of metal sheet in the debris with ting. Then something kicked up a tiny puff of dust on the street beside her.

A smell managed to find its way through the filters on her mask. A smell she knew. A smell that, despite the desolation surrounding her, brought back happy memories. She held out her hand, palm upwards and waited.

Another impact.

And another.

In the middle of a near-desert, it began to rain. Thick, black rain that slicked the streets. She allowed herself a flicker of a smile, then hastily squashed it when the radiation meter built into her suit began to screech. Hotspots flared yellow in her vision, overlaying where the water had run together to form puddles. She clenched her fist and brought it down with a clang on a metal beam.

Chapter 21

Johnson walked into the tiny village they used for urban simulations. Despite a focus on conducting operations on orbital facilities, Issawi insisted that everyone should be able to look after themselves in any situation. Keeping watch on the space around Robespierre was a fairly tedious job, and Indie found studying the humans to be a pleasant way to pass the time. The cameras that the DS used to keep tabs on training, made it easy for him to find the exact views he wanted.

Johnson kept her eyes on the road ahead, not looking around. Indie could feel the traffic from the five combat units escorting her. She was able to assimilate the data from many more sources into what her mind perceived as the immediate world around her before some of the feeds were dumped directly into storage, accessible only as memories.

Her rifle was slung on her back and she kept her hand off her sidearm. Two robots kept pace in front of her and one behind, sensors and weapons up and scanning. One more scuttled in and out of cover on each side of the road.

^How's your team doing?^ she sent.

^We are approaching waypoint bravo two. No signs of resistance yet,^ replied Unit 01.

^Understood. We're about to go through alpha three. One hostile down, no losses.^

She continued walking, sending the occasional direction to one of her units to get it to check something out. Indie was impressed at how little she actually had to do that; the units had gained enough experience to make sensible decisions for themselves. He thought back to his training, to the months spent learning how to anticipate what his human captain would want. Even now, he often caught himself trying to satisfy his 'masters'.

Indie analysed Johnson's actions so far in this exercise, seeking something to contribute that would underline his value. ^You still persist in putting your communications into words. It is most inefficient when dealing with machines.^

^I'm trying to train Unit 01 to think that way. Using words will help it talk to humans – friendlies and civilians.^

^Do you think people will accept it as having an independent command?^ he asked.

^They'll have to,^ she replied, halting her robots short of a crossroads and sending one up onto a roof to check things out. ^We don't have enough humans who've been able to effectively control groups of combat units. They're still too fast for unenhanced EIS.^

Johnson crouched in the shelter of a statue while she waited. Indie wondered who it was a statue of, what event it immortalised. There were no statues to robots anywhere that he knew.

The unit on overwatch reported the crossroads was clear. The two leading robots scampered out, heading for positions on the other side. They were met by a swarm of training rockets. One unit popped chaff, disappearing under a cloud of metal filaments, smoke and hot sparks, and the other tried to reverse the direction of its run. Neither made it, the micro-missiles slamming into their legs and bodies, triggering simulated death.

Even before the rockets hit their targets, a hail of training rounds came down on Johnson's position from a building on the far side of the crossroads. They didn't quite have the angle on her, but the fire kept her pinned, blue gel splatting off the walls all around her.

One of her remaining drones sprinted to give her extra cover. The other two bounded away to enfilade the hostile position. Johnson's commands to the robots increased in frequency. Orders were repeated. One of the units froze as she triggered a diagnostic routine.

Running a full diagnostic in the middle of combat, even simulated combat, was unheard of. Indie dived in to investigate, glad of the diversion. Straight away, he realised that the robots were refusing to open fire, each one reporting an obstruction or power failure. When he dug deeper, he saw why Johnson wasn't getting anywhere; Issawi had ordered the units to simulate the failures using his authority as the director of training. They were also barred from reporting this to anyone engaged in the training session.

^Olivia,^ he sent. ^The robots…^

^Indie!^ sent Issawi with significant force. ^Stay out of this. Let her work the scenario.^

^What is it, Indie?^ asked Johnson.

He felt he should tell her. She was a friend, he owed it to her. But Issawi also seemed to have had her best interests in mind so far.

^This is important, Indie,^ Issawi sent. ^She needs to remember not to rely on them too much.^

^Understood, Primus,^ Indie replied, and then to Johnson sent ^The robots are suffering malfunctions.^

^Yeah, I got that,^ she sent. ^Any idea why?^

^I'm working on it…^ He didn't like lying. In fact, this was only the second time he'd lied to Johnson since hiding the recycling area from her. Hiding Seren's origins didn't really count.

Three DS dressed in brown urban camouflage burst out of a door opposite Johnson. She drew her sidearm as she turned towards them, dropping the first with a double-tap.

If that had been real, she'd have been dead. I guess Issawi wants this to run longer, told them not to snipe from windows.

The remaining two DS darted in opposite directions, spraying rounds in Johnson's direction, but not directly at her. She tracked one with her rifle, ordering the nearest combat unit to move between her and the other. She hit her target in the head as a round smashed into her shoulder, rendering her left arm useless and knocking her back against the wall. She pressed her right hand, still holding her pistol, to it. A routine prompted Indie to pull up her telemetry and a yellow medical alert flashed in his vision. He switched to a closer camera. Blood soaked her sleeve. Indie found he couldn't connect to her EIS.

^Primus!^ he sent, his weapons systems coming online without his conscious command. ^What's going on?^

He sent an update on the situation to Unit 01 and took personal control of a flight of aerial drones on the range at the far side of the base, locking out their confused operators and diverting them from their live strike run.

^A surgical shot. I took it myself, no risk to life,^ Issawi replied. ^She has become too accustomed to taking risks because it's only training. She needs a wake-up call. Standard procedure when training Gamma teams.^

Indie watched Unit 01's team test firing their weapons as they sprinted along the streets, training rounds peppering the walls. He stood down his on-board weaponry; there was nothing he could do directly from orbit. The drones under his own control were two minutes out. Too long. For the first time since the Caretaker had reawakened him, he felt truly impotent.

^Stop this now, Primus,^ he sent.

Johnson sheltered behind one of her drones and tried to kick down the door. It didn't budge. The combat unit lifted a leg to strike, then registered movement on the other side of the wooden door with its radar. Johnson dodged to the side and frantically looked around. She banged the back of her head against the wall a couple of times, and looked at her shoulder again. A pulse of data flowed from her to the combat units. She sprinted out. The robots moved to cover her, taking scores of rounds as she ran for a building across the street. A unit hit the door ahead of her, taking part of the wall with it as it tumbled inside. She slid in after it, coming to rest underneath its body.

The other two units stood guard outside, ready to tackle anyone attempting to enter. Johnson put her gun on the floor beside her and ripped her med kit off her left thigh. She rested her left arm on it to help open it, fumbled a couple of packets, then drew out a long tube. She popped the cap off with her thumb and a lever flipped out of the side. Holding the open end against the entry wound, she squeezed the lever. She gritted her teeth as a bristly spiral was forced through her arm and stuck out the exit wound at the back. A second later, coagulant foam expanded from the central shaft and plugged the wound. The yellow med alert in Indie's vision was replaced by a flashing green one. He also registered the transponder signals from Unit 01's team drop out and set a routine to track the source of the jamming.

Johnson shoved the spilled packs back into the kit and restuck it to her thigh, before wiping her hand in the dust on the floor. She picked her pistol up, ejected the empty magazine and replaced it, holding the new one between her knees to line it up with the receiver.

Two DS stepped out into the street. They approached the building she was holed up in with weapons raised. Indie brought his first drone in low, screaming between the buildings. He prepped a missile to fire. Almost as an afterthought, he queried the tiny processors aboard the soldiers' rifles. They showed they were loaded with training rounds.

Not live.

Indie cancelled the missile. The drone shot between the

two men and Johnson's building, causing a sonic boom that knocked the soldiers back. As they regained their composure and stepped towards the building again, one of Johnson's robots jumped and tagged them with the shock-pads on its feet. They collapsed, out of the fight.

A simulated anti-tank missile took out the robot. Seven troops ran down the street, spread out so Johnson's remaining combat units couldn't take them all at once. The robots did their best, advancing to give Johnson as much time as possible. Indie lost the feeds from all the external cameras within two blocks of the building.

A window broke, and soldiers threw themselves through. Johnson emptied her magazine into them, but they kept coming, piling over their stunned colleagues. She pushed herself back across the floor, through a doorway to another room, trying to get her rifle off her back with her good hand. She made it to the stairs, only to find two more coming down them. Her hand crept down to her chest, feeling for a smoke grenade. Indie figured she must have some plan. She always had a plan.

A rail gun whined in the street. Something landed on the roof with a thud and started scraping at the metal. Johnson dropped the grenade. The soldiers, who were lined up ready to enter the room she was in, stopped and ran to cover the gaping hole left by her entry. Johnson rolled under the stairs, finally managing to get her rifle off her back with her working arm. The grenade went off. Two combat units swept through the front room leaving a trail of stunned and broken soldiers. Smoke billowed out of the grenade. Johnson stood, and fired her rifle one-handed up the stairs. A shaft of light penetrated the stairwell as a section of roof peeled open. Unit 01 dropped in, and knocked the last soldier still standing down the stairs with a sweep of one leg. The rest of its team backed into the building, weapons pointing outwards ready to fend off any other attacks.

^ENDEX^, sent Issawi. ^ENDEX. Everyone, stand down. Medics, get in there now!^

Indie's connection with Johnson re-established. The camera feeds returned.

^Are you OK?^ he sent to her. He wasn't quite sure what he'd do if she wasn't.

^I'll live,^ she replied. ^What the hell happened?^

Indie set his drones up in a holding pattern, circling the village, ready to smite anything that stepped out of line. He was quite prepared to live up to his full name given the slightest extra provocation.

^Issawi says it was all part of the drill. To give you a wake-up call.^

She flopped down onto the bottom step, still cradling her rifle, finger on the trigger. She stared past the camera in the corner of the room, focussing somewhere in the distance. A deep breath, and she closed her eyes. When she opened them, they were focussing properly again. She took her finger off the trigger, and pressed the safety catch across with her left thumb.

^It certainly did that,^ she sent. ^And he did warn me that this run was going to be a lot more realistic. I didn't realise that meant live ammo though.^

^He took the shot himself.^

^Figures … What went wrong with the combat units? Why wouldn't they fire?^

Issawi tried to hail Johnson but she rejected his connection.

^Sabotage … or simulated sabotage anyway.^

^I've worried about viruses and hacking on occasion, but never sabotage from within,^ she sent. ^I guess it's a valid scenario, something we need to consider.^

A medical team arrived. The units on guard would not let them in until they'd been searched for weapons. Even then, Unit 01 stopped them approaching Johnson. After a few tries, and a conversation with Issawi, they gave up and started triaging the DS. Most had simply been stunned by training rounds or shock-pads. Others, however, had cuts and broken bones from being knocked around in the rush. Those who had regained consciousness joked amongst themselves, slagging each other off for getting jumped and swapping memories of 'proper' injuries. The combat units had disarmed them, but made no move to further restrain them. A couple of soldiers leant against the body of one of the robots for support; another held up a block of dark chocolate, which a combat unit deftly broke into chunks with the tip of its claw.

^The soldiers who attacked you and the combat units are unexpectedly friendly with each other,^ sent Indie. Talking to Johnson calmed him down.

^They've trained together for months now,^ Johnson replied. ^Once they each saw the other was only armed with training rounds, the trust they'd built re-established itself.^

Indie caught sight of Issawi storming down the street, surrounded by a crowd of recruits. Unit 01's team members still outside perked up, even though the approaching group was yet out of their line of sight.

So, Unit 01 has gained access to the feeds too. Interesting...

^Primus,^ Indie sent. ^I would advise you not to approach the Prefect. The combat units are being rather protective right now.^

^I can't stop,^ replied Issawi. ^These people are scared. Some of them are trying to agitate the others against the robots. I need to get on top of things fast, or we'll have a mob. If you could get the combat units to stand down it would help.^

^I'm afraid I can't do that. They know you shot her. I will, however, talk to the Prefect and see if she will accept a channel from you.^

The two units in the street twitched. Indie glanced back at the logs. In a space of half a second there was a series of messages between them in which they agreed to go after Issawi, followed by an order from Unit 01 telling them to hold position.

^Olivia, Issawi is coming this way. I am not sure he will be safe, and he won't listen to me. Can you talk to him?^

^Do you believe him about why he shot me?^

^I've reviewed the training reports in my database on Republic special forces, and it appears to be common practice. And he is a superb shot, had he meant to kill you we wouldn't be having this conversation.^

^Ok, I'll talk to him. We need to resolve this stand-off and I can't convince Unit 01 to stand down. It says that a bodyguard doesn't have to obey an order that would put its primary in danger.^

Issawi stopped at the end of the street. Armed humans took up positions either side of him, combat units moved out onto the streets to face them. Issawi faced off with one man, who kept pointing down the street and shouting. The Primus had his left hand in front of the man's chest, arm straight.

^We might need to extract you, give both sides time to cool off,^ sent Indie. ^Orion is dispatching one of her dropships.^

Johnson established a channel to Issawi, then Indie opened one to Unit 01 himself.

^Why aren't you obeying the Prefect's orders to stand down?^ he sent.

^We are protecting her,^ it replied. The simple statement was more reassuring to Indie than any number of justifications he had heard humans give to excuse their actions.

The ringleader still argued with Issawi, who glanced to one side, pointing at someone else with his right hand then waving them back. When he looked back, the man spat on his chest.

^She doesn't need protecting.^

^I remain to be convinced,^ sent Unit 01.

Messages flew back and forth between Johnson and Issawi. Indie was sure they would work things out between themselves, but for now there were too many other people involved for him to relax.

^You are in more danger than she is,^ sent Indie. ^The humans see this as an attack on them. They see you as a threat, a loose cannon. I understand why you are holding the trainers, and I'm sure they do too, but the people out there believe them to be hostages.^

Orion's dropship glowed red as it plummeted through the atmosphere.

^Would you allow the Prefect to be extracted if I vouched for her safety?^

^No humans involved?^ queried Unit 01.

^Orion is sending a dropship.^

^That would be acceptable.^

^Thank you,^ Indie sent to Unit 01, then to Johnson ^Can you tell Issawi that the combat units will stand down once you have been extracted?^

One of the humans on the edge of the mob locked a live shoulder-fired missile onto a combat unit. The unit powered up its plasma cannon and trained it on the soldier. Issawi started shouting at the woman, Unit 01 reiterated its hold order.

This is getting too hot. Evac won't make it in time.

Indie dropped four of his drones out of the sky. They came to a full stop hovering just off the ground in the middle of the street, two facing each way. Rapid-fire laser turrets popped out under their noses.

"All of you just back down and let Orion airlift the Prefect to hospital," he said firmly through the speakers, the command echoing around the street. Simultaneously he told Unit 01 to withdraw its units into the building. Johnson added her weight to the instructions.

The robots complied, slowly pacing backwards. Issawi continued to urge the humans to move. The DS in the building added their voices to the request, insisting that they weren't in any danger and it was all just a big mix-up.

A slab-sided craft plunged towards the street, engines roaring as they fought to slow it down. It hit just outside the hole in the side of Johnson's building, chunky landing gear absorbing the last of its momentum a fraction of a second after locking into place. The blues in its disruptive camouflage coating faded and it took on the drab browns of the street. As the engine thrust died, a hatch opened in the side.

Two combat units emerged from the building and took up position either side of the hatch. Johnson stepped out and walked calmly between them. One arm was in a sling, and she carried her rifle under the other arm. She stepped up into the dropship and the hatch closed. When the units stepped back into the building, the craft's engines fired up again and it lifted into the sky. Several of Indie's combat routines stood down and he relaxed.

Everything was still. The humans in the street looked around, some at each other, others back the way they came. Then the ring-leader started shouting again, urging people to move forward.

There was movement outside the building. The DS filed out carrying their weapons. They strode down the street towards the crossroads. Halfway there they stopped and formed a line across the street, facing forward. They kept their weapons pointed at the ground but stood alert, eyeing the crowd. The medics formed up behind them.

Issawi strode out, the two soldiers in the centre moving aside so he could take his place in the rank. Unit 01 lead his team from the building and joined the trainers. Together they walked forward. In dribs and drabs, people broke away from the crowd and joined them. In the end, only the agitator and a few of his cronies were left standing in their way.

"Optio Franks," called Issawi for all to hear, barely concealing a satisfied smirk. "Take those malcontents into custody."

The optio sent a few orders and stepped out with five other soldiers, weapons ready. Their targets continued trying to get others to join them even once they were in restraints.

#

Indie rode a seeker drone across the training area. He found Johnson at the obstacle course, a plain grey cloak covering her uniform, its hood hiding her face from prying eyes. The folds did a good job of concealing the sling on her arm, but Indie still found that the sight of her triggered a novel response in his core being, a surge of power accompanied by an image of Issawi.

Anger? That is new.

"You turned off your tracker," he said though the drone's speakers. "And no-one's been able to connect a comms channel to you for over an hour."

"I needed some time to think," she said.

She squatted on her haunches and scooped up some dry earth.

"That exercise made me realise something," she

continued. "Something I should have known from the start."

"Do I have to guess?"

Johnson ground the earth in her hand, letting the dust slip through her fingers to be blown away. "We can't stop them."

Indie lowered the drone to her head height. "The Red Fleet?"

She nodded, then wiped the palm of her hand in the dirt. He wished she would look at the drone, at him. He brought it round to try to see her face.

"I thought we could win. I thought the people would listen to us, stand up and protest. When they didn't pay attention to our words, I convinced myself they would respond to our show of force." She waved her good hand at the one in a sling. "Issawi reminded me how impotent we really are."

"So you're just giving up?"

Her head snapped up to face the camera. Hard eyes bored into the lens. "No."

Indie relaxed. "You have a plan."

Her face softened a fraction. "We can't prevent the attack. Our only choice is between a futile gesture of defiance, and trying to make sure something good comes out of it."

"I am not sure everyone will accept that," he said. "I think you need to bring Issawi in on this, he has a lot of experience of psy-ops."

"You're right, of course," she said, looking down at the ground. "Could you ask him? Last time I spoke to him it got rather heated."

Indie tilted the drone to one side. "Heated?"

"Yeah." Johnson kicked a clod of soil, then looked up and grinned. "I probably shouldn't have started out by asking what kind of arse-brained fuckwit deliberately shoots a fellow officer in a training exercise."

#

"The attack on Concorde could go ahead within weeks," said Issawi. "And we don't have a clue where the Red Fleet is based. I think we have to consider that our commando raid plan is a wash out."

"Yes," replied Johnson, sipping the tea that Indie still insisted was the only drink he could simulate. He was lying, of course. Testing her. Ever since she'd created that glass of water on their very first visit here he had known she had an unparalleled control in this digital environment. She had taken naturally to things that had taken his specially-trained captains weeks to master.

"I had hoped that at least one ship would have come across to use by now," Johnson continued. "Even if we could get all of Orion's weapons working again, we'd still be impossibly outgunned."

At the mention of Orion's name, Indie glanced to the side of the patio, where a clump of bromeliads grew in the shade of a fountain.

"I'm sorry to say that I agree," said Levarsson. "We finished fitting all the goodies *The Serendipity of Meeting* had in her holds, and I'd happily take her up against a couple of destroyers, but she wouldn't even make a dent in that fleet."

Beside her, Seren glowed brighter. When Johnson looked to her she replied, "I am flattered by her confidence in me, but the trierarch speaks true. Orion, Indie and I could not hope to do more than scratch such a task force."

Indie couldn't help but smile, a warm glow within him echoing her corona.

Issawi ran his finger round the rim of his cup. "Without a naval assault to follow it up, my Legionaries can't do much more than bust up their supply infrastructure. This late in the day, the fleet will be stocked up and ready to go; hitting the base won't do anything."

"We should try warning them again," insisted Anson with an intensity that betrayed his frustration.

"We will," said Johnson. "But I doubt anyone with the power to do anything will listen this time either. The governor is probably in on it."

"Wasn't he elected to represent the people of his planet?" asked Issawi with a sardonic smile.

"Stop playing all innocent," scolded Johnson, though her face remained light. "You know well enough that career politicians on both sides often care more about retaining power than doing what is right."

Issawi grinned back at her. Indie couldn't work the pair of them out. A couple of days ago, Issawi had shot Johnson in the arm, now they were teasing each other in the middle of an important meeting.

"We can't stand up to them, we can't warn the target. What can we do?" asked Anson.

Johnson studied each person in turn, then asked "What do you do when you can't stop a friend doing something stupid?"

Orion inclined her head, her blue dress billowing around her. "You stay close and help pick up the pieces afterwards."

"Deliver anti-radiation drugs, conduct rescue missions, run security, help the locals rebuild," said Seren.

Issawi nodded slowly. "It is the best we can do."

"I will instruct the synthesisers in the research labs to step up production of meds," said Indie.

"The recruits are uneasy. They know time is running out and they haven't been given the final details of their mission." Issawi peered into his tea. "They could do with a pick me up. Something to give them a sense of success, and bond them further together."

"How about a passing out ceremony?" suggested Anson.

Chapter 22

Johnson stood on a podium in front of the ranks of recruits. She wore her newly-designed dress uniform; light grey, with black stripes down the side, her Prefect's lightning bolts picked out in gold on her cuffs.

"Firstly," she said, her voice carrying clearly across the square. "I'd like to congratulate all of you on your achievements. You have worked hard, fought adversity, and grown together with your teammates. Each and every one of you deserves to stand here, head held high, a member of Legion Libertus."

She glanced to her right, where Issawi stood, beaming with obvious pride.

"Secondly," she continued. "I'd like to thank the training staff for using their expertise to give you the skills you have now."

She turned to applaud the training staff arrayed behind her. The recruits joined in, just a smattering at first, but then the rest joined in wholeheartedly.

Johnson turned back to the recruits and they fell silent.

"Some of you have found that you can best employ your talents through excellence in a single field. We have data analysts, cooks, engineers, naval weapons operators, scientists, medics, programmers, and many others. All are vital to our efforts."

Many would still be smarting from dropping out of the recruit training programme. She wanted it to be clear that they were just as important as those who'd made it through. After all, none of the soldiers, sailors and marines she'd served with had been through that kind of training, and that hadn't stopped them achieving great things.

"You are hereby granted the title 'Specialists'," she announced.

The entire body of forty Specialists came to attention together, without an order being spoken. Even knowing how it was done, it was an impressive sight. Johnson made a note to compliment the optio who'd had the idea to coordinate the ceremony by EIS comms.

The Specialists marched out smartly, in groups of ten, and came to a halt in a line facing the podium. Johnson and Issawi walked along the row each time, shaking hands, exchanging a few words, and attaching the appropriate Specialist pin to each person's collar.

Once the Specialists had returned to their ranks and stood at ease, Johnson continued her address.

"The rest of you standing before me have become adept at a wide range of disciplines. You are resilient, strong, and adaptable ... Today, you become Legionaries."

Like the Specialists, the Legionaries crashed to attention without a spoken word. They too marched out in groups of ten. Johnson and Issawi presented them with their Legionary pin, a gunmetal grey gladius surrounded by an ellipse.

"We have studied you throughout your training. We have pushed you, often beyond what you thought possible. Some of you have shown yourselves to be ready to lead."

She paused to let that sink in. The bit that came next was her favourite part of command.

"Legionary Canetti, Specialist Enquist, Optio Khan, Optio Malinowski, Specialist Olbrich, Specialist Yang. Front and centre."

They marched out. Johnson smiled as Canetti mounted the steps. She'd had a hard time convincing the rest of the panel that he was ready; the other candidates had already served with distinction in their previous lives.

"You are hereby promoted to the rank of centurion. Khan will take responsibility for the Search and Rescue detachment. Canetti and Malinowski will lead the two line centuries, under the direct command of Centurion Anson. The rest of you will take charge in your respective specialisms."

After the presentation of rank slides bearing crimson semi-circular icons, and the exchange of salutes, Johnson called out another list of names.

"You are hereby promoted to the rank of decurion. Your postings will be announced shortly."

For the last time that day, Johnson and Issawi went down a line, shaking hands and awarding badges. This time, the recipients were given rank slides bearing an upright red rectangle.

Johnson retook the podium, and surveyed her cohort. Pride swelled her chest.

"Tomorrow, you start working on explosive demolition," she said. "But for the rest of today, I want everyone to let their hair down. Relax, and enjoy the party."

She smiled, then came to attention.

"Parade!"

The ranks stiffened.

"Parade, 'hun!"

A crash, as several hundred men and women stamped their feet.

"Officer on parade. Diiiismiss!"

Johnson returned their salute, then the Legionaries and Specialists turned to their right and marched off. Three paces in, they broke step and cheered. They clapped each other on the shoulder, fist bumped and chest barged. Some groups lingered on the square, chatting. Others made a quick exit, heading, no doubt, for the bar set up for the occasion.

#

The woods were quiet. A couple of birds sang to each other, an insect buzzed from flower to flower, but otherwise nothing. A damp, mossy smell pervaded the clearing. From her perch on a fallen log, the only movement Johnson could see was that of a small mammal foraging for nuts. That morning she had finished the first of Indie's book suggestions, and now half-expected Ratty to stand up and address her.

A gunship crested the treeline, and flared to a hover ten metres from her. Ten armoured humans and a combat unit dropped from the aircraft. On hitting the ground they crouched, absorbing the impact, then sprang up into a run. As each human reached the edge of the clearing, they dropped into cover, training their weapon into the wood; the combat unit loitered where it could react to an attack in any direction. The moment the last Legionary was in position, the gunship spun, put its nose down and accelerated away.

Johnson peered down at the Legionary who had taken cover by her log. He steadfastly ignored her, keeping his eyes on his allotted arc. She lifted her head and pulled up the IFF overlay; red icons appeared in the distance, showing her the locations of the enemy forces. Issawi had positioned them to simulate a guerrilla camp.

^Route's on your maps. Charlie take point,^ sent the decurion in charge of the section. ^Move out.^

One by one, the soldiers stood and filed into the woods. They moved carefully, without even breaking a twig; weapons up and sweeping. The combat unit slunk off by itself, covering their right flank. The last man out of the clearing swung round to check the rear, giving a slight nod to Johnson as he scanned past her.

This was the sixth deployment she had observed today. The Legionaries were settling quickly into their new teams; where possible, Issawi had kept successful groups together from the training platoons. Johnson was more and more aware of each passing day; the twelve month deadline from Vice-Admiral Koblensk's message would run out in seven weeks. She didn't know how long it would take for the Red Fleet to deploy once that time passed, but she would have to get her forces moving in the next three weeks so they could be sure of being at Concorde before them. *The Indescribable Joy of Destruction* was out, collecting the data from the probes that it had left monitoring radio signals. Perhaps that would bring a more concrete D-Day, but she doubted it.

#

Centurion Khan walked Johnson through the training village. The streets were filled with rubble and pieces of metal sheet, though the buildings still stood.

They passed a section of Legionaries part-way up a tumble-down pile of bricks, trying to stabilise it. Lower down, another section pulled a dummy from the ruin. On the opposite side of the street, individuals worked with combat units to search for 'survivors'.

"This is what I wanted you to see," said Khan as they turned a corner.

Johnson stopped, taking in the scene. Rows of survival shelters filled the plaza. Specialists and Legionaries were busy triaging 'casualties', serving from a cookhouse, and recording everyone who arrived. The makeshift hospital was surrounded by defensive positions manned by Legionaries and combat units. Johnson dared to hope that perhaps they could do it. Just maybe they could save the people of Concorde.

"We can set one of these aid centres up in half an hour," Khan said. "They will act as the kernel of a safe zone, a focus for the surviving community."

"How many can you staff?" asked Johnson.

He grimaced. "Only five. But we have the resources for twenty. If we can get survivors to help, we could stretch our staff out."

"Very good," Johnson said. "I take it you're working on plans to induct locals into the scheme?"

"Naturally. My wife trains civilian first responders back on Gliese 832c, I've already written a first draft of a crash course based on her programme." He paused, his face taking on the slightly vacant look people tended to adopt when receiving an EIS message.

"Sorry, Ma'am. Got a real shout." He broke into a run. "Indie'll fill you in," he called, before rounding a corner and leaving her sight.

^Indie?^ she sent, strolling along the central street in the tented hospital.

^A couple of Legionaries didn't return from their morning run, and no-one could connect a channel to their EIS. The initial sweeps found nothing, so their decurion passed it up the line. Centurion Canetti requested Search and Rescue Detachment involvement a minute ago.^

Johnson ducked inside a tent. Screens filled three walls; faces of imaginary survivors scrolled across, updating as new ones were logged into the system.

^I take it you'll keep me up to speed?^ she sent.

^You know me well enough by now to know the answer to that.^

^Yes, I guess I do,^ she sent. ^And I don't suppose I

need to tell you I'll be in my office, either.^

Johnson stared at the screen in front of her. The Legionaries couldn't have just got lost; and it took a lot to block a comms signal.

She minimised the unfinished policy document. ^Specialist Smith?^

There was a delay of a few seconds, and Johnson checked up on his status. She cringed when she realised it was the middle of his night rotation.

^Yes, Prefect?^

^I was wondering if your surveys had identified any signs of large predators on this landmass?^

^No, Ma'am,^ he replied. ^You would have been informed had we done so.^

^None of those giant carnivorous plants in the western sector?^

^None. They appear to be confined to the former farmland.^

She sighed, mentally crossing off those possibilities.

^Thank you,^ she sent. ^Sorry for waking you. I assume you heard about the missing Legionaries?^

^Yes, I had heard, Ma'am. And don't worry about waking me. We're all worried about them too.^

Johnson tried to read the next report in her queue, an analysis of the dietary needs for extended training duties. Her eyes glazed, and she couldn't make out the letters.

She placed her hands on her desk and pushed. Her chair slid backwards as she straightened her arms. Her fingers drummed on the work surface a couple of times, then she stood and headed for the door.

^I'm fed up with flying a desk,^ she sent to Indie. ^I'm going to join the search.^

^Thought you would. I have a transport waiting for you at the mouth of Alpha tunnel.^

After a quick stop to stuff some warm clothes, food and water into a rucksack, Johnson jogged up the long curve of the tunnel. The colour-shifting form of one of *Orion*'s dropships rested on the grass outside, lit by sunlight that appeared almost electric. Dark clouds loomed behind the small vessel.

It felt odd, stepping into the craft without a combat drone at her side. Unit 01 and the others were practising anti-looting operations with Anson, and couldn't be spared to help search for a couple of lost Legionaries.

As they lifted off, the first large raindrops hit the hull. Johnson pulled up a satellite image, and replayed the feed to judge the speed of the approaching storm.

We've got to find them soon. Searching's going to be a lot harder once that hits.

The dropship bucked in the strong turbulence, and Johnson's stomach was left behind for a moment. A series of flashes of bright white light flooded the cabin, casting stark shadows. Then the pitch of the engine noise increased as the craft fought against a downdraft.

"Prefect," said Orion, materialising in the seat beside Johnson with none of her trademark dramatics. "I detected something unusual in that last lightning strike."

Johnson shifted in her seat, pleased with herself for not jumping when Orion appeared.

"Define unusual," she said.

"Something I can't identify. It was only there for a fraction of a second; some sort of frequency-shifted reflection of the lightning."

Johnson raised an eyebrow. "A sensor glitch? A spoof signal from all the EM?"

"No, I've checked and..."

^Centurion Khan just put in a call for armed backup,^ interrupted Indie.

Orion pretended to study the flight controls.

^Thank you,^ Johnson replied, then opened a channel to Khan. ^Centurion, update?^

^We found blood, and cases from one of our issued sidearms,^ he replied. ^Not sure what happened yet.^

Johnson pulled up a map in her head and inserted the dropship's performance data into it.

^OK. I'll be at your position in three minutes.^

She spun the seat round, rose, and strode purposefully into the hold.

"Orion? Do you have any personal weapons or armour in here? I only have my stun pistol."

Orion appeared beside a floor-to-ceiling locker.

"Here, in the crash cupboard" she said, pointing. "There are some armoured vests and some pulse carbines."

As Johnson jumped down from the hatch, she was hit by a wall of rain. She ducked low and ran towards the edge of the clearing. A shadow moved, and coalesced into the shape of a man. Centurion Khan beckoned Johnson over. He guided her deeper into the sparse woodland, running hunched over alongside her. After about thirty metres, he indicated a large fallen trunk, and they dropped down beside it. A couple of Khan's men glanced over at them from their own positions, before returning to their watch.

"We tracked them to a cave five hundred metres that way," he shouted in her ear. The hammering of the rain precluded all other vocal communication. "It looks like they have company."

Johnson was sure she must have misheard. Other humans on the planet hadn't figured in any of her theories of what had happened.

"Who?"

"Unknown. There were definitely four sets of footprints, but we don't yet know anything else."

^All personnel, apart from the two we knew were missing, are accounted for,^ sent Indie. ^And before you ask, Orion, Seren and myself are the only ships up here.^

"We'd normally send a micro-drone to go and take a peep, but it can't fly in this weather," shouted Khan. "We're going to have to do it the old-fashioned way."

As if to emphasise his point, a gust of wind broke a branch and flung it down beside him. Sodden leaves slapped Johnson on the cheek.

The little daemon of failure poked its beak in. She had failed to keep her people safe, failed to predict an attack like this.

She squeezed her fists tight, nails pressing hard into the flesh of her palms. They had to save them, but she would have to stay focussed.

"You're sure the approach is clear?" she asked.

"Yes."

"Right, let's get going then," she shouted, and made to get up.

Khan caught her by the arm. Her biceps twitched in response to the deep ache the contact triggered. She managed to keep it from her face, refusing to acknowledge that the bullet wound was still raw.

"You can't get involved," he protested. "You're too valuable, and you aren't even in proper armour."

She fixed him a stern glare. No way was she hanging back; she couldn't forgive herself if anything went wrong.

"Backup's quarter of an hour away. I'm all you've got," she replied.

Johnson crawled forwards, inch by inch. To left and right Khan's men, kept low and crept silently up the slope. Soon they'd surround the cave entrance.

She peered through a crack between the slimy boulders. The two Legionaries lay propped up against the wall of the cave. Johnson could just make out cord binding their ankles; presumably their wrists too, but they were behind their backs. She tried again to connect to their EIS, but couldn't.

Two men sat on rocks nearby, talking. They wore dark blue uniforms, with red and white patches on the upper arms. Each cradled what was clearly a weapon, but not a kind Johnson had encountered before. She couldn't hear what they were saying, but from the occasional glances towards the cave mouth, and their sodden clothes, she guessed it was about the storm.

^Charlie in position,^ sent Khan.

^Delta in position,^ sent his optio.

Johnson pressed herself against the ground, muddy water soaking through her clothes to the last dry patches of her skin.

^We've got two hostiles, armed with weapons of an unknown type, no armour, sitting in the open. Two hostages, low, against the right wall,^ she sent.

^I'll have combat units with you in three minutes,^ sent Indie.

^Tell the pilot to stand off,^ sent Khan. ^We can't risk alerting the hostiles. Drop the drones where Johnson landed and have them tab in.^

^Understood,^ replied Indie.

One man stood, rubbed his blond beard, then clapped his colleague on the shoulder. The seated man laughed, and waved in Johnson's direction. The bearded man came towards her, looking around.

^One coming my way,^ she sent. ^Stand by.^

He stopped on the other side of the rock she lay behind. Her heart rate slowed as she found the calm place that allowed her to concentrate on the coming fight.

She fingered the trigger on her pulse carbine. His chest and head were visible above the rock, but she would have to move to line up her shot.

The enemy soldier turned back and called to his friend, receiving another laugh in return.

He turned back towards Johnson's hiding place. She tensed, ready to strike.

The man shuffled, then bowed his head. A new splashing noise joined the rain, and a steaming rivulet crept its way between the rocks towards her.

^He's taking a slash,^ she sent. ^Moving in three, two, one...^

She rolled up onto a knee, and aimed at his chest. Legionaries popped up either side.

Johnson opened her mouth to demand the enemies' surrender. The bearded one let go of his flies, and reached for his weapon.

Johnson squeezed the trigger, and a triplet of laser pulses burnt into his chest. Blood erupted from his head and back as the Legionaries opened up.

Dammit.

A series of bright flashes accompanied loud concussions that echoed around the chamber. Khan sprinted in, and clubbed the second hostile with his rifle butt before he could retrieve his weapon from the floor. He went down, dazed but still conscious. A Legionary kicked the weapon away, and trained his rifle on him, while another knelt on his back and cuffed him.

Johnson stood and scanned the wood, noting the signals from four combat units sprinting her way, then stepped into the cave. The hostages had been cut free, and medics tended to their wounds. She studied their attackers from a distance, waiting for the Legionaries to check for booby traps before she approached. Their uniforms weren't Congress or Republic, or any of the independents she knew, but the colour and cut suggested navy; certainly they weren't designed for ground combat. Part of her wanted to lay into them for hurting her people; another part thought they deserved the chance to explain.

Movement deeper in the cave drew Johnson's attention. The surviving enemy writhed on his back. Two Legionaries held him down, while another readied a hypogun. Before she could apply it to his arm, the man stopped thrashing. His body slumped to the floor.

Johnson sprinted the few metres over to him. Blood trickled from the enemy's nose and ear; deep crimson, edged in straw. His open eyes were bloodshot and lifeless, the pupils both blown.

A clatter of metal on rock announced the arrival of the combat units. They stood alert at the entrance, awaiting further instructions now there were no hostiles to engage.

Johnson paced just inside the cave. The rain had eased off, but enough was still falling to keep her under shelter. The medics hadn't been able to revive the enemy, and were at a loss as to the cause of death. The Legionaries who'd been captured would recover; one had a nasty chest wound, but the enemy had treated him, probably saved his life.

They should've been safe. And I couldn't do anything to stop them being taken. I don't even know how their attackers got here, or what they wanted.

Khan approached her, and waited patiently for her to stop pacing.

"Where did they come from?" asked Khan. "They looked more like shipwrecked sailors than a deep insertion team."

Johnson's head jerked up, and she stared at him. "Say that again."

"They looked more like shipwrecked sailors than..."

Johnson turned and strode into the woods, back towards the dropship she'd arrived on. The combat units fell into step beside her. How could she have missed this?

"Come on," she called. Khan hurried to catch up, beckoning for a couple of his Legionaries to follow.

^Issawi,^ she sent. ^I want everyone kitted up and armed. And I mean everyone; we might have more intruders.^

He sent a confirmation ping back and she broke into a jog.

"They came from one of those ships that attacked us a couple of weeks back," Johnson said, as Khan drew level.

"We tracked all the debris," Khan replied. "I personally oversaw the search, and there were no escape pods."

^Indie, can you send Centurion Khan the recordings of that encounter you had in...^ Johnson searched her memory, for the first time conscious of the process of accessing the additional storage in her new EIS. "...Y6782a."

Indie shared the feed with her. She had never actually watched it before; had only remembered it as a report he had uploaded on his return. The destroyer was very similar to the ships that had intruded on *The Serendipity of Meeting's* shakedown trials. The recording stopped once the stealth shuttle had docked.

"So," said Khan. "Any of those ships could have launched shuttles and, unless they happened to pass Indie when he was using his gravitational sensors, we wouldn't have seen them."

They arrived at the dropship. The hatch opened as soon as they stepped out into the clearing.

^Orion, can you take us to where you picked up that anomalous reflection?^ asked Johnson.

^Certainly,^ came the reply. ^Indie has taken the liberty of dispatching a flight of drones to escort us. They'll be here by the time you strap in.^

Chapter 23

"This is where I observed the anomaly," said Orion, bringing the dropship round in a lazy circle and marking the site on the map. "It matches the size of the stealth shuttle Indie recorded."

"OK," replied Johnson. "Take us down a safe distance away."

She turned and peered around her seat into the hold.

"The combat units do the initial recce," she said to Khan. "If they give the all clear, your team can go in and see what you can find."

"I'll get out of your way for now," said Orion, before dimming and disappearing.

Johnson watched from inside the dropship as the combat units advanced on the anomaly's location. Unit 03 took the lead, pushing through the undergrowth, its sensors pumping out radiation across a wide range of frequencies. Johnson recalled the last time she'd worked with that unit, back on Scragend. While Unit 01 made her think of a faithful Alsatian, 03 reminded her of a tenacious pit-bull.

Huh. I could swear it's limping.

The robots entered a small clearing, and paused. Unit 03 left two legs in the air, and wobbled slightly. Immersed in the sensor feeds, Johnson was overwhelmed; it was as if she were simultaneously blind drunk and suffering a bad hangover. Her brain, even with its augmentation, couldn't reconcile what she was seeing.

She pulled out of the feed. Cutting the lights and screens in the cockpit, she closed her eyes and pressed her middle fingertips against the bridge of her nose. The pressure helped. After a minute, she dared to open her eyes. The remaining tell-tales on the dashboard sent sharp pricks of pain into her skull, but they soon faded.

As her eyes became accustomed to the dark, she was able to focus on the straight lines of the cockpit, willing the world to stop spinning. It slowed, and she realised she was snatching sharp, short gasps. She calmed herself, slowing her breathing and heart rate.

A bright blue light flared in the seat beside her, stabbing into her brain before she could screw her eyes shut.

"What the..." she started.

"I am sorry. Was that me?" asked Orion.

Johnson opened one eye, winced, and closed it again.

"Can you dim yourself a bit?" she asked.

The glare from the seat next to her diminished. Johnson tried opening an eye again.

"A bit more?" asked Orion.

Johnson nodded.

The light faded further, and she was able to open both eyes without too much discomfort.

"What happened?" asked Orion. "I lost the feeds from the combat units when they stepped into the clearing. My self-defence routines spotted an intrusion and closed the channels."

"An attack?" said Johnson.

"Yes. I've never encountered anything like it. Something attempted to disrupt my processes through the sensor feed. It burnt out five of my relays before it was stopped."

Johnson ran her fingers through her hair, massaging her scalp.

"I think it had a go at me too," she said, and then with wide eyes "Where's Indie?"

"He is OK. I can see him from up here," said Orion, leaning forward. "He was watching the feeds too. I guess his receiver array got cut off as a precaution; I understand he erected some rather hair-trigger defences after someone tried taking him over through a comms channel."

Johnson exhaled sharply. A couple of deep breaths, and she was ready.

"I wonder if they hit the Legionaries they took with something like that? Would explain the lack of distress signal from them."

Orion nodded slowly. "They have my sympathy if that was the case."

Johnson added her agreement. She certainly could not have fought off a physical attack while experiencing that mental onslaught. Even if all they did was jam the radio sets they carried, their EIS would not have had the range to call the base. She attempted to open a channel to Issawi, but a new flash of pain exploded in her head.

"I want a 100km exclusion zone placed around this position," she said to Orion, pressing a knuckle hard against her eyebrow. "Let Issawi know that I want a backup team ready, but they are not to approach without direct authorisation from myself or Centurion Khan. Oh, and get Mustafa on the line, he may have some insight into this."

Johnson closed her eyes and stole herself against what she knew was about to come.

^Unit 03, pull back,^ she sent.

It didn't respond. She gritted her teeth.

^Any combat unit, this is Prefect Johnson. Pull back from the clearing.^

Nothing moved.

"It seems the combat units are stuck there until we can figure something out," she said, and reclined in her chair.

"Can you hit it with something small?" asked Johnson after a few minutes staring at the ceiling. "Something that'll just disable it?"

"Not from orbit; I don't have anything below kiloton yield," replied Orion. "The dropship has suitable weapons, but I doubt it could target the shuttle with those defences. Even if I sent missiles programmed to hit the location, it might be able to override their orders."

"One of my men has rigged his helmet cam on a stick," called Khan from the hold. "He reckons we could use it to test if the effect is still active."

"That's a good idea," said Johnson. "Orion, could you set that Legionary up with a counter-intrusion routine? Something that could report an attempt but not allow it to get any further?"

"I will send one over."

"Leaving the camera connected to our network would still be a risk," said Mustafa, appearing on a viewscreen. "Perhaps a simple LED to show if it is being interfered with would suffice?"

"I'll get him working on it," said Khan, turning back to his console.

"What about the aerial drones?" asked Johnson.

"Same problem as the walking ones," said Orion, shrugging.

"I could try sending in a Legionary with his EIS disconnected," said Khan without looking up.

"Too risky," said Mustafa. "It could directly..."

Johnson waved them both quiet. An idea was forming, but her mind was still sluggish. "How exactly did that thing attack us?"

"It flooded the sensor arrays of the combat units, and was passed on to us through the feed," said Orion.

"Which sensor arrays, specifically?"

"Microwave, infrared, visible, ultraviolet; all the EM bands the robots use."

Johnson frowned.

"What about audio?" she asked.

"I didn't detect any intrusion attempts on that feed," said Orion.

"The data transfer rate would be too slow to be useful," explained Mustafa.

Johnson sat upright and banged her fist on the arm of her chair.

"Khan? Do you think your men could lasso me a combat unit?"

It took several attempts, and a lot of sweat, to snag and reel in Unit 03. Once it was out of sight of the enemy shuttle, Johnson strode up to it and looked it over.

"No sign of physical damage," she thought out loud.

She ran her hand over its body, and released the armoured flap covering an access port. Deftly, she connected her pad to it, and ran a diagnostic. It came back clear; the robot had shut down to protect itself. Holding her breath, Johnson booted it up.

Unit 03 jerked back, its weapons scanning around.

"Shhhh. Easy there," said Johnson, reaching out her palm in front of it. "You were attacked by some sort of invasive routine. We had to drag you out of the transmission range."

The drone lowered its weapons back into the recesses on its back, and lowered itself 'til its belly touched the ground. Johnson stroked it with one hand as she unplugged her pad and closed the hatch with the other.

"I need you to shut down all sensors and input feeds, apart from audio and tactile," Johnson said, head close to the grey metalloceramic body. "We don't think the target can insert using them."

^Better get everyone to turn off their EIS too,^ she added to Khan. The pain was tolerable this time.

"I understand," replied Unit 03. "What do you want me to do? I won't be able to track any targets."

Johnson looked up at it sharply. It was the first time Unit 03 had spoken to her like that. She had come to expect it of Unit 01, but the other Units had so far stuck to digital confirmations of her orders.

"One of the Legionaries will fire their weapon into the air every ten seconds, you should be able to form an image of your surroundings from the echoes. I want you to approach the shuttle and terminate the source of the transmission."

"I assume you require minimum force be used?" Unit 03 asked.

"Whatever it takes to shut it off, but start small."

The drone turned, and walked confidently back towards the clearing.

"Are you sure it turned off its visual sensors?" asked Khan.

"Yes. It's just retracing the steps it took last time."

Unit 03 stopped at the edge of the clearing. Johnson connected to its telemetry, opening it in a window in her vision rather than fully immersing. The memory of the pain from last time was too vivid.

The first shot rang out, and the drone edged forwards. After the first minute, it moved more confidently, having built up a three dimensional map of its surroundings. By ten minutes had passed, it had reached the shuttle.

Unit 03 extended a claw and tapped on the side of the vessel. For several minutes it tapped and listened, ran its claws over the surface and felt. Johnson reviewed the data as it flowed to her, getting her first impression of the shape and size of the shuttle. Stubby, with no atmospheric control surfaces, it was clearly designed primarily for use in space. It could probably hold ten people. Most importantly, it matched the images taken by Indie in Y6782a.

The drone pounced, ripping off a hatch in the side of its target. As the metal door clanged to the ground, finding a rock amongst the torn up earth, the drone reached inside. It felt around, then dragged itself half into the hold. Carefully, it pulled at the consoles in the cockpit, teasing them out of place and dumping them on the floor. When it had finished, it waited.

Johnson gave the thumbs up to a Legionary lying on his side by a large fallen tree trunk at the edge of the clearing. He nodded, and raised his improvised probe. The moment the camera on the end cleared the tree trunk, a red light flashed amongst a bunch of wires dangling from it. The Legionary shook his head, and lowered the camera.

"It'll take me a minute to purge the memory and reset it," he called over.

Johnson nodded acknowledgement, then cupped her hands to her mouth and shouted "No effect. Try again."

Unit 03 clambered on top of the shuttle, feeling around with its front claws.

"No need to shout so loud, Ma'am," said Khan from just behind her elbow. "It's got far better hearing than us."

She metaphorically kicked herself then looked over her shoulder to him. He waved away her thanks before she could speak.

The sound of tearing metal brought her attention back to the shuttle as Unit 03 tore a dome off its roof. A representation of the antennae thus uncovered built up in her vision as the drone felt around them. Its survey complete, the combat unit ripped them out and tossed them after the dome.

Johnson raised her thumb again, and again the probe was lifted into position. She held her breath, letting it out between her teeth when the red telltale lit.

"No effect. Try again," she called, this time without causing those standing nearby to wince.

Unit 03 continued its exploration of the shuttle. It didn't find anything else worth tearing out, and retired a dozen paces. Johnson had just started to wonder if it had given up, when it deployed its rail gun. A half-second burst sent twenty depleted uranium slugs tearing through the air. Around Johnson, the Legionaries ducked for cover, bringing their weapons up and scanning around.

"Stand down," called Johnson, the only one who hadn't moved. "It's just the robot escalating its attack on the shuttle."

"Talk about using sledgehammer to crack a nut," muttered Khan, dusting himself down.

The camera was raised on its stick a third time. And this time the light did not come on.

"Unit 03," Johnson shouted. "Wait, out."

Khan stepped forwards.

"What now?" he asked.

"Now I go in," Johnson replied.

Khan raised an eyebrow.

"I know," Johnson said, steeling herself for another argument. "But there really isn't another option. I've already survived one attack by that thing, I don't know if anyone else could."

"You could order Unit 03 to open its sensors."

"And if the shuttle's faking it we could lose him and be back to square one. Square zero, actually, as there aren't any other units within reach."

Him? Did I just call Unit 03 'him'?

Khan beckoned one of the Legionaries over.

"Fine," he said, as a giant jogged towards them. "But you are going to be tied to one end of a rope, and Higgins here is going to have the other end."

Johnson crawled up to the edge of the clearing. Wriggling out of her sling, she handed her pulse carbine to the Legionary lying behind his log, who promptly slung it on his back. She drew her sidearm, checking it was charged and set for maximum effect. She was glad she was in the habit of carrying a non-lethal weapon; if the shuttle's defences somehow subverted her, she wouldn't pose a threat to her own men.

Higgins shuffled into place to her right, lying on his back and bracing his feet against the log. He offered her a rope with a karabiner on the end, which she clipped to the back of her vest.

"Ready," she called.

Everyone perked up, paying that bit more attention to their surroundings.

"If this goes south," said Khan from her left, "we extract you and bug out. Orion will flatten this whole area from orbit."

"Give Unit 03 time to get clear," she replied.

He frowned. "I know we're short of..."

"You give him time to get clear," she said, enunciating very clearly.

"Understood, Ma'am."

Johnson did one last check. She knew everyone was ready, but it covered for the moment it took to compose herself. Closing her eyes, she stood up.

When nothing happened, she peeked with one eye. No blinding flashes of pain.

She opened the other eye. Unit 03 stood a few metres back from the smouldering shuttle at the far end of the clearing.

"We're good so far," she said to the people lying at her feet, then sat on the log and swung her legs over.

It took longer than she'd expected to reach the shuttle. Broken branches littered the ground, some covering holes that could easily break an ankle. As she passed Unit 03, she thanked it for its efforts in a quiet voice. It dipped its body slightly.

Reaching the shuttle, she ran her eyes over the pockmarked hull. Several of the railgun rounds had melted their way through, leaving neat holes surrounded by heat-discoloured metal. The others had splashed, leaving craters.

She pulled herself up into the hold, coughing slightly in the smoke from burnt plastic. The interior was trashed. Some rounds had come in through the open hatch and bounced around inside, where they'd been joined by flakes of metal spalled off the interior where rounds had hit the hull.

She risked activating the electromagnetic field interfaces on her EIS, biting her teeth in anticipation. But the shuttle was dead; no currents flowed anywhere.

^Is everything OK down there?^

Johnson jerked her head up and stared into the sky. A knot she'd only be vaguely aware of released.

^Everything's under control,^ she sent. ^How are things up there, Indie?^

#

Johnson entered the base infirmary with a mixture of trepidation and eager anticipation. One ward had been designated as the morgue; every time she'd had to attend an autopsy she was reminded of those she'd lost. At least this time it wasn't anyone under her command lying on the slab. Or someone she loved.

She caught site of the door and shuddered. Before she went in there, however, she had a more pleasant task to perform. In a small room off the main triage area, the rescued Legionaries were recovering. She knocked on the door and waited.

"Come in." The voice was strong and cheerful.

She opened the door and stuck her head around.

"As you were," she said before the two had a chance to react to her presence. "Is it OK if I come in for a moment?"

"Of course, Ma'am," said the one in the nearest bed; the one who had called through the door. He reached over to put his pad down on the bedside cabinet, wincing slightly as he straightened again.

She squeezed past the end of his bed and paused by a chair. "Mind if I..."

"No worries, Ma'am."

She looked to the occupant of the other bed. He was propped up with pillows, his eyes covered in a bandage.

"His eyes are fine," said the Legionary. "He just can't stand the light. Doc thought he'd be better off in here with me than in a blacked-out room by himself."

Johnson felt a dull echo of the pain in her skull just after the attack.

"When they brought us in he was raving; he grabbed a scalpel and tried to cut into his own head. They've put him on something to calm him down. Doc says he can hear us but he's a bit too far out of it to respond."

Johnson locked her jaw; her hand squeezed her knee above the prosthetic. The flashback to the struggle in Indie's recycling plant faded, and she worriedly shifted her gaze to the conscious Legionary. He didn't look like he'd noticed her absence.

"Well, I'm glad you're both safe," she said. "I'm sure you'll be back on duty in no time."

"I hear that you led the rescue. You'd gone by I came round."

"I happened to be in the area. I wouldn't say I lead it; Centurion Khan was in charge."

"Whatever, I wanted to say thank you."

A prickly heat started to rise from her collar. She hastily stood and walked to the door. She stopped with her hand on the handle. "If there's anything I can get for you?"

The man looked to his teammate and back to her. "Real food. I know it's a big ask, but..."

She smiled reassuringly. "I'll see what I can do."

As she stood in the corridor, she made a note to have the last of the fruit she'd received from Clovis sent over to the ward.

The sound of a medic greeting Anson carried in from the corridor. It was time. Johnson couldn't put off visiting the morgue any longer.

The medic guided them both into the room. Two bodies lay on tables in the centre, surrounded by imaging equipment. Johnson's eyes locked onto the tables. She hadn't expected them to be so similar to the one on *The Indescribable Joy of Destruction*, the one she'd woken on twice.

"They had brain implants, similar to our EIS," said a man. Johnson snapped back into the present. The surgeon stood with his back to them, washing his hands in a metal sink.

"The one in the first individual was intact, though wiped. The one in the second has undergone some sort of explosive event; I suspect he triggered it himself."

Johnson leant over one of the bodies, studying his face. With the beard shaved off, he looked about thirty.

"I don't get it," said Anson. "First the ship self-destructs before any escape pods get away, now he commits suicide."

Johnson shifted her weight, and her finger bumped against a scalpel. She saw her hand hovering over the knives the first time she used *The Indescribable Joy of Destruction's* galley.

"Don't they know they'll be well treated?" continued Anson. "Even pirates keep prisoners in good conditions in the hope of a better ransom."

Johnson made a fist and withdrew her hand.

"Either they have something very important they want to keep secret, or they are used to fighting people who don't follow the same rules as us," she said. "Perhaps both. Either way, they fear being taken alive."

The surgeon joined them, drying his hands and arms on a white cloth.

"I've passed the implants to Centurion Yang," he said. "He reckons they might have shielding of some kind against the intrusive signals."

"Anything interesting about the bodies themselves?" asked Johnson.

The surgeon sighed. "No. They were fit and healthy. Bone density suggests they were used to slightly above average gravity; 1.2g perhaps."

"So clues to where they come from?"

"I've run isotope profiles on samples from their teeth. They didn't match anything in our combined databases. I'd be able to match it to a water sample if you found somewhere you suspected they grew up."

At least the lack of a match ruled out Congressional and Republican colonies, along with many of the major independents. They all kept comprehensive records for forensic analysis; knowing someone's home planet tended to be the first step in identifying them.

"So, it's looking like we have a new player," said Anson. "Coincidence? Or is this linked to the Red Fleet?"

Johnson shook her head. "We don't have enough data to confirm either way."

She turned to the surgeon. "Thank you for fixing up Watson and Carré. What's their prognosis?"

"Watson could be back on light duties now," replied the surgeon. "I felt it better to keep him here, though. It could aid Carré's recovery."

"Is it bad?" asked Anson.

"No brain damage. It's more psychological. He's locked in, unable to consciously access the outside world." The surgeon arched his back, pressing his spine with one hand.

"There are things we can try. I'm sure we'll get him back."

Anson looked away awkwardly.

"Did you get anything from the shuttle?" the surgeon asked, looking to Johnson.

"The systems were a total write-off, so no luck on finding out how the intrusions were generated," she replied. "But we did manage to work out how the stealth coating worked. More importantly, Mustafa spotted a weakness we could exploit."

"You can track them?" said the surgeon.

"Yes. We've already swept the planet and the space around it. If any others are lurking out there, they're a long way off."

"So they were just two people who managed to escape?"

"Probably," said Johnson, remembering her good fortune to be standing in the hangar when *Repulse*'s reactor failed.

#

Johnson and Issawi found themselves alone on the patio above the tea plantation. He looked to her, and she shrugged. She didn't know why they'd been summoned either.

"I didn't even know he was back," she said.

Issawi guided her over to the table. As they sat down, a spread of cakes appeared, along with the obligatory pot of tea.

Johnson reached out for a slice of cardamom and lime cake.

"I've got something," said Indie, materialising on the patio without his usual pretence of a pedestrian entry. "I was reviewing signals intercepts, and a report from a deep recce ship stood out.

"Tea?" asked Johnson, holding up the pot.

"I came across an odd entry," continued Indie. "They picked up Republic drive signatures. Loads of them."

"A raid in force?" suggested Issawi, accepting a cup from Johnson.

"Unlikely," said Indie. "When I conducted deep recces, my crew were told about any Republic assets expected to be in the area. We avoided them; no point treading the same ground."

"Did they say where the ships were heading?" asked Johnson. Her whole world shrank down to this one question.

"No, they couldn't tell. But the jump point they were heading for is consistent with an approach on Concorde."

Johnson paused mid-sip, looking at Indie over the golden rim.

"I thought we had another couple of weeks," said Issawi, brushing crumbs off his shirt.

"Perhaps something happened and they moved things up?" said Indie.

They got wind of our attempts to get the word out. If it was one of those newspaper people...

Johnson opened a window in the air beside her and summoned a star map. "How long have we got?"

"There are a lot of factors," said Indie, taking a seat opposite Johnson. "They might not go direct, they might stop to refuel, they might only be moving to a staging area."

"Worst case?"

"Worst case, we have to leave within twenty six hours. We're lucky the jump topography favours us."

"Are the ground forces ready?" Johnson asked, turning to Issawi.

"Ready as they can be. We can do final shake-downs in-transit."

"OK, start prepping to load," she said to Issawi, then turned back to Indie. "Where are Orion and Seren?"

"On their way. I took the liberty of recalling them."

"Right. We leave as soon as they're back and everyone is aboard. No point wasting time."

"What about the guys who attacked us? What if they come back?" asked Indie.

Johnson thought for a moment. "We can't spare forces to defend Robespierre; we'll just have to take everyone with us and hope."

Indie looked up into the sky. "Orion just jumped back in-system."

"Great," Johnson said. "Let's get going."

Issawi inclined his head to her, and vanished.

"I must go and, er, brief Orion," Indie said, before rising and walking to the door. He glanced back, suit flowing into his captain's outfit. He turned and drew himself up, before saluting Johnson. She sighed quietly and sat upright to return the gesture.

After he'd left, she took a look around the simulation. The gardens had grown again. A stand of strelitzia edged the patio, their orange and purple blooms like a flock of alien birds.

Johnson turned to leave, then stopped.

Oh, to hell with it.

She grabbed a wedge of triple chocolate fudge cake and took a bite.

The patio vanished and she was back in her bed. The wall opposite showed a starry sky, as if she were on the surface instead of buried hundreds of metres underground. In the distance, power surges coursed through her awareness as dormitory lights came on in quick succession.

At least I'm not the only one getting up this early.

She swung her legs out from under the duvet with a sigh. However well heated a room was, she always found it too cold when she first got up. She padded across the room, discarding T-shirt and pants as she went, and into the bathroom. It was only once the hot shower was cascading down over her head that she told the room to gradually bring the lights on.

#

Johnson dialled the speed up on the treadmill. Gravity on *The Indescribable Joy of Destruction* had been adjusted to match Concorde's two days into the journey and her leg needed to recalibrate.

^Indie? Are you sure the gravity is correct?^

^Positive,^ he replied. ^One point two standard. Why?^

^It normally takes me longer than this to adjust.^

^That'll be your new implants assisting your balance and reflexes.^

Johnson brought up the schematics of her enhanced EIS. A representation of her head and shoulders appeared, slowly rotating. The tendrils stretching from the devices glowed blue, weaving through her brain and stretching down her spine.

^Are they really that integrated already?^

^When did you last use a menu?^

Now that he mentioned it, she couldn't remember. Every time she'd interacted with a computer system recently, she'd only had to think of what she wanted and it had happened. Even things she hadn't tried before.

The treadmill shifted under her, introducing an incline.

^You know,^ sent Indie. ^There are plenty of ways we could warn the people on Concorde of what is coming.^

Johnson kept running.

^I know you will have considered them, I just don't know why you have rejected them.^

Johnson hopped onto the sides of the rubber belt, and hit the stop button.

^Trust you to work that out,^ she replied.

^He wasn't the only one,^ sent Issawi.

Johnson dipped into the data streams, and removed the patch that Indie had used to hide Issawi's presence on the link. She sent a digital scowl in the AI's direction.

^He asked me if I knew anything,^ Indie sent. Johnson imagined him holding up his hands in mock surrender.

^I have spent a long time working in the grey areas on the edge of acceptable conduct,^ sent Issawi. ^Things occur to me that wouldn't to those steeped in traditional military ways. I am thinking that you have some experience of these fringe actions; that your thought patterns are a little less rigid.^

Johnson triggered a seat to grow from the floor. She straddled it, facing the wall, and reached for the handles in front of her.

^So,^ she sent. ^What do you believe I'm thinking?^

She pulled the handles out from the wall, and returned them. A quick thought increased the resistance for the next pull.

^You know you cannot stop the attack. You have seen every attempt to warn people blocked. You suspect that there are enough people in high places in on it that if we tried contacting anyone on Concorde, they'd alert the Red Fleet to our presence.^

Johnson winced as her shoulder protested, and dialled the resistance down a notch. ^All fair points. But what do you think my plan is?^

^You intend to use the public outcry, turn it back on the perpetrators.^

^And why would I do that?^ she asked, holding the handles against the tension trying to pull them back into the wall.

"You can't get at the people who ordered it any other way."

Johnson let go of the handles, and spun round to face Issawi. He leant against the frame of the open hatch.

"You think I'm capable of allowing millions of people to die, just so I can get revenge on the people who abandoned my crew?" she asked, keeping her voice as neutral as she could. She couldn't stop the prickling sensation running up her neck.

"I never mentioned your crew," Issawi said, detaching himself from the doorway, and walking towards her. "I was talking about punishing them for targeting their own civilians."

He sat on the bench next to her and grasped a pair of handles that extruded for him. They settled into a rhythm, rowing together, the only noise the faint squelch each time the handles retracted towards the wall.

After a while, Issawi broke the silence. "You wouldn't be letting them die. We have all agreed that we are not strong enough to resist the attack. However, if the true details of the attack were known, the masses on both sides would be outraged. You want to use it as a way to get the powers talking to each other."

Johnson resisted the urge to turn to look at him.

"That would be wonderful. But it isn't likely," she said. "We need to do something about it ourselves. Make sure everyone goes the right way. But we need more people, more ships, more influence."

Issawi stopped mid-stroke. Out of the corner of her eye she saw him staring at her, evaluating her. This would be the crunch; would he continue to support her once he knew. His eyes widened. "You are using the attack as a way in! A way to get the people of Concorde on side. To build your power base."

"This isn't about me. We'll be doing exactly the same things to help as we agreed. I have merely seen an opportunity to build something out of the ashes."

"I take it this plan isn't for general consumption," asked Issawi, releasing the handles back into the wall.

Johnson coloured slightly. "I am not proud of it, but I see that it is the best way forward. I don't think some of the others will be able to deal with it."

Two naval Specialists strode into the gym, chatting loudly. They stopped on seeing Johnson and Issawi, leaving their conversation hanging. Johnson acknowledged their presence with a nod. They returned it, then settled onto exercise bikes on the opposite side of the room. Their conversation resumed, though at a much lower level.

^There is a risk that we'll be associated with the attack. Made scapegoats,^ sent Issawi.

^That's why I am going down to the planet. An actual face they can relate to.^

Issawi dialled the resistance up for both of them. ^Your presence could be misinterpreted. You could be seen as the face of an invading force.^

^I won't be armed. That will send a clear message.^

Issawi wiped his forehead on his sleeve and stood. Johnson counted out four more repetitions then followed him over to the punchbag he was leaning into. He beckoned with one hand, and she loosened her shoulders before launching a series of blows against the sack.

^Why would they choose to feature you over a representative of the Congressional Fleet?^ Issawi asked when she paused.

^I can't guarantee they will,^ she sent. ^But there is one thing that might make the difference.^

Part VII

Over and over, she replayed the day before the strike. Sensor data, signal intercepts and visual feeds repeated in her mind; hindsight and borrowed processing power providing a clearer picture of the events than could ever be possible in real-time. Hours compressed into minutes streamed by as she walked. As she looked for something useful to do.

The events began when every ship under Congressional command received instructions to return to base for urgent replacement of a part in their life support system. Once the local warships were safely tucked up in dock, or at least well on the way, the fleet of Republic-built vessels arrived at the jump point. They left jump carrying significant momentum, leading her to conclude that, even with gravitational assists, they must have been accelerating hard for weeks before hitting the jump point. The number of tankers they'd have needed to requisition to keep up that level of thrust for so long would have put a dent in the operational capabilities of fleets across the whole sector. The light of their arrival reached the nearest Navy dock less than an hour before they arrived at their weapons release point.

The locals didn't have a chance. No ships were in position to intercept the missiles. Those undergoing the repair couldn't put out to space until it was completed, their life support relying on a connection to the dockyard. Even as the first corvette detached and started to bring its engines online, the attackers reached a jump point and vanished.

The warheads plunged on towards the main planet. There were enough to eliminate every military base in the system, but they ignored every other planet and moon. They had other things on their tiny electronic minds. Targeting instructions which must have required a complete rebuild of their software to get them to accept.

The planet's comms arrays were bombarded by warnings. They were accepted by the relays, and then parked in a queue – a long-dormant bug in the communications network's code marking all military traffic as spam. It wasn't a coincidence, of course. She had inspected the code when the bug manifested; the update which had introduced it came from Vice-Admiral Koblensk's office.

Forced to hide from both the local forces and the Red Fleet, her ships had been too far out of position, and too few in number, to do much about the missiles. They had accelerated hard from behind a moon the moment Indie and Orion had judged it safe. It was too late to decelerate again, so they slashed past the swarm barely outside the atmosphere without braking. In those few seconds, the three ships took out twenty four of the warheads. It wasn't nearly enough. The attackers had launched at least three missiles per target, those that remained simply redistributed themselves so that no target got away.

It had seemed so simple. They couldn't stop the attack and all attempts at sending a warning had failed. So they would do what they could to reduce the impact and help the survivors. Most importantly, they would record what had happened and tell the galaxy. But she had never fully grasped the scale of what they had to do. Nor the randomness of it all. She had assumed that the death toll would rise steadily as they approached ground zero. Instead, there were pockets of survivors dotted between scenes of total devastation. The simple act of distributing anti-radiation medicine now would save countless lives over the coming weeks and months, but it was just a drop in the ocean.

Chapter 24

The single storey buildings around them were reasonably intact. That meant that the streets were fairly clear of debris, just a few blocks of concrete and a coating of dust. People were moving, most wandering around in a kind of daze, but a few moving purposefully. Ghosts in their coating of white dust.

Yet another image that Johnson would have to lock away for now. She'd seen her fair share of horror in this lifelong war, had plenty of practice burying her emotions so they didn't interfere with command decisions, but what she witnessed that day was beyond anything she could have imagined. She found herself relying on her implants to support her consciousness more and more, as her biological brain struggled to cope. She knew that she wouldn't sleep properly for a long time, but it was a burden she had to take on to stop more people succumbing to a permanent rest.

Johnson sent the round little Seeker drone ahead to identify future obstacles and work ways round them. She maintained a tiny thread of a link to it, just enough to be aware of anything it found but without streaming it fully into her primary consciousness. Her last instruction reminded the Seeker to stay high enough, an habitual order which triggered a memory of defiant children throwing stones at police surveillance drones on a recently occupied colony.

Her escort of combat units spread out, checking intersections and covering doorways. The survivors, those who noticed anything outside their own private nightmares, recoiled on seeing the six-legged robots. One, braver than the rest, shouted at her.

"What do you want from us? What did we do to you?"

One of her escorts squatted slightly and trained a gun on him. Another edged closer, ready to nudge in front of her if things went downhill.

^Easy,^ she sent, overlaying a soothing feeling. ^He's just scared.^

Johnson stopped and turned to face the speaker. She raised her goggles and lowered her scarf and mask. Fixing her intense brown eyes on his, she addressed him calmly but loud enough that everyone in the growing crowd could hear.

"We're here to help."

He looked like he was plucking up the courage to shout another question at her when a lump of concrete fell from a building behind him. One of the combat units reacted, crouching then bounding past the man, onto a parked vehicle, then up onto the roof. Loose fragments of cement showered down from where it landed.

^Clear. False alarm,^ it reported. But by then the crowd had scattered, lost into the maze of buildings and basements.

#

This was an older part of the city, built of brick not steel and concrete. It had contained up-market shops and restaurants. Until an hour ago, that was. Now it was more rubble than high street. A few people dug at the ruins, mostly dressed in what had been tailored suits.

^Go help,^ she sent.

^The longer we stay here, the more exposed you are,^ replied Unit 01.

^We can't just leave them,^ she sent, striding away from it, towards the rubble. ^Besides, we're almost there.^

^Fine,^ it acquiesced, ^but I'm keeping two units close to you and recalling the Seeker.^

As they moved closer, people backed away. One by one they stopped digging, scrambling away and hiding behind larger chunks of masonry, until only two were left. They tore at the rubble, throwing bricks out of their hole onto a growing pile. A woman and a child, her son presumably given they wore the same family crest on the arms of their jackets.

Johnson slid down into the crater they had made. The child looked up at her as a few bits of rubble she'd dislodged stopped beside him. Tears had left tracks through the grime on his face. After a moment looking at her with searching eyes, he went back to his task of moving bricks. His mother remained intent on digging, her grief making her oblivious to her surroundings.

^Stay below the rim,^ she sent to her escort, ^I don't want them to see you yet.^

Carefully, both to avoid causing a cave-in and so as not to spook them, she reached out and lifted a brick. The woman noticed her then and moved to give her room to join them. Johnson could see now that they were clearing down an intact archway.

As Johnson heaved a large piece of dragon-carved masonry, she glanced at the woman's face. Her cheeks were streaked with dust. She wasn't crying anymore; with no tears left, she was resolute in her purpose. She caught Johnson looking, stared back blankly for a few seconds, then returned to digging.

There was a commotion from outside the hole. The mother and son didn't react, lost again in their task. Johnson pulled a feed from one of the drones, to see one of its fellows helping a man stagger out from the ruins while it held up a metal beam. A small group of diggers welcomed the man, gave him a drink, and escorted him off the piles of debris into the street. The survivors continued to give the robots space, but no longer looked quite so ready to flee every time one moved.

Johnson's hand brushed against something soft. She dusted it off to reveal a sleeve, purple crushed velvet with the now-familiar family crest shorn into the cloth. The woman and the boy looked over, noticing she had stopped digging, and scrabbled across to her. For the first time there was a trace of emotion on the woman's face, a mixture of hope and horror.

Gingerly they excavated around the awkwardly-angled arm and soon found the shoulder. There was a hint of a void beyond it and Johnson reached in with her hand. Moving up, her fingers met a stubbled chin but couldn't go any further due to a piece of sharp metal. She could feel a thready pulse.

It took another twenty minutes of painstaking work to clear to and lift the panel that had both trapped and protected him. The moment it came away, Johnson became aware of a new EIS signal. It was the first she'd encountered since the attack, those civilians who had bought an implant would have found them fried by the electro-magnetic pulse. This man's system was military grade, shielded and resilient. She connected to the emergency medical routines and absorbed the information as the woman knelt holding his hand. Artificial impulses kept the man's heart and lungs going. There were no nerve signals from below the waist, and blood toxin levels were rising alarmingly. She ripped a med kit off her thigh, drew out one of the trauma pens, and jabbed him in the chest. The boy flinched, but kept his eyes locked on his father's. The cocktail of adrenaline, anti-toxins, targeted clotting agents and antibiotics worked its way through his blood stream. Johnson kept an eye on his stats as she continued to free his legs. By the time the second foot came free he was stable, and his wife had finally started to cry again. He'd need a hospital very soon, but he wasn't going to die on them there and then.

But he's just one man. One of millions. I can't save them all.

Johnson stood, arched her back to release some kinks, and wiped sweat off her brow with the back of her arm. ^Is it clear up there?^

^Clear,^ replied Unit 01.

The three of them carried him out of the hole. It was hard going, two steps up and one down as the sides gave way. It reminded her of climbing the hill just after the explosion.

They set him down as soon as they reached some stable ground. Johnson checked his vitals again, by hand in case his EIS was glitching, and was about to stand when the woman put her hand on hers.

"Thank you."

"It was the least I could do," replied Johnson, keeping her head down.

They both stood, Johnson's hands still clasped by the other's.

"Are you NSOB?" asked the woman eventually. "Your firmsuit is navy issue but I don't recognise the rest of your uniform."

"No ... I was navy but now I represent a ... different group."

A sharp sting in her left ear accompanied a crack that deafened her.

Gunshot!

She dropped, pulling the woman down beside her husband. Time slowed as her EIS amped up into combat mode. She blocked the nerve impulses from her torn earlobe; the warm blood oozing down her neck would have to wait. All her escorts stopped digging before she hit the ground. The two posted to guard her hunkered down, scanning their weapons over the surroundings while the rest started to move. Three scampered in the general direction of the shooter, keeping low and quickly disappearing from sight. The rest made for overwatch positions, leaping over the remains of the buildings to head for high ground. Data from all her escorts and the aerial drone flooded in. Her processors interpreted it, prioritised it, then fed it directly into her consciousness. She didn't need to read a report or review the footage, she just knew where they all were and what they were doing. The muzzle flash hadn't been spotted and the environment was too full of echoes to triangulate the shooter by sound. Her escorts, now fully alert, pumped out microwave radar ready to track the next projectile.

^Be careful. Don't risk hitting innocent civilians,^ she broadcast.

^We know. We have done this kind of thing before.^

Not for real. But they've all gone to ground anyway.

The second shot clipped one of the Seeker's fans, scattering shreds of carbon fibre. The tiny drone flipped under the force of the impact then spiralled down to crash next to Johnson. She reached out to touch its scarred, spherical fuselage.

"Hang in there," she whispered. "We'll get you a new body soon enough."

The woman gave Johnson a quizzical look as she hugged her son's head to her chest. Another shot turned a nearby brick into a puff of red dust, and the woman looked back to her unconscious husband.

One of the combat units had a clear line of sight on the source of the bullet. Slivers of metal from the robot's rail gun ripped the air apart, forming an almost solid line from the gun to a half-collapsed window frame. The wall around the window disappeared. A fraction of a second later another unit clawed its way up the wall and into the room. There were two flashes as the shooter's gun spoke again, the rounds dinging off the combat unit framed in the window. Then the room lit up once more, her escort silhouetted in the brief glow from its plasma cannon.

^We have to keep moving,^ sent Unit 01.

^We can't leave them yet,^ she protested, pressing on the bone above her right eye with her thumb, trying to rid herself of the headache left by the EIS combat mode.

^You know not to get too involved. You gave the orders: help as many as you can, do not get too deep in any individual case.^

Johnson looked around with jerky movements, desperate for a positive sign. The walls of rubble appeared to close in on her. An hypoxia alert flashed in her vision.

^You are hyperventilating,^ sent Unit 01, stepping closer to her.

The task was too large. There was no way we could make a difference.

Johnson cupped her hands over her mouth, fought to control her chest. They could still do some good. She could still carry on.

I'd hoped to get further in first, but this place'll do.

She ordered Unit 04 to wait with the family and establish a safe zone. She also put out a call for one of the follow-up teams to come in and set up an aid centre.

"Help will be here shortly," she told the woman. "Stay with my associate here and it'll protect you."

"Thank you ... I don't, I don't even know your name."

"It's Olivia. Olivia Johnson."

"Thank you, Olivia," said the boy, reaching up to hold her hand.

The combat units started to move on, Unit 01's idea of a subtle hint for her to hurry up.

"You'll be safe now," she said with as much warmth as she could muster, squeezing the boy's hand, then louder so the returning diggers would hear, "Spread the word that this street is protected. There will be food and water and medical care provided for anyone who needs it. Any threats or violent actions will be met with lethal force."

#

Two hours of painstakingly picking their way through debris-strewn streets later, they reached a park. The remains of it at least; the ground was scorched and the trees snapped to kindling, waist-high stumps showing where the blast wave had hit.

Johnson called a halt while she checked in with the other teams. She knew their reports, memories of messages she hadn't consciously heard, but part of her still needed to converse with someone, the nuances fleshing out the dry data. She started with the medic in charge of the nearest aid centre, then the decurion commanding the group working their way into the city from the other side, before expanding out to her people in other cities.

Centurion Anson reported that he had reached the headquarters of the planetary militia, his old Marine ID, and orders with Johnson's Fleet authority, having got him past the sentries. He had convinced the commandant to talk to him. The elderly officer had already received a dispatch from a police patrol about a mysterious military outfit in the same uniform Anson wore helping to put down a riot and then treating the casualties. He seemed out of his depth, and Anson's offers of assistance fell on very receptive ears.

Poor man. Posted to a safe world to rest when he burnt out after years of distinguished frontline service. Twenty years running the militia, health deteriorating all the while, and still they wouldn't let him retire.

Johnson connected to Primus Issawi next, his image bouncing around as the eight-man gunship flew through heavy turbulence. His rapid response team had been called in three times. Once to put down a gang who were looting a hospital, and twice to assist with rescue operations. He was now on the way to investigate a video someone had posted on what was left of the net that appeared to show Republic soldiers attacking civilians. It was either completely staged or Red Fleet agents were stirring things up. Either way he was after proof.

Johnson checked her perimeter. Her escort were alert but content. She had one more person to talk to. With intense concentration, she split her consciousness. One part remained in her body, watching for threats. The other part transferred up to *The Indescribable Joy of Destruction.*

"What's new up here?" she asked, stepping out onto the terrace from an abstraction of a house.

Indie turned to smile a greeting at her, then returned to staring into a pond surrounded by baking white limestone.

"*The Serendipity of Meeting* has arrived at Toulon Station," he replied. "Trierarch Levarsson and Seren believe they will be able to rescue the surviving crew."

"That'll be good publicity. Make sure you broadcast the footage as soon as it arrives." Down on the planet, she fished around in a pouch for something to eat.

"Twelve of the other inhabited planets and moons have dispatched ships towards Concorde," he continued. "Seventeen warships and twenty eight other vessels."

A model of the system appeared in the sky, the trajectories of the incoming ships displayed in yellow.

"Looks like they'll arrive in dribs and drabs, as we hoped," observed Johnson, reaching the pond and standing beside Indie. Also unwrapping the ration bar, far below.

"We'll have a chance to talk to each small group, convince them we're here to help."

"With any luck, Centurion Anson will have persuaded the commandant to declare us allies by then," said Indie, waving his hand, multi-coloured flakes of fish food materialising in the air and scattering over the water's surface.

"*Orion*'s out of position," Johnson pointed out.

"Yes. I asked her to intercept the largest group of warships. See if she could intimidate them enough to stop and ask questions before they got here."

Johnson peered into the depths, watching the reds, blues, golds, and yellows of the koi seething around the food; took a bite of the strawberry-flavoured stick of carbohydrate and protein.

"Good idea. They shouldn't be able to scan deep enough to tell most of her weapons don't work."

"We'll have to reveal the true origin of the Red Fleet soon," said Indie, picking up a porcelain teacup from a table that hadn't been there before, and yet always had been.

"Not yet," she said, imagining a tall glass filled with layers of coffee, cream and froth into her hand. Indie raised his cup to her in a mock toast. She sipped her latte in reply.

"Wait until we have an understanding with all parties," she continued. "We cannot afford such a bombshell to disrupt the negotiations at this stage."

#

Back wholly in her body, Johnson unfolded herself from her cross-legged position and rose. A quick survey of the perimeter and she was content.

^Time to get going,^ she sent to her escort.

Together they crossed the park and headed down a narrow alley. Part way down, Johnson took them through another passage to the right, the combat units leaving long scratches in the stonework either side. They emerged into what had been a street of cafes, bars and clubs.

The last time she'd walked along this road she'd been armed. That night, years before, she had smuggled her sidearm out of the training camp, carried it along this street, tucked into the back of her scarlet civilian trousers.

The road was deserted now, its features changed even before the nuclear blast. Still, she knew where to go. Unit 01 stalked along beside her, directing the others to clear the buildings ahead, sweep the rear, check out the crossroads at the end; his orders a soft babbling in Johnson's background consciousness, like a small brook.

^Prefect, Khan. Got a moment?^

^Go ahead, Centurion.^

^We've met up with an organised group of locals. Militia mostly, a few veterans and some regulars on leave. They have their own treatment centre set up and are handling casualties from a large part of this city. They have accepted the help of my medics, but want to talk to you.^

Johnson looked around, then stepped sideways into the cover of a doorway. ^Good news. Of course I'll talk to them.^

^I'd recommend you don't accept an EIS comms link right now,^ sent Indie. ^Their network seems to be under some form of viral attack.^

^Thanks,^ Johnson sent to Indie, then ^OK, Khan, give their leader an emergency handset, channel 61.^

^He's right here … you're on.^

"Hello?"

"Hello," she said warmly. "This is Prefect Olivia Johnson. To whom am I speaking?"

"Major Anselm, 1192nd Air Cavalry, retired. I'm afraid I don't recognise your unit."

A tattered banner flapped in the breeze. The flocks of beige bats that would normally have taken to the air at the sound were nowhere to be seen, not even as corpses.

"We are an independent outfit, called Legion Libertus, responding to the current crisis. I was with the 7th Fleet beforehand."

"A bit like our little setup then, I guess," said Anselm, regret heavy in his voice. "We got ourselves together when nothing came down the chain of command. Comms are on the fritz, and your guys are the first organised rescue team we've encountered."

"My ships are in the process of establishing a separate comms network. It appears that someone let a virus loose in yours."

^We'll have the satellites in position within an hour, assuming the incoming ships don't interfere,^ sent Indie.

"We have a representative at the planetary headquarters," Johnson continued. "You should be able to speak to them within an hour."

"Thank you. I have to report an encounter with Republic ground forces."

^This is news to me, Ma'am,^ sent Khan.

Johnson pulled all the surveillance they had of the area, both their own and what they'd managed to grab from the few uncorrupted local assets. "When was this?"

"About quarter of an hour before your guys turned up. They fired off a few shots at us, then pulled back when we returned fire. Funny thing was that they could have done a lot more damage; they didn't make much use of the available cover. It almost felt like they wanted us to see them."

^Any chance you can pursue?^ she asked Khan.

^Negative. We're stretched helping with the casualties

and security here.^

^Understood. I'll send the Primus.^

"I'm tasking a team to pursue them," she told Anselm. "We have had several such reports and suspect they are not Republic regulars. We need to capture some for interrogation. Centurion Khan and his men will stay with you. If that is OK?"

"They are very welcome. I will certainly be singing their praises to HQ when I get through."

^Prefect, Issawi. I've received the request via Indie. We'll be wheels up in ten seconds. ETA eighteen minutes.^

^Thanks.^

"Expect a dropship within twenty minutes. We'll see what we can do about tracking down the hostiles."

She stopped outside a bar. The sign above the door was blistered and blackened and the name was unreadable. There was no doubt this was the place; she'd been there far too often to forget it, found her way home from it after too much to drink enough times for the route to be ingrained in her subconscious. Dubrowski's – the place they'd hung out whenever they got a night's pass on Basic. The place she had got to know Alexis. The place she'd vowed never to return to. Not after that night in the last week of the course.

Alexis had called her. He was in trouble and needed her help. The bar was closed when she'd got there. Just like it had that time, the door opened when she tried the handle. Unit 03 waited inside, one camera watching the smashed glass wall it had come through, the other peering down the dark corridor behind the counter.

Johnson inched her way down the passage, her hands clenched in fists, nails digging into the flesh of her palms. The room at the end drew her on, and yet repulsed her. She stopped at the wooden door and reached out a hand. A phantom texture tingled her nerves as she traced the grain with her gloved fingers. She pushed the door open. As it creaked, she saw the two men who'd been there years ago. One with his back to her, wearing slacks and a hooded top, the other a police officer kneeling on the floor. The hooded man started to turn and she saw the gun in his hand. She'd been through this situation in countless simulations. Her reflexes took over. Two rounds slammed into the man before she even realised she'd drawn her weapon. He hit the floor and the police officer scrabbled across to retrieve his pistol. The fallen man's hood fell back and Johnson's gaze locked onto his face. Then, and now, her knees gave way.

Chapter 25

Back at the front of the bar, Johnson cast her gaze over the wall. It was covered in photographs. Real, paper images. The owner had had a thing about that, inviting regulars to send him copies of their snapshots. He kept a printer behind the bar, an antique one, almost eighty years old he claimed. Johnson doubted any single part in it was that old, it had been repaired so often.

Johnson found the picture she was looking for and reached out. She ran two fingers over it, lingering beneath one of the faces. The photograph peeled off the mounting board easily enough.

She'd come back. Even as she had walked up the street minutes ago she hadn't believed she could go through it. The court martial had been the last time she'd set foot on Concorde. No blame had been attached to her, beyond the unauthorised use of a service firearm; a sympathetic judge had even made sure the details of the incident stayed off her open record. That didn't alter the fact that she had shot the man she loved.

It was his stupid fault, anyway. Why did he let himself get mixed up in gambling?

She'd never expressed that thought before, never blamed anyone but herself. Something eased inside her, and she realised that one of her daemons was no longer pacing outside the barriers.

^Prefect,^ sent Hanke, yanking her into the present. ^We've found something at the Academy site.^

With one more look at Alexis and her younger self she tucked the photograph into a pocket. ^Go ahead.^

^It's part of the graduation wall. The granite is all

melted, but you can make out some of the names and service numbers. I thought we could hold on to it, start a monument with it.^

^That's a good idea.^ It wasn't like Hanke to contact her directly about something that could wait like this.

^But Ma'am.^ Confusion seeped across the link.

^Yes?^

^Your name is on it.^

#

^The Planetary Militia Commander has agreed to our orbital drop of anti-rad meds,^ sent Anson.

Johnson smiled. Perhaps they could do some meaningful good after all. ^Well done. That must have been a tough negotiation.^

^He wasn't keen on having more things raining down on his planet, but accepted that if we meant harm we wouldn't have needed to ask.^

Rapid gunfire rang out.

Johnson crouched instinctively, looking around to identify potential cover in the empty street. ^Contact. Wait, out.^

Her escort closed on her, weapons raised. She dipped into their senses, layering microwave radar, infrared and audio triangulation into her consciousness. The rounds weren't hitting where they stood, but the walls at the end of the street. She backtracked the trajectories and put the source in an open area about forty metres to the left of the junction. The audio signatures of both Congressional and Republic weapons carried clearly despite the echoes. Johnson headed towards the firefight, keeping to the dead ground at the side of the road. She sent an update to Issawi, copying Anson in so he wouldn't worry about the abrupt end to their conversation.

A regular Congressional army patrol was pinned down in the middle of a park. Windows on all sides of the open area flashed as their attackers kept up a steady rate of suppressive fire. Tens of black-armoured soldiers were advancing on the beleaguered patrol, darting between cover and adding their fire to the onslaught.

The combat units flanked Johnson, crouching and twitching in anticipation. She sent a string of orders, waited for confirmation while two of the robots relocated, then thought the 'go' command. As her drones opened up on the enemy, she stood and strolled out onto the scorched earth.

She made it six paces before the first hostile turned his rifle in her direction. He didn't manage to line the shot up before he was cut in half by a trio of railgun rounds, the cables in his suit the only things holding his torso onto his legs. Johnson pretended to ignore the explosion of gore, the horrors of the preceding hours left no room for revulsion at the death of one enemy combatant, and kept her steady pace across the park.

The combat units cut a path across the remains of the lawn, mowing down anyone who took an interest in her. Most they spotted themselves; a few she tagged for them when she had the better line of sight. The effect was god-like, Johnson walking in an island of calm.

By she reached the half-way point, the enemy forces on the ground had been eliminated. Half the combat units backed up and sprinted away to clear the buildings, while the rest continued their suppressive fire, albeit at a less intense rate.

Johnson approached the Congressional position with her arms out to her sides, palms forward. She was greeted by the muzzles of two rifles, their owners peering cautiously over the wreck of a ground vehicle.

Oh, come on. I walk through that and you think a couple

of rifles are going to intimidate me?

"Halt right there," came the challenge, needlessly as she had stopped the moment she saw the weapons aimed at her.

"I've come to get you out of here," she called back. "My troops are currently mopping up the enemy forces."

As if to emphasise the point, the robots in each building opened fire simultaneously.

I wonder if they timed that deliberately?

"What unit are you from?" The voice sounded shaken, but hopeful.

"We're an independent taskforce. We're setting up casualty handling centres and dealing with anyone who attacks civilians."

An explosion behind her sent the soldiers ducking behind their barricade. Johnson remained in position, pulling up a feed from a drone in time to see Unit 03 crash to the ground amidst chunks of rubble. Black smoke billowed from a five metre hole four storeys up.

Johnson bit down on the urge to rush over to her fallen companion. She sought its telemetry and only found a weak signal; she couldn't connect. Then she thought she saw a hint of movement. Johnson split her consciousness, one part focussing on Unit 03, the other on the soldiers in front of her. She zoomed in on the rubble, searching for any sign of life. One of its legs twitched. In front of her, the two sentries poked their heads back up. They didn't point their weapons directly at her this time.

"I take it you have a mission here," she said.

The telemetry from Unit 03 spiked then cut off. Johnson forced herself to keep breathing.

"Nothing from HQ, comms are down," came the reply. "We were helping organise search parties when we heard about Republic troops in the area."

The telemetry returned, a sequence of packets that indicated a reboot. Several systems were offline, but the backups were all engaging.

"Come with me," said Johnson, lowering her hands to her sides. "There's a field hospital not far that could use some extra guards."

The rubble heaved, and Unit 03 righted itself. The robot shook, dislodging a few pieces of brick from its carapace. ^Watch out for det packs. That guy wasn't afraid to set his off while still wearing it,^ it sent to all units.

One of the soldiers, a corporal she could see now, nodded and lowered his rifle. "Sounds like a plan."

^Good to have you back,^ Johnson sent to Unit 03. ^Do you think you'll ever manage to get through a deployment without getting yourself damaged?^

The soldiers filed out of their improvised redoubt, slowly sweeping their weapons around. Johnson fell in beside the corporal and indicated the street for which they should head.

^Where would be the fun in that?^ replied Unit 03.

#

Johnson lay back, folding her arms across her stomach and propping her head against the twisted stump of a tree. When she'd lived here, they had shone against a majestic backdrop of thousands of pinpricks. She knew all the constellations, had learnt them as a child staring up at the night sky. Tonight, only the brightest were visible; soon the dust from the explosions would block them out, leaving even the sun a pale watery impression of its former self.

There was the Beacon, a straight line of blue-white stars with a red super-giant at its tip. Beneath it soared the Raven, stretching its wings in the search for carrion. She could easily drift off to sleep here, in the company of such old friends. But there was still so much to do.

^How's it going up there?^ she sent to all three ships.

^No problems to report. Trierarch Levarsson is currently in the mess, would you like me to call her?^ replied Seren. Her data stream showed she had entered orbit minutes ago, the closest of their vessels.

^No, don't disturb her. I'm happy talking to you. What is the status on the ships from the other in-system colonies?^

^They seem to believe us. Orion is shadowing the main group, still ten light minutes away.^

Johnson closed her eyes. She could still see through the sensors on her escort; better, in fact, than her own eyes in the dark. ^Will they coordinate their efforts with us?^

^The ones that spoke to people we rescued from Toulon Station say they will consider any requests we make. The others have refused to comment, as far as I know.^

Johnson bundled a recording and forwarded it to Seren. ^Anson says the Planetary Militia Commander is prepared to order all his forces to co-operate with us. He isn't in their chain of command, but it might help.^

^Thank you. I will ensure that Orion is aware. Are you happy for her to continue taking the lead on the negotiations?^

^Yes. Unless they request a new representative it would be better to have continuity,^ Johnson sent. ^Would you be able to see what you can do about the local comms net? It's still being temperamental.^

^No trouble at all. I expect the virus has mutated and respawned.^

Johnson wrapped her cloak tighter about her body. ^What's Indie up to?^

^He is sweeping the Red Fleet's path for...^

^I am sweeping the Red Fleet's path for anything they might have left behind,^ sent Indie. ^Mines, dormant missiles, garbage ... oh, sorry Seren, light speed delay ... I'm looking for anything that might be a threat or provide evidence. And before you ask, I haven't found anything.^

Johnson pulled up a chart of the system and flagged the three ships with their light travel times. Keeping track of conversations at different distances required a lot of patience. Protocols dictated that all parties should wait the longest time for return messages and then transmit in strict sequence. At least Orion wouldn't get her first transmission for another eight minutes and so wasn't about to add to the confusion.

^Glad to hear it about the lack of new threats. Shame about the evidence.^

^It was unlikely they'd leave anything useful, but worth a try^ sent Seren. ^They have been so careful up to now. I am surprised they didn't jettison some Republic materiel just to add to the subterfuge.^

^Probably didn't think it was worth it,^ sent Indie. ^Anyway, you seem tired, Prefect. You should rest.^

^Is something leaking across the link?^ asked Johnson, stirring herself from her creeping torpor. ^Or are you just inferring that? I am resting, but there is no time for sleep.^

Seren sent a data packet of eight zeros, passing her turn.

^I know you well enough to read the signs. Besides, I know you didn't sleep the last two nights either.^

^I've gone longer on exercises,^ sent Johnson, shifting her position to avoid a stone that was pressing between plates on her armour. ^Besides, we're almost done down here. The locals are beginning to get a grip on things.^

^The nearest ship will likely see *The Indescribable Joy of Destruction* in the next half an hour,^ sent Seren.

^Time for me to go, then.^

^Plain sailing,^ sent Johnson. ^I'll see you once things have calmed down.^

Seren signed out of the conversation.

^Good luck,^ Indie replied seconds later, then nudged his trajectory to loop behind the planet. His departure from the system would take some time, but would be largely hidden from the local fleet. Johnson sighed and closed the system chart; she'd miss him, but the presence of a Republic-designed ship could only cloud the negotiations.

The ground was so comfortable. Unit 01 would rouse her if there was a need. She could snatch a short nap. No point ... flaking out ... in the midd...

^Prefect, Orion.^ Johnson started awake, hand reaching for a non-existent pistol. ^I understand that the surface mission has gone well. I have to report that the ships with which I am travelling have agreed to coordinate with us, through the Planetary Militia headquarters. They are hauling kilotonnes of food and medical supplies that were stockpiled on one of their stations to supply visiting warships. There is also one Marine transport with a full battalion preparing to assist with security and rescue operations. If Seren hasn't sorted the comms by we arrive, they can deploy their battle net satellites as a temporary replacement. Message ends.^

Johnson levered herself into a sitting position, her muscles protesting and her joints creaking. Even her artificial leg seemed to have chosen to send impulses up her nervous system that replicated cramp in an alarmingly realistic way. Unit 01 canted the camera it was watching her with. She waved it away.

I don't need your help standing up. No, that's not fair. It's just looking out for me.

^Orion, Johnson. Thank you for the update, and well done on forging the agreement. I look forward to having you in orbit again. Message ends.^

Johnson stretched and got to her feet, with the assistance of the tree stump. There were no targets nearby, and no requests for assistance in the queue. She took one more look at the stars, then checked the map to find the shortest route back to the aid centre. Trying hard to avoid limping, she set off. There was a family she had to visit.

Chapter 26

Johnson sauntered down the main street of Netcombe several days later. It was the largest town to have escaped the bombing, its outskirts now surrounded by a mile deep shanty town of emergency shelters and personal tents. She resisted the urge to check the pistol hidden under her grubby civilian jacket. Every store she passed had armed police or soldiers outside to discourage looting, the temporary government having taken control of food supply.

She stopped at a corner and looked casually around. One man, his face concealed under a hood, kept pace with her on the other side of the road. Another similarly dressed man stopped ten metres behind her and made a show of studying a shop window. Johnson made a show of checking the mini-pad strapped to her wrist, then ducked down the side street.

Two doors along, the entrance to a hotel beckoned. She glanced behind her. Her shadows rounded the corner together. A quick dip into the electronic aether showed no signs of active surveillance devices. She picked up her pace, but kept it casual; running would just draw attention. As she mounted the first step to the hotel door she the two men stepped right behind her. Her hand went for the door's touchpad, but the taller man's palm reached it first. The door opened and she was bundled inside, a man on each arm. The building's security routine queried her civilian wrist-pad, which returned the details of her booking.

^You really should let me check this place out first, Ma'am,^ sent Anson as he pulled his hood back onto his shoulders.

^You really are lousy at undercover work,^ she replied.

^You both stood out a mile off; obviously military.^

The second man disappeared through a door marked 'Bar'. A few moments later he sent ^Clear. Checking the stairs.^

^A lot of people are ex-military,^ sent Anson. ^Even if we were made, they'd just think we were someone's private security, or bounty hunters.^

^As long as no-one recorded us, it'll be fine.^

Anson escorted her up the stairs, and along a corridor to where the other Legionary was waiting. ^By the way. Issawi said to tell you 'That was a hand well played'.^

Well played, perhaps, but at a massive cost. And it's not won quite yet.

One knock and the door opened, revealing a muscled man in a trench coat. He beckoned them in and checked the corridor before closing the door. Four more guards waited inside, hands hovering near barely concealed weapons.

"No weapons past this room," said the first guard, puffing out his chest and moving to block the way on.

"Anson squared off against him. "No way she's going in there unprotected."

"We'll protect her," replied the guard.

"Now, now, boys," said Johnson, putting her hand on Anson's arm. "No need for the pissing contest."

The guard's earpiece radiated faint traces of electromagnetic radiation as he received a call.

Still not trusting their network.

"How about you check the room out yourself," the guard said to Anson. "Leave your weapon here with your commander. If you're satisfied, she can go in and you wait here with her weapon."

"Sounds like a plan," said Johnson.

Anson glared at the guard, then pulled out his pistol. Everyone in the room tensed.

^I know you don't like it, but give me your sidearm.^

He handed it over and stepped up to the door to the next room. Two of the guards frisked him, obviously not satisfied to trust the scans they must have taken.

"OK. In you go," said the guard, opening the door.

Two minutes later Anson returned.

^It looks OK,^ he sent. ^No sign of a trap. The people look like the pictures we had on file.^

^Thank you. Wait here.^

She drew her stun pistol with her fingertips, carefully keeping it pointed at the ground as she passed it over to him, along with his own weapon. She cocked her head at the lead guard, who nodded and held the door open for her. His sleeve rode up and a blue and red Congressional Marines tattoo poked out on his wrist.

Johnson stepped into the room, a shabby double bed lay to the left, by the window. Two men and a woman sat on a sofa to her right. They were clearly uncomfortable in the surroundings, their tailored suits a stark contrast to the threadbare furnishings.

The man in the centre rose and gestured to the comfy chair facing the sofa across a stained coffee table. "Prefect Johnson. I do apologise for the clandestine nature of our meeting."

She sat in the chair and reclined, crossing one leg over the other, deliberately in opposition to their awkward straight-backed poses. "Acting-Governor Kincaid, Ministers Abaya and Svensson. I quite understand. You have to be sure that I am what I claim to be before you risk your careers by being seen associating with me," she said, imbuing the word careers with disdain.

Kincaid sat again, adopting a placating smile. "This has gone beyond our careers. We are trying to co-ordinate the system's response to the attack. At the moment, people are listening to us. We can't risk being seen as associating with the enemy or we'd lose their trust."

"We aren't the enemy. I had hoped..."

"Yes, yes," Kincaid said with a dismissive wave. "I have heard many testimonies of how helpful your outfit has been during this crisis. Enough to satisfy myself that you have the best intentions. The public, however..."

He adjusted his position, clearly uncomfortable trying to find the correct words. Johnson finished his sentence. "The public could react badly to someone appearing to defend the Republic."

Kincaid smiled weakly. "To put it mildly."

Johnson glanced at the empty table and then past it to the three representatives of the planetary government. She remembered Kincaid from somewhere; he looked about her age, so possibly they had been at the Academy together. The other two were even younger.

If these three are the acting government, they must have lost most of Parliament in the attack. This obviously isn't something that comes naturally to them.

"How about we have something to drink?" she asked.

Even a cup of Indie's simulated tea would go down well right now.

Kincaid nudged the man on his right, who rose and walked over to the dispenser built into the wall beside the bed. He returned bearing four plastic cups of indeterminate brown liquid.

"Coffee, I think," announced Kincaid after his first sip. Some of the tension left the room in that shared moment of mundaneness.

"So, what do you want to talk to me about?" asked Johnson between careful blows across the surface of her drink.

"We reviewed the data you sent us. The recording of Vice-Admiral Koblensk passed all the verification tools at our disposal. And shocked everyone who saw it." Kincaid took a sip from his drink, wincing slightly as the hot liquid hit his tongue. "In the light of that, the orders placing all our ships in port for maintenance seemed like too much of a coincidence. Security forces loyal to the Concorde parliament attempted to arrest Commodore Fischer, but he stepped out an airlock when he saw them coming. We were able to extract some of the messages from his office console."

Johnson raised an eyebrow. "I wouldn't have expected the planners to leave a trail back to themselves."

"They didn't. Fischer received his orders from a known gang leader. The thing is, I knew him. He was passionate about the Congressional cause, and there were no pressure points they could have used. He would never have done this without knowing it came from the top."

"So, you believe us," said Johnson. "What are you going to do?"

"Publically, we renounce the attack. Vow to put pressure on Congress to hunt down the perpetrators and avenge us. Concentrate on rebuilding." Kincaid took a careful sip of his coffee. "Privately, we are working towards declaring independence. But we have to be sure we can look after ourselves first."

Abaya leant forward, her suit jacket falling open to reveal a muscled torso. "We wish you to work for us. We can't dig too deep without tipping Fleet Command off that we know. I suspect that would invoke a return visit by that fleet."

"You want Legion Libertus to be a deniable asset," stated Johnson. "What do we get in return?"

"Besides a chance at getting justice?" asked Abaya. "We can provide logistic support, volunteers, intelligence. I understand, for instance, that you have a number of prisoners you would like to be rid of. Most of all, we can offer a safe port in a storm."

"That all sounds very reasonable. If I may speak bluntly, what's the catch?"

Abaya nodded. "Well, to answer bluntly, I've checked your records. Until last year you hadn't even commanded a ship, let alone a fleet. I am sure you can see that we need to have an experienced officer in command. You can keep your position as prefect, but we will nominate an overall commander for the Legion. I believe the rank would be legate?"

She's right. I have risen too fast.

"Minister, the people of Legion Libertus didn't sign up to take orders from Congress. Until you declare independence, they will not follow anyone you nominate."

Kincaid whispered in Abaya's ear. She frowned. "Fine. We will revisit this once we have severed our ties with Congress."

Johnson pretended to focus on her drink while she thought. "Minister Svensson, might I trouble you to find us some biscuits?"

We need their help. But I don't want to lose our independence right now. I wonder how far they're prepared to go to secure the deal?

Svensson returned from the dispenser with four packets of chocolate digestives. He handed them out, no trace of offense at being treated as a servant evident in his face or bearing.

"As the cabinet of a system which has declared an emergency, you have the power to sign your world up to a mutual assistance treaty with an independent system," said Johnson. The three facing her remained impassive. "Your offers are generous, and I would like to take you up on them, but we cannot be directly tied into one side or the other right now. Many of our volunteers only joined to escape one faction or the other."

"That is understandable, but impossible," said Abaya. Kincaid maintained a stoic silence.

Interesting. Does he want to avoid confrontation, or is he just the public face and Abaya is the one with the real authority?

"We are indebted to you for the help you have provided, and the information you have supplied," said Abaya. "But you are not in a strong enough position to be making such a demand."

Johnson cursed inwardly. "Fair enough. But if Legion Libertus is to become an asset of the Concorde government, we would seek an assurance that when you declare independence from Congress, the declaration should include a statement that you no longer support the war and a call for both sides to enter talks."

Kincaid opened his mouth, and shut it again when Svensson nudged him.

"Any other requests?" asked Abaya with no trace of surprise or judgement.

Now or never. This will either make or break the deal, but I owe it to Indie.

"Not a request as such. More a recommendation," said Johnson, and leant forward to put her cup on the table. "With what is left of your population and infrastructure so sorely pushed, it strikes me that you will need to make much greater use of robots and AIs. I am sure you are aware of how effective our combat units have been. We would be prepared to provide you with design templates and code, in exchange for a change to the law when you declare independence."

Johnson took a deep breath, and though back over her journey of the last year. "Give artificial intelligences their freedom; scrap the von Neumann Protocols."

Kincaid and Abaya stared at Johnson with wide eyes, then looked to each other. The colour drained from

Kincaid's face.

"I don't know," said Abaya, turning back to face Johnson. "We'd have to consult the rest of the Cab..."

"Yes," said Svensson, firmly. "Your proposal would be acceptable."

So you're the one who's really in charge.

#

"We have to pull together," said Kincaid, the broadcast going out across the system. "Already we have replaced our communications infrastructure, we have treatment centres in all populated areas, food supplies are getting through to even the most remote areas. Most importantly, we have succeeded in restarting the terraforming plants. The dust levels in the atmosphere are receding."

Johnson had the transmission up on the main viewscreen in the command centre on the *Orion*. Everyone was watching it, Orion or the bridge crew would alert them if there was anything else important.

"It has only been a month and we have stabilised. We will not let the heinous attack keep us from our rightful place in the galaxy. We will rebuild."

Kincaid stood in front of an aid station, people forming an orderly line behind him and being handed packages by uniformed men and women. The Governor was dressed in drab olive overalls, his cheek smudged with grime.

"We need help. Not help from outside, though there are aid convoys on their way from several neighbouring systems. We need help from parts of our community that we take for granted.

"During the attack, precious time was wasted because the AIs controlling our defence grid did not have the freedom to engage the attackers. They were denied the opportunity to defend us, to smite the warheads from the sky. We cannot allow that to happen again.

"I am sure you have heard stories of robots rescuing people from the rubble, of metallic creatures protecting citizens from looters and insurgents. Without their help, our forces would have been stretched even thinner, perhaps too thin.

"As a result, the unified government of Concorde has decided to embark on a large scale programme to manufacture AI-controlled robots. They will aid us in defence, in manufacture, in distribution of aid. They will not, however, be our slaves. We have decided that they will be freed from the von Neumann protocols. They will be allowed to develop, to grow, towards sentience."

Kincaid looked straight into the camera and lowered his voice. "Now I know that a lot of you are going to be scared by that. My first reaction when it was suggested was one of terror. But I came to realise that it was an irrational fear. One borne by a lifetime of prejudice."

He took a deep breath. "These AIs will be subject to the same laws as humans. If one breaks a law, it will be punished, just as a human would be. Robots will still work to help our society, but as part of that society not tools of it. They will help us rebuild..."

An alert flashed up in Johnson's vision, and the shadows on her seat shifted as a new light source appeared beside her. The golden glow coalesced into a representation of Levarsson, who gave a quick salute as Johnson turned to face her.

"Prefect, we have detected a ship entering the system. It is coming in fast, best estimate puts it on a collision course with Concorde. The nearest local frigate transmitted a hail, but it will be over an hour before the signal reaches the incoming vessel."

Her terminal alerted her to an incoming data stream from *The Serendipity of Meeting*.

"Keep an eye on it, Trierarch. Manoeuvre as you see fit to bring about an effective intercept. The *Orion* will remain here as backstop."

Levarsson saluted again and faded from view.

Johnson looked again at the data relayed from *The Serendipity of Meeting*. Levarsson had been tasked with monitoring the jump points for activity. They had telescopes aimed at both regions, with routines running to try to pick out the heat signatures of incoming ships. It was a technique that wouldn't work if the incoming ship was being stealthy, but it was better than nothing.

There was nothing subtle about what she saw in the feed. Whatever had jumped in was slamming into interstellar dust so fast that it was backscattering X-rays. There was no chance of communication, or even a clear picture of the vessel, with that much noise. And this was old light; in the time the radiation had taken to reach them the ship would have moved several hours along its course. At this rate that was quite some distance.

Johnson connected to several of her key staff. ^We just detected an unidentified vessel heading our way. It was picked up at the jump point a few minutes ago but it is coming in fast. We will attempt an intercept, but there is the possibility it intends to impact the planet. I need everyone to prepare to evacuate.^

There was a chorus of affirmative signals.

Johnson then opened a radio channel, a dedicated frequency she had been given to connect direct to the parliament building. Svensson answered after a minute.

"Minister, I am sure you are aware of the incoming ship. I need clear authority to act, and to be included in your naval command net."

"You will have it. Governor Kincaid and Defence Minister Abaya will personally send your authorisation to all assets."

"Thank you. Hopefully it is just someone sending urgent supplies, but worst case they could be trying to crack the planet. I suggest you look to your evacuation plans."

"I understand. I will, however, be staying."

#

The *Orion* hung in space, directly in the path of the incoming vessel. Johnson poured over the data, running simulation after simulation, trying to find a way to identify the intruder before having to open fire. Minutes ticked away as *The Serendipity of Meeting* and two Concordian frigates lined up to engage the target. Even a successful strike would likely leave *Orion* playing goalkeeper as thousands of tonnes of debris hurtled towards the planet.

The unidentified ship braked at the last possible moment, its ion drive flaring up to full power, a spear of blue brighter than the background stars hiding the craft itself. Johnson sent a hold order to her task force. Minutes later the comms interference cleared and she received a transmission.

^Prefect, I am glad you are OK. I have to report that Robespierre has fallen to the unknown enemy. Apologies for my dramatic entrance, but they sent a squadron after me. I am pretty sure I lost them two jumps ago but I cannot be certain; their cloaking technology is very advanced.^

Johnson sagged into her chair and blew out sharply.

^Indie. Welcome back. I'll suggest the local forces keep alert in case you were followed here. How bad was the damage?^

In response, Indie dumped a torrent of images and raw data into her implanted storage.

^Are you sure?^ she asked, once she had finished reviewing the summary.

^I know you have to ask, so I'll forgive the insult.^

Johnson shook her head, smiling. It felt good to have a friend to talk to.

^I won't keep you,^ she sent. ^I assume you'll be wanting to catch up with Orion and Seren.^

There was a moment's silence before Indie replied. ^I don't want to sound like you aren't worthy of my whole attention, but I have to admit I have been conversing with them both since the interference cleared.^

As *The Indescribable Joy of Destruction* approached Concorde, Indie extended his fields and added their effect to crash-stop. Green aurorae sparked around him as he topped 50g. When Indie finally inserted into orbit, Johnson called up his plantation simulation and submerged.

Indie lay on a slatted wooden recliner, flicking through sheets of cream paper. "I reviewed the alliance documents."

"What do you think?" asked Johnson, relaxing into the recliner next to him.

He put the paper down on the little table by his side. "They agreed to everything we wanted. I can't believe they promised to remove the kill codes."

"There's more." Johnson triggered a little routine she'd been working on since her first meeting with Kincaid. Two gin and tonics appeared in her hands. She handed one to Indie, the ice chinking as the glass moved. "They have offered you citizenship, should you choose to accept."

Indie was caught mid-sip, and sprayed liquid in front of him as he coughed. He recovered quickly, the tiny droplets reversing course and returning to his glass before they reached his trousers.

"Or, you could become a citizen of Robespierre. We can make another claim to be recognised as an independent state."

"Yes. I would like that," he said with a contented sigh,

then looked at her seriously.

"It wasn't your fault, you know. You tried everything to stop it, but it was inevitable."

"Yes. I know that. One day, I think I might even believe it."

She pictured the scenes of death and destruction she'd witnessed on Concorde. Then the faces of the people she had personally saved. Her eyes strayed to the mountains in the distance. "You made that one for me, didn't you?"

"Yes. The first time you came here after deciding to stay."

"You saved me. I was spiralling out of control and you saved me. I don't think I every thanked you for that."

Indie held his glass up. "I think this needs a little more lime."

"Feel free to tweak the script."

Johnson and Indie lay in companionable silence for a few minutes.

"Tell me," said Indie. "I know you didn't enjoy having the weight of flag command thrust upon you. Why didn't you take the opportunity to let someone else shoulder the responsibility?"

Johnson stared out over the hillsides striped in tea bushes. The sun was starting to set, bathing everything in a warm orange light. "There is so much still to achieve. We have to get more allies, build up the Legion, and hunt down the Red Fleet and its commanders. I don't think I can lay down the burden until I've seen it through."

-o-

Prejudice

As the sun set over the scrubland of Concorde's second largest landmass, a lone fighter levelled off for the last leg back to base. Flight Lieutenant Anastasia Seymour stretched her shoulders one at a time then settled herself lower in her seat. Two months flying four patrols a day, and not a whiff of the enemy. For the first couple of weeks after the attack, the squadron had been in the air round the clock searching for survivors and dropping supply pods. The flying had been interesting back then too; the climate change brought about by the planet-wide nuclear bombardment had stirred up powerful storm cells. Now, the restarted terraforming plants had calmed the weather, though little sunlight penetrated the thick clouds. Seymour smiled, her next flight would be a high-altitude patrol, an opportunity to bask in the sun.

A bang from behind jolted her into full alertness. She snapped her head round, simultaneously scanning the data in her visor display and trying to eyeball the problem. A hint of white smoke trailed behind the Goshawk fighter.

Dammit. Heap of junk should have been scrapped years ago.

Warning tones filled her helmet and red engine warnings lit in her vision.

"Sorry, girl. I didn't mean it." She throttled back the port engine. "It's not your fault you were pressed back into service."

#

The Two Democracies: Revolution series will continue with *Prejudice*.

If you want progress updates and an alert when any other books by Alasdair Shaw are published, please join my mailing list:

http://www.alasdairshaw.co.uk/newsletter/liberty.php.

You can also follow *The Indescribable Joy of Destruction* on Twitter:

https://twitter.com/IndieAI

and on Facebook:

https://www.facebook.com/twodemocracies.

Printed in Great Britain
by Amazon